About Leap

The Wild Hunt L

Erotic paranormal

There's a reason why Cherise Sinclair is on my auto-buy list: she writes fantastic erotic romances with great stories and wonderful characters.

~ The Romance Reviews

She shifts for the first time on the day of her escape.

After a decade of captivity, Darcy MacCormac escapes the corrupt, clandestine organization called the Scythe, leaving family and friends behind. She must find a way to rescue them. Discovered by other shifters, the brand-new cougar gets two mentors. Blademage Gawain is an easy-going blacksmith with a steel-hard core. His brother Owen is a deadly warrior. Grumpy. Rude. And he doesn't like her.

They aren't the mates she'd dreamed of—they're more.

Powerful, dominating Owen protects the clan—especially the weak—and the only remnant of an abused childhood is his avoidance of females. Now he has to mentor one? Although Gawain soon falls for the dauntless little cat, Owen knows better than to lose his head. But Darcy has a gift for repairing everything…including damaged hearts.

Love isn't in her destiny.

In the brothers' arms, Darcy finds safety. Comfort. And love. But however much she longs for a future with Owen and Gawain, her people need her. Somehow, she must find the courage and skills to save them, even if the attempt demands her life.

If you haven't read a Cherise Sinclair book, you should certainly pick one up. Apparently, no matter the genre, you just can't go wrong.

~ Dark Diva Reviews

Here's how you can get notified on the day of a new release.
www.CheriseSinclair.com/NewsletterForm

Leap of the Lion

The Wild Hunt Legacy 4

Cherise Sinclair

VanScoy Publishing Group

Leap of the Lion
Copyright © 2017 by Cherise Sinclair
Print Edition
ISBN: 978-1-947219-03-8
Published by VanScoy Publishing Group
Cover Artist: Hot Damn Designs

Acknowledgments

Huge thanks go to my critique partners, Monette Michaels and Bianca Sommerland. Where would I be without you to keep my plots on the right trail?

A big squishy hug to Fiona Archer for enduring the worst year ever and still managing to perform a BFF's handholding duties. *Love you, girl.*

To my beta readers, Lisa White, Marian Shulman, and Barb Jack, lots and lots of kittens. (The li'l pouncers are an expression of gratitude. *Really.*) Seriously, though, y'all are amazing. Thank you so, so much!

Prologue

EIGHT-YEAR-OLD OWEN TREHARN closed the back door silently, heard his mother yelling, and froze. The kitchen was dark and empty. For once, he wasn't the one in trouble. Although the sound of her anger hunched his shoulders, he crept toward the living room to see what was going on.

No one would hear him. Sneaking was a survival skill he'd mastered already.

He peeked around the corner.

Two of his littermates were in the room—Edwyn on the couch, Bonnie standing motionless in the corner.

Face dark red with rage, Mother shook a broken bowl at Bonnie. "I liked this bowl. That's why it was on top of the refrigerator."

"Bonnie wanted the candy out of it." Edwyn gave her a taunting look.

Bonnie gasped. "I did not. *You* did. You climbed on a chair an' knocked it off when you were grabbing the candy."

Owen's fingers dug into the doorframe. Bonnie wouldn't steal candy. She never broke the rules. Even so, Mother would never believe Edwyn had busted the bowl. She thought Edwyn was perfect.

"How dare you blame Edwyn for something *you* did."

Mother slapped Bonnie across the face.

"No, Mother!" Bonnie screamed and cringed away.

No. No! Owen cringed, too. He glanced behind him at the back door and safety.

Bonnie was crying. Bonnie needed him.

Forcing his unwilling feet to move, he darted into the living room. Mother hit Bonnie again, and then he was there, between them. He shoved Bonnie toward the front door. "*Run*, Nee."

"Demon-spawn." His mother's cruel name for him hurt almost as much as her hand hitting his face. Pain seared his face, and he turned, covering his head with his arms.

She didn't stop.

Blow after blow struck his shoulders and back, burning through his skin, setting his world on fire. It *hurt*. Tears ran down his cheeks. Jaw clamped shut against the sobs, Owen bent his head and…endured.

A door slammed shut. Bonnie had escaped. She was safe.

Dodging the next blow, he tore for the kitchen, his mother on his heels. As he ran through the back doorway, she flung the broken bowl at him. It slammed into his hand, and blinded by tears, he fell down the back steps. His face ground into the dirt, scraping his chin and cheek. *Ow, ow, ow.* A sob broke out.

Mother stood on the steps. "You disgusting brat. Your sire was no good, and you're no better, Demon-spawn."

Gawain, his other littermate, was suddenly there. He yanked Owen to his feet. "C'mon, brawd."

They ran for the forest.

Every footfall sent pain through Owen's hand, and his eyes were so filled with tears, he kept tripping over branches.

Finally, Gawain slowed. "She gave up and went back to the house. Is here okay?"

"Yeah. It's good."

A sprite, wakened by their noise, chittered at them before

popping back in her hole.

Gulping back sobs, Owen crumpled down into the soft debris on the forest floor. With his good hand, he wiped the tears away, wincing at the sore spots on his face. He was too old to be crying. But his hand, shoulders, and face hurt. The names she called him hurt, too. Why did she hate him so much? She loved Edwyn. Most of the time, she liked Gawain and Bonnie. But she'd always hated Owen.

With a tired grunt, Gawain dropped onto the ground, his face was streaked with sweat and dirt, his blue eyes worried. "What made her so mad this time?"

"Edwyn told her Bonnie broke the candy bowl."

"Bonnie? She wouldn't take Mother's candy. He lied." Gawain was smart that way. He understood people better than Owen did.

"Yeah. He lied."

"Is Bonnie okay?" Gawain's eyes narrowed. "You let Mother beat on you instead, didn't you?"

Owen's shrug made his shoulders hurt worse. "Why does she hate me so much?"

"Dunno." Gawain sighed. "Maybe she'd love us if we looked like her. She loves Edwyn."

Edwyn and Mother had skin the color of milk, and their hair was as light as the pearl necklace Mother always wore.

Owen's thick, straight hair was as dark as the tree trunks around them. Where his arms weren't bruised purple, his skin was reddish-brown. And his eyes were the color of the evergreens.

Gawain had blue eyes, hair a lighter brown than Owen's, and his skin was golden with freckles.

Bonnie's eyes were brown, but her hair was as yellow as the sun.

Owen scowled. "Other littermates don't look much alike,

and their mothers love them." He wasn't saying it right—he wasn't good with words—but Gawain would understand. Gawain always understood him.

"I know. Mother's different. Maybe she only wanted one cub."

Owen closed his eyes. "Maybe." If she had to love only one, she should have picked Gawain or Bonnie. Edwyn was a liar and a cheat—and even if Owen loved him, he didn't really like Edwyn much. The sneaky weasel didn't *deserve* their mother's love.

And Owen didn't deserve her hate…did he? What had he done to make her scream at him and hurt him all the time? "She sure didn't want *me*."

"I think it's 'cause of your sire," Gawain said.

"Did he make her mad, so she hates me instead?"

"That's what Great-Aunt Sandy says." Face streaked with tears, Bonnie stepped into the clearing and sat down next to Owen. "I'm sorry Mother hit you."

"Better me than you." Owen tried to smile even though his swollen cheek pulled painfully. "What did Great-Aunt say?"

"She told the grocer lady how your daddy was one of the males Mother mated with during a Gathering, and later, she wanted to be his mate, but he didn't like her much. Only she kept bothering him until he made fun of her…and then he mated a really pretty female, and Mother got so mad she moved away to here in Pine Knoll."

Gawain chewed on a finger. "Being made fun of would make her really mad."

"Yeah." And Mother could stay mad a really long time. His stomach dropped lower in his belly. If she hated his father, she'd never like him, either. She'd keep hating him and hitting him.

Owen blinked back more tears. He was only a little cub. He couldn't hit her back. It wasn't fair.

But life wasn't fair, was it? He looked at his purpling swollen hand and felt the burning pain in his shoulders. No, life wasn't fair.

Bonnie leaned her head on his shoulder. "Great-Aunt Sandy says she's taking me away from here. From Mother. But I don't want to leave you and Gawain."

"Leaving?" Gawain gulped, swiped his sleeve over his eyes. "That-that's good. It'll be safer."

Lose Bonnie? Owen felt his own eyes burn. Cubs were often fostered other places, but only when they were older. Not at eight years old. He turned to tell Bonnie to beg them to let her stay—and saw the red welt on her face from Mother's hand.

Owen couldn't keep her safe. Not yet.

"Yeah, you should go."

Determination straightened his spine. He'd get bigger and older, and when he did, he'd take care of all the cubs and people who couldn't hit back.

Chapter One

ONLY HUMANS WOULD take two beautiful three-story brick manors and turn them into houses of horror.

Toolbox in hand, Darcy MacCormac stood on the front steps and looked across the grounds of...hell...or whatever this place should be called. Her friend Barbara who liked the old language called it a *priosan*. A prison.

If run by the government, the place would be termed a detention camp. But their captors, the Scythe, weren't with the government. Much to the contrary. Their mission was to manipulate the governments of the world. Holding hostages was one of their favorite techniques.

H Hall on the west held human hostages from all over the world. They'd been kidnapped to ensure their influential family members complied with anything the Scythe demanded.

Z Hall, which the guards called the *Zoo*, held the female shifters from Darcy's village. They were also hostages, not to keep CEOs and politicians in line, but for their fellow shifters.

Darcy walked down the front steps.

Encircling the entire property, ten feet tall, thick stone walls muffled the noise of Seattle and blocked any view of outside. Her shoulders rounded against the claustrophobic feeling.

It could be worse, though, couldn't it? When the shifters

first arrived, they'd been confined underground in animal cages. The adults, then babies had sickened and died before the Scythe realized the fatal effect of confinement and proximity to metal. Finally, they'd let the surviving children out of the basement, given them outside tasks, and housed them on the third floor of Z Hall. There they'd been imprisoned for over a decade.

Each year, each day, she felt more trapped.

Each year, each day, she grew weaker.

Stop. This was where she was—and no one escaped the Scythe. She pulled in a slow breath. The scent of cut grass hung heavy in the humid air, mingling with the briny breeze off Puget Sound and the overripe smell of late September apples that had fallen into the brambles. The years of captivity had taught her to ignore the stench of gasoline, metal, and other putrid odors from the surrounding city.

A cry of pain came from the right.

Hand to her cheek, twelve-year-old Alice, the youngest shifter, cringed from a uniform-clad guard. Long blonde hair pulled back, the youngster wore the Scythe-assigned garb of white T-shirt and cheap cotton pants.

Palms sweaty, Darcy headed that way, moving quickly without looking as if she hurried. "Can I be of assistance, sir?"

After so many years, maintaining a polite tone was habitual, despite feeling as if she was strangling down her shouts. Interrupting an abusive guard was never safe, but sometimes...sometimes she could redirect their anger from a cubling and toward her instead.

With a relieved look, the girl spoke to Darcy. "Manager said I can't have supper unless all the grass is cut. The mower was working, but I had to stop it to clear the blades, and now it won't start. Can you fix it?"

The guard grabbed Alice's shoulder and gave her a brutal shake. "You don't talk with other dirty beasts. Shut your mouth."

The girl's eyes went glassy with tears.

Darcy clasped her hands in front of her waist in an appearance of servitude...and to keep from belting the guard. Once, only once, had she hit a guard, trying to save a friend from a caning. Both she *and* Margery had been beaten into the ground with fists and boots and canes, thrown in separate cells, and left for days. Darcy's intervention had turned a common caning into an unspeakable nightmare.

No hitting. No shouting. Humbly, she looked at the guard and bowed her head to keep him from seeing the hatred in her eyes. "I could look at the motor if you wish. Sir."

After a second, the guard snorted. "Fix it, freak, or I'll take it out on your hide."

She kept her gaze lowered until he'd stalked away. Her mum would have called him a stupid, sprite-brained boggart. Being imprisoned had taught Darcy other terms—*the fucking, dickhead asshole.*

A sigh escaped her.

"You can fix anything," Alice whispered, trust glowing in her big blue eyes.

"Most mechanical things, yes." Not the important things, like illness, heartbreak, and imprisonment. She couldn't fix the slow wearing away of her life force. All the older captives from their village were weakening. Barbara had collapsed yesterday and been taken away.

Had she been taken to the ghastly research labs in Z Hall's basement? Despair filled Darcy. *The Mother keep you, my friend.* Because there was nothing anyone could do.

Do what you can, tinker, for the little one here, instead. Pulling her gaze away, she reached in her pocket and pulled out a wrapped piece of cake she'd snitched when fixing the dishwasher.

A quick look around showed no one was watching. "Here,

munch on this while I work."

The girl's eyes grew wide, and she turned so no one would see her stuff the treat in her mouth. Shifters received only enough food to stay healthy—never sweets. The cake had been baked for the staff.

Alice's eyes filled with tears. A treat. And kindness. Both were unknown in this place.

After patting the cub's shoulder, Darcy knelt beside the mower. It had gas, and the gas wasn't old. The air filter was clean enough. The spark plug—*ah-hah*—was wet. During the summer season, Darcy'd learned to keep extras in her toolbox. After replacing the plug, she gave the pull rope a firm yank.

The mower sputtered, and she adjusted the throttle for a healthy roar.

Alice hooted in glee and threw her arms around Darcy. The hug was bittersweet. The child should have been preparing for her first shift, should have been running in the mountains with her littermates. Should have been home. But their Daonain village was blackened rubble.

Although the Scythe's human hostages might eventually be freed, the shifter females would never be released. They'd slowly weaken and die in this grim institution, surrounded by stone walls, far from the forest.

Across the grounds on the west, the human hostages worked in their garden. Shifter females were restricted to the east side, human hostages to the west. Darcy, however, was allowed everywhere. She'd worked hard to become an indispensable handyman. She was always polite. Always obedient.

They thought her thoroughly cowed. Of course, it helped that the Scythe avoided bringing in outside repairmen.

There were other visitors though. Even now, a car pulled up to the closed wrought-iron gate. Darcy watched as a uniformed guard walked out of the discreetly placed guardhouse and spoke to the driver.

At Z Hall, Director hurried down the manor steps to greet the arrival.

So the guest was important and obviously approved since the car hadn't been shot into little pieces.

With a little smile for Alice, Darcy continued on her way. In front of the manor, she neared the first of the three semi-sunken guard posts that created hillocks in the front lawn. Anyone at the entrance would see only a dark slit behind which was a camouflaged machine gun "pillbox".

During her brothers' visit last week, Patrin had eyed the gun embrasures and said the interlocking fields of fire created a killing field. Anyone coming in the front gate to free the hostages would be easily slaughtered.

A narrow stairwell led down to the concrete box's rear door, and Darcy hurried past, then turned left between the two manor houses toward the rear of the property. The equipment building and generator shed stood near the back orchard. The last of the apples lay rotting, since no one could get to them. The orchard trees circled the inside perimeter of the stone wall, and a thirty-foot mass of blackberries and huckleberries had been allowed to grow wild around them. The thorny tangle created an effective barrier to escape or rescue. The only way in and out of the property was through the front gate.

Maybe.

She glanced to the west at a walnut tree near the side wall. The fruit trees were shorter, their top branches skinny, but the full-sized walnut had wide, strong limbs. If a super-coordinated male came in over the wall, he could possibly jump to the walnut. Over the years, she'd visually picked the sturdiest tree branches above the ocean of thorny brambles. So this imaginary male could...maybe...leap from branch to branch, around the perimeter of the wall, and eventually reach the apple tree that grew closest to the lawn. Even she could make the leap from the grass into that tree.

Next time she saw Fell and Patrin, she'd point out the zigzag route.

It was a shame she didn't have the skills to use the route. Then again, she couldn't. If the Scythe didn't have her as hostage to keep her brothers in line, they'd kill Fell and Patrin.

Focus on today, tinker. Don't think about what can't be.

After doing routine maintenance and running the emergency generator, she went into the equipment building to work on the chainsaw. Gathering oil, lubricants, and sharpeners, she set the chainsaw on the table and started to work.

She'd barely finished sharpening the chain when a foul scent came through the door. Darcy tensed and glanced over her shoulder.

Huber. The human who'd raped Fenella. Hatred roared up within her.

Sneering, the guard swaggered into the building and pulled his cane. "Slacking off again? Lazy cunt." The blow sliced across her shoulders, her cheap cotton shirt providing no cushion.

The long line of pain flared. Gritting her teeth, she didn't move.

Huber's smile was ugly with pleasure—and frustration. "The Director might let you run around like a real person, but we all know you're just an animal. A freak. One of these days you'll fuck up, and then I'll deal with you."

She didn't answer. His open lust nauseated her, but he wasn't allowed to do more than beat her.

A decade ago, after he'd molested Fenella, the girl's male littermates visited, went berserk with rage, and killed human after human before being shot down. With the loss of the littermate bonds, Fenella turned feral and attacked the Director himself. Unwilling to risk losing more shifter-soldiers, sex with shifter females was prohibited.

And this human male salved his thwarted lust with violence instead.

When he drew back for another swing, Darcy dodged and ran outside where those in the gardens, including the other guards, could see her. As a handyman, she was useful enough the Director wouldn't want her incapacitated.

Huber knew it. With an annoyed sound, he followed her. "Fucking unnatural freaks." Backhanding her to her knees, he attached the cane to his weapons belt and sauntered past her to continue his rounds.

The desire to tear at him with claws was a furious drumming in her blood. Her fingers curled...uselessly. She had no claws.

Had never shifted.

She couldn't trawsfur to animal form; none of the females could. The sense of loss drained away her anger.

When captured, she'd been twelve years old, wondering what animal she would be when she first shifted. She didn't know what her father had been, but she'd hoped to be a cougar like her mother.

She had daydreamed of running the forest trails with a beloved lifemate on each side, dancing in the moonlit meadows, and playing tag the tail. She'd live in a big house with her mates, all sleeping in a pile in a huge bed. And she'd someday swell with their cublings. She'd known she would be cherished and protected and in turn, would give her mates all the love in her heart and soul.

But her dreams of a sunlit forest trail had turned to an ugly concrete road. One she would travel alone.

Even if she were free, even if she could shift, she would never lifemate. Love required trust. The starry-eyed cub had matured into a scarred, realistic survivor.

The only person she could count on in life was herself.

LIGHTS WERE OUT, and each female's cell door was locked. In her tiny space, Darcy sweated as she completed another set of squats. From watching the guards' daily sparring sessions, she'd learned how to exercise, how to fight, and the very best curse words. From working on equipment around the human hostages, she'd learned current slang.

Her legs trembled as her muscles failed on the last squat—one less than she'd completed last week. Each week she lost more strength.

Why did she keep trying? The other females had given up hope.

But, as her mum had often said, Darcy was a tomfool tinker—and she never gave up.

Using the jackknife she kept hidden in her sock, she manipulated the old-fashioned window lock until it clicked open. Thanks to frequent waxing, her third-floor window slid up silently.

The security lights had come on at dusk, flooding the wide front lawn. Thank the Mother, she had a room in the rear where the spot lighting illuminated only the sidewalks and patches of the perimeter fence. The ivy-covered manor walls lay in darkness.

After shoving the jackknife back in her sock, she looked up. Black clouds covered the almost full moon.

What nice sneaking weather you have, tinker.

Carefully, she climbed onto the narrow ledge and gripped one of the vines covering the aged brick walls. After a forceful tug to check if the ivy would hold her weight, she swung out and curled her legs around the sturdy trunk. Vine by vine, she worked her way along the wall before moving downward to the second floor. The staff apartments.

She passed the library window and hesitated. Book lust caught her every time. But no, she'd already "borrowed" every book in there at least once. And it was too dark to read now anyway. Summer was the best season when the days were long enough to read far into the evening.

But it was fall, and she had snooping to do. She climbed to the window outside Director's lounge.

Soundlessly, she balanced on the ledge and peered in.

In the sitting area, Director sat across from the visitor. An older, rotund, balding human, Director was in charge of the entire *priosan*.

Darcy didn't know Director's real name. High status Scythe used simply their titles or ranks.

Reminding her of an ugly vulture, the visitor had a shaved head, sharp nose, and dead eyes. From the flurry of activity after he arrived, he was what the human girls called a *big shot*.

Perhaps the *big shot* had interesting news. Taking her...liberated...stethoscope from around her neck, Darcy pressed the bell to the glass and heard light conversation about politics and the weather. No problem. She'd wait...as patient as any cat at a mouse hole. A very cold, shivering cat.

Years ago, she'd risked much to steal black leggings and a black, long-sleeved T-shirt from the staff laundry room. Unfortunately, frequent contact with the rough brick walls had mangled the fabric, leaving holes for the frigid night air that blew off Puget Sound.

This high up, Darcy could see the faint glimmer of the Olympic Mountains, and her body hungered to be free of the enclosing walls. If she could only trawsfur and run the forests on four legs.

But, even if she could escape, she was stuck in human form. She'd hoped to be a cat shifter like Mum, but whatever the Scythe had done to her and the other captured females, none of them could trawsfur to animal form.

The bitter loss of that ability was…what it was. Perhaps having a cat shifter mother was the reason she enjoyed sneaking around. Of course, mountain lions ruled the forest and wouldn't be caught dead in a city. She was more like a cowardly rat. That hurt.

Louder voices brought her attention back. The humans had finally reached the reason for the visit. Keeping her grip on one vine, she listened to Director.

"That's right, Colonel. We don't know why Barbara died."

Died? Darcy froze, her chest tight with grief. A few months older than Darcy, Barbara had just turned twenty-four and was—had been—the oldest of the survivors. Tears prickled in Darcy's eyes. Barbara had been her one real friend in here.

Eleven years before, Darcy had been carrying moving boxes into their new Dogwood home and hating Mum for making them move. She'd felt so lost.

"*Hi. I'm Barbara.*" The slender blonde had walked right up to Darcy. "*I'm so glad you're my age. There aren't enough female cubs here. We're going to be friends, you know.*" And they had been.

As a drizzling rain began, Darcy bowed her head. Even the heavens should mourn when someone so special passed on.

Tapping the table with a finger, Director continued to talk. "For some reason, the creature wasted away, year by year. Nothing halted the progression, even though the doctor could find nothing wrong."

The colonel frowned. "Was this wasting similar to how the Dogwood adults died?"

"Exactly. However, Barbara's death took years. The adults were gone within a few months."

Darcy's jaw tightened. Mum had died in a cage. All the grownups had, one by one. Only the children between one and twelve had survived.

"How about the other females?"

"The older ones are weakening and growing thinner."

And they were giving up. *I won't. I can't.* As the rain soaked her clothes and ran down her face, Darcy shivered in the growing chill.

Director scratched his round chin. "You knew Barbara had died almost before I did. How?"

"Her cougar siblings tried to escape." The colonel's smile was grim. "None of them ever tried before—not since we made that demonstration video years ago. It proved most effective."

"That video." Director's mouth twisted. "Although they're beasts, the girls still look human, and effective or not, the way that child was tortured…"

Darcy snarled silently. These humans were the *true* beasts.

"They're abominations. We can't show weakness. Now each shifter-soldier *knows* that if he doesn't obey, we'll *skin* his sister. The threat is what keeps them in line."

A grumbling sound came from Director. "It's a useless threat without a hostage."

"True enough—and the cougar brothers somehow knew their sister had died. Next time a hostage is near death, tell us so we can dispose of her siblings first."

Dispose. If—when—Darcy died, these humans would *dispose* of her brothers. Would kill Fell and Patrin. Her hand on the stethoscope shook as she remembered her littermates as children. Blue-eyed, brown-haired, light-skinned Fell, all lanky and tall. Patrin with black hair and dark eyes like hers and a wicked sense of humor.

Now, her beloved brothers were hard-eyed, bitter soldiers. *Shifter-soldiers.* Yet, the over-protective Daonain males were vulnerable when it came to their loved ones. That was why Mum had told *her* to watch out for Fell and Patrin.

But how? *How*, Mum? As she turned her attention back to

the conversation, a rumble of thunder drowned the two humans out.

Director refilled the glasses. "Did Barbara's brothers get away?"

"No. Although their disposal was a bit tricky." The colonel made an annoyed sound. "The GPS devices pinpointed them, but they'd entered the forest. Even with tracking devices, it's almost impossible to catch the mutant beasts there."

Director gave a short laugh. "Well, that *is* one reason the shifters are useful. How did you catch them?"

"We didn't try." The colonel sipped his drink. "They'd entered a box canyon. We set the trees on fire and shot the cougars when the heat forced them into the open."

Tears burned Darcy's eyes. She'd played with Barbara and her littermates in Dogwood. The boys had been sweet and funny and always telling jokes.

"Hell of a waste," Director said. "Don't the idiots know you can track them? The female freaks here are fairly clever."

"Oh, they know. They sliced their biceps open to remove the trackers."

Feeling sick, Darcy ran her hand over her rain-wet upper arm and felt the round nodule. The foreign *thing* in her own body. How often had she wanted to cut it out?

"Then how did you locate them?"

"They've never learned that each shifter has *two* location devices." The colonel's smile was cruel. "The smaller is implanted deep in a thigh muscle. The animal would have to know it was there to palpate it and remove it."

What? Two? Dear Mother of All, she needed to tell the others.

Barbara had only been the first. All the females were failing in health...were dying. With a female's death, the bond between littermates would break as it had between Barbara and her brothers.

Darcy bit her lip. When she died, Fell and Patrin would know she was gone. They must be able to flee and not be tracked.

"Two devices. Nice." Director smiled slowly. "Such a shame you had to waste the cougar pair."

"Annoying, too." No grief showed in the colonel's dead eyes. "I had to give their mission to the MacCormac brothers and their team."

"Where's the mission?"

"Russia."

Darcy felt like wailing. Her brothers…so far away.

"Really. What's going on?" Director asked. Over the years, she'd learned he loved being in the know about the Scythe undertakings.

"Since our new US president is starting negotiations on commerce, the MacCormac team will create "incidents" to show how unpopular the US is with the populace. When the Secretary of State visits, it'll appear Russia has turned hostile. Then our nervous president and Congress will agree when we push for increased military spending."

Both men chuckled.

As the buzz of their conversation and clinking of glasses was drowned out by thunder, Darcy growled. Over the years at this window, she'd heard the Scythe big shots boast of manipulating everyone from presidents to helpless shifters. The organization steadily grew more powerful, the members richer.

The urge to break the window and tear them to pieces made her hands shake.

"I hope the MacCormac wolves make it back. In the past few years, we've lost too many of the creatures." The colonel poured the last of the alcohol into his glass. "I'd hoped we could manage to breed them or locate more."

Director frowned. "Are we searching for more?"

The rain increased to a downpour, making it difficult to hear. Darcy pressed closer to the glass, keeping the stethoscope on it.

"We haven't spotted others, and searching takes manpower since they blend into their surroundings so well. However, if we lose this batch, we need to find replacements. If there are any. For all we know, that village had all the mutants." The colonel pulled something out of his jacket pocket. "By the way, I brought you back something from Cuba. You mentioned you have a fondness for a good cigar."

"Fantastic." Smiling, Director shoved to his feet. "Smoking is discouraged in the building. Just let me open the window."

He headed straight for the window where Darcy was perched.

Oh no. She shoved the stethoscope behind the vines and dove off the window ledge into the ivy. And her grip slipped from a rain-slick vine.

Falling.

Desperately, she raked through the foliage for another hold. Caught one. The smaller vine tore loose from the wall. The next one did, too.

She dropped several feet—and a thicker trunk scraped her fingers. She caught it and jolted to a stop, gasping for air. Rain pattered around her on the leaves.

Shouting came from above her. Director had poked his head out the window and spotted her. "Guards!" he bellowed. "Guards. A freak is loose! On the house wall!"

Heart hammering, she half-swung, half-fell to the ground. A strident alarm blared over and over.

Guards charged out of their quarters in Z Hall and into the rainy dark.

Panting, Darcy dove into the narrow gap between the building's wall and the four-foot privet hedge. She crouched there, trying to think. Her skin was clammy with fear, her mouth dry.

Have to move. The lava rock mulch around the bushes crunched as she crawled along the side toward the back. She reached the rear and turned the corner. The jagged lava rocks ripped her leggings—then her knees.

Thunder echoed off the stone fence and brick walls as she wiggled into a hollow under a big bush.

What now?

Turn herself in? They'd suspect she'd heard about the GPS devices. But if they killed her while Fell and Patrin were in Russia on that mission, her brothers would break free. The Scythe couldn't risk that. No, the bastards would take her alive and cage her in the basement where she couldn't tell anyone about the second tracker.

She stared up at the third floor windows where the other shifters were. They needed to know what she'd discovered. Over her head, window after window came alight. The staff must be checking and securing the rooms.

A guard rounded the corner, and Darcy tried to press herself lower.

She couldn't get back to her floor.

More guards moved around the lawn.

If she stayed, she'd be caught.

She had to try to break free. No choice. Even if Fell and Patrin were overseas, maybe she could find their forest compound and warn the other shifter-soldiers about the trackers.

How could she escape?

She could climb over the front gate easily enough, but the entire front was flooded with light. When the guards spotted her, the machine guns would spray the entire area with bullets.

Forget the front. How about the back?

Darcy studied the grounds. In the heavy downpour, the

floodlights on the rear lawn were reduced to smaller circles of light, leaving pools of darkness between. It was the only way.

After smearing mud on her face and hands, she crawled out. Every time a guard looked her way, she froze. When she, Fell, and Patrin had played wolves-and-rabbit as cubs, they'd learned black-on-black disappeared and movement would be spotted.

She gained another few feet.

Terror shook her arms, and surely even human ears could hear her heart slamming against her ribcage.

Her hand came down on a thorny blackberry vine, and she barely suppressed a cry of pain—and victory. She'd reached the thorny hedge that circled the inside of the stone wall. Crouching, she crept along the edge of the bramble-filled orchard and stopped.

There was the apple tree that stood closest to the lawn.

As she straightened, a pair of guards trotted along the back sidewalk, flashing their lights.

No! She flattened herself on the ground in the shadows, presenting no silhouette, nothing to catch their attention. Fear clogged her throat as she waited for their shout of discovery.

They walked on.

Now. Do it now. Oh, Mother of All, she didn't know how to leap into trees; she only knew how to do slow, careful creeping.

Now, tinker.

She ran along the edge of the blackberry thicket, building up speed, and leaped. Her hands slapped against the low branch of the apple tree—and slipped. Terrified, she convulsively swung one leg up and over—and caught herself.

Gods, Gods, Gods. Heart hammering, she clambered onto the branch. The foliage was shaking, so she waited, trembling all over.

No one had noticed.

Next. She had the route mapped out in her head. But jumping in the dark?

No choice.

Suppressing her whimpers, she jumped to the next tree. In the dark and wet and cold. *Oh Gods*. To the next. And the next. Branch by branch, she worked her way to the walnut tree.

Her panicked breathing hurt her chest as she slowly climbed the walnut. There was the branch that extended toward the top of the wall. But...from this angle, she could see the distance was too great. Tears filled her eyes. She couldn't jump that far. She couldn't.

No choice.

Balancing carefully, she walked out on the branch. It sagged ominously, and a wave of fear shook her. She was tired. Weak.

And out of options. The Mother and the God held no sway in human cities, but she sent them a prayer anyway. And leaped.

Failed.

She landed belly down on the edge of the wall, knocked her breath out, and she slid downward. Frantically, she stretched her arms across the wall, trying to claw a hold into the rough stone and concrete.

Her fingernails caught. Her motion stopped.

Gasping for air, she clung with all her might. Ever so carefully, she swung her leg up over the edge and, inch-by-inch, wiggled onto the wall.

The streetlights revealed a grassy patch down below. She jumped—and landed on her feet. Maybe she would have been a cat shifter like Mum.

But...*ow*. Her ankles felt as if she'd crunched all the bones together.

Ignoring the pain, she broke into a run, darted across the wide avenue, and sprinted down the Seattle streets, turning left and right at random. Blindly running...always heading roughly east toward the Cascade Mountain Range where her village had been.

The guards wouldn't dream she'd escaped the grounds. Not for a while. They'd search the compound for at least an hour or two, and surely delay admitting to the higher-ups she'd gotten out. But the higher-ups would call in the people who did the tracking.

If she had the GPS devices in her body, they'd find her. So that was her next step. Go somewhere quiet and use the knife in her sock.

Being caught was more terrifying than cutting herself open.

Mostly.

THEY DIDN'T FIND her for a whole twenty-four hours.

Chapter Two

A T MIDNIGHT THE next night, Darcy limped down an empty street. A sock was knotted around the wound in her upper arm. She'd torn off her long shirtsleeves and wrapped them around the multiple slashes in her right thigh. The tracker in her leg had been horribly deep, and she'd had to cut and cut through far too much muscle to extract it.

For a second, she stopped to lean against a building, catch her breath—and try to find some hope.

Stupid human city.

She was so lost. Her goal of *head east toward the mountains* had sounded easy enough. From eavesdropping on the guards, she possessed a hazy idea of Seattle's layout. Her knowledge hadn't been nearly detailed enough. Last night, she'd had to detour around a huge construction area with chain-link fencing. Then a big river had blocked her way with one—only one—bridge in sight. She'd wasted time trying to find a less obvious one and had finally given up and crossed. To her relief, the Scythe hadn't been at the other end. So far, so good.

For hours, she'd been walking, angling south and east, through an industrial district, over an enormous huge highway, and finally back into residential neighborhoods. Horrible city. Why would anyone choose to live in an area bounded by concrete boxes and streets and stinking of gasoline?

Block after block after block. Eventually, she'd have to detour around some giant lake in the middle of the city…if she ever reached that point.

At the next intersection, the hair on her nape rose. She was being watched. A casual glance to the left showed nothing. To the right…

Parked at the curb, a black van with tinted windows waited. The disturbed air at the exhaust pipe showed the engine was running.

She turned to head the other direction and glanced behind her.

Another dark van rolled slowly down the street.

No, no, no. Her mouth went dry; her pulse roared in her head. How had they found her so quickly?

The bridge. The Scythe must have had spotters, cameras, or something.

Despair was a metallic taste in her mouth. She broke into a run, knowing her flight spotlighted her as surely as if she'd screamed *look at me.*

She sprinted down the sidewalk, turned into a one-way street, and lost the car behind her. Speeding through a barren stretch of smaller apartment dwellings, she spotted another Scythe vehicle.

Run faster.

The car's engine revved as she darted around another corner. Reaching the next intersection, she started to veer right…and scented green. *Trees. Forest. Water.* Within one breath, her body took over, yanking her left and straight for the wilderness. A wilderness in the center of a city. How could this be?

She ran past the signs at the entrance—*Seward Park*—and angled into the shadows beside the road.

The vans followed her in. Their tires screeched as they

stopped. Men erupted from the vehicles, shouting orders.

Sharp popping sounds came from behind her. The road ahead sparked and spat concrete at her. Bullets—they were shooting at her. Trying to bring her down.

A slicing pain burned into her already damaged right leg, and her knee buckled. She fell, rolled, and tried to scramble to her feet. Her leg failed.

Terror consumed her, complete and utter panic, and she keened with protest. Using one leg and her hands, she lunged forward, unable to stop, unable to surrender.

As she blundered out of the shadows, the light of the waxing moon poured down over her, spotlighting her to her enemies. The need for shelter, for escape, filled her until nothing was left.

Oh, please.

Then she was running. *Running.* She bolted into the underbrush, through the huckleberries, and far into the fir forest where the darkness was impenetrable. She tripped on something, realized it was her shirt, and bit at the offending fabric until it shredded under her teeth. Her shoes were gone. Her leggings had split and hung off one paw.

Paw? She had paws. And a tail. And—

The yelling behind her grew closer.

On three legs, she fled, fear digging its claws into her fur as she ran and ran and ran.

Chapter Three

THE SUN WAS well up when Owen Treharn left the diner on Cold Creek's Main Street. He stopped for a moment to stretch and try to shake off the ugly emotions rasping over his skin. Last night had been the full moon when shifters gathered to ensure the Daonain race would continue. From moonrise to moonset, he'd mated female after female. He didn't even know how many.

He shook his head. Who would have thought he'd ever tire of full moon Gatherings?

Admittedly, sex was enjoyable, sure, but wasn't there supposed to be more? And dealing with females? Fuck, he'd rather fight a hellhound.

The hours of mating hadn't helped his wrist either. Grimacing, he rotated his left wrist. Felt as if a beaver was gnawing on it with dull teeth.

He snorted. He'd always been willing to die for his people, and when the God had called him to serve as a cahir—a warrior of the Daonain—he'd been overjoyed. Funny how in the stirring bard tales of glorious sacrifice, the aftermath of battle and the irritating injuries went unmentioned.

At least the pain had eased up. And the busted bones had been for a good cause, since his attack had kept a hellhound from ripping Ben's arm off. His big grizzly partner had managed to break free, but the hellhound fractured Owen's wrist in the process.

The North Cascades healer, Donal, had closed the gory bites, but busted bones didn't fuse together quickly. It'd taken him two days at a slow human's walk to get to his remote cabin. Yesterday, he'd returned to Cold Creek in cat form, but the bones weren't quite healed, and mating all night hadn't helped.

Fuck, he was tired. Despite two cups of coffee, he felt as if his tail was dragging in the dust.

With a grunt, he scratched his stubbled jaw. He needed to shave. Feeling hair on his face reminded him too much of adolescence when he'd claw himself by accident, belatedly realizing he'd unexpectedly trawsfurred into a cougar. Damn embarrassing. His brother, Gawain, who'd rarely trawsfurred by accident, would merely grin in sympathy. His other littermate, Edwyn, had gloated, even though his control had been even worse.

Edwyn. Owen's mood ran downhill like an avalanche of mud. Spoiled rotten, Edwyn had been an entitled, unlikable brat. If denied something, he'd go after it anyway, no matter how much damage he caused.

But, by the God, he shouldn't have died. First, one female had ruined him from birth, and another had sent him to his death.

Owen shook his head and turned his thoughts from his past. Gathering night's enforced intimacies always left him feeling as if someone had skinned him and hung his carcass from a tree. This morning, his mood was as mean as a half-starved badger's.

He needed to go home to his isolated cabin. But…Gawain had been at the Gathering last night, and it'd be good to spend some time with him. *Maybe.* If he could figure out what to talk about, since it seemed as if Gawain had inherited all the conversational skills.

But damn, it was nice to see his brother again. Maybe he could just sit and let Gawain talk?

They'd both changed in the last...what...twenty-five years since they'd separated? When Owen had walked away from Pine Knoll at sixteen, Gawain had been apprenticed to a metalsmith. Pride swelled in Owen's chest because, somewhere along the line, his littermate had been called by the Goddess to be a blademage—a magical blacksmith.

Every cahir who had access to a blademage wore a magicked blade, because there were no finer knives in the world.

"Look, look!"

"Unca Wen!"

At the sound of his nephews' high voices, Owen stopped, and love swept through him. Smiling, he went down on one knee and braced. One tiny body hit him, then another, like the patter of acorns in a high wind. "What are you two doing in town?"

Luke bounced on his tiptoes. "We get b'ekfast at the diner. Da said Mommy is sweepy."

"Sleepy," their father Brady corrected with a grin. The male's eyes were half-lidded with both exhaustion and satisfaction. Owen figured the three lifemates had spent all night mating.

"An' Da Van is sweepy, too," Tyler said.

Owen smothered a laugh. As he rubbed his cheek over Tyler's soft hair, he noticed a human leaving Angie's diner with a donut box.

Bonnie had always loved chocolate donuts. His sister was an amazing female, not manipulative or self-centered—nothing like their mother. He'd never regretted moving here to be closer to her, and she'd given the Daonain two fantastic cubs. She deserved all the treats in the world. "Luke, Tyler, I saw chocolate-covered donuts in the diner. Why don't you buy some for you…and your mama?"

The screams of glee made him wince. Angie might nip his ears off if the tiny terrors disturbed her customers. "Cubs," he said sternly. "You have to be quiet as little mice to earn donuts. Can you do that?"

Vigorous nods.

Brady clapped a hand on his shoulder. "Thanks, cahir. You heading back to your cabin today?"

"Probably. Tell my sister I'll stop by when I return for dark of the moon."

Brady nodded, although his mouth flattened at the reminder of the dangers during moonless nights. Because of the human encroachment, more hellhounds hunted the North Cascades Territory. As a cahir, Owen stood between danger and his people.

Cahirs often died young. And yet—Owen ruffled Tyler's hair—was there anything more important than protecting the cubs?

With a nod to Brady, Owen rose and headed toward the wilderness lodge where he'd stayed yesterday. By now, the innkeeper Breanne would be serving breakfast.

A few minutes later, as he approached the lodge, he spotted a tiny pixie perched in a huge fuchsia bush, nibbling on a bloom. Not a sprite's favorite food, but summer's bounty was decreasing. Even the miniature roses in the porch planters were done flowering. But… He plucked a rose hip and tossed it over.

The pixie caught the marble-sized hip, examined it, and chittered happily.

This kind of female he could tolerate. Open and honest. No manipulation. When given a treat, a sprite openly exhibited her delight. A shame Daonain females weren't the same.

Inside, the tantalizing scent of bacon drew him through the

main lodge to a glass-walled dining room in the rear. Three shifter females at a window table were already chowing down.

Ignoring them, Owen walked into the kitchen.

"Hey, Owen." At the sink, Zeb, a fellow cahir, acknowledged his presence in a gravelly voice. Somewhere over the past centuries, a Native American human had joined the bloodline of the mostly Celtic shifters. Zeb had black hair, dark brown eyes, and his bronzed skin showed a wealth of scars, many from hellhounds' teeth and claws.

Shay, another cahir and Zeb's blood brother, nodded a greeting. Called by the God to serve, cahirs were gifted with additional strength and size, usually ending up around six and a half feet tall. The three of them made even the huge kitchen feel crowded.

And they dwarfed Zeb and Shay's pretty lifemate who stood at the stove.

Breanne smiled over. "I was beginning to think I'd have to send Shay to find you."

"It'd take a hellhound to make me miss one of your breakfasts." Owen returned her smile. Bree was a likable female. The rough time she'd had when first coming to Cold Creek had revealed unexpected courage and generosity of spirit. Although being lifemated to one female seemed a form of insanity, he had to admit his friends had been lucky to win Bree for their mate. "Gotta say, having one of your breakfasts after a Gathering makes coming into Cold Creek truly worthwhile."

The way she brightened made her almost radiant, and Shay grinned. "Pretty compliments get your plate loaded to the edges."

"Challenge accepted." Owen took the cup of coffee Zeb poured and leaned against a counter.

"Calum wanted a word before you left," Shay said. "He should be here soon."

"Food, first?" Owen gave the bacon-filled skillet an assessing look.

Breanne laughed. "Yes. Go have a seat, and Shay will bring it out in about five minutes."

Owen's stomach rumbled a complaint at the delay.

With a snort, Zeb tossed him a muffin from a pile on the counter. "Start on that."

Owen went out to the sunny dining room and paused.

The three other lodgers were still there, doing that giggling thing females did. High and shrill, the sounds reminded him of his mother whenever a lover had visited. His jaw locked. On one occasion, he had accidentally spilled his drink on a male's shoes and discovered how quickly giggles could turn to shrieks of rage. And pain...

Bah. What the crap was wrong with him? For years, he'd managed to keep Pine Knoll out of his mind. Was Gawain's presence dredging up these ugly memories?

Selecting a corner table far from the females, Owen turned his back and put his feet up on the windowsill. Nibbling on the muffin, he gazed out the window at the huge flagstone patio. The small playground Zeb had built was empty of cubs. On the far right, Zeb's latest project, a built-in seat wall, curved around what would eventually be a circular fire pit. Down the grassy slope was a gurgling creek where silvery undines swam in a flashing game of tag beneath the footbridge. Past the creek, the dense forest sloped upward into the mountains.

The sound of footsteps caught his attention, and he glanced over his shoulder.

Carrying a cup of coffee, Gawain strolled into the room. It was still a surprise to see him as an adult, but grown up he was. Only a couple of inches short of Owen's six-five, he had a full, neatly trimmed beard and wavy, light brown hair that reached surprisingly broad, muscular shoulders. Spotting Owen, he lifted his eyebrows in a silent question. *Up for company?*

Owen suppressed a grin as he shoved a chair out with his foot. Whereas Owen had the manners of a tactless dwarf, Gawain could be as courteous as their high Fae ancestors were reputed to have been.

Yeah, he'd missed his littermate over the years.

As Gawain crossed the room, the giggling from the corner began again. If Owen'd been in animal form, his ears would have gone back. He shouldn't be surprised the females had set their sights on Gawain since blademages were called by the Mother in the same way cahirs were called by the God. Females always pursued the God-chosen...whether they liked the male or not.

Owen studied his littermate. He and his siblings had been conceived during a full moon Gathering, which meant they had different fathers, appearances, and personalities. With light brown hair and fair skin, Gawain looked and acted like a sociable, easygoing Scottish laird. Owen's father probably had Latino blood—and perhaps the sociability of a wolverine, although Owen might have developed that trait all on his own.

As Gawain took a seat, Owen eyed him. "Maybe you should sit somewhere else."

"What?"

"With a cahir and a blademage at one table, how long before a female approaches to see if we want to fuck, even though the Gathering is over?"

Gawain shook his head. "You've grown rather cynical, brawd."

"Maybe." Owen's mouth tightened. Maybe he'd been more optimistic at birth—before their mother showed her hatred. Or before Edwyn's death when Owen had left with Bonnie and not returned. "Cynicism grows with experience."

Gawain took a sip of his coffee and glanced at the covey of females. "I don't mind being pursued. And Cold Creek's females are impressive."

"Nah, the females resemble those in other territories." Unmated males were urged to sow their seed in more than one territory, and Owen had done his share of traveling.

"In appearance, yes. But your Cosantir draws a high percentage of shifters with intelligence, flexibility, and acceptance into his territory."

Huh. "I try not to talk with the females I mate," Owen muttered. "But Calum *is* an unusual Cosantir."

"You try not to…" Gawain stared at him and shook his head. "Brawd, you worry me."

A scream of laughter sliced through their conversation as the females' voices rose.

"The healer adores big breasts." The buxom brunette cupped her breasts and bounced them. "Just think. He's got a nice house and money. I'd be set for life."

"Poor Donal," Owen muttered. "The predators are circling him like hawks after a chicken."

"I'd rather have one of the cahirs." The blonde fluffed her hair.

"Fat chance," the brunette told her. "The only unmated cahir left is that brown-haired one who never talks. He might be all right if he had a lot of money, but…"

"Owen's nice." The youngest bounced in her seat. "He liked me. I know it."

The brunette sniffed. "I doubt it. That cahir doesn't…" Her voice trailed off as she obviously remembered he was in the room.

When the females turned to look, Owen curled his lip in a snarl. "I'll let the males in town know you three are out for money and a house—and that, in my opinion, they might as well fuck a human."

They were shocked silent at the coarse insult.

He scowled at the youngest female, a slender redhead he'd mated with last night. "And I don't like you; I don't like *any* female. Unfortunately, I have no choice but to fuck you vultures one night of every month."

The younger one burst into tears and fled…followed by the other two.

"By the Goddess, Owen." Gawain shoved to his feet. "What is wrong with you?"

Guilt made Owen growl as he stood. "Did you hear them? Donal deserves better. Fuck, even *I* deserve better."

"You made that little female cry." Gawain grabbed his arm and yanked him forward. "You can't—"

"Back off, brawd." Owen slammed his palm against his brother's chest.

Gawain staggered back, knocked over a chair, and regained his balance. "You mindless moose." Head down, he charged Owen, his head impacting Owen's sternum. Painfully. A table and chairs crashed under their weight.

As Owen broke free and nailed Gawain in the jaw, Shay shouted from across the room. "By the God, stop!"

Not a chance. Adrenaline crooned a battle song in Owen's ears. He hadn't had a good fight—a fun fight—with anyone in years. A grin pulled at his mouth—until Gawain's fist wiped it away.

Scat on the trail. When had his brother learned to punch?

Blinking away the swirling stars, Owen spat, "Flabby feline, that the best you can do?" Readying an attack, he spotted a tall, dark-haired, olive-skinned, leanly muscular man at the kitchen door.

It was Calum. Oh *fuck.*

How long had the Cosantir been watching? "Stop, brawd."

Gawain halted. Looked. His hand relaxed, and he took a step back.

"Sorry," Owen said under his breath.

Gawain nodded, and a corner of his mouth curved up. Slow to ignite, the blademage's temper was hotter than the fire in his forge, but his anger died quickly, and he held no grudges.

Owen's anger didn't contain as much heat, but could take hours…days…to disappear.

Then there was Calum. The God-called guardian of the North Cascades Territory kept firm control over his temper, and his anger was as icy as the glaciers covering the highest mountain peaks.

Gawain's fury could be intimidating. Calum's wrath was deadly.

Might as well see how badly his whiskers were about to be trimmed. Owen gave a slight bow and attempted a smile. "Good morrow, Cosantir. Do you remember my littermate, Gawain? He's a blademage from Pine Knoll in Mt. Hood Territory."

Calum's normally gray eyes were dark with the presence of the God.

Owen heard his littermate make a soft sound at the impact of the black gaze.

"I remember Gawain," Calum said.

"Cosantir," Gawain acknowledged quietly.

Calum's faint English accent grew terser with his anger. "Three females ran from the room."

By Herne's hairy balls, females were more trouble than anything on the planet. What was he supposed to say? *I'm sorry* would be a lie. "They annoyed me."

"Nia was crying."

The youngest one. "She boasted that I liked her. She lied."

Calum's voice held a chill that matched his eyes. "If a young one has only experienced a Gathering or two, she might misread a mating for something more. Childish boasting is harmless. Even if irritated, an honorable adult doesn't cut down a tree to move a branch out of his path."

No argument could stand up. As Calum had noted, the female was young and inexperienced. Owen bowed his head. "I was overly harsh."

The evenness of Calum's voice was more menacing than a shout. "You are often overly harsh with the females. You may well regret your intolerance when you try to win a mate."

Owen stared at him. "I will *never* lifemate."

Calum lifted a brow. Rather than answering, he appraised the room, and Owen winced. Several chairs were busted. A painting lay on the floor, the frame broken. "It seems you are also angry with your littermate," Calum said. "Was there a reason?"

He hadn't done anything right this morning. "Not really, Cosantir."

An eyebrow rose. "Indeed. Aside from females, your judgment of people tends to be quite accurate. If you dislike your littermate so much, should I drive him from my territory?"

For Herne's *sake*.

Beside Owen, Gawain stiffened—and stood his ground.

"*No*, Cosantir. My brother is a fine shifter. Strong and honorable. A talented blademage. We simply have a history which lies uneasily between"—*no, that wasn't right*—"with *me*."

Gawain looked over and a corner of his mouth lifted, his emotions right there on his face for everyone to see. How could they have been birthed by the same female?

Calum's eyes narrowed. "History shouldn't become a weight tied to a shifter's tail." His attention turned to Gawain. "I've heard you and your Cosantir are at odds."

Gawain probably had cause. Last Beltane, Owen had watched the Pine Knoll Cosantir acting the fool.

Calum looked at Owen. "Cahir, you have risked your life for our people. I won't invite someone here who makes you unhappy."

Unhappy. That wasn't what he felt when his brother was around. Not any longer. Owen collected his laggard wits and offered his Cosantir the truth of his heart. "I would be pleased to have Gawain here. I would also be pleased to punch him when he annoys me."

The darkness disappeared from the Cosantir's eyes, and his quicksilver grin appeared. "That seems clear enough. Gawain, the North Cascades Territory could use a blademage. You are welcome to move here."

Gawain's eyes lit.

"He's only welcome if he and the idiot cahir clean up the mess they made," Zeb growled from the kitchen.

"We will, Zeb." Owen frowned. "Cosantir, Shay said you wanted to speak to me?"

"Aye. I have a task for you, cahir."

Owen bowed his head. "Your will, Cosantir."

"Although I'd considered sending Alec, now I believe you are a better choice." Before Owen could feel complimented, Calum added, "A visit to a city might remind you of what is important in life."

"A city?" By the God, cities were full of...humans. And metal and concrete. And *humans*. Where they gathered in large numbers, their putrid odors would make a skunk gag. Owen smothered his objections. Calum chose only what was best for the Daonain.

Didn't mean Owen would enjoy the assignment.

"A female cougar shifter has been seen in a Seattle park for a number of days." Calum frowned. "Possibly, she blundered into the city and can't find her way out, or she might be feral."

"No, not feral." Gawain's brow wrinkled with his dismay.

Owen suppressed his own hiss of protest. Feral shifters had to be killed, and cahirs did the killing. Over the years, he'd returned five feral males to the Mother, and he remembered each gut-wrenching death. Each name. But he'd never had to kill a female. Although most females he'd encountered were self-centered and sneaky liars, he'd rather rip off his tail than physically hurt one.

"After you pack, come to the bar to get the keys to the car," Calum said. "Tynan will meet you near the park."

Tynan. Healer Donal's littermate lived in the fucking city and worked as a cop for humans. The male must be crazier than a bee-stung badger. "You sure he knows what he's doing?"

Amusement lit Calum's eyes. "I daresay he knows better than you, cahir."

Ouch. Owen bent his head, said, "Your will, Cosantir," and retreated while he could.

Gawain fell into step beside him.

Owen stopped. "What's up?"

"I'll clean up the dining room and fix what we busted." Gawain hesitated. "Thank you for what you said to the Cosantir. I'd hoped to talk with you before meeting him."

"Talk about what?"

Gawain rubbed his hand over his beard. "Brawd. We haven't been... After Edwyn died, it was difficult to be together. Made his absence more painful. I know you felt the same. But the missing bond is scarred over now, and I miss you."

His littermate had always been appallingly upfront. Owen shut his eyes, remembering how it had felt as if a piece of himself had been ripped away when Edwyn died. Yet, as with a missing limb, the wound had closed. "What did you want to talk about?"

"I'm moving out of Pine Knoll no matter what. But if my presence here causes you pain, I'll find a different territory."

"No. Stay." The Cosantir was right that the territory needed a permanent blademage. The last one had been ancient, rarely worked, and had recently moved to Elder Village.

And it was time Owen stopped hiding in a corner like a wounded cub. He scrubbed his face with his hands as if he could groom the awkwardness away and tried a smile. "I've missed having someone to fight with."

"Oh. In that case, far be it from me to deprive you of your fun." With an evil grin, Gawain casually shoved Owen face-first into the wall.

Well, fuck. Owen gingerly shook his head, ears humming as if he'd bumped into a beehive. The fucking blademage had put on some serious muscle.

THE TRIP TO Seattle had taken so long that Owen's skin felt infested by a thousand fleas. It was a shame Gawain hadn't been assigned to this damn trip instead. The idiot enjoyed human forms of transportation and didn't see anything insane about trapping a body in a small metal box on wheels. Then again, blademages loved metal. Crazy fools.

Owen's foot twitched on the gas pedal, but the Cosantir had warned him about speeding. If caught exceeding the posted "speed limit" numbers, he could get locked in a small iron cell with no view of the sky.

The thought made him want to curl into a ball.

Almost there. Off to the right, the setting sun glinted off a spindly mushroom-headed tower that rose from a forest of atrociously tall buildings. "What a fucking ugly place."

A few minutes later, he escaped the multilane highway called I-5 onto quieter streets. As instructed, he drove past the Seward Park entrance and parked a short distance north.

A man in jeans and a hoodie leaned against a parked car. Around six feet tall. A bony face with a square jaw. Short, brown hair with reddish tints. Tynan had visited Cold Creek a time or two to see his littermate, the healer.

Owen parked, jumped out, and tucked the car key into his knife sheath. Along with the stench of the city, he could smell lake water, freshly cut grass, fir trees—and the faint wild scent of a shifter. "Tynan."

"Good to see you, cahir." The cop held out a thin hooded sweatshirt. "Put this on."

Frowning, Owen did so. "Why? And why meet this far outside the park?"

"Because this section of the road has no street cameras. Closer in, there are people and cameras. Pull the hood up, keep your head down, and let's go." Doing the same, Tynan led the way down the sidewalk. Nearing a black van with darkly tinted windows, he said in a low voice, "This is one of the vehicles hunting the female. Slouch and keep your head turned."

As the hair on the back of Owen's neck rose, they passed the van. Humans were within. And he caught the scent of gun oil.

Avoiding the park entrance, Tynan crossed the grass at the northernmost corner into the park. His voice held a distinct Irish lilt as he said, "It's a pretty park, this old growth forest in the city's heart, and I often run here of a morning."

Owen wanted to ask what kind of fucked-up Daonain would live in a city, but this wasn't the time...if there ever was one. He'd rather expected the notorious city-living shifter to be wild-eyed and half-crazy. Instead, Owen could feel the rock-solid nature of Tynan's personality. For whatever reason the wolf chose to live surrounded by humans, it wasn't because he was insane.

Following Tynan, Owen strolled past bushes, various buildings, a parking area, and finally into a forest that would have been at home in the North Cascades Territory.

"Have you figured out what the female is doing here?" Perhaps she was a youngster who'd taken a dare to enter the city and gotten herself lost.

"I don't know why she's here; I do know why she hasn't left. Vans—like the one we passed—are parked at the entrance and along the adjacent streets, monitoring every person who leaves. When I scouted yesterday, I also discovered some humans camping out." Tynan glanced back, and anger simmered in his eyes. "They're hunting her."

Fury rose in Owen. Humans were hunting a female of the Daonain? "Do they believe they're out to capture a wild animal—or a shifter?"

"Oh, and the hunters know she's more than a cougar. Animal removal would normally be handled by the Department of Fish and Wildlife. This group isn't with the state, yet they obtained permission from someone. The company name on their vehicles is magnetic—easy to put on and easy to remove."

"Anything else?"

"The park caretaker says they've been here two or three days. Last night, they brought in hunting dogs."

Owen barely suppressed a snarl.

As twilight faded into full dark, Tynan veered onto a deer trail, moved through the dense underbrush, and stopped. "Right, we'll leave our clothes here."

Owen nodded. Most of the city stink had disappeared under the moist green fragrance of the forest. Douglas firs and orange-barked madrone towered over ferns, vining blackberries, and huckleberries. After stripping, he moved his hunting blade from his calf to his forearm, seeing Tynan do the same. The magicked weapon sheaths would trawsfur with them and be inconspicuous on their furry forelegs.

Tynan studied him for a second. "Alec calls you *ghost cat*. Says, on a hunt, you're the most cunning, silent shifter he's ever seen. So I'll get us close to the humans, and you can lead us around them."

Owen nodded. When he, Alec, and Ben worked as a cahir team, they dumped the sneaky undertakings on Owen. "Works for me."

Tynan shifted into a heavy-boned, muscular, silver-gray wolf.

Owen sniffed, trying to catch the female shifter's scent, but only caught the stench of humans. "Let's go find her."

WAY TO GO, TINKER.

Darcy wanted to cry—but, hey, not an option for a cougar. It was so amazing that she'd actually trawsfurred. Only…the miracle had turned into a disaster. Because she couldn't shift *back*.

In the chilly September night, she lay curled up and shivering in a dirt hollow above a tiny stream. Her right hind leg, right foreleg, and ribs throbbed angrily. The gunshot wounds and the areas she'd cut with her knife were oozing and smelled foul. The wounds were infected.

And she was trapped.

Over the past…however long it had been…she'd kept trying and trying to trawsfur back to human form. No luck. As the humans would say, she was screwed. With her injured legs handicapping her and no experience, she hadn't caught any food in the forest.

As far as she could tell, Seward Park was a tiny peninsula, a "finger" projecting out into a huge lake. Whenever she'd tried to escape the park, the Scythe had blocked her escape. Yesterday, they'd brought in hunting dogs and more men.

From experiments on the Dogwood captives, the Scythe

knew tranquilizers drove shifters berserk, which explained why the hunters were shooting real bullets, aiming to disable her. They'd spotted her at dawn, and a bullet had grazed her ribs, slowing her even more. She'd escaped only because the park had opened, and the hunters retreated to their camp.

They'd find her tonight.

As her despair deepened, she rubbed her chin on her forepaws. She'd only be free and alive for a few more hours. When they realized she wouldn't let them take her alive, they'd shoot to kill.

Well, if she died tonight, at least she'd gotten to be a cougar. She closed her eyes, feeling the breeze ruffle her fur. As each hair tip moved, the wind's touch felt like a caress.

Her ears swiveled to catch the sound of a rustle in the grass. Ears that turned were so strange. And difficult to control. If she actually tried to make her ears or tail move, nothing happened. But now, with sickness and exhaustion overwhelming her, her feline instincts were taking over.

A louder noise caught her attention, and she lifted her nose to scent the breeze.

Only the forest fragrance.

Last night, she hadn't caught the scent of any Dogwood shifter-soldiers with the Scythe's humans and dogs. What if the male villagers showed up to hunt her tonight? Her stomach knotted. To keep their littermates safe, they'd follow orders and capture her. However, in cougar form, she couldn't speak to tell them about the second concealed tracker.

Could her escape have gone any more wrong?

Sure, it could have. Other shifter females or males might have been hurt during her breakout. That would have been intolerable.

As almost silent footsteps sounded, her ears pivoted. She smelled the air, but the wind was wrong, blowing her scent toward whatever was coming.

A naked man stepped out of the brush, sniffed, and his gaze fixed on her hiding place.

On *her*.

Cold terror flooded her. *Run!* She leaped out of the hollow toward the thickest underbrush. Pain stabbed into her wounded legs, and she hissed. Gathering herself, she leaped toward the—

A cougar smashed into her, knocked her onto her side, and came down on top of her. He was heavy, so heavy, and more pain shot through her.

Her claws emerged, and she twisted to bring them to bear.

A terrifying growl reverberated in her ear. Teeth closed on the back of her neck, and each time she moved, his jaws bit down. The animal could sever her spine if he wanted.

Panting in dread, she went limp.

Her worst fear had come true—the Scythe had sent the shifter-soldiers.

Tell them. She had to tell the males about the trackers right now. Her paws twitched as she tried to trawsfur back to human.

Nothing.

She lay still under the male and trembled.

The naked human walked out of the brush. He was tall with short brown hair and a square jaw. His lack of clothing indicated he was a Daonain shifter and not human.

"Conclusions, Owen?" the male asked. "If she's not fighting you, I'd guess she's not feral?"

The cougar holding her down made a chirrup-purr of agreement.

When the naked shifter drew closer, the teeth on her neck tightened to ensure she couldn't attack the unarmed male.

"I smell blood. Did you damage her?"

The cougar made a low growl of no.

Keeping his distance, the naked male circled her and made a

grunting sound. "Her right hind and foreleg have infected wounds. Got a bloody graze across her right ribs deep enough to show bone. Either she has been poking herself with sticks or someone shot her. More than once."

The rumble of anger from the heavy cougar filled Darcy's brain, and she flattened her ears, wishing she were as tiny as a mouse. A mouse might have a chance.

The naked male stared down at her. "You need to trawsfur to human so we can figure out what to do."

The order was like a kick to her belly. Everything in her surged forward, trying to do as he asked...and failing again. The sound she made was more of a kitten's whimper than a cougar's snarl. Her shivering increased.

"By the Lady, we don't have time for this." The male frowned at her. "*Now*, female."

The teeth clamped on her neck released her. As magic tingled in the air, the cougar on her back was replaced by a huge male in human form. He rose to his feet.

The shorter male put his hands on his hips. "Got a suggestion, Owen?"

Darcy tried to stand.

"Don't move, female." Even in human form, the one named Owen had a growl that shattered her courage. Several inches over six feet, he had straight, rich brown hair to his shoulders, dark stubble along a strong jaw, and thick, dark brows. He looked...mean.

When moonlight glinted across a blade-shaped scar on his cheekbone, she went still. Every Daonain knew the symbol for a cahir—a warrior of the Daonain.

He looked at the other male. "Tynan, I don't think she *can* shift."

"Of course she can shift. She's fully grown, not some thirteen-year-old girl."

"Uh-huh. I'm sure if you explain that to her carefully, she'll trawsfur right back."

Tynan gave the cahir a narrow-eyed look before turning his attention back to her. "You can't change to human form, lass?"

Darcy shook her head from side to side. If they were Scythe, they wouldn't talk with her. Although maybe their friendliness was a trick. If only her brain were working better. Still, why would they bother to talk? They wore knives and could simply cut her throat. Or bite through her spine. No discussion needed.

"Getting a wounded cat past the dogs and hunters will turn into what Calum's mate calls a clusterfuck." The annoyance in Owen's low, rough voice was oddly reassuring...because he was on her side.

"No choice." Tynan's voice had the lilt of an Irish accent. "Cosantir's orders."

Cosantir? Darcy pulled in a breath of relief. A Cosantir, the God-empowered guardian of an entire territory, would never work for the Scythe. These males couldn't be Scythe shifter-soldiers. Whatever were they doing in a city?

Oh, if she could only talk with them.

"Are you going to come with us nicely, female?" Owen's question was blunt.

There was nothing she wanted more...but this was wrong. They couldn't get her past the Scythe guarding the exits. She'd tried. The thought of putting these males into danger made her heart hurt. But she couldn't speak and explain.

More importantly, they were offering her a chance to save the other villagers. She had to let them try. She nodded to Owen.

And if she died trying to escape? By the Mother's sweet blessing, she would die in the company of her own kind.

"You know the area. Shift and lead us out, Tynan." Owen trawsfurred and waited for the female to follow the wolf before bringing up the rear.

Tynan retraced their path for a while, then angled north to keep their scent from the encampment.

The little female—and fuck, she really was little—limped along without a sound. The air brought him the scent of her illness—sick, infected, starving. She was weak and wouldn't be able to run long at all.

How could he sneak her past the encampment without the hunting dogs catching her scent? If it came to a chase, he might manage to wipe out the canines, but the animals were backed up by humans with weapons.

Anger ran through him and sang for him to enter their fucking camp and teach them the dangers of threatening a Daonain female.

Being sensible sucked. With a huff of disgust, he put his mind to devising a better plan than *shred them all*.

When Tynan finally halted and glanced back, Owen scuffed the dirt. In the paw language used by cublings during games, the gesture meant *stay here*. The cop might be competent in the city, but Owen lived in a forest—and hunted hellhounds. He'd do the reconnoitering.

Shifting to human, Tynan stepped in front of the female. The guards were too close for explanations, so the cop gripped her scruff and went down on his haunches, showing her that they'd wait.

After a second, she sank, belly to the ground.

Good. She was trying, and Owen appreciated that. On the trail, when she'd stumbled and thumped her wounded leg against a log, she hadn't made a sound. Even now, as tremors shook her body, she stayed silent. She was sick—and scared—and by the God, she was a brave little thing.

He gave her a nod of approval before sliding silently into the brush and moving upwind.

Before approaching the camp, he circled to approach from

upward, crept closer, then took to a tree. From the high vantage point, Owen watched the hunters form a long line of men. The dogs were readied to go. Two guards were chatting near three black vans and two pickups to the right of the tents. *Vehicles. Hmm.*

Averse to metal, shifters rarely became mechanics. But as a teen, Gawain had learned to hotwire cars to help shifters who'd gotten themselves into awkward situations. City-dwelling Tynan might well know the trick.

Plan formulated, Owen headed back toward where he'd left the others, pausing to deal with one sentry. He generously put the human to sleep rather than gutting him.

Tynan and the female were still where he'd left them.

Owen shifted and crouched to murmur, "So, cop. Can you hotwire a truck?"

"That I can. Stealing a vehicle is your plan?" Tynan glanced at the female. "Right. I doubt she'd be able to walk out."

"I doubt it, too." Owen gestured to the south. Downwind. He'd be able to draw the dogs and men away from the cars and keep them entertained. "I'll create a diversion over there. The vehicles are on the north side. Take the pickup closest to the road, head for the exit, and I'll catch up."

Tynan's displeased expression showed what he thought of driving away without Owen, but he nodded.

Owen pointed to the path they should take. "The guard there won't bother you."

"We'll be off, then." Tynan stroked the female and motioned for her to follow. After shifting to wolf form, he led the way down the trail Owen had indicated.

Time to hunt.

A few minutes later, Owen reached the end of the south sentry line and dropped out of the tree on top of the scent-impaired idiot. A quick slash-slash resulted in rewarding shouts of pain.

He leaped back into the trees, skipped the next sentry, and chose one who was walking in terrified circles. The scent of fear was gratifying.

His own scent should be drifting to the dogs about now.

Crouched on the branch, Owen waited for the right moment. The tip of his tail lashed. His haunches tensed.

The human turned.

Without a thought, Owen sprang, landed on the man's back, and drove him onto his face. When Owen sank his fangs into the man's shoulder, the pain-filled scream of terror was long and loud.

Shouldn't be anyone asleep in the camp now.

Between the scent of cougar and the screams of pain, the dogs went into a frenzy. With several men shouting orders, chaos ensued.

Unheard in the uproar, an engine started up.

Huffing in satisfaction, Owen nipped the hunter's ear to provoke another scream. And realized his mistake when shots peppered the area, *snicking* the leaves, and *thwacking* the tree trunks.

Owen snarled. The idiots were firing blindly, even with their own soldier in the line of fire.

A bullet hit the human, and his scream of agony sparked more gunfire.

Something thumped Owen's leg—and pain burst like wildfire though his hind leg. A hiss escaped as he fought his cat instincts for control. The squirrel-brained humans had *shot* him.

Fuck, it *hurt*. His claws emerged, digging holes in the human beneath him. More screams.

Growling low in his throat, Owen darted into the underbrush. His leg flared with pain with every movement. He pulled in a deeper breath. *Suck it up, cahir.* He knew how to deal with pain. When killing hellhounds, a cahir fought—no matter how badly he was damaged—or that cahir died.

He needed to shake off the dogs and quickly. Trotting into a creek, he headed northward, staying in the water until the wind no longer blew his scent toward the dogs. With a grunt of pain, he sprang into a tree directly from the water, leaving no scent markers on the bank. A keen hound might catch his scent, but the wind was now in his favor.

Behind him, the shouting grew less terrified and more frustrated. Some idiot was still firing a weapon.

Traveling through the trees was slow going, and after a brief time, Owen dropped to the ground, winced when his foreleg almost gave out—damn broken bones—and raced for the road.

Satisfaction filled him at the sound of a pickup farther ahead. The cop had gotten the female out.

As Owen caught up, the truck showed no headlights and was going slow. Owen leaped into an empty spot in the truck bed, landed, and pain stabbed into his foreleg. Then his wounded hind leg bumped into a pile of crates. By the *God.* Hissing at the pain from fucking everywhere, he moved forward and pushed his muzzle against the rear cab window.

The female was curled in a miserable-looking ball on the floor.

Tynan met Owen's gaze in the rear-view mirror. The cop touched his finger to his forehead in a salute, and the pickup surged forward.

As the distance from the humans' encampment increased, the noise of shouting and firearms diminished. Tynan turned the headlights on.

The pickup approached the park entrance, which was bracketed by window-darkened black vans. The humans there sported rifles and holstered handguns. Leaving the tinted window up, Tynan slowed only slightly.

Smothering a snarl, Owen crawled under an overturned crate.

As Tynan drove past the vans, the guards didn't attempt to stop them. It *was* their vehicle, after all.

A couple of minutes later, the pickup rocked to a stop beside their own cars.

Chapter Four

THE ONE NAMED Owen had been shot. Because of her. Darcy hated that he'd gotten hurt and she was so, so grateful to him.

She was *free* and leaving the city.

After abandoning the Scythe pickup and putting her in Owen's car, the males had driven their two cars to a parking lot. In a deserted corner, the men had dressed. Tynan bandaged Owen's leg and said he'd drive them to Cold Creek in Owen's car. When Owen insisted he could drive, Tynan rapped two fingers on the cahir's swollen wrist. Owen's pain-filled snarl lost him the argument, and he grumpily climbed into the passenger seat.

Darcy stayed stretched out on the back seat.

With Tynan driving, they headed north and onto the freeway.

For what seemed like hours, Darcy lay flat, tense with nerves. Car lights flashed by. Air brakes hissed on the massive trucks. Horns blared sporadically.

Then they were out of the city.

As the land rose, the car engine hummed a lower note, and the stench of gasoline and chemicals faded. First, there was the dusty scent of end-of-summer grass, then the sharper fragrance of evergreens. With a happy sigh, she curled into a ball and fell asleep.

Itching roused her. It felt as if ants were crawling all over her body. In the front seat, Owen absentmindedly rubbed his arm, and watching him made her itch worse. She lifted her hind leg to scratch her neck—and pain battered her senses. She snarled. How could she forget her leg had multiple holes in it?

Owen glanced back. "I'm surprised the itching didn't wake you sooner. Damn vehicles."

What did he mean? As she adjusted her position, she watched him rub his back against the seat cushion. Itching. Vehicles? The metal. Of course. She should have recognized the feeling from when she worked with engines. But then she only did repair work with her hands not her whole body. Closing her eyes, she set herself to endure.

"I'm surprised you can stand it," Owen said to Tynan. "Constantly around metal. Surrounded by humans. Too far from the forests."

Using the rear view mirror, Darcy could see Tynan's grim smile. "Since I have blademages in my ancestry, I have more tolerance for iron than most Daonain. The city is irritating though."

She tilted her head, enjoying the sound of his Irish accent.

"So why do you live there?" Owen asked.

"Well and someday maybe I'll tell you. This isn't the day."

As silence fell, Darcy lowered her head and let herself drift off to the low hum of the motor and the throbbing burn of her wounds.

Dawn was breaking when Tynan pulled the car to a stop.

"I need to call and report we've arrived," Owen said. "Be with you in a minute."

"I'll take her." Tynan slid out and opened the back door. "Let's be getting you into the house, lass. The healer's expecting you."

A healer. Dogwood had been too small to have a healer. Carefully, Darcy jumped off the backseat to the grassy lawn. The shooting pain of landing flattened her ears and made her hiss.

"On with ye." Motioning her toward the house, Tynan took out a phone and started punching in numbers.

The door to the house opened, and a tall, thickly muscled male strode down the steps and to the car. A trim brown beard covered a strong jaw, and his wavy light brown hair hung to midway down his white cotton shirt. The porch light showed a scar on his cheekbone—a blade resembling a cahir's but encircled by a full moon. As Darcy tried to recall what the symbol indicated, the male opened the passenger door and frowned at Owen.

Owen shoved his phone into his pocket. "Gawain."

"Mother of All, brawd. You're a bloody mess. What've you done to yourself?"

"What've *I* done? Wasn't me filling the air with bullets." Owen's annoyed growl had Darcy trying to back up.

Without any fear, his muscular brother lifted the cahir out of the car and to his feet.

Owen spotted her. "Can you make it, little female?" His tone was gruff, almost a snarl, and yet…despite his own pain, he was making sure she was all right.

Unable to answer any other way, she took a few steps forward.

"Good enough. Let's go get patched up." Leaning on his brother, he headed up the sidewalk.

In the front doorway waited a tall, lean male with chiseled features like sharp mountain cliffs. He had a tinted scar in the shape of a crescent moon on one cheek. A healer.

Surrounded by the God-touched, Darcy wanted to cower.

"Come on in, people." The healer motioned them through the door. As Tynan came up the walk, the healer asked, "Are you coming home finally, brawd?"

Tynan clasped the healer's forearm, and his flashing smile was unexpected. "I am not. I cannot even linger. Alec is driving me to Seattle before the humans notice my car's been in the parking lot too long."

Owen turned. "Thanks for the help, cop. I owe you one."

Tynan's voice took on an added Irish lilt. "Just keep an eye on this lost little female so she doesn't stray back into danger." He ruffled her fur gently, slapped his brother's arm, and strode back to the street.

"Come, shifters. Let's get this done." The healer led her, Owen, and his brother Gawain into a pale green room with a tall rectangular table in the center. A long wooden bench ran along the wall by the door. The far end held sinks, counters, and cabinets.

Darcy limped in.

"Let's take a look at you, cat." The healer crouched in front of her and scowled. "What in the God's green forest did you do to yourself?"

At the anger in his voice, she tried to retreat—and bumped into Owen who stood directly behind her with his brother.

Owen growled low and mean, and Darcy cringed. She shouldn't have—

"You're right, cahir. I was rude." The healer cupped her muzzle gently. "Sorry, female. I forget not everyone is used to my blunt ways. I'm Donal, the healer in Cold Creek."

Owen hadn't growled at her, but the healer. Why? Because he thought the healer had hurt her feelings? The sense of being cared for was so strange she wasn't sure what to think.

Taking his time, the healer looked her over, and his mouth flattened. "That's a bullet hole in your hind leg. And another across your ribs."

"We will need information about how those injuries occurred." The resonant, English-accented voice came from the doorway behind Darcy.

When she tried to turn, her legs failed. She sank to the floor, panting, and looked over her shoulder.

Silent as a panther, a male had entered the room. Black hair, gray eyes. Tall and lean. The air around him crackled with power.

"Cosantir. Good timing." Donal inclined his head and rose.

A Cosantir. Dread constricted Darcy's lungs. In the city, humans had known she was a shifter and chased her. Would the Guardian of this territory listen to her—or banish her for putting the Daonain at risk?

She couldn't explain, not in this form.

The Cosantir's gaze met hers, and she could feel the wash of power. "When Owen called, he said you were unable to trawsfur back to human. Is that true?"

Would he kill her if she couldn't?

She hated that she knew more about humans than about her own people. It was her brother's fault for being such a blabbermouth that their mother had stopped talking about the Daonain.

The Cosantir was still waiting for her answer. Shifters "shift," and she couldn't. She was…defective. Her head lowered in shame.

"Hmm."

She could feel his gaze on her. He took a seat on the bench against the wall, and she eased herself around to face him.

"There's a door—something akin to a door—in the back of your mind," he said. "Can you see it at all?"

Oh, she could. The door was overgrown and blocked with vines. How many hours had she spent tearing at those vines with mental claws? Her ears flicked in an unspoken affirmative.

"Will the door open?"

She shook her head.

"I see." He leaned forward, put his hand under her muzzle,

and lifted her head. "Look at me, little female." His soft voice held a ruthless command she couldn't oppose.

Her gaze met his.

His eyes were darkening, turning black—black meant something, she knew. She tried to pull back, but his grip tightened. There was no escape possible. His voice deepened. No one could fail to recognize the infinite voice of the God. *"Trawsfur."*

The power he held blazed into her, filled her mind with terrifying flames. The vines holding the door shut shriveled and turned to ash. As the door banged open, a gust of wind and heat pushed her through.

Her head spun, and she gasped for air. Her arms collapsed, dropping her to her elbows. *Elbows.* She opened her eyes and stared at her hands. Dirty, scratched…hands. "I'm human."

"Aye." The Cosantir's voice was grim. "Now, turn around, find the door, and trawsfur back to cat. On your own."

No. She never wanted to go back to being a cat. What if she got stuck again? She stared at him. "B-b-but…"

"Now."

His eyes were still black, and a shiver ran up her spine. *No, no, no.* Yet, denying him was impossible. Her gaze lifted to the other men.

Standing near her, Gawain looked surprised.

Owen sat farther down the bench, injured leg extended, swollen wrist in his lap. His harsh expression matched that of the Cosantir's. "Do it. Now. Find the door."

Her hands closed into fists, but she mentally turned. She frowned. The door had closed again, darkened, and somehow moved away from her. So far away. As she headed for it, her energy drained away like water.

Finally, she reached the door. Her hands flattened on the ancient, scarred wood, but this time when she shoved, the door opened with a rasping creak into brightness.

As she stepped through, a wave of…of love ran from her paws into her whole body. It was as if her mother had returned and enfolded her in a hug. She realized she was lying on the floor in panther shape—and purring.

"Thanks be to the Mother," the Cosantir murmured. "Excellent. My assistance didn't break the connection. Trawsfur back, and you can stay human."

With a sense of relief, Darcy turned in her mind. The door was there, plain as could be, and she stepped through.

"Very good." The Cosantir sat back on the bench.

To her surprise, Owen's brother came over with a soft blanket. "Come, let's get you warm." Wrapping it around her, he helped her stand.

Her leg gave out immediately—and she realized she really didn't feel well at all. His arm around her waist was the only thing holding her up.

"Easy, pretty panther." Gawain's voice was a composed rumble. He scooped her into his arms.

After a second of jarring pain, she relaxed, feeling the iron bands of his arms beneath her shoulders and knees. His chest was immense and hard—and he carried her as if she weighed nothing.

He smelled of musky male and the compelling wildness of a shifter with a curious iron tang. She wanted to bury her face against his chest and sniff.

"On the table, please," the healer said.

The counter-high table was a heavy, dark wood. Not metal—it wasn't metal. Yet the size and height matched a Scythe laboratory table. Her stomach twisted, and she clutched Gawain's shirt. "No. No, please, don't strap me down."

His blue eyes darkened with his frown. He looked at the table. "Aren't any straps, catling."

No straps? She took a breath and looked. With an effort, she unclamped her fingers from his shirt. "I… Sorry."

Very gently, Gawain set her on the table, then touched her cheek and moved away, leaving her with a sense of abandonment.

"Little female." The Cosantir walked up to the table. His eyes were now gray, not black. "I'm Calum and Cosantir of this territory. Can you give me your name?"

Her name. She had to push through the remnants of terror to remember it. "Darcy. Darcy MacCormac." Hauling in a fortifying breath, she recalled the manners her mother had tried to teach her. "Ah, it's good to meet you."

His lips curved up slightly. "Darcy, can—"

A throat was cleared.

The Cosantir glanced over his shoulder, and his lips twitched. "Yes, Donal. I do recall. Healing before answers." His gaze returned to her. "I'll return in a while."

"Yes, Cosantir."

Calum turned. "Cahir, let's talk in the other room."

Owen pushed to his feet.

No! He was the only person she knew, although, she didn't…really…know him. But he'd fought for her. Saved her. She clenched her hands to keep from calling him back.

Owen glanced at her and stopped, studying her more slowly. "Gawain." The one word was low.

"Aye." Gawain moved forward from his place against the wall. "I'll watch over her, brawd."

Donal snorted. "I wasn't planning to slaughter her, cahir."

Ignoring the healer, Owen met her eyes again. After a long moment, he nodded at her and left.

Loss swept through her, and she made a noise that sounded far too much like a whimper.

"Shhh. You're going to be fine." Owen's brother put an arm around her waist, bracing her against his hard, warm body.

"Another female, half-starved, dehydrated, and injured." Donal stood in front of her. "This is growing familiar. I hear the males found you in Seattle?"

She tried to answer, but her voice had dried up. Now she was in human form, and the pain was increasing, taking over her world.

"That's what Owen said," Gawain answered.

"That benighted city." Donal made a disgusted harrumph. "Don't you know better, girl? Cities drain your magic faster than you can devour a mouse." He pulled the blanket off her right side, studied the bullet's furrow over her ribs and the gouge in her arm she'd made to remove the tracker. Then he checked her right thigh and the bullet wound in her calf. The lines in his face grew deeper. "Whoever shot you got you good."

The healer's eyes shone startling silver in his tanned face. "Have you ever been healed before?"

"I've never even *met* a healer."

His chuckle was smooth. "I hope you're properly honored. Now, there is good and bad news. The good: I can heal your injuries. The bad: because it's been so long since you were hurt, you'll have scars. And…" His mouth tightened.

"And?" Dread curled in her stomach.

"It will hurt when I clean the wounds, and when I take the bullet out." He nodded at Gawain. "Can you hold her?"

Rather than answering, Gawain moved to where she could look at him. "Darcy. Will you let me hold you so you don't move when the healer is working on your injuries?"

His eyes were a quiet blue, as calm as a high mountain lake.

"Yes," she whispered.

SUCH A BRAVE little female. Gawain had noticed that, despite being forced into a trawsfur and questioned by the Cosantir, the little female had been most terrified by the table. He wrapped his fingers around Darcy's small, cold hand and studied her.

Black wavy hair fell to her low back and was streaked with dirt. Her heart-shaped face was pretty, but her cheeks were hollowed from lack of food. Beneath her tilted upper lip, her full lower lip trembled. Her dark brown eyes were wide, and the scent of fear hung in the air.

She was still scared. When he put his arm around her and she leaned against him, the act of trust squeezed his heart.

Donal set a bunch of ominous healer instruments on a wheeled table-tray. "Would you prefer to lie down or remain sitting, Darcy?"

Her gaze never left the tools. "Sitting, please."

"Gawain, from behind, bear hug her with your arms over hers."

Restrain her, but with muscle rather than chains. Gawain stood at the head of the table and slid her toward him until her back was against his chest and waist. Carefully, he wrapped his arms around her and pinned her arms to her sides.

She didn't struggle, but he could feel her breathing speed up.

"This liquid helps with the pain." Donal squirted something in the furrow across her ribs. "If you haven't been healed before, you might not know we don't use human pain medications. They blur a shifter's mind, and if you're scared, you're liable to shift to cat form." His lean face held a sardonic amusement. "A pissed-off cat, no less."

Yeah, Gawain didn't want to find himself holding an annoyed cougar.

Darcy's resonant voice was husky with pain. "I understand."

When the healer picked up a massive water-filled syringe with a narrow tube on the end, Darcy made an appalled sound.

To divert her attention, Gawain quickly asked, "Why did you think Donal would strap you to a table?"

"I want the answer to that as well." Calum walked to the

table opposite Donal.

Limping back into the room, Owen dropped onto the bench and put his leg up. Gawain nodded at him, thinking his littermate must have given Calum a very short report. Then again, Owen wasn't much for chatter.

"Good timing, people. All of you can keep her occupied. I fear this is going to hurt." Donal gave Gawain a warning glance.

As Gawain tightened his hold, the healer forcefully squirted water into the bullet gouge, holding a towel to catch the dirty, bloody fluid.

Gasping, Darcy jerked, but Gawain kept her still. When tears filled her eyes, he wanted to knock Donal across the room.

"You were going to tell us about a table?" Owen's rough voice was oddly gentle.

After a second, she said in a hoarse voice, "They—they call themselves the Scythe. They strapped the adults to the tables. Cutting away pieces. Dissecting us. They killed many of the grownups, trying to discover what made us shifters. The rest died in the cages."

The Cosantir's face turned icy cold, and the same chill spread through Gawain's bloodstream.

"Where did this happen?" Calum asked.

As Donal flushed the wound again, she whimpered and muffled it immediately.

By the Hunter and the Mother, she was a brave young female.

She pulled in a breath. "My home is—was—Dogwood. It was a tiny village, and all of us were captured by the Scythe."

"Dogwood?" Gawain frowned. "Up in the mountains in Mt. Hood Territory?"

"You know it?" she asked.

"I lived in that territory until recently."

Calum frowned. "Did they take both humans and

Daonain?"

"We had no humans there. The population was all shifters." Her breathing hitched. "They shoved us in trucks and burned the whole village. I could see the flames as we were driven away."

DARCY STRUGGLED NOT to break down. But even the healer's cleaning job was less agonizing than remembering the bodies in the streets. Their cozy cottage engulfed in fire. "We—Mum and my littermates—had only lived in Dogwood a couple of months."

The healer put his syringe down. "All clean. Let's get this wound closed, so you have one less place hurting you." He flattened his palms over her ribs, bent his head, and closed his eyes.

Deep in the wound, a heavy tingling awakened. Like the slow melting of snow in the spring, the pain receded.

Donal lifted his hands. "One down. Take a minute to recover while I check Owen over." After rewrapping the blanket around her, he motioned the cahir to precede him through the doorway.

A second later, the healer's voice came clearly from the other room. "Did I not order you to take it easy with your foreleg? You've re-broken your wrist, you gnome-brained idiot." The volume increased. "And what is this hole? By Herne's hairy balls, you must have been moving slower than a drunken dwarf for a human to put a bullet in you."

Head tilted, the Cosantir listened to the ranting with a smile tugging on his lips. Then he looked at her and his amusement disappeared. "After you were captured, Darcy, where did the Scythe take you?"

"Somewhere in Seattle. At first, they kept us in a basement." She pulled in a breath. *Be clear, tinker. This is a Cosantir, and the*

Daonain need to be warned. "In metal cages, below ground. For a…I'm not sure…for months?" They hadn't been allowed to talk, to be together. Could only hear the screams coming from the rooms with the metal tables. "Everyone who was over thirteen, who had shifted at least once, they all died. The babies died. When the children who were still alive got sick, the Scythe moved us out of the cages and the basement."

Gawain's embrace had changed from restraint to reassurance, and his every exhalation held a growl.

She took strength from his anger and concern.

The Cosantir frowned. "Where are your littermates? I see your bonds to them are intact."

He could tell? When Mum died and the mother-cub bond had broken, Darcy'd felt as if her heart had torn apart. But deep within, the warmly glowing links to her siblings still remained. "My brothers—and all the males—were kept somewhere else. Because they're useful. The males were able to trawsfur when they got to thirteen or so. None of us females could shift, and no one knows why."

Gawain's body tensed. "When the males got to thirteen? Darcy, how long ago were you captured?"

Every year felt like a boulder piling onto her body. "Over ten years ago."

As the color in the Cosantir's eyes darkened, she kept talking, and the words spilled out like water from a broken faucet. "The Scythe are using the males as soldiers and spies. Shifter-soldiers. All the females are kept in the Seattle *priosan.*"

"If they can't use the females as shifters, why didn't they kill you?" Calum asked in an even voice.

"We're hostages." Hatred tasted bitter in her mouth. "As long as they have a male's sister, they can make him do whatever they want."

The ache in her heart increased as she told them, "They told

Firth to assassinate some politician, and he refused, so they…they tortured his sister until she died. Broke her…" Darcy swallowed despite her dry throat. "Ripped her s-skin off. They made us watch and showed the video to the males. After that, everyone cooperated."

The growls behind her turned deadly, and she felt Gawain's blazing anger.

The Cosantir didn't speak. The power around him was an unsettling thrum in the air before he simply turned and walked away, brushing past Donal and Owen as he left the room.

Feeling as if ice was filling her, she pulled the blanket closer.

Owen was watching her with eyes the dark green of a forest at night. "You were imprisoned for over a decade?"

She nodded.

Donal walked up to the table. "That partly explains why you couldn't trawsfur. Breanne didn't shift until she was over twenty—because she lived in the city and took those drugs." He moved the blanket off her wounded leg. "Let's get the rest of these holes closed up."

Still leaning against Gawain, she had her legs straight in front of her. The healer gripped her right leg and poured the so-called numbing liquid into the gunshot wound in her calf.

Pain. It felt as if he'd shoved a red-hot stick in her leg. Her leg tore from his grip.

"I'm going to need both hands, so Owen, could you could hold her leg, please?"

"Aye, Donal." Owen curled a big hand around her ankle and his other above her knee, then added his weight to press her leg against the table. "What drugs were you on, Darcy?"

"I don't know what you mean. We didn't take any medicine or drugs."

"The stuff that keeps females from having children." Donal turned to the equipment table, ready to start.

Oh Gods, more pain. Darcy tensed.

Gawain's arms tightened around her. Behind her, his body was a warm, breathing wall. She rested her head back against his shoulder.

"Medicine?" Owen prompted.

Stuff to keep females from having children? "You mean birth control? Yes. After a human raped a shifter, they stuck something in our arms to make sure none of us got pregnant. They used to replace it every few years, but the nurse was killed, um, about four years ago. Since then, a medical person only visits if someone's injured."

"Breanne took pills, but what you're talking about sounds like a hormone implant." The healer ran his palms up and down her arms. "There it is. It would be best to remove this right away. May I?"

Hormones. Trackers—and hormones. They kept putting horrible things in her body. "I hate this," she whispered, then looked at the healer. "Yes, take it out."

"I'm sorry, Darcy. If you grit your teeth, I'll be as fast as I can." When she nodded that she was ready, he picked up a razor and sliced her arm. The pain made her gasp, but within a second, he'd plucked out the implant and healed the cut. Only a tiny pink line remained. He'd even healed the spot where she'd removed the tracker.

Darcy blinked. He really had been fast. Her arm didn't hurt any longer, and the trackers and foreign implant were gone. Each breath she took was freer. Her body was more and more her own, except for one spot. "Can you take the bullet out of my leg now, too? Please?"

Obviously braced for her to ask the opposite, Donal gave her a nonplussed stare.

Gawain chuckled. "Never underestimate a female."

Still holding her leg, Owen studied her, his brows pulled into a line.

"All right, Darcy. Since you're ready…" The healer examined the ugly hole in her calf, and his expression darkened.

She could see the skin around it was crimson and puffy. Red streaks of infection extended upward. "I'm ready."

After the healer cleaned the hole out, the true torture started.

As Donal used forceps to dig for the bullet, fire erupted in her leg, and she clenched her teeth to keep from screaming. Sweat broke out on her face, tears ran down her face, and she…endured.

"Almost…" With a pleased sound, the healer pulled out the forceps and dropped the bullet onto the instrument table. "By the Mother, you're a brave female. Didn't even try to claw me."

"She is brave, isn't she?" Gawain released her and ran his hands up and down her arms.

At her feet, Owen studied her.

He'd been so brave, had drawn off the dogs, had run for the truck on a broken foreleg. And she was sitting here bawling. *Sit up and act like an adult, tinker.* With a shaky breath, she wiped her face.

"One more minute, and I'll have this closed." Donal bent his head, his hands on either side of her leg wound, and she stared as the hole filled with tissue, as the skin grew over the hole.

Donal straightened, ran his finger over the slightly dented, shiny pink skin, and scowled. "I'm sorry, lass. This one will have a scar."

"Sorry?" She stared. "I'm alive. You got the bullet out and closed the hole. What do I care about scars?"

Owen's gaze met hers, his surprise obvious.

Not noticing, Donal laughed. "You're a prize, my sweet. Now, since healing takes a toll, you'll be sleepy for another day, tired for a week. You can—and should—trawsfur to cat and back. Since the repaired tissue remains fragile for a few days, take it easy. You're underweight, so eat more, especially meat. Am I clear?"

She nodded. "Yes, sir."

"You sound like Calum's Vicki."

The scary Cosantir had a mate? Her mind boggled at the thought. The female was probably over six feet tall, hugely muscled, and as scary as Calum himself. Maybe the female was a grizzly shifter or—

The Cosantir walked in, and Darcy flushed, feeling as if she'd been caught doing something embarrassing. Calum's gaze ran over her, and he glanced at the healer. "Donal, are you finished?"

"Almost. There's just this mess on her thigh." He poked at it, making her wince, and clucked his tongue. "Were you in a knife fight? Why did someone stab you several times in the same spot?"

"I stabbed myself. There was a GPS tracker in my leg, and I couldn't find it at first." Yawning, she sagged against Gawain. As her fear waned, so did her energy. Somehow, the table had turned into quicksand, pulling her down into its softness.

As her eyes closed, she heard Owen ask, "A tracker. Is that something they could use to locate you?"

"Mmmhmm. I removed it and the one in my arm and smashed them with a rock."

She felt the healer's fingers run over the wound, and pain flared. "There's nothing in there now." Heat tingled deep in her thigh muscles, moving outward as he healed the sliced flesh.

"I need to find the shifter-soldiers. To tell them…" Her thoughts drifted away despite her attempts to cling to them. "I need to find them."

"Check for other surprises," the Cosantir said quietly.

The healer ran his hands over her, head to toes. "Help me turn her over, cahir."

She was slid down on the table and rolled over. They were being very careful not to hurt her. Wasn't that lovely?

Light hands ran over her scalp. Her neck, shoulders, and down. "Nothing else, Calum. I'll check on her tomorrow, but I'm done for today."

"Excellent. Owen, Gawain, please take Darcy to the Wildwood Lodge. Zeb and Shay have a room for her in the main cabin."

"Aye, Cosantir." That was Gawain's smoother voice. Owen made only a sound of assent.

Donal cleared his throat. "Cosantir, save me some work and order your cahir to take a few days of rest. At the lodge, not his cabin. His broken wrist and the new wound need time to heal—and he's more stubborn than a boggart spotting salt."

Calum huffed a laugh. "You heard the healer, cahir. Consider that an order."

Darcy thought Owen's rude response wasn't nearly as muffled as it should have been considering he was answering a Cosantir.

She tried to open her eyes to see how the guardian had reacted to being snarled at, but...someone had tied boulders to her eyelids. That was discourteous. Honestly, she needed to get on her feet. To find Fell and Patrin. To help...

Her thoughts faded away like mist dissipated by a warm sun.

Chapter Five

B Y THE GOD, Calum had a nerve, ordering him to stay in Cold Creek. Growling under his breath, Owen led the way up the stairs in the Wildwood Lodge. Behind him, Gawain carried the female—the one who had caused all this fucking trouble.

Wait, had he actually thought that? Talk about badger-spirited meanness. He gave himself a good mental shake. The female hadn't asked for any of this to happen. He'd sure run down the wrong trail when he figured she'd been in the city on a dare.

Captured as a cubling and held prisoner for a decade. Ripping her arm and leg open to remove the human devices. She was a fucking brave little cat.

Shay'd given her the room near the end of the hall. Owen opened the door and then turned the covers back on the bed.

Gently, Gawain laid the female on the mattress. Despite the bumpy gravel road to the Wildwood, she hadn't woken once. She was exhausted. Poorly fed. Young and fragile and incredibly determined.

Unable to help himself, Owen touched his fingertips to her cheek. Silky soft…and overly warm. "She's running a fever."

"Not surprising. Her leg looked nasty." Gawain tucked the

covers around her. "She'll shake off the fever now the infected wounds are clean and closed. The healer looked competent."

"Aye, Donal's incredible." Fuck knew the healer had saved his ass more than once. Owen frowned down at the female. She was so tiny and helpless, and he wanted to settle into a chair and keep guard until she woke. Talk about being an idiot. He shifted his weight and caught his brother watching him.

"Want to stay?" Gawain asked.

"No. We got her delivered." As off-balance as if he'd put a paw into a gopher hole, Owen headed out the door. Quickly.

"Herne's antlers, Owen, slow down." Gawain followed him down to the ground floor. "She's a female, not a rabid skunk."

He grunted.

A laugh halted his flight.

Shay and Zeb were in the sitting area near the stairs.

Grinning, Shay asked Gawain. "Was there ever a time Owen liked females, or was he born this way?"

Gawain stopped dead.

Ice in his gut, Owen stared at his fellow cahir. As far as he knew, his mother had despised him at birth. He had no memories of love, only of the stinging slaps she had dealt out. The hatred and the screaming, swearing abuse.

Shay's smile faded. "*A brathair-faoirm*, I didn't mean to…"

"Way to step on your own tail, brother." Zeb always sounded as if he'd eaten rocks for breakfast. "Did the female wake up?"

"No, she's sound asleep," Gawain said.

"Sorry, cahir," Shay said, still looking at Owen. When Owen nodded, he continued. "I didn't get a chance to tell you, but we put you two in the large corner room next to hers. It has two oversized beds."

Owen shook his head. "I'll stay in the cabin I rented, thanks."

"Cosantir's orders." Zeb's black eyes held open amusement. "He said the female trusts you, and she doesn't know anyone else here."

"He also said to remind you that you're to remain on two legs and rest." Shay's smile faded. "I don't know what's going on, but Calum sounded like a pissed-off wolverine. Made my fur stand on end."

"Fine, I'll stay for a day or two." It was too much work to argue. Fuck, he was tired, and it seemed nothing was going right today. As if Calum's orders had sucked away his energy, Owen sank into the nearest chair. Come to think of it, he'd just been healed. Like Darcy, his tail would be dragging for a good day or so.

Gawain gave him a concerned look and asked Shay, "Mind if I scrounge up some food for him from the kitchen?"

Before they could answer, the front door swung open, and Bree hurried across the room. Her pretty breasts bounced with every step, and her hair was such a golden yellow it seemed as if the sun had entered with her. "Vicki said the Cosantir sent over a hurt female. Is she badly injured? Has Donal seen her?"

Shay snagged her hand, pulling her into his lap. "The healer tended her. Gunshot wounds. Am I right, Gawain?"

"Aye. Infected. He had to remove a bullet."

"Well, my God, who shot her?" Bree's eyes narrowed as if she were ready to take on the attacker.

"Humans." Zeb's eyebrows lowered. "Glad I wasn't there at the healer's. Even strong shifters yell when Donal digs for a bullet. A female's screams would break my heart."

"She didn't scream," Owen said slowly. "Though she had tears streaming down her face, she was completely silent." By the God, she'd been amazing.

"Impressive." Shay squeezed the female on his lap. "Calum said she's underfed, which means she's in the right place, aye?"

"She's in exactly the right place. Donal and I have been working out the optimal nutrition for post-healings." Bree's nod held the determination Owen had come to expect from the pretty blonde.

Humans called her a chef. Considering what she created in a kitchen, he'd call her a magician.

Zeb smiled at his mate, a rare sight in the lethal cahir. "She's asleep, but Owen could use some food now. He got shot rescuing her, and Donal patched him up."

"I remember how crummy I felt after being healed." Bree jumped to her feet. "One big sandwich and the fixings coming up."

Gawain gave her a pitiful look. "I didn't get shot, but…any chance you have more food in there?"

"For you? Always." Laughing, Bree headed for the kitchen.

Owen snorted. His littermate could charm pixies out of the trees and gnomes out of the sewers. When Gawain grinned at him, Owen couldn't help but laugh. Yeah, despite the faded echo of Edwyn's broken bond, it was good to be with his brother again. Their own bond had thinned over the years apart, but still held together. "Want to come back to my cabin when I leave?"

"Ah, about leaving…" Shay eyed Owen warily. "Calum also said you and Gawain were to mentor Darcy."

Owen's mouth dropped open. "Me? Mentor a female?"

When Zeb burst out laughing, Owen glared. "What's so funny?"

"You, pigeon-brain. You insulted a female right in front of the Cosantir." Zeb snorted. "You should have expected some fucking nasty consequences. I'd say you got off easy."

Mentor a *female*. Owen's fingers curved as he imagined clawing a nice set of stripes down Calum's ribs. Of course, the Cosantir would kill him dead, but still…

By Herne's holy antlers, this wasn't fair.

THE PILLOW SMELLED of soap and lavender. Eyes closed, staying immobile, Darcy regulated her breathing as she tried to figure out where she was.

Had the Scythe caught her?

There was no sound of traffic, no planes overhead. She wasn't in the city. The tang of conifers perfumed the air along with the aroma of roasting meat. And she could smell one…no, two…males.

"I know you're awake, little female. Might as well open your eyes." The guttural voice sounded like the *priosan's* biggest chainsaw when the motor ran rough.

She knew that voice. Her muscles relaxed, and she opened her eyes. The mean looking shifter, the one called Owen, sprawled in a chair with his denim-clad legs stretched out. Very long legs. She'd heard cahirs were huge—this one sure was. His darkly tanned skin brought out the disconcerting green of his eyes. He'd shaved away the dark stubble, revealing the angular line of his jaw. Thick, dark brown hair touched his shoulders.

He shot her a sharp look. "How do you feel?"

"Well…" Her wounds no longer burned, but throbbed slightly as if bruised deep within. The rest of her ached almost as bad as the first time a guard had beat her senseless. "I'm fine."

He snorted his disbelief. "Sure you are. You——"

"What time is it?" she interrupted hastily.

"You slept the day away. It's after supper."

Her eyes widened, and she looked around. A bedroom with a sturdily constructed dresser and dark wooden nightstands. The hardwood floor was covered with a beautifully woven rug. It didn't have the smell of the healer's house. "Where is this?"

"The Wildwood Lodge, a fishing camp that rents out cabins and a few rooms. It's run by shifters."

Rent? "I can't stay here. I don't have any money." If she pulled the covers over her head, would the world go away?

"The room here is free for shifters in need. Don't worry."

Worry was all she had. How could she manage with no money? No food. She didn't even have any clothing.

However… Her lips curled up slightly.

"What are you smiling about?"

He sounded so grumpy. The male needed an *attitude readjustment*, as the human girls would have said.

"Because, even though I'm broke, at least I can turn into a cougar. With the infection gone, I'm sure I can figure out how to hunt and feed myself." Her smile widened. As a cougar, she could head toward the mountain range where the shifter-soldiers had their compound. Eventually, she'd find them.

"The Hunter should just trample me now," Owen muttered.

"What?" Just looking at him took her breath away, as if the lethal grace of his cougar had somehow translated to his human form. But, from his irritated expression, someone should fetch the male some coffee or something.

"Listen, female, you're not to go into the forest by yourself." He rose and paced around the room. "Calum assigned me and Gawain to mentor you while you get control of your shifting. We'll teach you to hunt and how to be safe in the wilderness."

Exactly what she needed. Yet no lessons were more important than saving her brothers and the others.

She waved her hand in the air, although doubting the cahir would shoo off easily. "I'm sure I can figure it out, and I won't be here anyway. I have to leave now." When his frown grew, she added a belated, "But thank you, anyway."

The deep rumbling laugh came from the doorway. Gawain carried in a tray of food. "Guess she told you, brawd." He set the tray on a table near the bed. "Let's get you sitting up so you can eat."

Without waiting, he leaned over and, with his hands under her arms, pulled her up to a sitting position. His hands were powerful, and the easy strength he displayed took her breath away. Compared to him, the Scythe's human guards were underfed rabbits.

When he picked up the tray, she shook her head. Her bladder had set up an urgent demand. "I need to…um, use the—" How in the world did non-prisoners talk about…needs?

"The what?" Owen demanded.

Gawain laughed. "Brawd, you've got to get out of your cabin more. She wants the bathroom." He put a long arm around her waist and lifted her out of the bed and onto her feet. The covers stayed on the bed.

She was naked…in front of two males.

"What are you *doing*?" Jerking away, she ripped the quilt from the bed. She'd barely managed to wrap it around herself before her legs gave out, and her butt landed back on the bed. She stared up at the two huge males. She couldn't even stand on her own and…

Both of them looked at her as if she were crazy.

Gawain frowned. "What's the—"

"She's scared." Sniffing the air, Owen took a step back. "Why are you scared?"

"I…you…"

"You're men, and she doesn't have any clothes on. Duh, guys." A blonde woman stood in the doorway, hands on her hips. "Didn't you tell me she spent the last decade with humans? Humans don't do naked."

"Really?" Gawain tilted his head. "How do they mate then?"

The woman choked as she started laughing and held up a hand for patience. Her shoulders were still shaking when she said, "Why is for later. Please ask Shay, not me."

Gawain frowned. "But—"

"For now, how about you help her, *with* the blanket, to the bathroom before she bursts?" The blonde grinned at Darcy. "I'm Breanne—or Bree—and I left a T-shirt and sweatpants beside the sink. They'll be big, but they're comfy."

Fears fading, Darcy smiled back. She'd forgotten so much about the Daonain. Of course, shifters would be comfortable with being naked since clothing didn't trawsfur.

A new fear slid into her heart. Would she ever be able to fit in with the Daonain again?

She would. She was free now; she could manage anything. "Thank you, Breanne. That's very nice of you."

The blonde made a throwing away gesture. "All part of the Wildwood service. If you're up to it, come on downstairs after you eat. Or take another nap, and we'll see you tomorrow."

As she disappeared, Gawain bent down. "Let's try this again." His arm wrapped around her waist, and he lifted her to her feet, supporting her when her knees wobbled. "The bathroom is at the end of the hall."

Owen still hadn't said a word. Brows together, he watched her with the same wariness she watched spiders.

She bit her lip. "Owen. I'm…uh…sorry for over-reacting. And for how you were hurt rescuing me. I meant to say thank you. Are you all right? Did the healer fix your leg and wrist?"

His brow furrowed and then he nodded. "Aye, I'm fine. Thank you." He glanced at Gawain. "You got this. I'll be downstairs."

As he stalked out, she stared after him in dismay. It was pretty obvious he didn't like her. But what had she done?

"Come on, catling. Your food is going to get cold." Gawain's deep voice held the rolling sound of thunder. Firmly, he guided her down the hall and into the bathroom.

The bathroom had a *shower*—and she could feel every bit of grime sticking to her skin. Could smell her own fear and pain sweat. She almost shook with the longing for hot water and soap.

Gawain still stood in the doorway. "I'll wait for you here."

Looking into his blue eyes, she saw only concern. Oh, she really did like him. "Honestly, I can manage—I'm not dizzy any longer. And I'm sorry I kind of yelled at you."

The sun lines at the corners of his eyes crinkled with his smile. "Not to worry, sweetling. However, neither Owen nor I are familiar with human customs, and we're to be your mentors. Will you tell us if something makes you uncomfortable so we can work around it?"

Hugging him wouldn't be appropriate, would it? No, her brains were surely scrambled. She nodded instead. "I will. Thank you."

As he strolled down the hall, she closed the door. *Shower, shower, shower.*

WRIST THROBBING, OWEN sat on the lodge's back patio, nursing a beer and a bad mood. The little female had grabbed the blanket and looked at them as if she were a bunny cornered by hungry wolves.

Then, he'd braced for hysterics, for screaming, for her to throw things as their mother had. Instead, she'd apologized. And acted as if she was worried about him. Him, a cahir.

Why couldn't she behave like a normal female?

Maybe he didn't know what a *normal* female was. Bree hadn't yelled at him or Gawain either; she'd laughed.

Come to think of it, he knew other good females. His own sister, for one. Then there was Ben and Ryder's mate, Emma, who'd taken on a hellhound to save their tiny girl.

And Vicki. Despite her small size, Calum and Alec's female

could give any male a run for his prey. He'd understood right away why the two males had chosen her for their mate.

Gawain walked onto the patio, beer in hand. "Did you see how both females turned red?"

Owen started to grin. "They did. It's a pretty color on a female. But who ever heard of being embarrassed for not having on clothes?"

"Eh, human customs. Who can figure them out?" Gawain took a good gulp of his beer. "Do they wear clothing to bed, then? Even when they're mated?"

Owen snorted. "Brawd, you're asking the wrong shifter."

"She kicked me out of the bathroom. Is that a human deal, too?"

"She's not in her bed?"

Gawain shook his head. "She said she could get back to her room. From the way she looked at the shower, I think she wants to clean up."

A shower? Owen frowned. As a blademage, Gawain had probably experienced burns, cuts, and bruises, but possibly never a serious wound. He might not know how, after a healing, a person's energy could slide right down the drain along with the hot water. The tough little female might not realize the danger, either.

He set his beer down. "I'll be back in a minute."

At the door of the bathroom, he listened. The shower was off, but he heard no movement. "Darcy?"

The soft sound wasn't a reply, but was good enough for him. Stepping inside, he glanced around the big bathroom. Long wide counter, one sink, a wooden chair at the end. A toilet stall. An open-doored shower.

And there she was. Like a withered flower, she'd weakened and dropped to her knees in the shower. Her hair hung in long black tangles, not quite covering small up-tilted breasts.

He headed for her and stopped short. *Naked.* He wouldn't stick his paw in that trap a second time. Snatching up a big towel, he bent and wrapped it around her. By the God, she smelled even more fragrant than a meadow of clover after a rainstorm.

"Up you come." As he lifted her to her feet, she clung to his forearm, determinedly trying to stand on her own. Stubborn female.

"I can help you into the clothes Bree left," he said. "Or take you back to your room in a towel and tuck you in."

"I can do—" Her voice died under the look he gave her.

"Guess not, huh." She sighed. "I'm sure not going to walk out there in a towel. Clothes, please."

He had to admit he found her low voice damned appealing. It had a furry timbre, as if every word contained a purr.

After sitting her on the chair, he grabbed another towel. Gently, he squeezed the water out of her hair and patted off her shoulders and back. He handed her the towel to rub over her front…although he wouldn't have minded drying her breasts himself.

Even with his courtesy, she blushed.

"Look how red you get," he murmured, running a finger over her cheek to see if the color came off.

Her tiny growl made him grin.

He helped her into the loose T-shirt, then squatted and dried her legs off. Pretty legs. Too thin, but she had some muscles. She'd get more when they worked on her hunting skills. "Can you stand and dry off…the rest?

The red increased. Fucking cute, actually.

He didn't wait, but pulled her to her feet, and stabilized her as she wielded the towel. Her ass was rounded and tempting. Her pussy was hidden by glossy black curls, and he could scent her lightly feminine musk.

He had a craving to smell the fragrance of her arousal as well.

No.

Surely, he wasn't interested in this female. In any female.

He went down on his haunches and held the sweat pants for her. "Hold onto my shoulder and step in, little female."

When she did, he pulled the pants up at the same time he rose. "There. All dressed."

And still red.

He ran his finger over her cheek again. The red did make her skin hotter.

Her eyes narrowed. She sure didn't seem afraid of him, at all.

If he teased her, would she scold him in her husky voice like an early-wakened pixie? Tempting, but she was tired. This wasn't the time. *Behave, Treharn.*

Biting the inside of his cheek, he kept his mouth in a straight line, put an arm around her waist, and guided her back to the bedroom. She gave him a suspicious look, but let him help her into bed. Silently, he set the tray on her lap.

When he left, he was grinning. Herne help him, he hadn't had so much fun in a couple of moons.

Chapter Six

THE NEXT DAY, Darcy managed a shower and made it down the stairs all by herself. Her legs wobbled only a bit—a major victory. Now she wanted a nap after her strenuous endeavors, and how pitiful was that?

She didn't have time to lie around. There were things to do, beginning with talking the Cosantir into rescuing her villagers. Two-pronged strikes would be the only way. If either the *prìosan* or the shifter-soldier compound were attacked alone, the Scythe would kill everyone at the other site. She frowned. A simultaneous rescue would require a lot of shifters.

Still, Calum had a whole territory, so he must have lots of cahirs. And he was powerful himself. Once the *prìosan* and compound were located, surely he'd send his warriors to free the hostages and soldiers.

Look, my brothers, I found help! She wrapped her arms around herself, feeling as if she could fly.

The foot of the stairs opened to a wide sitting area with a couch and chairs grouped around a huge fireplace. Very wilderness rustic, but beautifully done with a high ceiling and gleaming hardwood floors. Red and black Native American blankets and rugs added a cozy warmth. The open design led to the reception area by the front door with rooms off to the left.

As compelling aromas caught her attention, she turned toward the rear of the building. *Bacon. And fresh bread.* Her stomach growled. Sniffing as loudly as a dog, she followed her nose past a window-filled dining area and into a huge country kitchen.

Breanne was making scrambled eggs.

Darcy's stomach gurgled loudly enough to catch the curvy blonde's attention. She laughed. "You're hungry—and have excellent timing. I was going to bring your breakfast upstairs."

Spotting bacon piled on a plate, Darcy stared. "Bacon? For *me?*"

"I don't think I've ever seen anyone look at bacon as if it were Christmas and Easter rolled into one." Breanne offered the plate. "You must really love it."

Darcy bit into a piece and purred as the flavors filled her mouth. "When I was young, it was our weekend treat." At twelve, Darcy and the boys had reached the age where they devoured everything in sight, and they could go through a pound in one breakfast. Poor Mum had been looking forward to when they could hunt some of their meals. "I haven't had any since…since we were captured."

When Breanne took the plate of bacon away, Darcy sighed and wished she'd stuffed another piece in her mouth.

"Why don't you sit at the table in here?" Breanne scooped the scrambled eggs onto the plate and added buttered toast before giving the plate back. "I'll have another cup of coffee and keep you company."

The plate of food was heavy. "This is all for me?"

"Sure. Donal told Shay you needed to eat." Breanne eyed her. "I can see you're not up to fighting weight, so eat it all, if you can."

"Thank you." So much bacon for her? Darcy sank into the chair and tried to swallow the lump in her throat.

"What's wrong?" After handing over a glass of orange juice,

Bree poured herself coffee and sat across the table. Her big blue eyes were worried. "Darcy?"

"My friends back at the *priosan*, the other females, they'll all be eating oatmeal. Since the Scythe won't waste money on *filthy animals*, our meals were always the same. Oatmeal for breakfast. Vegetable soup for lunch. Hamburger stew for supper."

Bree set her cup down with such a violent thump that coffee sloshed over the sides. "For half your life? I-I don't know how to say how furious that makes me." Her face had gone red.

Darcy stared for a second and then smiled. "I know it sounds strange, but seeing someone else angry is nice."

"Be nicer if I could shred some humans." Grumbling, Bree picked up her cup and wiped the sides with a napkin.

After two more bacon pieces, Darcy started on the eggs. Best eggs ever. "When Donal healed me, he said birth control pills kept you from trawsfurring."

"True. Apparently birth control pills and shifter chemistries don't go well together," Bree said.

"You lived in Seattle?"

Bree smiled. "I did. Being an orphan, I came here, hoping to find information about my parents. Getting out of the city—and off the pills—let me trawsfur. But I'd never heard of the Daonain, so when I shifted into a wolf, it was a shock to everyone…me most of all."

"I can't even imagine how scared you must have been." At least Darcy had known who she was. What she was. "Did you move here and never go back to Seattle?"

"Actually, I did return once, but it was awfully close to being a disaster." Bree frowned. "Before I left, a hellhound had attacked me, and afterward, it preyed on my apartment complex. A boy lived there who I'd once babysat. It was stupid, but I went back to try to save him and kill the hellhound."

Darcy frowned. Weren't hellhounds horrifically dangerous?

Yet how could anyone sit by if she knew a child would die? "Did you save him?"

"Not the way I'd planned, although the hellhound did die." Bree's mouth twisted in a rueful smile. "Zeb almost died, too. He and Shay came after me, even though Calum had ordered us to stay out of the city. I hated the Cosantir so much right then."

Darcy stiffened. "But…why would the Cosantir forbid you to go to Seattle?"

"Because the Daonain survive only because humans don't realize we exist." Bree shook her head. "I understood, mostly, but I'd never imagined an entire town of shifters could be attacked. Or how horrible it must have been. I'm so sorry, Darcy."

Houses burning. Bodies in the streets. Caged in a basement. Her mum dragged into the laboratory. Dying there. "My village was called Dogwood." Named after a grove of the white flowering trees. She'd only lived there long enough to see them bloom once. Now even the name of the village was dead.

Her breakfast had lost its appeal, and the eggs tasted like ash. Darcy set her fork down. "Calum thought humans might discover the Daonain just because you went to Seattle?"

"He had reasons, I'm afraid. Cities are full of people and cameras, and a person turning into a wolf—or bear or cougar— would be impossible to cover up. I was a new shifter with untested control."

Darcy scowled. She was a very new shifter and probably had atrocious control. "Why didn't he send Zeb and Shay? They look incredibly strong."

"Humans aren't a Daonain concern, especially ones who don't live in a territory." Bree sighed. "And cities make shifters weak. Herne's power doesn't extend outside his territories, so the cahirs don't have their added strength."

"Oh." Darcy forced herself to finish the eggs, swallowing

past the tightness in her throat. Her dreams of an army storming the *prìosan* and the shifter-soldier compound were sputtering to a stop like an electric motor in the rain.

"Our territories are filled with females and vulnerable cubs. Calum couldn't risk our people to save a few humans, especially humans who weren't in his guardianship."

The Dogwood villagers were shifters but not in Calum's territory. Dogwood had been in Mt. Hood Territory in Oregon, and she'd never met the Cosantir there. Would either Cosantir take the risk of rescuing the captured villagers?

The dangers were real. Darcy stared down at the table, imagining the black vans driving into village after village. Like in Dogwood. *Human soldiers pouring through the streets, shooting their lethal weapons. Snarling horribly, a male falling, blood soaking the front of his shirt. In the street, gory, tangled remnants of people. Over the shouting sounded children's high, piercing screams. Everywhere, there was only death and burning buildings.*

If the Scythe discovered more shifters existed, they'd search the forests. Would find Cold Creek.

As fear pierced her chest, she pulled in a shuddering breath. Right now, the Scythe couldn't track her and probably didn't realize others had helped her escape. They'd think *Darcy* had attacked the hunters since a human couldn't tell one cougar from another in the dark. A vehicle had driven away, but she might have been the driver. When doing the Scythe vehicle maintenance, she'd learned to drive—although only on the property. But her driving out of the park wouldn't be impossible.

Right now, the Scythe didn't know if more shifters existed. A concerted rescue of the Dogwood females and shifter-soldiers would reveal the truth.

"Darcy," Bree said softly. "I'm sorry. Did you hope Calum could send shifters into Seattle?"

Darcy nodded. "I wasn't thinking of anything but freeing my

friends and littermates. I hadn't thought of the consequences."

"Of course not." As Bree rose, she leaned over to squeeze Darcy's hand. "Owen should be back any minute, and I'm making BLTs for his lunch. Do you have room for a bit more to eat?"

"No, thank you." Darcy managed to smile. "It was great, though."

After putting bacon on to fry, Bree sliced some bread and started to put it into the toaster. With an exasperated huff, she laid the bread in the oven and turned on the broiler.

"Um, Bree? Why don't you use the toaster?"

"The stupid thing broke yesterday. It burns everything I put in it."

Darcy's spirits lifted. "If you have some tools, I can take a look at it. I'm pretty good at fixing things."

"That'd be wonderful." Bree disappeared and returned with a small tool caddy. "This is the house set."

As Bree returned to cooking, Darcy started working on the toaster and felt more…settled. The *priosan* had regimented every moment of her day. Here, she had no idea what would happen next. What was she supposed to do today? Tomorrow? The uncertainty left her off-balance.

At least for the next few minutes, she had a job. "Do Owen and Gawain live here?"

"No, Owen has a place way up in the mountains, someplace not even accessible by road. But after a hellhound broke his wrist a couple of weeks ago, he kept reinjuring it. Calum ordered him to stay here until he healed up."

"Oh, right. I kind of remember hearing that." Owen would be here for a few days…and the relief she felt was confusing. The male was a grumpy cougar who disliked her. Why in the Mother's world should she feel better with him around?

Darcy frowned. "Doesn't Gawain live with Owen?" Littermates usually lived together.

"Huh-uh. Gawain lived down in Oregon, but he's moving to Cold Creek. He'll be staying in the lodge while he house-hunts."

Both of them were here. Darcy opened the bottom of the toaster. "Gawain seems really nice, and I owe Owen a lot for getting me out of Seattle." Darcy huffed a laugh. "Although, when I tried to thank him, he—"

"He probably glared at you, right?"

"In a way." Darcy examined the toaster interior and found pieces of bread stuck to the heating coils. No wonder it wasn't working. "He kind of just walked away."

Bree rolled her eyes. "The idiot. When it comes to interacting with females, he's got the disposition of a boggart."

"Oh." Maybe Darcy wasn't the only person who raised his hackles.

"Owen scared me some when I first met him. He stared at me like he thought I'd steal his wallet, although I think he likes me well enough now." Bree rolled her eyes. "You know, with other males, he's a whole different cat—relaxed and fun."

Had Darcy ever seen him look relaxed? "That would be different. But I do know how brave he is." And she'd put up with a lot from the shifter who'd saved her from the Scythe.

However, she might smack him on the nose if he got too grumpy.

AS OWEN STROLLED past the Wild Hunt Tavern parking lot, he noticed the young redheaded female he'd mated with at the last Gathering. She and her two loud friends were leaving, having probably gone for a trail run. The tavern's underground cave system extended into the forest and provided a safe entry for town-dwelling shifters.

After goodbyes, the noisy friends got into a car, and the redhead crossed the lot to hers.

Owen scratched his jaw and then raised his hand to attract her attention.

She flinched.

By the God, he wasn't planning to claw her. Walking over, he tried to arrange his expression into something that wasn't a scowl. It would help if he could remember her name. In all reality, he doubted he'd even asked.

Wait, hadn't Calum called her *Nia*?

Showing courage, no matter how foolhardy, she lifted her chin. "Owen. Is there something I can do for you?"

Perhaps not behave as if I bit off your tail. He found a better response. "Yes. Accept my apology for my rudeness the other day. Please."

Her mouth dropped open, and she looked even more immature.

From now on, he'd confine his matings to shifters closer to his age or older. Older would be good. No one under forty-two, at least. "Nia?"

"Why were you so nasty anyway? All I said was I thought you were nice and you liked me."

So. Fucking. Young. But he owed her the truth. "The way females talk about the God-called pisses me off. It's all about hunting status and money—not a male to care for. You think cahirs and healers are all just prey."

She blinked. "Oh."

Right. Oh. "But I regret having taken a swipe at you."

"Forgiven."

"Thank you." He took a step back.

"Did you realize you act like the females you just criticized? It seems as if you lump all females into one group and think we're all equally awful."

The expression on his face must have changed since she took a hasty step back.

Pulling a breath through his nose, he gave her a short nod and stalked away. By Herne's giant balls, he disliked the young ones.

Especially when they dispensed a Mother's wisdom.

THE MORNING HAD been frustrating, and as Gawain walked into the lodge, he sincerely hoped the afternoon would improve. Changing towns and territories was more involved than he'd anticipated.

Still, no matter the effort, it would be a joy to live close to his brother and sister. For over twenty years, he'd kept his bargain with their mother—as long as he remained in Pine Knoll, she'd leave Bonnie alone. But last summer, he'd discovered his sister had mated two sturdy males who would never allow their manipulative, abusive mother to upset her.

Gawain pulled in a long breath. Finally, he was free. With any luck, their mother would never learn his location.

He could make a new life here.

Hearing his brother talking with Breanne in the kitchen, Gawain went in search of the female they were supposed to mentor.

On the flagstone-paved patio, Darcy was settled at one of the redwood tables. Barefooted, she wore jeans and an overlarge T-shirt that said Seahawks. The bright October sun teased blue glints from her raven-colored hair.

She was watching the gurgling creek, and the look of peace on her face made him smile.

Seeing him approach, she smiled back. "Good morning."

"Good morning, pretty cat." He ran his hand down her

thick, wavy hair. *Soft.*

She jumped, then relaxed. It was interesting how her expression changed to both a cat's pleasure at being stroked…and wariness.

Giving her space, he turned away to check out the stream. Long, finned shapes glinted under the water, swirling and leaping in a happy game of tag. Undines, hmm? With long, sleekly scaled bodies and silvery hair, the water elementals were even more mischievous than pixies.

He'd definitely keep his dangling bits out of that section of the creek.

Sensing him, one undine sent water arcing toward the patio.

Darcy had a beautifully husky laugh. "They didn't do that before. I think they're trying to get your attention."

"Probably. They're more children of the Mother than the Hunter—and She is strong within me." He settled into a chair and stretched out his legs with an exhausted sigh. "I think I walked every street in Cold Creek this morning."

"For exercise or another reason?"

"I'm house-hunting. Calum gave me permission to move here and—"

"Permission?" Her delicate dark brows drew together. "Does a shifter need permission from the Cosantir to move into a territory?"

"Most shifters, no. For the God-called, it is courteous to check first." When she still looked confused, he elaborated. "For example, it would be wasteful to have three healers in one territory if other territories had none."

"Oh. Right." As she studied him silently, he did the same.

Her eyes were such a dark brown even the sun didn't lighten them…and the pain of her years of captivity lay in the shadows.

She tilted her head. "The scar on your cheekbone. It's different than Owen's."

He touched the silvery-tinted scar of a blade encircled by a full moon. "Aye. Mine is for a blademage."

"I'm afraid I don't know what a blademage does."

"Never met one of us, eh?" He smiled. "Your mama wasn't lifemated?"

"No, she said she'd never met any male she loved enough. My littermates and I were"—her eyes narrowed—"Gather-bred. Is that the word?"

He nodded.

"I've forgotten so much." She made an adorably exasperated sound. "For the first years of captivity, I tried—we all did—to remember everything about being Daonain. But thinking of the outside made the walls higher. So I tried, instead, to forget and live in each day with no future and no past."

Amazed at her strength, he took her small hand in his. "I can't imagine being imprisoned, especially in a city. I think I'd go mad." He stroked his thumb over her palm, finding scars and calluses. She'd had a rough life.

"A couple of the females did go crazy." Her eyes darkened before she straightened her shoulders and pulled her hand away. "So, Gather-bred is correct?" Efficient as a housekeeping brownie, she tidily brushed away the messy emotions.

"Gather-bred means conceived during the full moon Gathering, so aye, you have used the word correctly. My siblings and I were Gather-bred as well." His jaw clenched. Four children, four different sires. And their mother had treated each child differently because of those sires. "Among other things, blademages make lifemating bracelets, which are a symbol of love. If the Mother approves of the match, she blesses the bracelets." Now he and Owen were reunited, maybe…someday…they could find a lifemate.

Darcy wrapped her hands around her coffee mug. "I used to daydream about finding my mates."

"Used to?"

The sadness in her laugh was heartbreaking. Again, she brushed away the emotions. "Have you been a blademage long? Do you meet lots of shifters who are lifemates?"

"I've been a smith since the age of sixteen and was called to serve the Goddess a few years later." He frowned as the years turned into decades. "I've met many, many lifemates."

"Then you'd probably know… I've always wondered if people fall in love instantly, or is it a process that takes time?" Her eyes were alight with interest.

"A few do fall in love upon meeting." He stroked his beard as he thought. "Perhaps they were mates in a previous lifetime and simply recognized each other."

"Oooh," she sighed. "Wouldn't that be wonderful?"

For a moment, he could see the starry-eyed cubling she would have been. All feelings and passion. But now the little female kept her emotions under careful control, and his heart hurt for the change. "After most shifters meet, there seems to be an adjustment period. Their beliefs and habits change in tiny ways until everything matches seamlessly."

"Change?"

He smiled. "It always reminds me of how I create a knife shaft for a blade. I'll adjust the size, working at it little by little, until the haft slides into the wood for a perfect fit."

Someday, he and Owen would find their perfect fit.

"THANK YOU, BREANNE. You're going to ruin me for stalking my own food." As the pretty blonde chef laughed, Owen swallowed the last of the bacon-lettuce-tomato sandwich and headed out of the kitchen.

Through the dining room windows, he spotted his brother

and Darcy on the patio. Sunning sounded good, but he'd have to converse with a female and… He winced, remembering Nia's accusation. "…*you lump all females into a group and think we're all equally awful.*" By the God, he'd become the kind of a person he abhorred. The realization was as painful as a reprimanding swat from the grizzly cahir, Ben.

True, his childhood had given him reasons to avoid females, yet not all were like his mother or the ones who chased after the God-called merely for status.

Time to change his ways. To observe each female with the clear eyes of a hawk rather than a snake's vision, which would note only moving prey. And he needed to learn to be polite.

He walked over and set his hand on Gawain's shoulder, smiling as his blood and muscles recognized the soul that had shared his mother's womb. "Are you two ready to go for a run?"

"A run?" Darcy's expression was that of a cub considering how far to venture from the den. Anticipation, excitement, anxiety. "I guess?"

When Gawain laughed, she smiled ruefully. "I thought I was supposed to stay put and heal."

"Shifting helps the healing process, since the magic gives everything a lift," Gawain told her.

Owen nodded. "Since you've had problems with shifting, it's best if not much time passes between trawsfurs."

"Oh."

When Gawain took her hand, she startled, then let him pull her to her feet.

Gawain kept her hand in his, and Owen noticed she didn't tug away. His littermate had apparently exerted his charm.

"We can use the side door here since the exit was designed for shifters." Owen led them inside. His healed wrist could use the magical boost, and he'd make sure he and Darcy took it easy today.

Down the back hallway, the door at the end was marked *Private*. Owen punched in the code for the door lock, which had been added after a cub used the door. In the tiny changing room, he and Gawain started stripping.

Darcy's face lost the soft flush of color. "Um. You two go on ahead."

Females. Didn't they... Catching himself running the familiar trail of disparagement, Owen skidded to a stop. Altering his ways might be more difficult than he'd anticipated.

"Gawain and I have seen hundreds of females without clothing." He tried on a smile. "You all have the same parts. Today, you will be shifting several times as you learn how to survive in the wild. This is your first lesson: Lose the embarrassment."

She'd listened, nodded, but at his final words, an irritated red swept into her face. "Fine." The sideways slant of her mouth held the same warning as the lashing tail of an irritated cougar.

Ah-huh. Like his mother, her words said one thing and her body language another. Was any female honest?

"Although my brother has the manners of a drunken dwarf, he's correct, catling." Gawain took her hand again. "You don't live with humans any longer. It's time to learn shifter ways."

Her jaw relaxed. "You're right. I'm sorry for holding up the lessons." Without further ado, she stripped quickly, folded her clothing, and set everything on the shelf next to Gawain's pile.

She *apologized?* Owen watched her simply getting on with the task at hand...and it took him a minute to recover.

OWEN WAS WATCHING her with dark green eyes sharper than any emerald, and Darcy felt like a mouse facing a hawk. Because she was naked.

He was naked. Gawain was naked. Feeling the heat in her face, she stared at the floor.

Feet appeared in her field of vision, and she jerked her head up. Owen stood in front of her. When his hand came up, she flinched. Just a little. Hardly at all.

But more than enough for the observant cahir. "I'm not going to hit you, female," he growled. "No male would hit a female."

She snorted, thinking of the beatings and canings she'd endured.

Gawain cleared his throat. "Unlike with humans, it's extremely rare for a shifter male to hurt a female. The shifter would have to be crazy."

"We did have a crazy one, once," Owen muttered. "When Calum found out, he sent the male straight back to the Mother."

Back to the Mother. Calum had killed a shifter? For hitting a female?

Owen set his fingers against her ribs over the healed bullet gouge and pressed. "Does this still hurt?"

"No, it's good."

He went down on one knee and curled powerful fingers around her right calf, just below the healed bullet wound. His hand was warm—but when she tried to move away, his grip tightened to steel.

She stared down at him.

The cahir's shoulders and arms were so powerful and ripped; she could see each striation of the muscles. He was sleekly lethal and yet strong. Not a lightweight sports car, but a streamlined SUV, capable of…anything.

Gawain pulled her attention away as he walked around her to unlatch the door. He was even more muscled than Owen. Probably not as fast, but she'd bet he'd plow through any obstacle like a military tank.

The two of them were a bit scary.

Owen traced a finger around the pink area on her calf and

told Gawain, "It's healing, but we'll have to keep this lesson short."

"Aye." Gawain's voice sounded…odd. Dark and angry.

Darcy looked over her shoulder.

As Gawain stared at her back and shoulders, his every exhalation held a growl.

After a second, she realized he'd seen the spattering of scars on her back.

His gaze lifted to meet hers. "Those scars aren't from claws."

"No." Her laugh sounded as if she was choking. "Humans don't have any claws worthy of note."

Owen joined his brother and ran one finger over her scapula. "From a whip?"

"Cane. The *prìosan* guards used them to keep the hostages obedient."

Owen's growl was as deadly as his brother's. "I look forward to meeting these guards."

"As do I." Gawain patted her arm and then gave his brother a rough shove. "Let's be away. I need to run."

With a shoulder, Owen pushed him back and walked out the door first. "Look around, Darcy. See how private it is?"

She could see how the tiny clear spot outside the door was enclosed by tall evergreens and head-high underbrush. "Yes."

"If you don't have anything as private as this, then the tavern has a portal through caves beneath it. Everyone in town is careful to shift only in designated areas—or they hike well into the forest before stripping and trawsfurring. The Cosantir is very strict about this."

Even as she nodded her understanding, she felt sick to her stomach.

"A shame other Cosantirs aren't as strict. In Mt. Hood Territory, the Daonain are pretty careless, and our mother is one of the worst offenders." Gawain shook his head.

Owen was silent, and his face had gone expressionless.

After a glance at him, Gawain winced. "Let's get moving." He frowned at Darcy. "What's wrong, catling?"

"That's how they found Dogwood." She pushed the words past the nausea in her throat. "I heard Director. The Scythe use wilderness areas to train their human forces and had a camp near Dogwood. Some soldiers spotted a few new teenaged cubs shifting and followed them back to Dogwood. They did surveillance on the village and figured everything out. And later, attacked."

Owen's expression was grim. "I wondered how it had happened."

"Yes." She shook her head. "Everyone in the village was Daonain, so...they weren't as careful as shifter-human towns are."

"That was...an ugly price to pay for carelessness," Gawain said softly. He glanced at Owen."

Oh, it had been.

"Shift, Darcy." Owen glanced at his brother and nodded.

Gawain grinned at her, and a second later, he was a cougar.

She stared. He had to be close to two hundred pounds, and his feline body was as thick with muscle as his human one. As with most panthers, his throat and chest were white, and his muzzle stripes, the fur behind his ears, and the tip of his tail were black. She smiled because his tawny pelt was the same color as his beard.

Setting a giant paw on her foot, he rubbed his jaw and cheek over her bare leg, marking her with his scent.

Unable to resist, she stroked his head. Short, plush fur, prickly whiskers.

He purred, low and beautiful.

"Back up, brawd, and let her shift," Owen said.

Right. She needed to trawsfur. *Okay, then.* First, find the door. Darcy looked inside her mind and found the dark wooden door, now clear of any barriers. But would she be able to open it? She had to do this correctly. Carefully. Not mess it up. Really, it should be simple. Walk to the door in her head. Find the—

"Darcy. Less thinking, more action." Owen's voice held impatience.

Honestly, didn't he know things needed to be done properly? That people got…hurt…if others lost control and simply acted? But she could do this. *Pull open the door.*

Take a step.

As she changed, the full force of the Mother's love hit her, flowing up from the ground, through her paws…so achingly beautiful her heart swelled.

When she lifted her head, she saw Owen had trawsfurred as well. Although taller, he was sleeker than Gawain and moved with a lethal, predatory grace. Gawain's pelt held a few claw and bite marks from fighting. Owen's darker fur showed so many scars she wanted to weep for the pain he must have endured.

The cahir had fought and survived—and grown only more deadly. The knowledge should have made her fearful.

Instead, when he stalked over to her and put a big paw on top of her neck, she sank to the ground, curving her neck as if in invitation. What…what had she just done? Yet the purr filling the air was her own.

Owen rubbed his furry chin over the top of her head. When his deep, rough purr joined her own, the sound filled the gaps in her heart. His raspy tongue smoothed the fur behind her right ear.

Gawain chuffed at him, as if laughing.

Owen turned. His tail lashed, once, twice, and he sprang at Gawain.

No! Don't fight! Darcy danced in anxiety as the panthers

rolled on the ground.

Gawain's hind paws scrabbled at Owen's pale belly fur. On-ly…his claws were sheathed. They rolled again and leaped apart, curveting away from each other in a sideways dance, which was as funny as it was graceful.

Playing. They were playing. They'd probably had mock-fights since their first shift at thirteen or so.

Regret seeped into her. She, Patrin, and Fell should have spent the last decade learning how to be cougars. Playing games and pouncing on each other. Fell would have been awesome at hide and seek. Patrin loved heights and would have lurked on low branches. Her? Undoubtedly, she'd have gotten caught up trailing something, and they'd both have ambushed her.

Because of the Scythe, they'd missed all that.

But she'd get them free. She would.

TURNING TO LOOK at her, Owen chirruped and trotted forward, taking an almost invisible trail through the brush. She glanced at Gawain.

He waited for her to go next.

All right then.

As she trotted across the space, she realized they'd been right. She did feel better, just from trawsfurring. Happily, she leapt after Owen in long bounds.

Soon, the undergrowth hid him almost completely. All she could see were occasional flashes of movement, a flash of dark ochre fur, and the black tip of his tail.

He disappeared entirely.

She stopped and looked around.

Joining her, Gawain made a *huh-huh* sound. He was laughing at her.

Her ears flattened, and his huff grew louder. He shifted smoothly to human form and stood straight. "You kept him in sight longer than I thought you would. But Owen's better than anyone I know at disappearing. Alec, one of his cahir partners, calls him *ghost cat*."

Her tail lashed. Weren't they supposed to be running together? He'd *cheated*.

"This is a lesson, Darcy." Gawain's voice was patient. "What should you do when your prey disappears?"

She stared at him. *Oh.* In Seward Park, when she'd stalked a rodent, it had faded into the brush. She never did find it.

She shook her head to show she didn't know the answer to his question.

"Learn to use your other senses. You see, the human form relies almost entirely on sight. As a cat, you'll want to use your nose and ears, as well." He grinned. "The lesson on whiskers will come later."

Whiskers? She realized she could feel the long, stiff hairs on her muzzle. Could move them. Could—

"Can you hear anything moving?" Gawain tilted his head. "Point your ears and listen."

Her ears swiveled obediently forward and sideways. The rustle came from something tiny—maybe a mouse or shrew. The wind stirred the tops of the conifers. Bird song came from farther away, probably by the creek. There was the smack of an axe against wood from someone cutting firewood.

Nothing related to Owen. Giving up, she looked up at Gawain. Was she missing something?

"I can't hear him either," Gawain said, easing her worry. "Use your nose. You should know his scent." The male grinned. "He rubbed it on you before we split up."

Oh. Both males had, and she'd recognize them anywhere now, whether human or cat. Lifting her head, she inhaled, caught a whiff of bitter minerals and smoke, and wrinkled her nose.

Gawain's eyebrows lifted, and he sniffed. "No, that's not Owen. I'd guess there's a dwarf hall around. Try again."

This time, she caught something elusive on the wind.

There.

"Good. Let's go." Within one heartbeat, Gawain was a cougar, tail lashing as he waited for her to lead out.

With no hesitation, she bounded forward. Oh, when she found sneaky Owen, she was going to bite his ear.

His overwhelmingly male scent drifted to her, and when the wind shifted, Gawain taught her to sniff the trail for scent markers left by cat paws.

Farther on, she found the stinky urine Owen had obligingly provided on a tree. *Ew.*

She discovered a faint trace where he'd brushed against a huckleberry.

The forest opened into a sun-filled meadow. They were so high that much of the grass was still green, and a tiny stream rippled through the center.

Owen, still in cat form, was sunning himself on a flat rock. The jerk looked far too comfortable.

With three swift bounds, she sprang across the clearing, landed on him, and tumbled him off the rock.

Success. Delighted, she grappled with the cougar, pretending to bite on his ear, clinging with her paws to his muscular shoulders. Huge shoulders, she realized, as his giant paw curled around her neck.

Suddenly Gawain joined the fray, and she was squished between two huge panthers. Unable to *move*.

A second later, she was in human form. *What?*

Stepping away, Gawain shifted.

Freed, Darcy scrambled away from Owen. The late season meadow grass stabbed her bare feet painfully as she retreated farther. "I…I…what happened?" She stared down at her arms.

Her human hands. "I didn't look for the door."

Gawain's dark beard showed his white teeth in a smile. "It happens with new shifters, some more than others. I enjoyed teasing Owen back in the day."

She blinked at Owen as he shifted to human form. The deadly cahir had accidentally trawsfurred? "You?"

Owen's grin was a revelation. Had she ever seen him simply enjoying himself? "Aye, me. Frustrated me no end until I finally got control."

"I bet." She'd been terrified when she couldn't shift back to human for all those days. And now she was trawsfurring accidentally? Her jaw clenched. No, she wouldn't have it. Just, *no*.

"Catling, accidents happen," Gawain said gently. "Within a few months, most Daonain get enough control that they won't unexpectedly shift."

Most, but not all. She remembered the Scythe basement. The guards had dragged a young male of about seventeen into the laboratory. He'd been begging. *"No. Please."* He'd shrieked in pain…then human screaming came from the room. *"A bear. He's a bear."* The guards had rushed in, shooting. She and the rest of the children could smell the blood. The death.

Her heart ached even as anger made her growl. She wished the young werebear had killed more of them. *All* of them.

Suddenly she was a cougar again.

Oh, bloody scat.

Chapter Seven

O N SATURDAY AFTERNOON, Owen entered the Wild Hunt
tavern and stopped to swipe his sleeve over his wet face.
The fall storms had begun. Outside the sturdy 1800s log
building, thunder rumbled, and the early October rain drummed
pleasantly against the windows.

As he waited for Gawain to arrive, the scents of popcorn
and roasted peanuts made him wish he'd eaten more than the
mouse he'd snatched up when out with Darcy earlier. Being a
polite male, he'd let her eat all of the rabbit she'd caught.
Actually, he'd been as pleased as she had been with her successful hunt. She'd done well.

He glanced around the room. Near the massive fireplace to
the left, a shifter was reading a book. Two regulars were playing
pool in the alcove on the right. At a center table, a male whose
clothing stank of fish sat with another human and boasted in a
nasal voice about his success on the stream. The rest of the
heavy oak tables and chairs were empty.

Behind him, the door opened. Gawain stepped in and shook
his wet hair, spattering Owen with water.

"You mangy-tailed maggot." Owen wiped his face
off…again. "You're not a dog; stop acting like one."

His littermate grinned and glanced around. "So where's

Calum?"

"Behind the bar." Owen pointed headed toward where the gleaming wooden bar that extended across the back with a mirrored wall behind it.

"A *Cosantir* is a *bartender*?"

"Keeps him up on all the information. What he doesn't hear, his brother Alec, the sheriff, does."

Gawain scratched his beard. "Interesting and rather sneaky. Nice."

Noticing their arrival, Calum motioned toward the end of the bar before crossing the room to serve the fisherman and his companion.

As Owen settled onto a wooden barstool, Calum returned. "Can I get you something?"

"Coffee would be great," Owen said, and Gawain nodded.

Calum poured coffee for all of them and slid over a tray containing cream and sugar. "How are you feeling, cahir?"

"Good. My leg's fine. The wrist is…close." It tweaked his tail to admit Calum's order to rest and heal had been appropriate.

"Excellent. How is Darcy doing?"

Gawain picked up a cup. "Fair to middling. Unfortunately, her healing is slower since she was so physically run-down. Donal ordered her to take it easy for a while yet."

"I see." Calum frowned. "How about her shifting and control?"

"Her control is normal for having her first trawsfur only a week ago"—Gawain grinned—"although she's more frustrated than a pixie unable to reach a flower."

"She is." Owen snorted. "Most new shifters expect they'll screw up. Not being a youngster, Darcy figured she'd be perfect by now."

Gawain studied Calum. "Owen mentioned your mate was

human before the Death Gift transformed her to Daonain. Did being an adult speed up her control over shifting?"

Owen blinked. Good question.

"Victoria achieved control quickly, but it wasn't due to her age," Calum answered. "Years as a soldier gave her a superb mastery over her body, which extended to her ability to shift. Breanne, however, went through much of what Darcy is experiencing."

"Darcy will get there, even if not fast enough to suit her." Owen's lips twitched. The female was fun to watch when she got frustrated. He took a sip of his coffee. "You wanted to see me, Cosantir?"

"Aye. I want to discuss where you live."

"My cabin?" Owen frowned. What was wrong with his place? The Cosantir had visited a couple of times in the past years and admired it. Had even helped Owen learn to brew his own beer.

"Not your cabin, but the location."

"Owen showed me on a map where his place is." Gawain shook his head. "Insane cat. Admittedly, I don't want my den side-by-side with someone else's, but a dozen miles of wilderness seems excessive. I'd rather be able to stroll down to a tavern or restaurant in the evening."

Owen sighed. He'd hoped Gawain would come and live with him. Littermates belonged together. Silently, he absorbed the disappointment.

"Your cabin *is* far away, cahir, and I have a couple of concerns." The Cosantir's gaze rested on Owen. "Yesterday, on Main Street, some shifters found a hellhound's scent."

"Yesterday?" Gawain straightened. "I thought they only appeared when it's moonless."

Owen's gut hardened. "They shift to their hellhound form only at the dark of the moon; they're in human form otherwise.

This one could be scouting Cold Creek and targeting vulnerable shifters." The thought was worrying. Although the cahirs patrolled on moonless nights, if a hellhound was prepared, his prey might die before help arrived.

Calum frowned. "And even in human form, the demon-dog might attack someone. Violence trails a hellhound like a coyote after a lame rabbit."

Owen nodded. The Cosantir was right to be worried. "You said you had two concerns?"

"Aye. In addition to a hellhound in town, there is the danger of the Scythe. Darcy's former captors are undoubtedly searching for her."

"But her trackers were removed," Gawain said.

Calum nodded. "However, if they have any suspicion she was rescued, their experience with Dogwood will point them toward the closest wilderness areas. This territory."

"You want me to move into town," Owen said slowly.

"I do." Rather than trying to persuade him, Calum walked away to fill another order.

Owen swirled his coffee, gazing into the black liquid. After years of peace, Cold Creek was being threatened by multiple foes. He was a cahir—called by Herne the Hunter to defend the Daonain and given increased strength and size to do so. He'd seen what was left after a hellhound attacked a shifter—gore, shattered bones, and eviscerated corpses.

It seemed that being several hours away from the people he was guarding was…no longer possible.

"I don't like living in towns," he muttered. He loved his isolated cabin. *No power lines, no phones, no cars—*

"Aren't you supposed to defend your people?" The question came from behind him.

—and no females. Recognizing the smoky voice as Darcy's, Owen turned. "What did you say?"

"You're a cahir, right?" When Darcy set her hands on her hips, Owen felt his muscles tense. Now would come the screaming, hitting, and throwing things.

Rather than rising to a shriek, her sultry voice lowered. "The Scythe are searching for shifters. Do you want to come back and find your town burned to the ground? All the Daonain gone? What's wrong with you?" She gripped his arm and actually tried to shake him.

He plucked her hand from his arm and held it—and her—in place. "I didn't say I wouldn't move. I said I don't like towns. I'll be moving here." He glanced at Gawain. "Females. Always jumping to hasty conclusions."

Darcy made an annoyed sound.

"Mmmhmm. You making a remark like that? Sounds like the ocean calling a lake *wet*." Gawain's smile faded, and he hesitated. "Ah...I've missed you, brawd. Since you're moving to town, want to get a house with me? Try living together?"

"Yeah." The answer came so easily Owen knew he'd been burying his feelings deeper than he would his own scat. Sharing a room at the lodge with his littermate was comfortable. Home-like. No, better—since they'd never had what could be called a home. There was no stress in being with Gawain, just familiarity. "As long as we can find something near the edge of town."

Gawain nodded. "Aye. And I need a place for smithing. We'll find something that works."

A tug made him realize he was still holding the female's hand.

Her eyes were the darkness of a lake at midnight...and nar-rowed. At him.

"You're glaring at me, little cat." By Herne's holy antlers, she was pretty when she was pissed-off. He had to say, it was refreshing not to be treated like a stud male...or feared. "Are you still angry with me for finding your hiding place this morning?"

"For finding me? No. For knocking me into the creek? Oh, yes." The fiery snap in her voice made him grin. The screech she'd let out had been amazing and then she'd lost control and shifted to human. Fuck, she'd been angry. Yet her voice had never risen above a whisper as she spewed a stream of very interesting human curses.

She tugged on her hand again. "Please let go." Even now, her voice was low and polite.

Her personality was remarkably restrained. Why did that spark a perverse need to shake her up? Rather than releasing her, he kept her hand imprisoned. Such a delicate hand, and yet her fingers held calluses that spoke of hard work.

"Darcy, thank you for coming." The Cosantir smiled at her before glancing at Owen, then her hand in an unspoken order.

Well, scat. His fun was over. He opened his hand.

Moving closer to Gawain, she cast Owen a fulminating look. With her strong personality, it was easy to forget her size. And whenever she was steaming mad? He could swear she grew almost a foot.

Still left her a fuck of a lot shorter than he was.

Wisely holding back laughter, Gawain winked at him before asking, "Darcy, are you in the mood for some coffee?"

"I…" She pushed her annoyance aside with impressive skill. "Sure. I'd love coffee." Her smile curved her cheeks, created dimples beside her mouth, and totally transformed her face.

He realized interest hummed in his blood, and he was watching her as a male would a female he wanted to mate.

No. Owen stomped on the emotion with a ruthless paw. *Absolutely not.* Maybe if she chose him at a Gathering, he'd enjoy her favor then. And only then.

DARCY CAUGHT THE dawning masculine appreciation in Owen's

gaze before his expression went blank and his eyes shuttered. The loss seized her before she regained some common sense.

She didn't want to attract a male. This wasn't the time or place. There probably would never be a time or place. She couldn't afford to rely on a mate—or anyone. Not really. She'd learned to stand on her own two feet…and now she had four paws. Four paws were wonderfully stable, far better than feet any day.

Well, they would be more reliable if she could regulate when she had paws and when she had feet. Honestly, inadvertently shifting was—

"Here you go." Gawain set a cup in front of her and slid the cream and sugar closer. "Owen said you hunted well this morning."

She couldn't have asked for a better opening. "I did. In fact,"—her attention turned to the Cosantir—"I'm ready to go search for my brothers and the shifter-soldier compound."

"Indeed. Are you in control of your shifting?"

Under the Cosantir's level gray gaze, she couldn't lie. Getting dumped into cold water had made her trawsfur. And just this morning, she'd rolled out of bed, landed on four paws, and realized she'd changed in her sleep. She shook her head. "Soon, though."

She couldn't wait forever. "Cosantir, the male villagers—the shifter-soldiers—*must* be told about the hidden trackers right away. Since the males visit the female littermates every few months, they—"

"Why the visits?" Owen asked. "Why show captives that mercy?"

Mercy? Darcy's laugh came out bitter. "Not mercy. The Scythe think they have to let us visit. You see, humans can't *feel* their bonds to family or lovers. If they're parted too long, apparently the love dies. So, the shifter-soldiers visit the prison to ensure each male continues to love his sister and won't put her at risk by trying to break free or refusing an order. It also proves to the males their sisters are still captives."

"Clever and effective." Gawain tilted his head at Owen. "Face it, we'd do just about anything to keep Bonnie from being hurt."

Owen looked like he'd bitten into a sour huckleberry. "Yeah."

"When the males visit the *prìosan* in two to three months, my brothers won't find me there. They'll revolt—and the Scythe will kill them." The thought made her breathing go all funny, and she closed her eyes.

Her hair was given a stern tug. "Stay human, Darcy," Owen growled.

She froze, realizing that, in her mind, she'd opened the door to the wild. Had been about to trawsfur. Appalled, she slammed the door shut and edged away.

When she looked up, Gawain's hand was on her back. Owen's fingers were wound in her hair, keeping her from doing something stupid.

"Thank you," she whispered.

With a grim nod, Owen released her hair and moved back.

Well, that sure showed the Cosantir she couldn't leave yet. Her breath escaped in a long unhappy sigh.

Gawain squeezed her shoulder. "You'll get better, catling."

"Tynan is searching for the property where Darcy was held," Calum told Owen. "But she couldn't give much of a description of the location or property. Two three-story houses surrounded by a high stone wall. Somewhere in Seattle to the west of Lake Washington."

Gawain snorted. "If I were chased through the streets without a map and no knowledge of cities, I'd do no better."

Gratitude for his understanding welled within her.

"Aye. Human cities are pure chaos." Calum frowned. "From what Darcy's said, even if Tynan finds the location, we cannot rescue the females until we—"

"You'd help? Help get the villagers free? Even though they're in a city?" Hope rose like a fountain.

Calum considered her thoughtfully. "Having any of our people—especially females—held by humans doesn't sit well with me. Yet I can make no promises, Darcy. Danger lurks on every path I can see, so at this point, we are merely collecting information."

Her hope drained away. For a moment, she had childishly hoped for miracles. Unable to speak past the disappointment clogging her throat, she nodded her understanding.

Calum turned back to Owen. "Rescuing the females before finding the soldier's compound won't work. If the hostages are lost, the Scythe would undoubtedly eliminate the males as an uncontrollable risk."

No, no, no. Her hands closed into fists as she fought the need to shift and run and find her littermates. Owen's lean hand landed on her shoulder and kept her focused.

Although the cahir wasn't touching her for comfort, but to prevent problems, she couldn't help but feel thankful.

"I can assist, Cosantir," Gawain said. "Maybe Owen and I could do some scouting for the males' location."

Owen nodded. "Agreed. Where should we start?"

Sheer surprise left her speechless.

The Cosantir shook his head. "I fear your search will take you out of Herne's domain. There are no unknown shifters in my territory, and when I contacted the Washington and Oregon Cosantirs, they verified the same."

"How do you know that so quickly?" Darcy asked.

Owen answered for Calum. "A Cosantir can sense every shifter in his territory. It's one of their powers."

Her teeth ground together. Wasn't it appalling how much she didn't know about her own people?

"Permission to leave the territory and search, Cosantir?" Owen asked.

Calum nodded. "If you and Gawain find time from setting up your household, I'd appreciate if you searched for the shifter-soldiers."

Owen grinned. "We'll need a break from that moving shit anyway."

"Do you have any suggestions on where to start hunting, Darcy?" Gawain asked.

She'd already spent time trying to determine her brothers' location. "Fell and Patrin mentioned doing training at Twin Sisters Range. Since they called their place a forest camp and forest compound, it's in the woods. But they never spoke of having to hike to get out, so I think the barracks are probably close to Highway 20. I'm afraid it's all guesses, though."

Calum's fingers tapped the top of the bar as he thought. "My territory ends east of Mt. Baker and not nearly to the Twin Sisters, so that will narrow the search."

A sound from the other side of the bar drew Calum's attention, and he turned. "Excuse me, please." After drawing two drafts of very dark beer, he carried them to a table in the shadows.

Darcy stared. *OtherFolk—here?* The two at the table were shorter than she was with long beards and gnarly faces like old trees. "Dwarves come to this bar?"

"There's a dwarven hall nearby, and some of them get a kick out of sampling what's on tap," Owen said.

Wow. She frowned. "Don't the humans ask questions about the strange-looking visitors?"

"Not unless they have the Sight." Gawain shook his head. "Dwarves have a *don't-look-at-me* magic in the same way sprites and gnomes do."

The Cosantir tilted his head, the dwarves bowed slightly, and the Cosantir disengaged. Returning to the bar, he picked up his cup of coffee. When he looked at her—and she was probably gawking—his eyebrow went up.

"I don't think our catling has run into dwarves before." Gawain covered her hand with his.

She took a step back and then stopped herself.

Frowning, he picked her up hand. "Does it bother you to be touched?" Both her mentors often took her hand, squeezed her shoulder, or tugged on her hair.

Owen turned to look at her.

"It's a habit. In the *prìosan*, contact between captives wasn't allowed—although those of us who were older would sneak hugs to the children when we could." She'd earned a few canings that way.

Gawain's clear blue eyes held concern. And wasn't that wonderful?

She tried to lighten her tone. "If I'm not expecting to be touched, my first reaction is to move back and check for guards watching. But I like being touched." *Like* was such an inadequate word. Sometimes it seemed as if her entire body had been waiting forever to be stroked or held. As if her skin drank in the feeling of someone else touching her.

With the back of his knuckles, Gawain stroked her cheek. "I like touching you, so I'm glad you enjoy it."

Owen made a low growl. "I look forward to meeting those Scythe bastards." To her surprise, he pulled her back against his chest long enough to rub his cheek over hers.

A panther mark of affection...from the grumbly cat.

The surprise left her silent, and as her mentors turned to discussing their upcoming move, she stood between them, feeling content.

Chapter Eight

ON MONDAY, GAWAIN spotted a turnout on the forest service road and pulled the car into it. Time for shifter-soldier hunting as they'd promised Darcy.

Yesterday, they'd let her practice on her own while he and Owen had run up to his littermate's remote cabin. The setting was beautiful—a tiny mountain valley with a stream at the front door—but also what the humans called "off the grid". No electricity. No road.

While Gawain had looked around, his brother had figured out what belongings he wanted to move to town. After a few hours of savoring the peace, Gawain suggested Owen keep the cabin. Having a quiet sanctuary was good for shifters—especially introverts like his littermate.

This morning, over breakfast, they'd listed out what they each needed and wanted in a house, and shared some of their experiences in the years apart. Gawain glanced over at his brother, seeing the scattered scars on his arms, face, and neck. Owen had been far too nonchalant about the dangers of a cahir's life.

Sliding out of the car, Gawain looked around and gave a sniff. Odd how the air smelled different outside of Calum's territory. Even the feeling of the land was strange—thinner or less rich or something. Perhaps the lack was because the Gods had no influence over the Twin Sisters Range.

As Owen stepped out of the car, he was absent-mindedly scratching his neck and arms.

Being resistant to the effects of metal, Gawain didn't suffer from vehicular-induced itching. But he knew better than to laugh. In fact, it had been a very quiet drive, since his itchy littermate had been as grumpy as a dwarf without any gold to his name.

Speaking of dwarves... "Did Calum find out if the dwarves had seen any shifters around here?"

"They weren't any help." Heading into the underbrush, Owen unbuttoned his shirt. "Their only hall this far north is within the North Cascades Territory, so they don't know any more than Calum does."

"That's a shame."

"We might get more help, though. Tynan, Donal's littermate, lives in Seattle. Did you see him when we brought Darcy to the healer's house?"

"Big male? Square jaw and Irish accent?" Gawain followed as Owen led the way into the underbrush.

"Yeah. The cop doesn't come to Cold Creek often. He worries if he's ever exposed as a Daonain, someone might track his movements back to the town. But he misses other shifters—he's a wolf—so he and Donal want to join us next time we come to search."

The poor bastard; wolves weren't meant to den alone. "I don't know how anyone could tolerate being in a city surrounded by humans. Of course they can join us."

Reaching a place well hidden within the brush, Owen shed his clothes.

Gawain did the same and then tied the car key around a branch and out of sight.

Owen raised an eyebrow. "Why not leave it in your pocket?"

"This way I have a car, even if someone steals our clothes." He shook his head. "And, having learned the painful way, I keep extra jeans and a shirt in the car."

Owen snorted. "Painful? Like when Edwyn got revenge for our going to the lake without him?"

"Exactly." Edwyn had never dealt well with being left out. He'd followed, and they'd returned to find their hidden clothing ripped to confetti. It had been a hot sunny day—and the ancient vinyl car seats had scorched their bare skin. "I think I had blisters on my ass for weeks."

"Fuck, I couldn't sit down for a day afterward."

"That little weasel." When Gawain's gaze met Owen's, they both grinned. The thought of Edwyn no longer caused agonizing pain, and even more, Owen had spoken his name with a smile. Time healed.

After Owen trawsfurred, Gawain did the same and followed his littermate down a tiny animal trail. The fir needles were damp and soft under his paws. He slowed to snatch a few tart huckleberries from a bush before loping after his brother.

The breeze came from the north and west. He could scent several deer, fairly distant. Coyotes had used the trail recently. No humans were anywhere close.

No shifters, either. His ears flattened with worry. What would Darcy do if they couldn't locate her brothers?

He couldn't imagine how it would feel to have Bonnie held hostage. It was such a joy to spend time with her again. He'd missed her almost as much as he'd missed Owen. But...by staying in Pine Knoll, Gawain had given both his littermates time to heal from their mother's abuse.

And he'd figured those dues were his to pay. After all, it had been his fault Edwyn had died.

Chapter Nine

TIME PASSED FAR too quickly, Darcy thought, as she strolled toward downtown. A week had passed while Owen and Gawain searched for the shifter-soldier camp. In Seattle, Tynan was hunting for the female captives.

As for Darcy, her trawsfurring was improving, and she no longer shifted randomly. Unfortunately, her control still disintegrated if she was startled or hurt. Yesterday, while repairing the lodge's refrigerator, a loose wire poked her arm. A second later, her clothes were trying to strangle her, and she dropped the screwdriver…right onto her furry hind paw.

Shay and Owen had come in, seen her, and laughed their fool heads off.

She grinned. Okay, it'd probably looked really funny. And it had been fun to hear Owen let loose. For such a grumpy cat, he had an awesome gravelly laugh. Just hearing him was worth a bit of embarrassment.

He still had her puzzled, despite all the time they spent together. He and Gawain took her out in the forest almost every morning. Of course, they didn't spend much time conversing while in animal form. Afternoons, the guys drove off to search for the shifter-soldier camp. Evenings, they'd all go house hunting.

Darcy waved at a child playing in a big leaf pile and continued on to Main Street. As a chill wind whipped around her, she zipped up her sweatshirt. The mid-October weather had been more dry than wet, but that seemed about to change. After a rain shower earlier, a thick layer of gray clouds dimmed the sun. Just as well she had a day off from the morning hunting. Wet fur was icky.

Although…she missed her time with the guys. Who knew she'd grow so fond of them? Much like a wide mountain meadow in the sun with nothing hidden, Gawain was exactly who he seemed to be—an honest, caring, strong, brave male. He enjoyed people, was easy to be around, and was delighted with being in Cold Creek. In return, the townspeople were delighted to have gained a blademage.

Rather than a meadow, Owen was a mountain at night, full of moving shadows and hidden hollows to trip up the most careful of paws.

She smiled. Her mentors had taken her for a midnight run soon after she'd arrived. At the forest's edge, she'd been stunned at the sight of moonlight on a still, black lake, cupped in the hollow of the mountains. The beauty, the peace… Owen had that in him, as well.

As she walked past the downtown businesses, she shook her head. Getting to know her mentors had reminded her that not all males were as vile as the *prìosan* guards.

"Good afternoon, Darcy," Angie called from inside her diner. The wolf was one of Bree's closest friends and had stopped by the lodge yesterday. "Are you running errands in town?"

Poking her head in the open door, Darcy saw the older blonde female wiping off the tables. "Breanne's cookbook order came into BOOKS, and I'm picking it up. There's a new recipe for fudge in it she wants to try."

"Tell her to save me a sample." Angie said. "Her candies are fantastic."

"Seems like anything she makes is amazing." Sweets were at the top of the list. When Darcy'd mentioned the *prìosan* never served desserts, Bree baked a different treat each day.

At a loss for how to repay such kindness, Darcy had fixed and tuned every appliance and power tool at the lodge. This morning, she'd been cleaning a cabin when Owen and Gawain found her. When they gave her permission to visit the downtown area by herself, it felt as if she'd gotten a gold star on her report card.

Angie grinned. "I love Bree's desserts, too. And even more, I love that I don't have to bake them."

Darcy laughed, knowing Bree supplied all the desserts for the diner.

With a wave goodbye, she continued down the street. Cold Creek was a quiet, high mountain town surrounded by evergreen forest. Since the Daonain hated car-induced itching and preferred to walk, they'd made the downtown pedestrian-friendly. Main Street's lanes were divided by long islands filled with trees, benches, and the last of the summer's flowers.

Smiling at the greetings she'd received from everyone, she entered the bookstore and spotted the owner. Bree had described Joe Thorson perfectly. Older, lean, mean looking. His forearms and the backs of his hands were covered in fine white scars. From fighting, she figured. Why did males fight anyway?

"Hi," she said and realized she'd been staring. *Bad kitty.*

He nodded, unsmiling.

"I, ah… Breanne asked me to pick up her cookbook order."

"I have it in the back." His voice was even harsher than Owen's. "Hold on."

"Thank you." She waited, breathing in the fragrance of coffee and the even headier perfume of books. The forbidden books had been one of her few joys in captivity. She couldn't count the times she'd almost been caught raiding the Scythe library.

When Thorson returned, she held out the money Bree had given her.

After he tucked the money into the old-fashioned cash register and handed the book over, she turned to leave.

"Nothing for you?" His grizzled brows drew together.

Darcy shook her head. No matter how much she lusted after books, she didn't have the funds for…anything. Breanne had tried to give her more money than what the cookbook would cost, and Darcy'd refused. She already got free room and board. It had been somewhat of a relief when Breanne explained the territory's funds reimbursed the lodge for her food.

"The lodge has books in their library room." Darcy found her smile again. "In fact, they have all the Agatha Christie mysteries."

Thorson chuckled. "Zeb's stash. In that case, enjoy."

Heart lightened, she stepped out onto the street and choked at the horrible stench filling the air. Something must have died or something. Or maybe a garbage can filled with rotting food had spilled?

"*Darcy.*" The yell came from Owen over a block away. "Get inside and tell Thorson to lock his damn door. *Now.*"

Startled, Darcy jumped back into the store and shouted to the old male, "Owen says to lock your door."

"By the God." With a savage scowl, Thorson hurried to the door and—rather than locking it—stepped outside.

What in the forest was going on? Darcy followed him out onto the sidewalk.

He sniffed the air and growled, "Stay in the store."

"Right." She obediently took a step back.

"*No.*" A young female screamed, "Leave me alone!"

"Get the fuck away from my kid, you bastard!" A woman

shouted from the alley around the corner.

"Jamie, Vic!" Thorson dashed that way.

A child in danger. Trouble. Darcy started after him. Stopped. *Bad* trouble. She dove back into the store, grabbed the fire extinguisher from the case inside the door, and chased after the old male.

Thorson moved fast. He disappeared around the corner. A roar of fury came from him followed by thuds and horrendous growls.

Owen charged past her and into the alleyway. She turned the corner and saw him attack a huge man.

The man wasn't a shifter—no shifter stank like carrion.

Thorson lay slumped against the brick wall near a pregnant woman and a teenager.

Growling and cursing, Owen and the man wrestled and then the man punched the cahir. Knocked away, Owen stumbled on some debris and fell.

Even as the cat shifter rolled back to his feet, the stranger pulled out a pistol.

No! Darcy charged. "Hey, dumbass!"

As the pistol swung toward her, she pulled the trigger on the fire extinguisher, aiming for his head. As the white cloud enveloped him, she threw the metal can at his head and dove to the right.

The pistol fired with an ear-hurting bang.

A second later, Owen was on the man. A cracking-crunching sound made her stomach clench.

The man fell limply to the concrete.

Such utter limpness. He was dead. Like ten-year-old Cecily whom a guard had hit too forcefully. Like her mother on the cart as it was pushed past the door, her arm hanging limp, and her blank eyes staring at Darcy.

The alley filled with noise. People were shouting. Darcy

couldn't look away from the unmoving human-sized heap.

Dead bodies didn't move.

"Little female, you shouldn't… Darcy? *Darcy.*" Warmth touched the side of her face; a firm hand turned her head.

She blinked and stared into eyes the color of forests, of leafy growth, of life.

Owen's hard eyes softened. "You with me?"

"I…" She swallowed and tried again. "Are you all right?"

A crease appeared in his cheek. "Thanks to someone putting out a fire. Nice job, kitten."

The approval in his rough voice was unexpected and bracing. She hauled in a breath and looked around—anywhere except toward the body.

On his feet, Thorson was brushing off his clothes.

In a tan uniform shirt, a male as big as Owen had his arms around the pregnant woman and the girl. He snapped low-voiced orders to a younger cop.

"Aye, Alec." The young cop crossed the alley to deal with the people amassing at the entrance.

After hugging the two females, Alec handed them over to Thorson and sauntered over. "Good hunt, Owen. Calum will be pleased."

"The thanks go to Darcy." Owen's big hand rested on her shoulder, lending her strength. "The demon-dog pulled a handgun. Would've shot me dead if she hadn't hosed him down with a fire extinguisher and bounced the container off his skull."

"That was fine thinking, miss." Alec went down on his haunches in front of her. "I smell blood. Did he hit you?"

"No." After a second, she realized her hands hurt. Turning them over, she saw her palms were scraped raw. "When I threw the can, I kind of dove to the side, just in case."

"Smart. I appreciate smart." The cop's grin was as easy-going as Gawain's. Apparently, death wasn't something that bothered him overly much. "I'm Alec, the sheriff here."

"Um. Nice to meet you?"

He chuckled and turned. "Thorson, can you escort my vixen and Jamie to the Wild Hunt? Owen, you take Darcy there, and everyone can report in to Calum. Tell him I'll see him after I tidy up here."

"Good enough. I hate cleanup." Owen rose, reached down, and hauled Darcy up like a puppy. Before she'd taken a step, she came face-to-face with the bookstore male.

"You all right, Joe?" Alec asked.

"Aye." The grizzled old male gave her a firm nod and a slight smile. "You did well, girl. Welcome to Cold Creek."

KEEPING A FIRM hold on the little cat's arm, Owen used his other hand to text his littermate about the attack. Darcy could use someone to hold her hand, and fuck knew, Owen wasn't much of a nursemaid.

This female deserved a bit of pampering.

She was silent as they walked out of downtown and uphill toward the Wild Hunt on the outskirts of town. He'd expected hysterics…tears, at the very least. Instead, he got a pulled-into-herself reserve.

He studied her. Her color usually matched his tanned skin, but now her face was pale gray, her dark eyes looked glassy, and she was trembling.

"Darcy."

She didn't respond, didn't seem to have heard him.

The knot in his gut tautened. After a vicious battle, he knew how to support the other cahirs, to extend silent sympathy or joke them out of a mood. But she was shaking…harder.

Silent sympathy wasn't helping. He could see joking wouldn't work. What would?

She was female. He handled females well enough on Gathering nights—mating was simple. But he wasn't used to spending time with them or giving them…comfort.

And she was definitely owed all the comfort he could give her. She'd heard Jamie scream and had run to the rescue, knowing she was headed toward a fight. She'd attacked a hellhound with a fire extinguisher.

He shook his head. Females just weren't so appallingly courageous.

Only some were, weren't they? *"…you lump all females into a group and think we're all equally awful."* He had the brains of a gnome, dammit. This little cat was not only bloody courageous, but had saved his life.

And now she was a mess.

Feeling as awkward as an undine out of water, he moved closer, until her hip rubbed the side of his leg. "Come here, Darcy," he murmured and put his arm around her shoulders. Fragile bones, tiny female. He drew her closer, shortening his stride so they walked in step. Through the thin shirt she wore, he could feel the chill of her skin.

Still wasn't enough.

She looked as pale and shaken as his two normally feisty nephews had after nearly falling off a cliff.

He'd known what to do for Luke and Tyler. Could he treat her like a cubling? This comforting business felt more hazardous than crossing the river at spring thaw with ice cracking under his paws. Barely breathing, he drew her into his arms and guided her head down against his shoulder. Unmoving, he let his body heat warm her.

She stood as stiff as a wild kitten, then sighed and relaxed against him.

With Herne the Hunter's grace, he'd done the right thing.

Now what? His chin rested on the top of her head, and the breeze blew her silky hair against his neck. Each breath brought him the wild scent of a shifter female, but with the quiet fragrance of a mossy green riverbed and a hint of metal like Gawain.

He ran his hand down her back. Since coming to Cold Creek, she'd gained weight, making her curves more pronounced. However, the soft flesh against him was quivering. Holding her wasn't enough.

She was female. They wanted to talk. And talk. And talk.

Well, didn't they?

Why wasn't she crying? Or talking?

Maybe she needed him to get her started? "Ah...did I remember to thank you for the help?"

She didn't react for a second and then gave a half-laugh. Her throaty voice was rougher than normal. "You're welcome."

He understood this kind of wry humor. With a smile, he tilted his head to rub his jaw against her silky hair. "Did you know that was a hellhound?"

A long pause.

Her responses were still sluggish. Yeah, he'd been in that condition before, although not for something as mild as this fight. Still, how many fights could she have seen while she was in a prison?

"A hellhound," she whispered. "Even though Calum said there was one here, I didn't really believe they existed."

"They do." He had the scars to prove it. Thank fuck Donal rarely was out of town on the dark of the moon, or he'd have more.

"That man—hellhound—was awfully strong. Is that why Calum was worried?"

"Yeah. When a fight starts, a hellhound will go berserk and only death will stop it." Owen softened his voice. "Is its death what bothers you?"

Against his chest, she nodded her head.

"You haven't seen anyone die before?"

This time her laugh was bitter. "Oh, I have. I really have."

And in the way a sunny spring day could turn to a drizzly rain, her silence turned to sobs. She never put her arms around him, simply let him hold her as she bunched his shirt in her fists and wept.

Feeling useless, he stood strong, one arm around her waist and the other—he realized he was stroking her shoulders, as if an action so useless would help what sounded very much like grief to him.

Heart-breaking grief. The little cat had loved and lost.

SHE'D CRIED ALL over Owen. Darcy couldn't believe the way she'd lost control of her emotions. And how…nice…the huge cahir had been. Talking softly, holding her, letting her bawl as if she were a child.

At least her weeping fit hadn't lasted too long.

When she'd pulled back, Owen had simply kept his arm around her—probably thought she couldn't walk without his help—and simply guided her to the tavern. As she'd regained her composure, the deadly cahir hadn't tried to make conversation, hadn't tried to joke, and yet his silence was more of a comfort than another person's chatter.

When he led her into the tavern, Thorson and his charges had already arrived. Face rigid with anger, Calum stood near the bar, his arms around the pregnant female and the girl who'd been in the alley.

The pregnant one had a hand on her large stomach, and all Darcy could do was thank the Mother the female hadn't been hurt. Or the cubling, either.

Blonde and blue-eyed, the girl was about the age of Alice,

the youngest of the captives.

Alice. The youngling was still a captive. Darcy hadn't gotten the females released—hadn't done *anything*—and the guilt was like a hand squeezing her chest.

"Hey." The pregnant female motioned Darcy over. "We didn't get a chance to talk. I'm Vicki, and this is Jamie."

"You did great with the fire extinguisher." The girl bounced up and down on her toes. "That was so cool. MomVee's been teaching me about using whatever is around in a fight. Stuff in the house or on the street, but you were in a store and, hey, you could hardly bring an armload of books to a fight, but I'd never have thought about using a fire extinguisher."

Darcy almost laughed. The girl hadn't even taken a breath. "I'm Darcy, and those sound like useful lessons you're getting." But didn't a male usually teach fighting? She eyed the Cosantir dubiously.

Reading her expression, Calum flashed a grin. "My mate became Daonain with a Death Gift. She was a soldier when human."

"Please…I was a *Marine*. I'm sorry I wasn't more help. Carrying a baby…babies…a *litter*"—Vicki glared at Calum—"sure takes the fun out of a good fight."

A good fight? A soldier? The female was barely an inch taller than Darcy.

Arm still around Darcy, Owen was chuckling.

The door opened, letting in Gawain. "Darcy, are you all right?" He was at her side in an instant, turning her to face him. His gaze ran over her face, her body.

"Mostly good, but her palms need attention," Owen said in his gravelly voice.

Gently, Gawain gripped her wrists and turned her hands over. "You've got dirt in those scrapes." He glanced at Calum. "First aid supplies?"

"In the kitchen. Jamie, can you bring the kit to Gawain?"

"Sure, Daddy." The teen had the grace of a panther shifter as she bounded across the tavern to the back.

"Sit here, Darcy." Owen pulled out a chair and firmly guided her down.

She didn't get a chance to object before Gawain sat beside her, still holding her wrist. Owen moved behind her chair, standing so close she could feel the warmth of his body. She was being *sheltered*. The realization made her breath thicken in her throat.

"Did you have questions for us, Cosantir?" Owen asked.

"Actually, I wanted to thank you and Darcy for your actions." Gaze soft, Calum looked down at his mate, then smiled as Jamie trotted back out. "You protected my mate and child. Thank you."

Owen made a deprecating sound low in his throat, and Darcy almost laughed. He sure wasn't comfortable in the spotlight, was he?

She smiled at Calum. "I'm glad they're safe. But, since I'm here, may I ask what's happening with the people from my village? Have we made any progress?"

"Mostly in elimination, I fear." Calum tried to help his mate sit, got an elbow in his ribs, and chuckled as Vicki seated herself.

Seeing Darcy trying not to laugh, Vicki grinned. "He and Alec started off too protective. Now that I'm pregnant, they act as if I can't walk across the room by myself. They're driving me bat-shit crazy."

Calum ran his fingers through his mate's hair with a slight smile. "Sorry, *cariad*. But new life is a gift from the Goddess— every instinct in a shifter is to protect that life and the life of the mother."

When he kissed the top of his mate's head, Vicki rubbed her cheek on his hand.

Darcy's tears burned her eyes. There'd been a few lifemates in Dogwood, and she'd always been mesmerized by the extra…something…about them. Most mates showed affection, but with lifemates, the bond of love almost glowed.

As she watched, Calum and Vicki turned toward the door to smile at the sheriff, and the love encompassed Alec as well.

Lifemating. Not for her. The Scythe would hunt her forever. And hey, she wasn't a starry-eyed cubling needing someone to protect her.

Alec dropped into a chair next to Vicki. "The hellhound will be disposed of in the canyon. The alley is cleaned up. And the gossip is some tourist tried to mug Jamie and ran into Vicki." He grinned at his mate. "No one was surprised when we said the guy had to be escorted out of town, and we doubted he'd ever return."

"You've got quite the reputation, love," Calum said.

"Quite the bloody one." With an evil smile, Thorson sat down at an adjacent table.

Darcy gave him a careful look. The older shifter's shirt was torn and his jeans scraped up, but he was moving without obvious pain. Spotting blood on his forearm, she frowned.

He followed the direction of her gaze. "Just a scrape, lass. I get worse running past blackberries."

Jamie set a bowl of water and washcloth on the table next to the first aid kit.

"Thank you," Gawain said. He turned Darcy's hand over and started to wash away the dirt.

She hissed and tried to ignore the pain as she turned her gaze back to Calum. "Progress?"

Calum leaned back in his chair. "Tynan continues to hunt in the city. Because the females haven't gone through First Trawsfur, they won't carry the scent of the wild. He has to rely upon matching your description of the property.

As she fought the need to run out and do the searching herself, her muscles tightened. Owen's hands pressed against her shoulders as if he could read her thoughts.

Gawain's deep blue eyes held sympathy and understanding—although his hold on her wrist was unbreakable.

They wouldn't let her leave.

"But…" She had to clear her throat. "It's taking too long."

"Faster would be better, but this is what we have," Calum said.

"Owen and I wondered if you can sense your littermates at all," Gawain said.

Darcy turned to face him. "Sense?"

Gawain nodded. "I can usually tell where Owen is—at least the general direction."

"I didn't know that was possible."

"Some littermates can, some can't," Owen said. "Try."

Bossy cat. She closed her eyes and tried to search for her brothers, then shook her head. "I can't feel anything."

"That's a shame." Gawain patted her hand. "Of course, the distance might affect your ability to sense them."

They might be out of the country, true. But it was more likely the fact that she'd spent very little time with them in captivity. A few minutes every few months didn't nurture a bond.

"Could we ask Wells for help?" Vicki asked Calum. "If the Scythe are attempting to influence our government, they're more than a simple mercenary organization. Wells needs to know, and he has resources we lack."

There was a silence for a moment.

"All right. He might, indeed, be able to help." Calum touched her cheek. "It will also give him an excuse to check on his Sergeant. I think he misses you."

Vicki's eyes filled with tears. Saying a foul word under her breath, she wiped her eyes and told Darcy, "Don't get pregnant.

The hormones suck the big one."

"Ah. Right." Darcy smiled at the Cosantir's mate. Such a tough female, and her embarrassed frustration made her all the more likable.

When Alec slid his chair closer to his mate, Vicki gave a husky laugh. "I'm all right. I'll give Wells a call." Her voice hardened. "He'll be very interested in the bastards."

"Darcy." Gawain waited for her attention and warned, "This part might hurt." Holding her hand open, he spread ointment over her abraded palm.

A yelp of pain almost escaped despite the warning.

"Sorry, sweetling," Gawain murmured...and continued. He was as stubborn as Owen was in his own steel-cored, calm way.

She pulled in a breath and asked Vicki, "Who is Wells?"

"He was my boss when I was a"—Vicki grinned—"you'd call it a spy."

A spy? And a soldier? "Oh."

"Wells is a human version of Thorson," Alec said. "Mean, sarcastic, anti-social, extremely competent, and deadly."

Thorson nodded, more pleased than offended.

"Wells heads up a covert operations force." Vicki smiled. "Since the Daonain have been here since the country was founded, he knows they—"

"*We*," Alec corrected with a tilt of his eyebrows.

"Right, *we* aren't a threat, and he helps keep us undiscovered."

Darcy nodded. Undiscovered was always good.

"There you go," Gawain said, giving her hand a pat. "All fixed up."

"Thank you."

Leaning forward, he ran his fingertips over her cheek. His calm eyes held hers. "You're most welcome, pretty panther."

As a flustered quiver woke in her center, she dropped her

gaze, but then she couldn't avoid seeing the broadness of his chest, the strength in his corded, thick forearms. He had a blacksmith's muscles...and her fingers wanted to touch.

A wave of heat rolled up and right into her cheeks, and she tore her gaze away. What was she thinking? She couldn't get interested in a male. By the Mother's breasts, she wouldn't even know what to do with one...although from the intimidating confidence in his gaze, Gawain knew exactly what to do with a female.

Chapter Ten

THE PROSPECTIVE PROPERTY was off the main road and a couple of blocks from the tavern. Owen yawned as he walked with his littermate down the private graveled lane. Last night had been dark of the moon when the cahirs patrolled the town all night. It'd been quiet, but his tail was dragging today.

He'd have slept longer, but both he and Gawain wanted to check out this two-story log cabin. Yesterday when they'd complained about turning down all the houses shown by the realtor, Calum had suggested this place. He'd also warned that the house was in bad shape.

How bad could it be?

"At least with Calum in charge of the property, the paper-work should be quick." The last owner—a shifter—had died without an heir, so the property had gone to the Cosantir to manage for the good of the Daonain.

"Why should the legal stuff be faster than normal?" Gawain asked.

"Calum was a lawyer before the God yanked him into being Cosantir. According to Alec, his littermate wasn't at all pleased with the change in his profession."

Gawain grinned. "The God does what the God does. I take it the Cosantir is used to babysitting Daonain property."

"I don't know how many places he has, but the Wildwood Lodge was one. Zeb and Shay had managed it before they talked him into letting them buy." Owen shook his head. "In the purchase contract, Calum added a clause so the Cosantir of the territory would always have one room to loan out—free—at his discretion."

"There's a lawyer for you." Gawain glanced over. "Darcy has the free room?"

"Um-hmm." As they approached the cabin, Owen studied the layout. The driveway made a lazy circle allowing access to a converted barn, then the house.

According to Calum, the property had been tended loving-ly…until the last generation turned it into a rental. Owen scowled at the run-down appearance of the cabin. Even if he hadn't needed a place, he'd have bought the place just to bring the house back to the way it should be.

Gawain climbed the porch steps and frowned as a board cracked under his weight. "Got our work cut out for us."

"So it seems." Owen tried the door, but the deadbolt was engaged. Calum had said the key was lost. "Let's find a window to crawl through. I'll bring tools to change the lock next time."

"Hold on." Gawain flattened his hand over where the dead-bolt connected to the metal plate.

Owen took a step back as power radiated from his litterma-te.

A minute passed. Turning the handle, Gawain set his shoul-der against the door and pushed.

Owen shook his head. "Brawd, that's a deadbolt. Not—"

The door opened, something thudded on the floor, and Gawain walked in.

Well. Owen knelt to check out what had fallen…and it was the actual deadbolt. The metal had melted into a teardrop shape.

Blademages were rare, secretive, and more powerful than

he'd known.

Owen walked in.

"Nobody's been here for a long time," Gawain called from the living room.

Owen sniffed in interest, but took his littermate's word for it. Gawain's nose had always been the more sensitive.

In the living room, the solid hardwood floor was in good shape. The walls...not so much. Someone had used one wall to write down phone numbers. Fists and boots had left holes and dents here and there.

There was garbage everywhere.

He frowned at a bare ceiling light bulb dangling from a frayed wire. One spark and the whole place would go up. "Brawd, we can't live here until an electrician checks it out. And until the litter is gone."

Gawain's expression held disgust. "Agreed."

"Ben, one of the cahirs, is a general contractor. We can hire him for anything we can't handle."

"I'll tell Shay to book us at the lodge for a while to come." Gawain shrugged. "Since we're mentoring Darcy, it's just as well. It's not good to leave her alone too long."

"True enough." The female looked as frayed as this house's electrical wiring. He couldn't even imagine how he'd react if Gawain or Bonnie were imprisoned and he couldn't rescue them. He'd be clawing things apart before a day was up. Actually, Darcy had been a marvel of patience. He grinned at Gawain. "When we're not out in the woods with her, let's put her to work here."

"I'd say you're taking advantage of free labor, but she does need to keep busy." Gawain studied him. "I'm impressed you're willing to have a female underfoot."

"Eh, she's not all that bad." He ignored his littermate's grin. "Let's check the upstairs."

With Gawain behind him, Owen walked up the stairs, making mental notes. The railing needed to be replaced. The hole-ridden carpet on the stairs and hallway should be ripped up.

The second-floor rooms were designed in traditional Daonain fashion. Down the left hallway, the female's suite was encircled by three smaller male bedrooms. The hallway to the right led to bedrooms for cublings.

The place was designed for a big family. Owen frowned. Having just him and Gawain here was a waste. Fuck knew, he had no intention of lifemating. Although…how did Gawain feel about mating and children? It was something they should discuss someday.

Maybe after they'd lived together for a decade or so.

A glance at the various bedrooms gave an idea of what would be needed to make them habitable. Wallpaper was peeling away in long strips. The carpets had holes and rips. There were leak marks around the windows. Several windows were broken. Debris was strewn everywhere.

Gawain walked around silently, his expression disgusted. "I've seen cleaner gnome-holes."

Since gnomes brought their garbage back to their dens, that was quite an insult. Owen couldn't disagree. "Want to pick a room?"

"The east-facing one, if you don't mind. It overlooks the barn."

"Fine with me. I prefer one closer to the forest anyway."

"Why am I not surprised?" Gawain chuckled. "Let's see the kitchen—although the thought makes me cringe."

Cringe was right. Whatever yellow color the walls had been had turned to a sickly urine tint. Mold and grime covered the wood countertops.

"Who could live like this?" Gawain shook his head. "Think we can hire some older cubs to clean out the garbage and strip the walls?"

"Better them than us. It'd be worth the money."

Although receiving a stipend from the clan, he and Gawain worked at other jobs...as did most God-chosen. Owen sold his carvings; Gawain sold metalwork. Since neither of them lived extravagantly, they had ample funds to toss at this problem.

"Let's check out the barn. As far as I'm concerned, the shop space will be the make or break."

Once outside, Gawain walked to the back of the faded-red massive barn and grinned when he saw the covered carport with an extremely high roof. "I bet someone built this for an RV. It's perfect for my outdoor forge."

Owen ran his hand over the barn wall. The wood was in fine shape. "The barn's a lot newer." They went in the smaller door to the side and looked around. Still holding the faint odor of hay, the huge open space had a tack room and bathroom in the back. No litter—the renters must not have bothered to use it.

"I can work with this. I say let's take the place," Gawain said.

Owen smiled as pleasure rose inside. He'd be living with his littermate again, and they were making themselves a lair. Although mountain lions didn't tend to create permanent dens, the human side of a shifter had a profound influence when it came to homes. As a result, werecats were almost as den-happy as werebears. "Agreed."

Gawain turned in a circle and frowned. "We'll need to put in windows, though."

"Easy enough." Owen glanced around. Plenty of space. One corner was all he'd need for his carving stuff.

"How about I take the left side of the barn?" Gawain asked. "There's a door to the covered area, and I can set my outside forge up under there. Then I can set up a ritual area in the grassy space on the left."

"Sure." Owen grinned at the light of anticipation in his brother's eyes. The blademage had obviously been missing his tools. "I'll take the back right corner. I mostly need a quiet area and storage."

"Sounds good. I figure I can set up enough to handle blademage requests within a few days, although it might take a while for people to realize I'm here."

"It's a small town and an underpopulated territory. You'll be surprised how quickly the news gets around." Owen glanced at the driveway. "Having our businesses just off the main highway will help."

"This is true." Gawain's smile widened. "Actually, we should put a sign out there on the road. Something eye-catching. What are the chances I can talk you into carving a sign for both of our businesses?"

Now there was a fine compliment. "You design it. I can carve it."

"Perfect." Gawain sighed. "How about we check out the other rooms in the downstairs. Something tells me the plumbing will need work, too."

"And you said *I* was the pessimist."

After thoroughly inspecting the entire house again, Gawain went into the kitchen to finish the to-do list.

Owen wandered through the big downstairs, envisioning how the rooms would appear once clean and furnished. He stopped to brush dust away from the beautifully carved trim beside the kitchen door and murmured, "We'll get you fixed up, house. Don't worry."

Despite the neglect and mess, the place had a good feeling to it, as if years of contentment and happiness had seeped into the wood.

He looked forward to living here. Working here. Although…a touch of guilt edged in. Would he and Gawain be letting the house down by not filling the empty rooms with cublings?

Chapter Eleven

D ARCY HAD SPENT Thursday afternoon helping Owen and Gawain clean up their house. A hoard of teenaged shifters had shown up to assist. It had been fun watching the two males work with pups. Gawain, big and confident, was so friendly the cubs were quickly at ease and telling him all their stories. And Owen… Was it her imagination or was he more relaxed? Laughing easier? Thrilled to be hired by the deadly cahir, the youngsters worked vigorously to get his rare word of praise and flashing smile.

Admit it, tinker, the cubs aren't the only ones striving to earn his smile.

The day had been a success. The walls were stripped and all the garbage was gone.

And she'd been in the shower forever, trying to remove the stink and grime.

Finally, when all she could smell was soap and shampoo, she got dressed in jeans and a pretty teal shirt. The innkeeper and Angie at the diner had rounded up a wonderful assortment of outfits for Darcy. Fun, bright clothes. What a pleasure it was to be free to choose what she wore each day.

After brushing out her damp hair, she trotted downstairs, hoping for some company. Gawain and Owen were planning to work on their house all evening, but maybe Bree would be up for some conversation or Zeb would want to discuss mysteries.

She'd miss her mentors, though—and her lessons on how to play pool.

Really, they all were enjoying being together in the evenings. Maybe because all three of them had spent their nights alone in the past. In the *priosan*, she'd been locked in her cell every evening after supper. Although sociable, Gawain had lived alone in Pine Knoll. Owen had his isolated high mountain land.

Since the lodge had a big screen TV and DVDs, they'd been sampling human entertainment. Some of the movies were hilarious. But why were there so many stories about werewolves and none about werecats or werebears? How insulting was that?

She stopped at the foot of the stairs and considered. Watching a movie alone had no appeal, and the long leather couch would feel awfully empty. Originally, she'd sat on the couch, the males in chairs. One night a gory movie had her shaking harder than an aspen leaf, and suddenly, she had a male on each side of her.

Even after that night, the guys had never returned to their chairs. And she'd soon grown used to being sandwiched between their warm bodies. She could feel them breathe. Gawain would hold her hand if she was worried. If she started to tremble, Owen would put a big arm around her shoulders and pull her close.

Nothing in the world had ever felt as…wonderful…as sitting between the two of them.

Hearing voices outside, Darcy walked into the dining room…and then silently retreated. Zeb, Shay, and Bree had lit a fire in the new fire pit and were cuddling on the stone bench, obviously enjoying a quiet twilight together.

Bree had once said that while the outside cabins were usually occupied, the inner lodge rooms were rented out as a last choice.

What with her, Owen, and Gawain living in the lodge, the innkeepers hadn't had any time alone. She should give them that.

But now what? Darcy frowned. Owen, if on his own, would retreat to his room and read. Gawain, however, would probably wander into town and find someone to talk with.

The tavern wasn't very far.

A few minutes later, having taken the tiny footpath from the lodge, she pulled open the heavy tavern door and stepped inside. Midweek, the place was only two-thirds full.

Breathing in the fragrance of roasted peanuts, popcorn, and beer, she listened to the babble of conversations and clink of glassware. Thumping noises came from the pool tables in an alcove to the right.

She wiped her clammy hands on her jeans and told her nerves to settle down. Who would have thought her first night out—all by herself—would be so daunting?

Move the feet, tinker. She shouldn't stand frozen in the doorway as if planning to flee.

Stupid feet didn't move.

A feeling of being lost swept over her. In *prìosan*, her world had been bound in time and space. She'd had her place, fixing things and helping people. Here, she was the one needing help.

In *prìosan*, she'd known everyone and everything. She glanced around the barroom, not recognizing anyone.

And each day here was different, as if she'd walked into an entirely different world. One where she wasn't in control of anything.

But she'd manage—she *would*—because that was what she did.

"Hey, Darcy!" In a cozy chair by the huge fireplace, Vicki, Calum's pregnant mate, waved her hand and tried to rise.

In relief and delight, Darcy motioned for her to stay seated and crossed the room.

The stubborn female was still trying to stand up.

"I'm here. Stop trying to get out of that chair." Darcy stopped in front of her.

"Have I mentioned that I fucking hate being pregnant?" Vicki's voice was a low growl.

"No...really?" asked a blonde, brown-eyed female sitting on the couch to the right. Amusement danced in her eyes. "Who would have thought?"

Vicki's growl deepened and then, with a yielding laugh, she collapsed back into the chair, hands on her belly. "I give up. When I need to stand, I expect you all to yank me out of this bottomless pit of a chair."

"Not a problem." The third female in the conversational area was big-boned, tall, and lushly curved. Her tawny coloring was that of the last golden days of summer. A guitar rested on the couch next to her. She turned her attention to Darcy. "Hi, I'm Emma."

"Sorry," Vicki said. "I had to bitch before making introductions. Darcy, meet our bard and bear, Emma. Her mate Ben is a cahir and patrols with Owen. Ryder, her other mate, has an adorable cub."

Emma's smile was beautiful and kind. "Welcome to Cold Creek, Darcy."

A bard. Wow. "I've never met a bard before. It's nice to meet you."

The other female lifted her drink. "Welcome, Darcy."

Vicki nodded to the short, brown-eyed blonde. "That wolf there is Bonnie, who is the sheriff's dispatcher, and she has two cublings full of more mischief than a den of foxes, and...oh, she's sister to Owen and Gawain."

Darcy had to laugh. "You have a talent for introductions."

"My boss taught me to be succinct and informative." Vicki patted the chair beside her. "Join us, so the cats will outnumber the others."

"Hey!" Bonnie said indignantly. "Wolves are supposed to have the majority. It's a rule."

"Rules were made to be broken." Vicki smirked. "What are you drinking, Darcy?"

"Um." At the lodge, she'd sampled the various beers. "I'm not exactly familiar with alcohol, although I've discovered I don't like beer."

"What...didn't the Scythe assholes share their alcohol with their prisoners? Rude bastards." Vicki grinned. "No worries, we'll find something you can enjoy." She twisted to look at the back of the room.

Darcy followed her gaze and saw Calum behind the bar...watching. He nodded at Darcy before lifting an eyebrow at Vicki.

His mate's circling gesture encompassed the drinks on the coffee table, then she pointed to Bonnie's drink and held up two fingers.

As Calum tilted his head in acknowledgment, the warmth in his smile could have kept a female nice and cozy all through a long, long winter.

Darcy sighed. He still scared her, but she had to envy Vicki just a bit.

"So, Darcy." Emma leaned forward. "Bree told me you fixed all the appliances at the lodge—and her washing machine doesn't make a *thump-thump-thump* sound anymore."

"Well, yes." Darcy bit her lip. "I wish I could do more to help."

"Oh, girl, she's enjoying having another female around." Bonnie shook her head. "Her best friend-roomie died before she got here, and she gets lonely for females. I wish we could get together more often, but I have the cubs. Emma teaches cublings during the day. And Vicki is a bit...ah...less mobile than she used to be."

Vicki shot her a deadly look.

"Bree says she loves having you there." Emma smiled. "But, actually, I was wondering if I could hire you to repair something at our place?"

"Of course. Fixing things is the most fun in the world." Relaxing, Darcy leaned back. "Mum said she knew my sire's identity just from the way I was always messing with machines. Then again, my coloring might have been a clue." Black haired, black-eyed Daonain were rare.

Bonnie tilted her head. "Native American like Zeb?"

"Roma. Mom said my sire hated the word *gypsy*." She grinned. "He didn't like the word tinker, either, but that's what Mum called me." *"My tinker cub."*

"Ah." Emma smiled. "You inherited the skills of a *tinceard*— a tinsmith. In ancient days, villages begged the tinkers to visit. It's a shame the word has fallen out of favor."

Tinceard. As Darcy turned her tongue around the word, Calum appeared with a tray of drinks.

"Quite correct, bard. The Daonain have always prized those who can build or repair." Calum gave Emma and Bonnie fresh drinks and set a glass of wine in front of Darcy. "You are very welcome in my territory, *tinker.*" His English accent gave the word an exotic flavor.

The warmth of his welcome was an unexpected, lovely gift.

"Water for you, *cariad.*" He handed his mate a glass with lemon floating in it, then panther-quick, headed back to the bar before she could respond.

From his mate's grimace at the water, she might have had a few choice words to share. "Gah. I hate water."

"Poor Vicki," Emma said with a grin.

Darcy could understand Vicki's irritability over the inconveniences of pregnancy, and yet... "You know, the three females who were pregnant when we were captured lost their cubs before birth. No one knew if it was being underground or the cages or the horrible experiments they tried. But those females would have given anything to have been able…" Her voice trailed away as she saw the looks of horror.

Darcy shook her head. *What had she been thinking?* "Oh my Gods, I'm sorry, Vicki. I don't know what—"

"Don't apologize for being honest," Vicki said quietly. "Or for smacking me upside the head for whining."

Darcy wanted to crawl under her chair. How could she inflict her ugly memories on other people? What was wrong with her?

"It happens, Darcy. To me, too." Emma gave her a sympathetic look. "Bad memories have a habit of pouncing at inopportune moments."

"What a horrid time you had," Bonnie said. After she took a sip of her drink, her lips curved and she started chortling.

"What?" Emma asked.

Bonnie pointed a finger at Darcy. "My oh-so-blunt brother is mentoring her." She grinned at Darcy. "Thank the Goddess, I think he's met his match."

"Hey, Owen's been…" Well, nice wasn't the word she'd use. Although he had hugged her once. "He's been…" Wonderfully kind sometimes. "He hasn't…" Giving up, she took a big drink of her wine.

Emma made a snorting sound. "Owen has been a good friend to my mates—and me—but no one in the territory would call him polite. Or sweet. Especially to females."

Bree had mentioned his dislike for females. "Why? Females are mostly likable, aren't we?" Darcy took another drink. Wine surely was different from the beer that tasted worse than musty, liquefied bread. This wasn't sweet, but crisp with a lingering fruity smoothness.

"We are likable," Vicki said firmly.

"Bad experiences, maybe? My Ryder didn't trust females because of one especially vile one." Emma frowned. "After meeting her, I understood why he was wary."

"Huh. I've never seen Owen hanging out with a woman." Vicki frowned. "It seems as if he only talks with unattached females at Gatherings. When would he have had a bad experience?"

"As a cub. Our mother was…is…a ghastly person. And abusive to Owen. Actually, I'm not sure she's even sane." Bonnie huddled down on the couch.

Darcy recognized the defensive posture. The cubling captives would curl up like that after a beating. "She hit you?"

"Oh my Gods, yes. There were four of us in the litter. She adored Edwyn. Usually tolerated me and Gawain well enough. And she hated Owen from the minute he was born."

"But why?" Emma asked.

"The gossip was that Owen's sire got annoyed at the way she chased him and humiliated her so badly she left town. My aunt says Owen looks like him."

"She took her anger out on a cubling?" Darcy scowled. "That's just wrong."

"It *is*," Bonnie said. "Owen never had any mother's love—only abuse."

Darcy tried to imagine the big cahir as a child. His skin was almost the same shade as her olive tones. As a cub, he'd have had bright green eyes and tangled brown hair, would have been skinny and…and adorable. Who could hit him—or any cub? "I've hated the humans so much for hurting the cublings from our village. To find a Daonain abused her own children makes me feel as if the ground is a marshland."

"I love my cubs so much," Bonnie said. "And I don't understand my mother at all. Owen—he's a good person."

Emma nodded. "He and Ben and Alec have saved more lives than anyone can count."

"I worry about him, my grumpy, domineering brother." Bonnie waved her glass. "Sometimes he barks out orders as if he's decades older than me instead of maybe two minutes."

Darcy grinned. What a perfect description.

"But even when he was waist-high, he was bossy and over-protective." Bonnie shook her head. "When our littermate Edwyn died, I was living here in Cold Creek with Aunt Sandy. Since she and her mates were out of town, I just took off without telling anyone and traveled as a wolf back to Pine Knoll."

"That's a fucking long way," Vicki commented.

"Stupid teenager, right?" Bonnie's grin faded. "Showing up there was a mistake. Mother acted as if I owed her for moving away. She wanted me to fix her hair and give her money and clean the house—as if she was the child instead of me, and she got hysterical if I left her for even a minute. I didn't know what to do."

"Did your Aunt Sandy come and get you?" Emma asked.

"She was still gone. Owen rescued me. Mother and I were in a restaurant where she was weeping about Edwyn dying. Owen came in, and Holy Herne, she had this violent meltdown and started throwing dishes at him."

Emma's eyes widened. "In a *restaurant?*"

"Mm-hmm. Thank the Gods, Gawain arrived. Even as a teen, that boy could calm an earthquake if needed. As she was crying all over him, I ran after Owen and begged him to help me."

Darcy knew the answer before Emma asked, "Did he?"

Bonnie laughed, although her eyes were damp. "This is Owen. Of course he did. He was all of sixteen and still, just took charge. He escorted me all the way back here...bossing me around and coaching me on my hunting skills. At Sandy's, he told me to finish growing up and disappeared."

Vicki frowned. "Disappeared?"

"I didn't see him again for…maybe fifteen years?" Bonnie smiled. "He left Pine Knoll, apprenticed somewhere else, and later wandered from territory to territory. I think he checked on me a few times, but when he showed up a decade ago, Calum spotted him. Owen was a cahir by then, and the Cosantir snatched him up for the North Cascades Territory."

Vicki smirked. "My mate is quick that way."

"He really is." Bonnie grinned back. "Anyway, once Owen was here, we became closer. It's so fun to watch my cubs turn him into a gooey-sweet mess."

Darcy snorted at the thought—and was dying to see Owen with his nephews.

Bonnie swirled her wine and frowned. "It worries me that he never talks about our childhood. Ever."

"Maybe he will someday. When more time has passed," Emma said.

Eyes narrowed, Darcy counted years on her fingers. "He's— you're—in your *forties*?"

"Mmmhmm. Low forties."

Well, no wonder he and Gawain often treated her as if she were a cub. Darcy let out a small sigh. She didn't feel much like a cub when she looked at Gawain…or Owen. Although she wasn't sure what her body was saying, it felt an awful lot like wanting to do male-female things.

And…she was hoping she'd found some friends here. She glowered at the others. "Am I the youngest, then? Are you all decades older?"

"You worry too much, cubling." Emma sounded as if she was at least fifty.

Darcy slumped back in her chair.

Laughing, Emma tossed a napkin at her. "I'm at least…oh, a couple of years older."

"You—you are evil," Darcy sputtered.

"Bards. They can play a person easier than they do their harps," Bonnie said.

Grinning, Vicki drank some of her water before offering, "I have a few years on you—not many—and Alec and Calum are older than Owen."

"Older?"

Vicki wrinkled her nose. "Imagine my shock, especially since I was raised human. Where are their pot-bellies and bald pates?"

Emma and Bonnie were snickering—because Alec and Calum were lean and muscular and drop-dead gorgeous.

"You know, I forgot that healthy Daonain look about the same from late twenties to about a hundred. But still," Darcy grumbled, "my mentors have twenty years more experience than me. They'll never take me seriously."

Thank the Mother, she had never hinted she might want them to be more than mentors. If she did. She didn't. Really, did she?

Right. Just keep lying to yourself, you turkey-brained tinker. Every time Gawain or Owen spoke to her, her insides whirled and curled like a salamander in a roaring fire.

"Ah-hah, so you want my brothers to take you seriously." Bonnie had a slight smile on her face.

Oh my Goddess, she was lusting after Bonnie's *littermates.* Her entire face turned hot with her flush.

"I totally approve," Bonnie said firmly.

Darcy's mouth dropped open. "You *what?*"

All three females grinned at Darcy.

Giving up, she slumped into her chair, took a big sip of wine—and grinned back.

Had she ever felt so at home with anyone? They'd accepted

her, advised her, and they liked her; she could tell.

And she liked them. At the lodge, Bree'd mentioned Emma's trials as a cub and adult. Vicki had been a soldier and spy—not easy professions for anyone. Bonnie'd come from a background of abuse. None had waltzed through life to arrive here, yet all three were strong and balanced. And they could still laugh.

If the Scythe ever tried to capture Cold Creek as they had Dogwood, she had a feeling the humans would regret it.

Darcy wiggled in the chair, getting comfortable, and drank more wine as the conversation moved to planning the Samhain festivities at the end of the month.

Would she even be here then?

As soon as her villagers were found, she'd have to leave. And she'd never dare to return and endanger these wonderful people.

Chapter Twelve

THE MISTY FOREST clearing was quiet except for the slight rustle under a serviceberry bush. Ignoring her pushy animal instincts, Darcy ran through a mental checklist.

There was the rat. *Check*.

She tensed her muscles, wiggled her butt, and lashed her tail.

Body is ready. *Check*.

As everything came together, she pounced. Her front paws landed on the woodrat. *Gotcha*. Her jaws closed around its body. A high squeak made her cringe even as she felt the satisfying crack of bones. Fresh, hot blood filled her mouth.

Paw on the body, she ripped off strips of flesh and swallowed. Chewing? Nah. Within a minute, the woodrat had disappeared into her belly.

As she cleaned her muzzle, delight was a bubbly froth in her veins. Catching her own lunch still simply amazed her...aside from the *ewww* factor.

Recalling her surroundings, she shifted to human form and looked around for Bree.

The wolf sat on her haunches across the clearing.

"I can't believe I just ate a rat," Darcy said to her.

Breanne opened her jaws in a doggy laugh, shifted, and found a seat on a flat stone. "Although you took a rather long time before you pounced, you did great. Better than me, since I didn't get good at hunting for ages. And even then, I refused to eat my kill. Zeb had to finish off what I caught. It was embarrassing."

"I can understand why a chef might not want to indulge in rodent *tartare*." In fact… Darcy swiped a hand around her mouth to make sure she cleaned away every icky drop of blood. "Now what are—"

Holding up a hand, Bree sniffed the air. "There's a cougar around."

Darcy inhaled and smiled. "It's strange how a person's animal form smells almost the same as his human form. That's Gawain." He must be following their trail, so he probably wanted to talk to her, which meant she shouldn't shift back to furry.

Only, she didn't want to talk to him without any clothes on. Where was a convenient bush to step behind when she wanted one?

Darn it, when she was immersed in lessons, being naked around her mentors didn't bother her. They were simply her teachers. However, outside of lessons, she couldn't ignore that they were incredibly masculine, potent, desirable males.

With a scowl, she crossed to kneel beside Bree.

Gawain bounded out into the clearing, spotted them, and padded across the sparse grass. Halfway across, he trawsfurred smoothly to human.

Wow. Just…wow. Every time she saw him undressed, her mouth went dry.

As the muted light from the sun glowed on his mist-dampened skin, it shadowed the hard-packed muscles of his wide chest. His wide shoulders tapered to a narrow, taut waist. His legs were solid, lightly dusted with hair. And his male shaft was…well, she'd guess proportional. Maybe more than proportional, but what did she know? It curved downward, long and thick, over large, round testicles.

Bree cleared her throat.

Staring. Darcy was staring at his cock. She jerked her gaze up to meet Gawain's amused—heated—eyes.

"Ladies," he said smoothly. The male was rarely at a loss for words. "I stopped at the lodge to ask Zeb for some help with a fan, but Zeb said he doesn't fu…mess with mechanical tools. He said to ask you, Darcy, since you have a talent with the human-made devices."

A compliment from terse Zeb; that was lovely. Darcy pulled in a breath of delight, and saw Gawain's gaze drop to her chest. To her breasts. Embarrassed heat ran from her all-too-exposed breasts right into her face. "Right. I'd be happy to take a look." She glanced at Bree. "Was there more we needed to cover?"

Bree didn't even try to conceal her grin. "Nope. We got to the end of my list of what to teach."

"Fantastic." Gawain smiled. Damp from the wet foliage, his hair and beard had darkened to a rich brown, making his eyes even bluer. Each breath brought her his masculine musk, shifter-wild, mixed with the tang of iron and smoke.

He turned his attention to Darcy. "Are your clothes at the lodge?" His shaft grew, thickened…

What would that feel like in her hand?

"Answer the question, Darcy." Bree nudged her.

Darcy felt the blush sear her cheeks. Again. What was wrong with her? Her words came out in a stutter. "Clothes. R-right. Yes, at the lodge. Meet you there."

Too embarrassed to continue, she shifted. As her front paws dropped onto the grass, love flowed upward from Mother Earth. With a lash of her tail, she bounded down the trail. By the time she arrived, she would have herself back under control.

Why did he have to be so…so masculine?

THE PRETTY PANTHER female was moving so fast she'd disappeared into the forest before Gawain could speak. Wasn't she cute?

He took a slow breath. The fragrance of her beginning arousal still hung in the clearing, and the appreciation in her gaze had been better than anything he'd felt before.

When he'd reacted accordingly, she'd been unable to keep from staring at him.

Didn't that make a male feel proud? Even better, he'd seen no signs of fear in her, just interest.

He smiled at Breanne. "Sorry to interrupt your hunt day."

"Not a problem. Shay planned to visit the lake, so I'll join him for a while." All round, soft female, she smiled at him, belying the sternness in her voice. "From what Darcy has told me, aside from her littermates, she's only met males who were human, which means she might never have felt desire before. I know from experience how excitement can feel wonderful and terrifying—and confusing. Please be careful with her."

Gawain could only stare. Never knowing desire? By the Goddess, he'd never considered what living entirely surrounded by humans could mean. He bowed solemnly. "You have my word, Breanne."

DARCY GLANCED AT Gawain. Strolling beside her, he wore one of his old-fashioned white shirts, long sleeves rolled up, shirttails tucked into his jeans. Such a flat stomach and tight butt and…

Stop it, turkey-brained tinker. She'd already made a fool of herself once. Behaving worse than a cat in heat, she'd stared at his…male parts and, when caught, had fled like a cub from a hungry wolverine. But he didn't seem to be upset with her.

After joining her at the lodge, they'd walked down the highway, past the Wild Hunt tavern, and turned off at the small gravel lane leading to his and Owen's house.

The lane circled past the large log cabin and red-sided barn. She noticed the chinking between the logs had been restored. The porch repaired. The huge garbage bins were gone. "You've done a lot of work in the last few days."

"Still needs a lot more. Whoever lived here last was a…" He bit back a nasty word. "To neglect your own den, especially one so beautiful, is a crime." His anger was intimidating, yet appealing. He was a male who would carefully tend anything given to his care—a home, his work, a family.

"At least the lazy slugs didn't mess up the barn." With a warm hand on her low back, he guided her to the barn she hadn't seen yet. "Owen and I are still setting everything up; it's going to be a great place to work." He flipped on the lights.

"Wow." Amazed, she wandered across the massive space. To the left, the long workbenches held a mixture of power and hand tools. In the right far corner, a wealth of carving knives and tools hung on a long pegboard. Blocks of various woods were arranged to one side. The floor and wall shelves displayed finished carvings.

She put a hand to her chest; her heart ached at the beauty.

A two-foot wolf sat with muzzle raised, so realistic she could almost hear its grief-stricken howl.

A waist-high grizzly was turning over a log to look for grubs.

Two teenaged panthers were playing king of the rock.

Eventually, she pulled herself away to join Gawain on the other side of the barn. "You do magnificent work."

"I do, yes, but Owen is the carver. He likes wood. I work with metal."

"Owen did those?" The rough, rude, deadly cahir had created such beauty? She turned to look at the sculptures. Some seemed a celebration of play and…connection. Others held such loneliness she wanted to cry. "I…"

Gawain's mouth curved into a wry smile. "You're not the first to be surprised. He rarely shows the side of himself that comes out in his art.

She'd thought she was getting to know him.

Like a mountain range, reticent people would willingly display their stony cliff faces and verdant forests. But their hidden canyons, mossy glens, and trickling streams were revealed only to those with the heart to look deeper.

Turning back to Gawain, she asked, "What did you want me to work on?"

Gawain motioned toward the far wall. "This exhaust system. When smithing, I need the air moving to avoid a build-up of carbon monoxide."

"Sure. Let me take a look." She walked over. The front panel had to come off. "Do you have a Phillips screwdriver?"

He lifted his eyebrows. "No tool kit?"

"I had one at the *priosan*." She grinned. "I must have forgotten to grab it when I leaped the wall."

"Careless of you." He tsked at her. "I'll ask Angie at the diner to check around. People always have spare tools. Meantime, use this. It's perfect for traveling." He picked something up from the workbench and set it in her hand.

"A knife?"

"A multi-tool." He opened it…and opened it…and opened it, showing the needle-nose pliers, the two screwdrivers, the punch, the—

"This is *amazing*."

"Yeah. It fits in a pocket, so you're never without the essentials." He smiled at the device with the delight of a true handyman. "I have another. You can keep this one."

She pulled out the screwdriver, then the knife. Wouldn't this gadget have been useful in the institution? Occasionally, she'd climbed the ivy with a big screwdriver tucked under her bra. "Thank you."

"My pleasure, catling."

Well, the best way to pay him back would be to fix the broken fan. "Let me get started. With luck, I'll have it running quickly."

"That would be great." Smiling down at her, Gawain tucked a lock of her hair behind her ear, leaving tingles behind.

How could just a touch make her breathless? "Are you working on a smithing project now?"

"Aye. Zeb and Shay teach a hellhound fighting class, and some of their students need cahir blades."

She frowned. "Why don't cahirs buy knives from a store?"

"A human-made knife has a few limitations." Gawain picked up a blade and held it to the light. A lighter metal made a fancy filigree within the dark steel. "A blade custom-made for a cahir has runes of silver forged into the steel, so they can wear the metal without irritation. The silver also makes it more effective against hellhounds."

"Oh."

"The sheaths are leather, but the straps are of the same silver we use for lifemating bands and are magicked to adjust when a cahir trawsfurs, since most cahirs want to wear their blades even in animal form."

Come to think of it, Owen wore one—usually strapped to his arm, sometimes his leg. When he shifted, it was almost invisible on his foreleg. "I bet you make sure the sheath matches the male's fur, don't you?"

"You're an observant lass." He grinned. "The knife is also balanced for throwing." He took the knife by the blade and threw it across the barn. With a thunk, it lodged in the target tacked to the wall. Right in the bulls-eye.

Startled at how swiftly and silently the knife had flown, she stared at Gawain. Had he even aimed?

"Is anyone here?" The shout came from outside.

"In the barn," Gawain called.

A young male poked his head in. "Are you the blademage?"

"That's me."

The male trotted over and looked up at Gawain.

Quite a ways up.

Darcy blinked. Next to Gawain, the male looked awfully short, but was actually average in height. She'd usually seen the blademage around Zeb, Shay, and Owen, all cahirs with extra God-given height and strength. Gawain was only a couple of inches shorter than the huge cahirs—and easily as muscular.

"I'm Gawain." The two males clasped forearms. "What can I do for you?"

"Grady." Bouncing on his toes, Grady had a huge grin on his face. "Calum said we had our own blademage now, and you make lifemating bracelets. Can you make some?" His face was so full of hope that Darcy held her breath as well.

"I can. There's nothing I enjoy more." Gawain turned and ran his hand down Darcy's arm. "Will you excuse me for a bit?"

"Sure. I'll get started on the fan if it won't disturb you."

"That would be most appreciated."

As Darcy took off the front of the exhaust fan, she positioned herself so she could watch what was going on.

GAWAIN LOVED THIS part of being a blademage.

Taking his time, he quizzed Grady about his littermates, Griffin and Grant, and their intended mate. As the male gushed with praise for his beloved, Gawain dug through the pile of moving boxes to find the dozen silver bracelets he'd made last month. He always kept some on hand since, once males found their lifemate, they grew extremely impatient—and making the bracelets wasn't something Gawain would ever rush.

He selected three heavy bracelets for the female to give to her new mates and three delicate ones for the males to give to their female.

At this point, the bands were merely silver discs and silver wire—although he could always feel something of himself in his creations.

Most Daonain hated metal, especially iron, but a few loved the song of the metals. Iron—so stubborn—crying its harsh melody, as fire and pressure and carbon transformed it into steel. Silver sang with the high, sweet sound of the cold, swift winds off Mount Rainier. There was nothing like working metal.

With talent and skill, he created beauty. When he added his power, he could make magicked objects—cahir blades and the trawsfur-flexible metal bands. However, to transform a bracelet of silver discs into a true lifemating band?

That called for a goddess.

"Come with me, please." Gawain guided Grady outside to the consecrated ritual area. Although not complete, the small space held the essentials.

The boundary had been demarcated by knee-high river stones. He'd diverted a segment of the creek so a tiny stream of water flowed through the stone circle. *Earth and water.*

After cleansing the sacred space with a pine branch broom, he lit a fire in the brazier and tossed on a mixture of cedar, lavender, and yarrow. *Fire and air.*

As the coals smoldered, a translucent sylph appeared over the brazier, its sinuous dance swirling the thin smoke into mesmerizing spirals.

Holding the lifemating bands in the fragrant smoke, Gawain opened his heart and mind and soul to the Mother of All. When a wave of love heralded her presence, he presented to her the names and images of the young mates. Unable to resist, he also shared how the young male was simply glowing with his love for his littermates and their chosen female.

The Mother's pleased acknowledgment and warmth skimmed his palms as the discs were imbued with the Mother's love. No matter how many years would pass, a lifemating band always carried a hint of the Goddess.

For a second, he lingered, unwilling to move. Although he'd been a blademage for decades, he'd never lost the sense of wonder that She would come to his call, that She took such joy in each new bond between males and their female.

When he opened his eyes, tears were running down Grady's face. "I never knew... I felt Her, even more than when I trawsfur. It was as if She was here."

"She was." Gawain smiled. "And She approves of your mating." He set the lifemating bands into the male's hand. "Blessings upon you and yours."

Grady beamed, his joy a soft hum in the air, and took his leave.

Unable to stop grinning, Gawain headed back to the barn.

In the doorway, Darcy stood, her dark eyes wide. She pressed her hands to her chest. "I felt...it was like my mother had come back and tucked me into bed and—"

Unable to help himself, he put his arm around her shoulders. "Love is a gift of the Goddess, especially a mother's love for her cubs. When the Goddess is near, that sense of being cherished is what you feel."

"Yes." Her eyes filled, not with joy, but with loss. "I haven't felt that since...since my mum died. I miss her."

This one had the capacity to break his heart. He pulled her into his arms. "Of course you do, catling. But life goes on. You will find others to love and who will love you in return."

Bending, he touched her lips with his, tasting the salt of her tears.

When she made a tiny sound and her lips parted, he deepened the kiss, teasing his tongue against hers, enjoying the softness of her lips and the way she melted against him.

More. Purring, he molded her soft body against his—and took more.

"What happened?" The low growl of his littermate broke into the stillness of the barn.

Darcy tried to jerk back...and Gawain didn't let her. "Brawd."

"What happened?" Owen repeated. Undoubtedly scenting Darcy's distress, Owen had a hand on his knife and—typical cahir—was hunting an enemy to attack.

"You're chasing the wrong prey." Looking down, Gawain used his fingertips to wipe the wetness from Darcy's cheeks. "I charged lifemating bracelets, and our catling is missing her mother."

"She's... Oh, right." Owen's hand fell from the dagger on his forearm. His gaze ran over Darcy, undoubtedly noting her pale face. "Forgive me if I scared you, little female, and I'm sorry for your loss."

She pulled in a shaky breath. "Thank you."

A corner of Owen's mouth curled up cynically. "At least you had a mother worthy of mourning." Spinning on his heel, he stalked out of the barn.

Darcy stared after him. "Is...is he all right?"

"Mostly. Around him, saying "mother" is akin to poking a grizzly with a sharp stick. Our mother mistreated him." *Be honest, mage.* "More than that. She was cruel to him." Guilt slid a sharp blade into his gut. He hadn't suffered the same way.

In fact...

The Mother's love flooded him with every lifemating bracelet he made. In contrast, as a cahir, Owen knew only blood and death. Although he'd feel the Goddess's touch when shifting, his littermate had never known how much love a real mother could give a cub.

No wonder Owen had little tolerance for females.

Chapter Thirteen

OWEN SAID IT was easy. Gawain said it was easy. As Darcy eyed the tree limb, her tail lashed back and forth. Carefully, she calculated her trajectory. The branch wasn't that high. She'd grab it with her claws, lean forward, and her back claws would catch the bark.

I can do it. It's easy—they said so.

She sprang.

No, too high! Frantically, she clawed at the bark—and kept going. Twisting in midair, she managed to land on the ground in one piece.

For the Mother's sake, what was wrong with her? She'd been more competent as a kid—in *human* form. Cats weren't supposed to have problems with jumping.

But she sure did.

Staring up at the tree, she felt her spirits sag. Her legs were sore and aching, her paws scraped, and she'd almost pulled a claw out. She was done.

Wearily, she padded down the forest trail toward the lodge.

Owen and Gawain were working on their house this morning and had told her to enjoy a run all by herself. To see how she did.

Well, she'd done just fine until she'd decided to practice her leaps.

Near the lodge, she stopped at the creek to lap up a drink. The undines playing near the lodge spotted her, darted through the water, and did a few leaps to demonstrate their own skills. And splash her.

Fishy show-offs. Although, the water felt good on her sun-warmed fur.

When she didn't dive into the creek to chase them, the undines swarmed back through the water to their favored spot near the footbridge.

As her fur dried, Darcy watched them resume their games…and her gaze caught on the huge trees—a spruce and an oak—which shaded the patio and small playground. The oak tree had a lovely low branch, didn't it?

Hmm.

No, you tomfool tinker.

She couldn't use that tree for practice. Human fishermen often rented cabins at the lodge.

But no one was out on the patio today, and the oak branch was lower and thicker than any she'd found in the evergreen forest. Surely, no one would notice if she practiced.

Owen would have been proud of how well she crept through the trees to the oak.

She sprang.

Failed.

The sprite in the spruce tree chittered its laughter.

Stupid pixie.

She sprang.

Failed.

In open mockery, the sprite threw a couple of tiny twigs down on Darcy's head.

She sprang.

Success!

Securely perched on the branch, Darcy flirted her tail in triumph and clawed the rough bark to leave her scent. *Darcy was here.*

Level with the sprite, Darcy wrinkled her nose—and watched the pixie pop back into its hole. Poor loser.

Warm sunlight streamed through the leafy canopy and, unwilling to leave her—*her*—branch behind, Darcy stretched out to nap. Eventually she'd go in. When she was ready, she had a mystery to read as well as a history book from Owen's bookshelves. The cahir did enjoy his history. Gawain preferred fiction, especially thrillers, but he owned a ton of ethics and philosophy books. Darcy loved mysteries, but the *priosan* library had been so small, she'd ended up reading every book there, no matter the subject.

What with their varied personalities and interests, she and her mentors had enjoyed some crazy discussions. Owen was a cynical pessimist with an overprotective attitude. Gawain, an optimist who delighted in people. She considered herself a realist…although Owen accused her of being a closet romantic.

Add in alcohol… Well, after the movie *Casablanca* ended, they'd spent hours debating how it *should* have ended.

Darcy still thought Ilsa should have joined the fight—with both Rick and Louie. She rubbed her chin against her forelegs and settled down for another few minutes, imagining the three of them, taking on the entire German army.

Sometime later, the sound of the back door roused her. To her dismay, Owen, Shay, and a huge male walked out onto the patio. The stranger apparently wanted to check out Zeb's new fire pit and bench.

Oh, bloody scat.

If she moved, they'd spot her right away. But if she stayed still…since she could smell them, probably the wind wasn't sending them her scent.

Please leave so I can get away. I won't do this again. Promise.

"How's the new cougar doing?" the big stranger asked. "Emma says she's something special. Says she's a tinker—a fixer."

Aw. Pleased, Darcy rested her muzzle on her forelegs.

"A tinker, huh? That makes sense." Owen rubbed his chin. "You know how no shifter messes with mechanical shit? She does. She's as talented with machines as Gawain is with metals."

Owen thought she was talented? A purr started in her throat.

"Yeah. Last week, while I was at a job site, she visited Emma and fixed our lawn mower." The big stranger had a slow Texas drawl. "Gotta wonder though—are those humans going to come here looking for her? I'm fine with taking them on—it'd purely be a pleasure. But what's the risk to Emma and Minette?"

Darcy felt her breathing stop. Had the Scythe been seen? Was she putting her friends—the town—in danger? *Oh, no no no.*

"Can't say. The Cosantir is…" Owen straightened, sniffed, and turned. His gaze ran over the oak tree—and met hers.

Oh my Gods.

Mouth in a straight line, he stalked over to stare up at her. "Got a good explanation for being in this form at the lodge?"

How could she answer in panther form? With a huff of despair, she hung her head.

"Yeah, you should be ashamed." He jerked his chin toward the side of the lodge. "Go shift, get dressed, and I want you on the patio in five minutes." It was his displeased mentor voice—bossy, growly, rough.

The trouble was she fully deserved the scolding she'd get.

Turning, she jumped down and crept through the underbrush without disturbing the foliage. Normally, she'd be pleased with her improving skill. Right now, all she wanted to do was sneak off and hide.

Once dressed in jeans and a T-shirt, she took another minute to work her courage up before she could walk out onto the patio. She'd broken the rules.

The males were watching the undines play tag with a couple of young trout. Hearing her, Shay turned.

"I'm sorry, Shay." She pulled in a breath. "The high branches defeated me, so I wanted to practice jumping to a low one, but I shouldn't have done it anywhere close to the lodge."

"Aye, you screwed up." His normally friendly face was unreadable.

Owen's arms were folded over his chest.

The strange male was…huge, taller than Shay and Owen by inches, and had even more muscles than Gawain. "That was pretty risky behavior, girl, especially with that bunch watchin' for hints of you?" His voice was as low a rumble as Gawain's, but with a Texas accent. He raised his hand.

Bracing for the blow, she turned her head and closed her eyes.

No blow came.

"By the God of the Hunt." His appalled voice was as soft as the wind from the south. "Li'l cat, I've never hit a female in all my born days."

She opened her eyes, feeling creaky, as if someone had forgotten to oil her joints. Her voice sounded creaky, too. "I'm sorry. Just…reflex."

His massive hand was still in the air, and he slowly lowered it to her shoulder—what he'd obviously planned to do all along. He gave her shoulder a gentle squeeze before he dropped his hand and stepped back. "Darlin', I just wanted to ask you to be more careful. We'll"—he motioned to himself and the others—"defend you, but—"

"But it would be far better if it weren't necessary," Shay finished for him.

No, it would be far better if she weren't here at all. Her throat closed. "I'll be careful. I'm very sorry." Her delight at gaining the branch seemed awfully far in the past. Her victory had turned to bitter dirt in her mouth. She'd risked the safety of all these people just to make things easier for herself.

The huge male was right—the Scythe were already looking for her. How could she have been so thoughtless? So selfish?

As she turned to leave, she glanced at Owen.

He frowned. "Darcy." He took a step forward, reaching for her.

No, she didn't want to hear the disappointment in his rough voice. Fleeing like the cowardly person she was, she hurried into the lodge and up to her room.

She wouldn't come down until she'd thought through everything and knew she could do better.

Until she wouldn't disappoint anyone again.

As Darcy—the little tinker—fled into the lodge, Owen shook his head and dropped his hand. He'd been reaching for her, wanting to take her hand, to pull her closer. From her shattered expression, he'd known she was judging herself far harsher than any of them were.

He glanced at the others. "I need to give her Calum's news."

Shay nodded, his eyes worried. "I hope we didn't make her cry."

Owen froze. Cry? She'd wept before, and the pain of hearing her tears had almost fractured his chest. "She…wouldn't be crying."

Ben's gaze held sympathy. "Good luck, cat. You'll need it."

He would, dammit. She was already upset. What he had to say would make it worse. By the God, this was like going into battle without claws or teeth.

When he knocked on her door, there was a sharp inhalation,

then silence.

"Open the door, little cat. I have information I need to share."

The door opened, and he looked down at her. Such a tiny female. Her head barely reached his shoulder. No tear streaks showed, thank the God.

The way she wouldn't look at him was less heartening.

He put his hand under her chin and lifted her head. "Darcy. No one is angry with you."

"Of course you are. I put the entire town at risk—first with my escape, then with sheltering here, and now with being stupid and lazy and careless."

Yes, this young female would always judge herself more harshly than anyone else. *Way to go, Treharn.* He should have sent Gawain to talk to her. His brother was far nicer, far better with the words females considered so important.

Hugging her had worked before, when she'd been suffering the aftermath of a fight. Maybe she needed him to hold her. Carefully, he put his arms around her and pulled her against him.

He feared she'd pull away, but after a shuddering breath, she leaned into him. Her trust was a heady gift.

Rubbing his chin on top of her head, he tried to think of the right words to ease her guilt. "Risk is made up of many parts. Aye, the Scythe are undoubtedly searching for you because you escaped."

The sound she made held despair.

"Yet, because you escaped, we know what happened to Dogwood. We know the Scythe exist and are targeting shifters. It's extremely dangerous for us to be unaware of an enemy, aye?"

"Oh." She relaxed infinitesimally.

"With your information, we've learned how the weasels work and have an idea of where to search for the captives.

You've told us what dangers we'll run into in getting them free."

Now her weight was fully against him, all warm skin and soft curves. He ran his hand down her back and—

Don't get distracted.

"Being in animal form close to the lodge—yeah, you fucked up."

She flinched.

"Everyone fucks up, kitten." He huffed a laugh. "Since ancient times when the Fae's Wild Hunt shifters first bred with humans, every Daonain cub has fucked up and been scolded for being reckless. Me, included."

He knew he was getting through when she looked up. Her damp dark eyes could break his heart. "Are you sure? Shay was so angry. And you were—"

"We wanted you to see that. Like any cub who indulges in risky behavior, you got nipped. Because it *is* dangerous."

Her head moved against him in a nod. "I can't believe I was so stupid."

"I can." He stroked her hair—thick and soft as a cub's pelt. "New shifters are prone to being careless. The animal mind is all about visible danger, not future threats. Eventually, the animal/human thinking finds a balance, but it takes a while."

Her arms crept around his waist, and she…snuggled…against him, and it was nice. Very nice.

Sometimes females hugged him during the full moon, but this was different. Not sexual. He pulled her closer, oddly pleased to know she found comfort in his arms.

Unfortunately, with his news, she was going to be upset all over again.

"By the way, I stopped at the tavern to ask Calum for an update on your villagers." He realized he was holding her snugly against his body. "Since you said females died in the prison, Tynan searched the police records of unclaimed bodies."

Her breath hissed out. As she stepped back to look at him, she wrapped her arms around her own waist. "Wh-what did he find?"

"It appears the Scythe are tossing the females into Puget Sound. Some bodies have washed up, ones that aren't on any missing persons lists. One female was pulled out of the water recently. Blond. Blue eyes. About your age. She had a woven leather band around her right ankle."

"Barbara. She was my only real friend in Dogwood." Darcy's voice was only a whisper. "She died the day I escaped." Grief turned her eyes a molten darkness.

"I'm sorry, Darcy." Why didn't she yell? Shout in anger? Even cry? Had he ever met anyone more restrained? It was as if she was the very opposite of his mother. "I'll have Calum tell Tynan you identified her."

"Yes. Thank you."

By the God, he hated to see this muting of her spirit. "Gawain was going to the tavern for a beer and wanted me to bring you along."

"I'm not going to be good company right now."

He snorted. "I'm never good company. Doesn't matter, little female."

"I'm short, Owen. Not *little*."

"There's a difference?"

Her huff of annoyance made him grin.

Pleased, he gave her shoulder a light shake. "Do you want to brush your hair or do some female thing before we leave?"

She stared at him. "Some female thing? Don't *you* brush your hair?"

"Of course I do, but..." He eyed her. "A lot of males complain their females require hours to prepare to leave the house. I was being...thoughtful."

Her lips curved up. "Oh. Got it." She swiped her hands over

her damp cheeks. "I'm ready—I guess that means I'm not very female."

"You," he breathed, "are very female."

When her eyes widened, he gave her hair a light tug and opened the door.

As she preceded him down the hall, he smiled. He'd come awfully close to stepping in his own scat there, but he'd done well enough. She was coming with him—and smiling.

Males might be wrong about female preparation time, but they were certainly on scent when they said no male could understand one.

Chapter Fourteen

BREAKFAST TIME WAS over in the lodge, and the fishermen and vacationers from the cabins had dispersed. As morning sunlight streamed through the dining room windows, Darcy finished wiping down the tables—her self-appointed chore. Taking charity was like chewing on sand, but she couldn't job hunt when she was being hunted and might have to leave.

Frustration made her want to kick something as she carried her cleaning caddy into the kitchen.

Across the room, Bree loaded the dishwasher, assisted by Shay.

Darcy glanced at the small hole in the baseboard. "I thought you had brownies to clean up." She'd caught glimpses of the little housekeeping OtherFolk. Bree's kitchen was always spotless.

"Oh, we do," Bree said. "They won't touch electrical appliances though. I only run it after breakfasts when there are so many dishes from serving the lodge guests."

"She feels guilty if she leaves too much of a mess." Grinning, Shay pushed his shaggy brown hair out of his eyes. "So, Darcy, what are you going to be up to today?"

"Well…Gawain said I need to learn to hunt something bigger than rats and rabbits."

"Aye, you cougars have a fondness for deer." He nodded to his mate. "Bree does amazing things with venison if you want to try."

"That'll give me a goal." Out of habit, she glanced at the calendar and frowned. Almost to the end of October. She'd been in Cold Creek nearly a month. Too long. Were her brothers back from Russia? Surely, the Scythe wouldn't kill Patrin and Fell until the last minute. Would they?

Life held no guarantees.

"How is the search going for my brothers—for the shifter-soldier camp?" She should have asked Owen or Gawain yesterday, but they'd headed off to bed soon after supper. Guilt swept through her. In addition to directing the search for the camp, the two males were fixing up their house and mentoring her as well.

"Nothing yet, but Calum's called in more shifters to help. Owen will be handing out assignments. Come and see."

Darcy followed Shay into the dining room and to the "map wall." Three maps showed the nearby fishing spots and hiking trails. Another map was their small county—Azure—and the surrounding Whatcom and Skagit counties. Next to that was a map of Washington State.

Shay pointed to the Twin Sisters Mountain Range and made a semi-circle around the South Sister with his finger. "They've finished the west area and are working their way south and east. It's slow going. There's a lot of ground to cover, and they have to avoid human hikers."

Darcy studied the map silently, seeing the tiny tent symbols indicating camping areas filled with humans. It was amazing Calum could get *any* shifters to search there.

She felt so useless. "Thanks, Shay. It helps to know they're trying."

He gave her a pat on the shoulder. "They are, Darcy. Give 'em time."

Offering a weak smile, she headed upstairs to her room. She wanted to be patient, but her brothers were running out of time. What could she do? Her control wasn't perfect yet—she still shifted to cougar if she got scared or hurt.

It was her job to look after them. Of course, they thought it was their job to protect her, like when they'd moved to Dogwood and two bullies found her picnicking, knocked her down, and stole her food. Humiliated, she'd slunk home, but Patrin had spotted her and coaxed the story out of her. Then he and Fell had found the two big boys—almost twice their size—and taught them a bloody lesson.

I can't let them die. She had to do something.

Each day, Gawain, Owen, and the others drove to the Twin Sisters to search in animal forms. What if there was a better way?

Gawain had said he could usually tell where Owen was, and when she hadn't sensed her brothers, he'd said the distance might affect her ability. What if she got nearer to where her brothers might be?

Her mouth flattened. She couldn't go with the searchers in their cars, not since she'd have to be in human form. But the Twin Sister Range wasn't that far if going cross-country, only around thirty or forty miles. A panther moving quickly could be there in…maybe two days? If she stayed in animal form and kept away from humans, there wouldn't be any risk to the Daonain.

Besides, her mentors had said she should spend more time in her animal form.

Picking up a pen, she started to write a note.

Chapter Fifteen

AT LEAST THE weekend was over, and most of the humans
had left the Twin Sisters area. Owen growled under his
breath. Avoiding hikers was a pain in the tail.

A long day's search had yielded no signs of the shifter-
soldiers. Calling it quits, he and Gawain met up with Tynan and
Donal, changed to human, dressed, and were jogging down the
animal trail to where they'd parked their cars.

Leading the group, Owen could hear the rustle of the three
shifters behind him.

"Pick it up, Owen," Donal called from the rear. "We don't
have long before the moon rises, and I want to arrive early
enough for the Samhain festivities."

Owen glanced at the rapidly setting sun and picked up his
pace. They'd all prefer to get there in time to chow down on the
festival food.

And then there was the Gathering. Although a male's need
wasn't as strong as a female's if there were no aroused females
within scenting distance, they'd still be fucking uncomfortable to
be in a car after the moon rose.

A second later, at an intersection of hiking trails, he caught a
whiff of a scent and stopped so suddenly Gawain ran into him.

"Herne's antlers, brawd, what—" Gawain sniffed. "Darcy?"

Her feminine fragrance hung in the air. What in Herne's name was she doing here? He pointed toward the vehicles. "You have the better nose. Can you see if she went that way?"

As Gawain jogged down the trail, Tynan joined Owen. "I know that scent. The female we rescued from Seward Park, yes?" His Irish accent was always thicker after he'd shifted from wolf.

"Aye." Owen lifted his nose to the breeze. No other shifters. No stench of humans. "She's supposed to be in Cold Creek."

Had she come all this way as a cougar? If so, she must have traveled all day yesterday. He and Gawain had returned late last night, or they might have known she wasn't in the lodge.

Gawain returned. "She didn't take the trail toward the cars."

"Decided to take matters into her own teeth, did she?" Donal sounded amused. "She didn't seem the type to leave her littermates' fates to others."

Owen crouched to study the marks at the intersection of trails. It appeared she'd been traveling east to west, heading toward the mountain, not toward Cold Creek. "What about her own fate, healer? It's full moon tonight."

Silence fell as the others grasped his concern. Tonight was the full moon. Every full-grown Daonain female would go into heat…and be driven inexorably to find males to mate.

A new shifter, unused to the overwhelming need, might—would probably—do something stupid.

Donal frowned. "We'd best find her quickly and see if there's time to get her back to Cold Creek."

After a quick sniff, Gawain sighed. "I can't scent her, so she's quite a ways off. We should trawsfur if we want to catch up to her." He motioned toward the area where they'd stashed their clothes before.

Exasperation mingled with fear as Owen led the way back to the massive tree. A female. Alone and out of the God's territory.

What was she thinking? This was the behavior of a careless female, doing what she wanted, no matter the cost.

By the God, he didn't want her to pay the cost.

THE SUN HAD disappeared behind South Twin Mountain and its lower neighbors.

In the twilight, her sides heaving with each breath, Darcy halted at a trickling stream with bitingly cold water. After drinking until her stomach rumbled, she sprawled on the mossy bank and absently started washing a bloody scrape on her side.

Her paws hurt. Her muscles ached. She had bruises on bruises mixed with ugly scratches. *Poor tired tinker, you're a mess.* The outings she'd had with her mentors hadn't prepared her for long, grueling travel. All day yesterday. Today, going mostly uphill had been worse.

Disappointment was a heavy weight in her heart. She'd really hoped to feel her brothers and sense their direction in the way Gawain had said. But nothing. She had no idea where her brothers were. She'd failed, totally.

Not long ago, she'd caught the faintest trace of a shifter. A werewolf had urinated on a bush in a cool, moist grotto sometime in the past. No other scent markers remained. Perhaps he'd only been on a training hike. Still, maybe the shifter-soldiers had been here less than a month ago.

Maybe their camp was somewhere near here, perhaps closer to the main highway. Tomorrow she'd work her way south toward Highway 20.

Lifting her nose in the air, she sniffed. Again. The chill air off the mountain glacier held a tang of conifers and a green fragrance from the moss on the bank. And then the compelling wild fragrance of shifters drifted to her.

She'd *found* them. As her heart set up a jubilant tattoo against her ribs, her nose lifted higher.

Oh, no, no, no.

Not her brothers, but the Cold Creek males on search. The scent was Owen's. And Gawain's. Was that Donal? Another male was there—the one from Seattle. Four males—none of them would be happy to see her.

For one second, she considered fleeing. Then her ears caught the sounds moving quickly toward her. They'd already caught her scent and were tracking her.

With an unhappy sigh, she sank back down. As the human hostages would have said, she was *so* screwed.

First into the clearing was a huge, darkly golden cougar. *Owen.* Tynan—the wolf—was behind him followed by a sleek, tawny cougar. Donal? Loping easily, Gawain brought up the rear.

All of them shifted at the same time. Four males stared down at her.

"Weren't you told not to leave the Cosantir's territory?" Gawain asked, brows together.

Answering questions meant she'd have to trawsfur to human form. She hesitated. After her years among humans, she was beginning to doubt that she'd ever be completely comfortable when naked.

Donal didn't appear upset, but Tynan and Gawain were annoyed. And Owen...even the air around him was trying to escape his irritation.

There was no escape. She trawsfurred to human and remained on the ground, arranging her legs to shelter her private parts and crossing her arms over her breasts. "No one said I *couldn't* leave. I mean, I know it would be bad to be around humans before my control improves. But I only lose control when I'm in human form. So I stayed in cougar form all the way here and avoided any human areas, and even if there *were* humans around, they'd simply spot an animal that belongs here."

Owen made a growling sound.

"Darcy, what would happen if you got hurt?" Donal asked quietly. "Branches fall. Cliffs give out. Poachers shoot. There are reasons why Daonain leaving the territories try to travel in pairs."

Well...he had a point. She opened her mouth to apologize.

Owen studied her and then shook his head.

She flinched at the disappointment in his gaze.

Gawain's face was grim; Donal's usual smile was absent. Tynan looked pissed. She'd obviously screwed up really, really badly.

Everything in her cringed, wanting to hide and... She felt the magic and a second later, saw her furry forelegs. Paws. Her tail twitched. She'd trawsfurred. By accident.

Oh, Mother of All. Shamed completely, she shifted to human, wrapped her arms around her waist, and tried to find the words to apologize.

Owen glanced at his brother. "I'll guard the camp." And without looking at her again, he walked away, shifting to cougar as he slipped into the underbrush.

Darcy blinked back tears. He couldn't even stand the sight of her.

Once again, she'd messed up. Bad. Nonetheless, she wasn't a cub to break down and bawl. "I—" She steadied her voice. "I'm sorry. You're right—I didn't allow for the possibility things might go wrong. I didn't mean to cause trouble or endanger anyone."

"I know, sweetling." With a sympathetic nod, Gawain moved away and started picking up firewood.

Donal leaned against a tree, face unreadable.

Tynan, though, still stood over her. Like many shifters of

Gaelic heritage, he was tall, big-boned, and broad-shouldered. His long face was clean-shaven with a square chin. His light brown hair was cut military short, reminding her of the Scythe guards. "Right, do you remember me from Seattle? Tynan, Donal's littermate."

"I remember. I hoped to see you in Cold Creek so I could thank you again for the rescue." Darcy frowned. If Donal was his brother, why didn't the healer's house hold this male's scent?

"I don't live in the North Cascades Territory." His voice was beautiful with a lilting Irish accent. "The God sent me to work in the human city." Shadows flitted across his face, darkening his eyes. The city wasn't where he wanted to be.

"But...why?" Why would any shifter want to live among humans?

"Why doesn't matter here." His expression hardened. "Do you realize what—"

"Brawd," Donal said. "Pad lightly. Moonrise is in a few minutes."

Tynan glanced eastward, and his face changed. Through the forest, the foothills could be dimly seen, lit from behind by the rising moon. "Aye and so it is. This was not the Gathering I had planned."

GATHERING? ABSENTLY, DARCY combed the tangles from her hair. That was some sort of moon celebration, wasn't it? "It's a full moon tonight?" When she was a cub, her mother had always left the house on full moon night to go to a "grown-up party". Did Cold Creek have similar celebrations?

More guilt piled on her shoulders. "I'm sorry. I didn't mean to make you miss the party."

Gawain dropped the firewood into a pile and studied her. "The party?"

"You don't need to stay for me. I promise I'll head back to

Cold Creek. If you hurry, you might still get in some fun."

The way the three guys stared at her was disconcerting.

Tynan's brows drew together. "If all the males leave you here, what will you do tonight?"

She sputtered. "I told you, I'll head back to the territory."

"I mean when you come into heat, how will you—"

"May the Mother save me, she's as uninformed as Breanne was. Raised human. I bet Darcy's never experienced a full moon heat." Donal narrowed his eyes at her. "You lived in a shifter village until you were twelve, right? What were you told happens at these…parties?"

An edgy discomfort stole over Darcy. She was obviously missing something. "Um, one of my brothers was…" This felt like a betrayal. "As a cub, Fell loved sharing secrets…with everyone."

"You mean he shared information about the Daonain?"

"Unfortunately. We grew up in a mostly human town, and after some close calls, my mother stopped talking about our Daonain heritage. When we neared the age of first trawsfur, she moved us to an all shifter village, so it wouldn't matter if Fell talked about shifting. But then the Scythe got us."

"And you learned nothing more." Donal rubbed his eyes. "This is bad."

Such a doomsayer. Darcy scowled. "Just tell me. Why is a Gathering party so important and what's a full moon heat?"

"Gods help us." Gawain sat beside her. When he captured her hand, the warmth of his concern relaxed the uncomfortable knot in her belly. "Under a full moon, adult female shifters come into heat—which is an overwhelming compulsion to mate. Over the course of the night, each female mates with the males who please her." He smiled slightly. "We males strive—and occasionally fight—to be chosen by the females we want."

Wait, wait, wait. Darcy loved being a cougar, but this…this was carrying animal instincts way too far. As panic welled, she said slowly, "You said males as in more than *one*? In a single night?"

"Aye, catling. More than one."

Donal moved to sit on a log a short distance away. "Myth says the Fae shapeshifters who made up the Wild Hunt didn't go into heat. But some of them interbred with humans, and their mixed race descendants acquired the quirk."

Some *quirk*. "You're saying I'm going to have an urge to mate a bunch of males? Like whoever is around me?" Like *these* males? Outraged, Darcy stared at Donal. "I hardly know you. Any of you."

"When the heat hits, you won't care how well you know a male, Darcy." Tynan sat in the grass and leaned against the log beside his brother. "Mating multiple males under a full moon is not only biology, but tradition and law, as well. The Daonain are too few. With our severe lack of females, our race can't afford monogamy."

Law? "A female has to do this forever?"

"Until past childbearing. Of course, if a female falls in love and lifemates, she'll have no interest in any males other than her mates." Gawain smiled. "For whatever reason—maybe because of the Mother's approval—lifematings have the highest blessing of cublings."

Darcy scowled down at where Gawain's hand engulfed hers. In captivity, a smart person avoided thinking about the past. Or about how Daonain litters always had two or three males to one female—or no female—and the implications of that lopsided ratio.

She inhaled slowly. If she'd learned nothing else in *prìosan*, it was to choose her battles wisely. Fighting biology, tradition, and law would be stupid. But oh, she didn't want to do this—any of it. "Okay, so what happens next?"

The males exchanged relieved glances. They'd been afraid she'd go into hysterics, hadn't they?

Gawain squeezed her hand in approval. "When you want to mate—and you will—simply choose a male. After you finish mating, you'll return here. If another male appeals to you, you pick him. If you're not interested, nothing happens."

"Nothing?" She gave him a suspicious look. "In *prìosan*, a human man...used...a female from my village." Fenella had been *raped*. The word wouldn't come out. "Fenella didn't want him, and he hurt her badly."

"*Humans.*" Tynan almost spat the word. "Be easy, lass. A Daonain male's response—and erection—is set off by a female's arousal. If you're not aroused, neither is he."

"Oh." Her erratic heartbeat smoothed to an even rhythm. "That helps, Tynan. Thank you."

She didn't have to choose any of them, did she? But, oh Gods, then the poor males would just...sit. The Gathering in Cold Creek would have lots of females. Guilt sliced across her spirit. "I'm making you miss the Gathering. I'm really sorry." *Because I'm not planning to participate.*

"Catling, we've all missed Gatherings before, for one reason or another." Gawain massaged her cold fingers as if to rub her guilt away. "If you don't want to do anything more than talk, we'll simply have a pleasant evening by the campfire. I'm fond of talking with you."

His honest, steady blue eyes met hers. And when he smiled and tucked a lock of hair behind her ear, she could only smile back.

AFTER THE LITTLE cat had relaxed and started to talk with Donal, Gawain wandered away to collect wood for the fire Tynan was building. The cop shifter wore a magicked blade similar to Gawain's, but also carried a pen-sized ferrocerium fire starter rod in the sheath. Good thing since this was going to be a long cold night. In animal form, they'd have been comfortable, but flirting, choosing, and mating were done in the human form. Since no one had clothing, a fire was a necessity.

Strolling through the trees, Owen appeared with an armload of firewood.

"Are you through acting like a bee-stung badger?" Gawain asked. "You almost had her crying."

Owen flinched. "I know." He dumped the stack of wood into Gawain's arms.

"Thanks." Gawain shifted the awkward mess to a better balance. "I assume you were listening." In feline form, Owen would have been able to hear every word.

"Aye and looked, too. Her paws are raw, fur's bloodied. She was just trying her best to save her friends and family—and she sure doesn't understand the dangers, let alone what the Cosantir might do. We should have explained better." Owen scrubbed his face. "I owe her an apology."

Owen had the temper of a moose, but his sense of fairness was as reliable as moonrise and moonset. "'Fraid so. Are you going to rejoin us?"

"Eventually. I'll pretend to guard the camp for a while yet."

"Why?" They both knew there was no need for a sentry, not this far into the wilderness.

Owen glanced toward the stream. "Her emotions are already a tangle—I'm not a good choice for her first mating."

"Heh—you're assuming she'd pick you at all."

His littermate snorted...with good reason. Like starving wolves, females in heat pursued all the God-chosen—cahirs, Cosantirs, healers, and blademages. Then Owen grinned. "Or she might well decide she hates the God-touched. In which case, Tynan will have her favors, and you'll have an aching dick."

Gawain laughed and felt the stretch of the Goddess's scar

on his cheekbone. "Cantankerous cat."

"Lethargic lion."

Gawain paused for the next voice to chime in—but no, Edwyn had returned to the Mother. There would never again be a childish, three-part insult-fest. With an effort, he pushed the ache of loss away. One brother was gone, but he had Owen back again.

Owen slapped his arm and motioned toward the clearing. "Go on, brawd. I'll see you in a few hours."

"Later then." Gawain headed back. A shame they wouldn't be together later. It had been decades since he'd shared a female with his littermate, and he'd been looking forward to the Cold Creek Gathering. But tonight wouldn't be the time—not with a new female to tend.

Yet, as he walked away, he felt closer to Owen than he had since Edwyn's death.

In the clearing, Tynan had built a fire in the hollow area left by an aged, fallen tree. The massive root ball served to reflect the warmth of the flames to the three around it.

Although a log had been dragged over, Darcy was sitting in the grass with Tynan and Donal sprawled on each side of her. She looked better. Donal had apparently healed her deeper cuts and scrapes.

As Gawain dumped his firewood into the nearby pile, Darcy jumped. Her face was flushed, her lips redder than normal.

Even as a needy hum started to simmer in his blood, he noticed the heavy circle of the moon rising above the forests. "How are you doing, catling?"

A shiver shook her, and goosebumps rose on her skin. "Um…"

Gawain frowned. If merely the sound of his voice caused a response, she was well taken with the heat. He glanced at Donal, surprised neither of the males had led her to the tiny mating area they'd created.

"Tynan and I waited, in case she wanted to start with her mentor," Donal said softly.

Gawain blinked. Setting aside the instinct to compete for a female's favors in favor of keeping her comfortable showed impressive control as well as kindness.

"That was a generous thought." Gawain pushed down his own need to fight the others, to prove himself worthy of mating this beautiful cat. As the other males rose, he stepped to Darcy's right side, leaving room for them.

Under the silvery moonlight, Tynan knelt in front of Darcy with Donal to his left.

"Sweetling," Gawain murmured and went down on one knee on the other side. "I love seeing you in the moonlight."

Darcy's hair streamed down her back like a midnight river, and he ran his hand over it. Thick as a winter pelt. Her big eyes were wells of darkness as she looked at him. When he stroked the wayward locks from her face, he heard her swift inhalation.

"Gawain," she whispered. "I feel so strange."

His imagination tried to give him an idea of what she must be feeling. He knew it was something akin to what a male felt when he wanted a female and discovered she was interested in him. Perhaps very similar to what he felt now as his cock rose and throbbed with urgency, as the skin on his body felt abraded, as his palms itched to run over her soft curves. Shoving his need down, he glanced at Tynan.

The cop nodded and took Darcy's hand.

When her fingers curled around the wolf's hand, Gawain had to suppress a growl. *Mine.*

"Your body wants to mate, lass." Tynan kissed her fingers. "I would love to spend this time with you, but the choice is yours. Is there a male here ye fancy?" Tynan motioned to Gawain, Donal, and himself.

"No. I don't want…" Darcy shook her head. "That's a lie. I do want."

Gawain smiled. How rare to find someone who faced up to his or her own feelings and even admitted them aloud? He motioned for Donal to speak.

"Darcy, the choice is yours." Donal stroked her bare leg, letting her feel his skin, catch his scent. "You're an amazing female, and it would be a delight to be with you."

She leaned toward the healer, then stopped and looked at Gawain.

Mine. Gawain took her hand, and rubbed his scent over her fingers, inhaling hers. A purr escaped him because she smelled like mossy forests and intoxicatingly female. "Pretty panther, I want you more than I can breathe. But the choice is yours."

The startled delight in her eyes was as charming as it was distressing. She'd never known the dance of flirtation, the give and take before mating, the growing anticipation in the day or so before the full moon. By the God and Goddess, damned if he wouldn't do everything in his power to give her a first Gathering night to remember.

They all would. Even his female-hating brother wouldn't be able to hold out against her sweetness.

She was starting to squirm, her color increasing. The scent of her arousal was heady. An experienced female would have already given in, chosen a male, and dragged him toward the mating rooms. But Darcy didn't know enough to make a decision about her own needs, did she?

"I want…" She didn't release his fingers.

A glance at the other two showed they agreed, and he realized he was purring louder.

He kissed her palm, then her wrist, inhaling and savoring the increase in her interest. Rising slowly, he leaned forward and took her lips. Soft and yielding, opening to his. Her skin had a heady flavor, spurring a need to taste her…everywhere. Drawing back slightly, he looked into her eyes and saw only desire. For him.

DARCY'S PULSE THUDDED hard and fast in her ears. Each breath brought her the scent of the males—as intoxicating as the champagne she'd read about.

And their voices. Tynan's Irish lilt held the patter of a soft rain; Donal's velvety smooth voice was a slow, sliding caress.

Gawain's resonant voice was the rumbling of a thunderstorm that shook her to the bone.

She gripped his hand, feeling the calluses. Those strong hands created useful, beautiful tools. And he could call upon the Mother of All. She'd never met anyone like him.

With each breath, she caught his scent—the wild musk of a male cat shifter with a tantalizing hint of smoke and metal. His shoulders were thick with muscle. Curly brown hair covered his broad chest, not quite hiding the flat male nipples, then narrowed to a line down his ridged stomach until reaching…

Startled, she jerked her gaze back up.

"Yes, I'm interested in mating," he said gently and drew her to her feet. The strength of his arm that curled around her waist made her knees go weak.

He led her away from the fire to a tiny clearing, one barely large enough for the moon to illuminate the grassy space.

"What…what do I need to do?" she asked as he sat and drew her down to straddle his lap. His erection pressed against her stomach and sent hot shivers through her.

"You need to kiss me, sweetling," he whispered. His big hand tangled in her hair and pulled her closer, until her mouth touched his. His lips were gentle, teasing, skilled.

Her breasts pushed against him, and his chest hair teased her nipples to an aching hardness. The entire world seemed as if it were tilting, so she wrapped her arms around his neck and held on.

He covered one breast with his hand and deepened the kiss. When he cupped the back of her head, holding her firmly as his tongue plunged in, the feeling of being taken swamped her senses.

Desire was a rising tide within her, sweeping everything before it, scouring away every thought and concern.

He moved, laying her on her back in the grass, and knelt beside her. His straight hair hung loose, shadowing his chiseled features. "You are so beautiful."

Was she? She hadn't wanted to be beautiful, hadn't wanted to attract human attention, but now…she wanted to be beautiful for him. To please him. "So are you," she whispered and made him laugh.

His low baritone melted her bones into hot puddles.

His lips grazed down her cheek, her neck, her upper breasts, and when his hot mouth closed on one nipple, the exquisite sensation was too much.

A tremor ran up her spine, and the urgency in her core grew and grew. "I need…" She couldn't find the words. "I need."

"I know, catling," he murmured. "But have you had a male inside you before? Ever?"

"N-no." What did that matter? *Inside?* All of her seemed to chime at that word. "Inside. Yes. That's what I want.

His chuckle made her center clench. Should any male have such an amazing voice?

"Let me get you a bit more ready."

He didn't understand. She was perfectly ready and needed…something. Him. Now.

Running his hand down her stomach, he touched her private area and slid a finger between her folds. The intense pleasure stole the very air from her lungs.

His finger swirled around and around in her slickness, each movement a shooting star of ecstasy. He pressed a finger inside her—oh, such a feeling.

One finger was in, but when he tried to add another, she felt an uncomfortable pressure, as if her body was denying him entry.

No, let him in.

Her body was vibrating like an overheated motor, whining with effort. *Need more.* She closed a hand over his cock. *Oh, amazing.* How could anything have an inner iron core and such velvety skin outside? She tried to pull him to her.

"Goddess help me, you test my control," he murmured. "No, sweetling, I'm going to make everything soft and ready, first."

To her frustration, he removed his cock from her hand, spread her legs widely apart, and moved to kneel between her knees.

"Gawain…"

He brushed his soft beard over her inner thighs, making her tremble. Then…his tongue licked over her clit.

Oh Gods. She gasped, and her core clenched in a way that spread smoldering heat along every nerve.

He didn't stop. His hot, wet tongue teased the tiny nub until her thighs were trembling, until the coil of pressure at her core tensed more and more.

Need him inside. Gripping his long hair, she tried to pull him up her body, to make him use his cock, but his huge hands stayed closed around her hips, holding her immobile as he swirled his tongue in big circles around her clit and entrance.

A pulse pounded in her head, and her urgency grew until all else disappeared under the sensation of his tongue.

Slowly every muscle in her body grew taut. Her hands fisted in his hair. Even her breathing stopped.

He chuckled again and set his tongue right on top of the swollen nub of nerves—and wiggled.

The amazing sensation sank deep, deep to her center, expanded—and slammed through her like a massive wave, and sheer, unadulterated pleasure flooded every muscle and cell in her body.

Helpless in the mage's implacable grip, her hips tried and tried to buck, but his tongue never ceased until he'd pulled the last spasm from her.

Her muscles went limp.

She was still gasping for air when he eased himself down beside her. Propping his head up on his hand, he studied her.

Her arm shook as she lifted her hand to caress his lean cheek, stroke the soft, short beard, and touch the hidden cleft in his chin.

Her scent mingled with his—and an additional fragrance. From sex? She frowned—tried to frown, although her lips kept curving into a pleased smile. "That wasn't what I thought happened during a mating."

The moonlight showed his slow grin. "Everything can happen during a mating, pretty panther. Although eventually we do have to join, there can be many other…additions."

"But I feel fine now. I don't…um…" Her mind felt clear again—and with a jolt, she realized he'd given her wonderful pleasure, and she hadn't done a thing for him. That wasn't right. "Can I do…? Will you tell me how to make you feel good, too?"

The corners of his eyes crinkled with his smile. "We're not finished yet. Just resting for a moment."

A rest sounded fine. Although the seething heat of her body had disappeared, Gawain was pressed against her closely enough to keep her warm. His free hand stroked her hips, stomach, and breasts as though he enjoyed simply petting her.

"You can do that as long as you want," she said. The *priosan* had kept the captives from speaking or touching, leaving her feeling like a spindly plant deprived of the sun. How she'd longed for someone to pat her arm, kiss her cheek, hug her—anything. Now, as he caressed her, she basked in the joy of being touched.

She could touch in return.

Holding her breath, she ran a hand up his thickly muscled forearm to trace the bulge of his biceps, the bisected muscles over his shoulder, the… A tingling grew, deep within her. The air warmed, and she looked to see if the bonfire had moved. Her breasts began to ache.

As her nipples bunched under his palm, he paused.

"Gawain?" She didn't have the vocabulary to ask him what was happening.

"Easy, sweetling. Under a full moon, you'll come into your need several times."

"More?"

"Lots more." As he kissed her, he moved on top of her until his rock-hard body covered hers, and his legs were between hers. The head of his shaft pressed against her entrance before he slid it in her wetness and over her clit.

Tremors of excitement shook her.

"This time, I'm going to take you—and since it's your first time, it will probably hurt some. I'm sorry for that, sweetling."

Although she nodded, fear curled inside her. Fenella had screamed when the human forced himself into her. The pain must be horrendous. But this…this wouldn't be the same, would it? As urgency burned within her, she couldn't think. But she trusted Gawain. She did.

"I'm ready."

"Not yet, but you will be." He shifted to one side, and his fingers circled her clit again. Hunger raged through her, even as he took her lips in a kiss. As his weight pressed her down into the soft grass, his shoulder muscles were bunched hard under her hands. His tongue teased her lips; his fingers teased her clit.

Sensations engulfed her and filled her. As her excitement grew, her hips lifted, trying to meet the cock she had to have.

"Gawain." Her voice came out a whine. A demand.

"Yes, catling, it's time." He gripped his cock, set it against her entrance, and pressed—met the barrier—and mercilessly drove through.

Torn. The shocking pain seized her. Digging her fingers into his shoulders, she bit back a scream.

He was inside her, huge and throbbing, filling her until she wasn't sure she could draw a breath.

But…he didn't move. Braced on knees and forearms, he kept his weight from smothering her. His gaze was on her face, a weight of a different kind. "Breathe, pretty panther."

The order slid into her, and she pulled in a breath, then another.

He nuzzled her cheek, kissed her temple. His hips remained immobile.

Although her core still throbbed around the intrusion, the pain eased from burning to a mild stinging. And then the feeling changed… Her center contracted around him as her clit wakened again. She tried to rub the nub of nerves against him, to ease the craving.

His smile appeared. "*Now* you're ready."

He eased out. The tiny burst of pain disappeared under the slickly wonderful friction. Slowly, he slid in and out, each time moving deeper. Filling her fuller. Desire bubbled upward in an amazing broth.

"More," she whispered. Demanded. Dug her fingernails into his shoulders.

He chuckled. "All right." Gradually he increased the speed, and oh, sweet Mother, it was heavenly.

Everything in her body was celebrating the feeling of being filled and fulfilled.

Lifting his head, he looked in her eyes, reached down, and touched her clit.

As his finger slid over and around it, as his cock plunged in, pulled out, and plunged in, her center clenched, tightened, and exploded into overwhelming sensation. "Oh, oh, oooh." Each wave hit the heavy shaft within her, setting off more and more detonations until she was drowning in an ocean of pleasure.

His erection grew thicker as he hammered into her, fast and forceful. Then his shaft pressed deep, ever so deep within her, and filled her with heat.

This time the rippling pleasure was so intense that it seared every cell in her body. His huge body pressed her into the ground, his cock filled her completely, and all she could do was grip his shoulders and shudder with the waves of sensation.

Sometime later, when the roaring in her ears lessened, she heard his rumbling laugh.

"What?" she mumbled.

"Thank you, sweetling, for sharing with me." He moved to her side and grinned when she whimpered at losing both his weight and his cock. Taking her hand, he kissed her fingers. "I've never enjoyed being with anyone more."

"Oh." The warmth of his compliment was in an entirely different class from desire—and yet much the same. "Thank you for being so patient." Would any other male have been as careful? As caring?

"My pleasure." He kissed her slowly, taking his time, as if to show her he liked her as much after mating as he had before.

When he lifted his head, she ran her hand over his arm and, as always, was surprised at the hardness of the muscles there. "Now what?"

"Now we clean up in the stream, settle by the fire, and chat with the others."

Why did she get the impression he wasn't saying everything. Hadn't he said a female took more than one male? She gave him a suspicious look.

"Easy, sweetling. You simply do what comes naturally. This isn't a night where thinking will do you any good."

Not think? That would be the day. She gave a resigned sigh. "All right."

As he pulled her to her feet, she looked up and saw the moon glowing above, full and round and beautiful.

Chapter Sixteen

LATER THAT NIGHT, Tynan carried the small female away from the campfire. The moon had traveled far enough to shine fully into the small mating area.

Tynan laid Darcy gently on the soft grass and covered her with his body, sharing his warmth. This far up in the mountains, the nights were far too cold to be in a naked human form. Bracing himself on a forearm, he smiled down at her. Olive skin, black hair and eyes. He wondered if she had some of the old Romani blood that had come to the islands with the Travelers. Gypsies they'd been called in the old days. He'd met many when he was fostered in Ireland.

She set her hands on his shoulders, and her eyes were as dark as the night sky. "Tynan."

"Yes, lass?"

"When does this stop?" She pressed her face against his chest with a soft moan.

Pity slid through him. Although her body wanted to mate, her mind was obviously in a tangle.

He understood, having spent the last decade fighting his own body, living in Seattle, rather than a forest where he belonged. "The heat will disappear at moonset." A glance at the sky told him that she had a while to go. Gawain had said Owen would return, so the little female would have another male to see to her needs if she wished.

And for the next few minutes, he would enjoy satisfying her. She was small and delightfully built, fragrant with her arousal, and sweet, as well. He stroked her cheek, down her neck, and captured a firm, round breast. The way she arched into his hand made him smile. As he kissed her swollen, ripe lips, she wrapped her arms around his shoulders.

Even if his schedule had permitted travel to Gatherings, he rarely visited shifter towns. Any law enforcement officer knew how easily a tech-savvy hunter could track someone through satellites, GPS devices, and street cameras. No one suspected he was Daonain, but that could change the moment he put a paw wrong. He'd leave no back trail to be sniffed out.

Yet he'd missed attending Gatherings and spending time with Daonain females.

Darcy squirmed under him in an unspoken demand that he move. Her body wanted a cock.

He grinned. This pushy little kit would probably walk all over younger, less knowledgeable males—and coerce them to fuck her immediately.

Unfortunately for her, she only had very experienced males tonight. She wouldn't be getting any *slam-bam-thank-you-ma'am* quickies. Mature males preferred to savor their matings.

How soft she was. He ran his knuckles along the underside of her breast, feeling the tender skin, hearing her shaking inhalation, seeing her dusky nipple pucker to a rigid peak.

She tasted of female musk and the mint that Donal had found growing along the stream. The healer knew his herbs.

A shame Darcy was so new. If she were more experienced, Tynan and Donal would have taken her together, extending their time, and pleasing them all.

Ah, well.

Ever so slowly, Tynan kissed his way down her body, smiling at the way her belly quivered under his lips. He wouldn't stop until he had her entire body trembling and her cries became incoherent.

And then he'd take her and satisfy them both.

AFTER HER THIRD mating of the night, Darcy's legs had turned to jelly. When she tried to stand, Tynan had to grab her or she'd have crumbled right then and there. She felt her face redden with her flush. "Sorry."

"No need to apologize, lass." He scooped her up and carried her to the stream to wash off.

Setting her on her feet in the water, he held her up with an arm around her waist. As the shallow creek flowed around her calves, she was still so overheated it was surprising the icy water didn't start to steam.

A cougar padded out of the bushes, and Owen's scent reached her a second before he shifted to human. "I think you could use some help."

"I could, it is true." Tynan moved to stand behind her, wrapped both arms around her waist, and held her against his warm body.

Owen stepped into the stream and went down on a knee in front of her.

She frowned. "I thought you were mad at me."

"I was." His deep voice was as rugged as the surrounding mountains. "You screwed up. But so did I. I should've realized you didn't know the dangers. And that you were acting on your concern for others. Can you accept my apology?"

Shocked, she stared down at him.

In the moonlight, his hair appeared as dark as her own, and

beard growth shadowed his jaw. Even down on one knee, the rough, deadly cahir was so tall his head came level with her shoulders.

And he wanted her to forgive him. She hadn't lost him for a friend. Relief made her voice shake. "Accepted."

Tynan handed him a handful of the leaves plucked from the banks, and Owen ran the soft bundle over her body, releasing the scent of mint. When he cleansed between her legs, ever so gently, the mint added a tingle to the coolness of the water against her swollen, sore flesh. She sucked in a breath.

"Sorry, kitten," he murmured, not stopping until he was satisfied.

He rose. "Let's go back to the fire and give you a chance to warm up."

Tynan scooped her up, kissed the top of her head, and, to her surprise, handed her to Owen. "Her legs are getting wobbly."

"I'm not surprised."

Darcy stiffened. "I'm sure I can walk now." Surely, the cahir didn't want to lug her around.

He didn't put her down. His arms were thick with muscle, and he carried her easily, holding her so close his body warmed her.

At the fire, Donal and Gawain moved aside, making a space for Owen to set her down.

As she curled her legs to one side in the soft grass, he sat behind her. Right behind her. His chest pressed against her back, and his long legs bracketed her sides and thighs. With the fire in front and Owen behind, she felt toasty warm.

And oddly happy.

The wind was a light breeze against her body. The fire crackled cheerfully, and a salamander was dancing in the flames. Its tail sent a spiral of pretty sparks upward into the black sky.

With a sigh, Darcy leaned back, and Owen's arms came around her waist.

And she felt his cock thickening against her buttocks. She tensed and tried to…unobtrusively…scoot away.

With a huffed laugh, he pulled her more firmly against him. "Little cat, a male rises if he gets even a whiff of interest from a female. Doesn't mean anything will come of it."

"No?"

"No, you're not ready for anything at all right now. If and when your need returns, you make a choice again—and you may or may not want me. Just relax and let me keep you warm." His gravelly tone held no room for argument.

In all reality, she was so tired all she really wanted was to be held.

Only…

"Do you even like me?" she asked, whispering the pitiful question.

Owen's muscles tensed as if she'd slapped him. "Darcy, I—"

"Never mind." Blinking back unexpected tears, she looked down, feeling more alone than ever before, even in captivity. Wasn't it horrible that sometimes she missed the lack of change she'd had in the *prìosan*. Maybe she'd never have discovered how many other kinds of pain were in the world.

No, she was being childish. Foolish. Her thinking was messed up by all the needs rioting through her system. The males were probably laughing at how naïve she was.

Biting her lip, she studied the scuffed-up dirt around the fire…and wanted to scream. Heat was already rising within her, and she did want Owen. She always had.

She'd just hoped that he liked her…a bit. She didn't want to be with someone—even him—if she disgusted him. Would his body, his own needs, make him mate with her even if he hated her?

The thought made her want to throw up. "This is awful."

"Let me ex—"

"Maybe I don't like you either."

Owen leaned forward so his cheek rested on hers and his unshaven chin scratched her shoulder. "Listen to me, little cat. Even with a full moon heat, if a female dislikes a potential partner, she doesn't get aroused. Your body and mind must agree."

"But I would never have mated"—she shook her head—"so many males."

"Mmm, numbers are irrelevant. Right now, the only question in your body and mind is: *Is this male worthy of a child of my body? Do I want to carry a cub from this male?*"

"Oh." Truly, that was an entirely different matter. Against the rising haze of need, Darcy looked around at the males.

Donal, the healer, whose knowledgeable touch had roused her completely—and who had been so very kind.

Tynan, who saw things in black and white, and fought for what was right. He had been slow and incredibly, sexily thorough.

Gawain, called by the Goddess, was like the blades he made, sparkling silver over a steel core. He'd made her first mating something beautiful.

She would be proud to carry a child from any of them.

Then there was Owen.

Her body was filling her with need already. With each brush of his hands against her skin, she smoldered with the desire to have him cup her breasts. To kiss her.

The cahir had rescued her from the Scythe in Seattle. Had come after her here in the forest. Would protect her with everything in his power. He was blunt and bossy and…would never lie to her.

Yes, she would love to carry his cub.

When she tried to push to her feet, he rose and helped her up. Silently, he waited, leaving the choice to her—and she knew this was the difference between humans and the Daonain. A Daonain female couldn't control coming into heat, but the decision regarding who she would mate with was all hers.

She extended her hand and held her breath. Would he want to be with her? Truly?

His dark wicked eyebrows were drawn together, making him look harsh, yet the corner of his mouth tipped up. A second later, his big hand engulfed hers in warmth.

IN THE TINY mating clearing, the moon danced on the edge of the trees. The light wouldn't last long, and wasn't that a shame; Owen wanted to see the little female. It had been a long time since he'd truly enjoyed mating. But Darcy was special. Being with the little cat was…different…somehow.

He laid her down on the soft meadow grass and stretched out beside her, propping his head up on his hand. "You asked me a question."

"I noticed you didn't answer." In the moonlight, her eyes were liquid pools of night. "You told me a female wouldn't mate someone she disliked. But I bet males are different."

Did she have any idea how appealing her clever mind was? "'Tis true males are less discriminating. He can mate someone he doesn't particularly favor. In a way, we see it as our duty to the race."

Her tiny sniff said she knew this would be the fact.

He grinned. "However, there is a wide gap between like and dislike. No male can rise for a female he hates."

Her soft lips formed an O.

He ran the back of his knuckles over her softly curved cheek, feeling the increasing warmth. As he moved down, he found the pulse in her neck was delightfully rapid. Her collarbone gave him a path to her sternum and down to rest between her breasts.

She was holding her breath.

He gave her the honesty she'd asked for. "I like you, Darcy."

At the release of her held breath, he smiled despite the ache in his chest. He was an ill-tempered weasel for making her doubt her appeal.

Awkwardly, he gave her the rest of the truth she was owed. "I was...poorly treated...as a cub and somehow figured all females were manipulative and self-centered. Since I'm gnome-stupid, it took me this long to realize not all females are the same."

Her expression held compassion, and she stroked his shoulder in a way he enjoyed all too well. "I'm sorry you had such a rough time, and your mother was so cruel."

She knew about his mother. By the God, the females had been gossiping about him. He started to pull back, then closed his eyes and wanted to groan. Aye, he was an idiot.

"Even knowing better, I keep seeing females as the enemy." He laid his palm on the side of her face. "Please grab me by the tail and yank if you see me fall into the trap."

Her lips curved. "Now there's a nice invitation."

He knew this female had the courage to tell him when he was messing up.

And now...after all the unkind words he'd given her, he owed her the good ones, as well. He stroked a finger over her lips. "I like your honesty—how you come right out and say what you want, what you're feeling."

Her startled look was a delight.

He trailed a finger down her pointed...stubborn...chin. "I like that you don't cave in, and you have the courage to do what you think needs to be done." He snorted. "Although the Cosantir might not be as appreciative."

Before she could overthink his warning, he took her hand, kissing the callused fingers. "I like your talent with those human devices. Your delight in making something work reminds me of Gawain's pleasure in a finely crafted blade."

Whether with tools or lives, this little tinker tried to fix whatever was broken.

Ah, the smile had reached her eyes.

He put his hand between her lovely breasts. "Perhaps more than anything, I like your loyalty to your villagers and your brothers. Even when you're afraid, you press on."

Her lips were soft under his, and he took his fill before lifting his head long enough to whisper, "Yeah, I like you, Darcy."

And he wanted her with a need that throbbed through him from his paws to his whiskers. His balls ached as if a gnome was squeezing them.

Still... He was going to take his time and enjoy every second he had with her. He kissed her cheek and nibbled on her jaw, under her ear, and down. The hollow at the base of her neck held her scent, the fresh green of oak moss after spring showers. He tasted between her small breasts, kissed the undersides, and licked over the puckered nipples.

She gasped, and her back arched up.

Nice. He could spend some time here. He licked around one nipple, then closed his lips around the peak and sucked. Nibbled, sucked.

Under his hand, her heart was beating violently against her sternum. Her moan made him smile.

He fondled her beautifully formed breasts, enjoying the firmness and the softness, feeling them swell until the skin was tight and the nipples long and pointed.

"Please. Please, Owen, I need more." She tugged on his hair, interrupting his play, and reminding him of his duty. In the moonlight, her dark eyes met his straightforwardly.

And he realized this one night wasn't going to be enough for him. He hadn't lied to her…he *did* like her, and he would want her even when the moon wasn't full. It might be fun to mate a female not influenced by the full moon heat. A female—*this* female. "All right, little cat."

"I'm not *little*, damn it."

His lips twitched. Fuck, she was cute. "No, you're definitely full grown." And he would thank the Mother for the gift of her. "And I'll give you more."

But, rather than impaling her on his cock as she'd obviously hoped, he moved down. As he licked her belly, he was pleased to see her ribs were now hidden under beautifully soft flesh. When he rubbed his chin on the crease between her thigh and pelvis, she inhaled sharply, and her hips started to rise.

"Oh, none of that now," he murmured, breathing her in. Her fragrance here was richer, more sensual, redolent with her excitement. Under his hands, she was almost quivering. "You'll have more fun if we take our time."

"You-you dumb dumbass, I don't want to go slow. Take me, dammit." Her voice—he did love her sultry voice. Instead of her tone rising to shrill, her cute demands were even more throaty than usual. The smoky sound laced around his heart.

He ran his hands up and down her legs before settling between her soft thighs. "I will. When I'm ready." Smiling, he teased his tongue over her pussy, savoring the musky taste of her—and silencing her completely.

Her hips squirmed enough that he ruthlessly pinned her down. Wasn't it nice his cahir's hands were so big he could hold her in place as well as use his thumbs to part her folds?

The moonlight showed the sweet nub of nerves was swollen and ready for his tongue. He puffed a warm breath over it—and she jolted upward. She'd need a light touch.

Using just the tip of his tongue, he teased around the nub,

wanting to bring his fingers into play, as well. However, new to mating, she would be tender inside.

Instead, he'd tease her in a different area.

MOTHER OF ALL, every drag of Owen's tongue sent her higher. Oh, she needed more, wanted him to take her.

But his hands mercilessly pinned her hips to the ground, and she couldn't even move as he teased her to the brink, then slowed, then teased her to the edge again.

Her clit was impossibly sensitive and so swollen it throbbed. Nothing had ever felt so good, if only he'd let her come. Why didn't he let her come? Just a tiny extra…

He moved a hand down and her breath caught as she waited for him to touch her pussy, to enter her. His hand slid lower, and he slid a finger between her buttocks.

She stiffened. "What…?" She felt his finger circle her anus. "Not *there*."

His lips closed around her clit—and his laugh vibrated through the exquisitely sensitive nub until nothing else registered. Then his finger moved again right there, engulfing her in strange tingling sensations that somehow only added to what she felt from the front.

He licked around her clit, and his finger circled back there, and a clawing need rolled through her in an entirely new way. *Oh, oh, oh.*

As he sucked in teasing pulls on her clit, the pressure at her core increased until she trembled on the precipice. Every nerve in her lower half was awake and needy.

His finger breached the tiny rim of anal muscles.

Oh my Gods! The shocking sensation flung her right off the precipice into a molten lake of pleasure. Wave after wave of sensation surged through her, flooding her from toes to scalp until everything in her body simmered with satisfaction.

"Ah, now, what a nice reaction." Like a cougar setting a giant paw on a cub, he held her down with a hand on her pelvis and studied her with intent eyes. He licked over her clit and watched her as she shivered. Licked again.

"It'll do for the moment. Come here." Lying down beside her, he pulled her over his body as if she were a blanket.

Her head spun for a second. She was on top. Of Owen. His body was a furnace beneath her and so, so hard.

Freed of the full moon need—for a minute or two—she propped herself up with her forearms on his chest. She had questions.

OWEN SMILED AS the soft waves of her hair spilled over him in a black wave, cool against his skin.

She frowned at him. "You touched me…behind. It felt so strange."

Inexperienced. Embarrassed. Yet so refreshingly straightforward. Fuck, he really did like her. Reaching up, he gathered her silky hair and rearranged it down her back, letting the last of the moonlight illuminate her face. "I did. You're undoubtedly getting sore, so I used the other hole." He paused and decided to be equally honest. "When shifters share a female, they often use both holes. I wanted to see if anal sex was something you might eventually enjoy."

"Share a female?" The moonlight showed her cheeks darkening with a flush. "Sex with…" She shook her head, muttering to herself. "Of course they would. Don't be a stupid tinker."

"You're not stupid, little cat." He combed his fingers through her hair, releasing the lingering scent of her shampoo. "Far from it. Did you think you would learn all about the Daonain in a month?"

Her exasperated grumble made him grin.

"You don't smile enough," she murmured, running her fingers over his lips, tracing the lines beside his mouth. "So, what you're saying, brothers mate a female at the same time. Do only lifemates do that?"

"Anyone. If the littermates want and the female agrees. Most littermates believe enjoying a female together makes a mating more special."

"I thought you and your brother had been apart since you were teenagers. How do you know?"

"Females don't reach maturity until early twenties. Males are old enough somewhere between sixteen and eighteen. Gawain and I attended two Gatherings before our lives went separate ways."

"Oh."

Those two Gatherings had been quite educational for him and Gawain. Their experienced partners had taught them exactly how to please a female—and how to share a female for the enjoyment of them all. "We were energetic, enthusiastic and"— he gave her a rueful smile—"we mated so many females from moonrise to moonset that our dicks were raw when we finally staggered out into the morning sun."

Her eyes widened, and she burst into husky, infectious giggles.

His dick throbbed, letting him know it wouldn't mind some energetic exercise.

As her laughter faded, her gaze lowered. As she traced a finger over various scars on his chest, she bit her lip.

He gave her hair a tug. "Ask, Darcy."

ASK, HE SAID, as if talking about this stuff was easy. Maybe it was for normal shifters, but not so much for ones who'd been brainwashed by neurotic human inhibitions. As she tried to figure out how to phrase the question without revealing her own neurotic anxieties, she traced a long silvery scar from his shoulder down his chest. A light scattering of silky dark hair covered his contoured, solid pectorals—and didn't conceal the myriad of past wounds he'd taken.

He laid his hand over hers, and his voice deepened to a growl. "Darcy."

Fine. "Donal and Tynan are littermates. So are you and Gawain. But none of you wanted to…share me." *Did I do something wrong? Is there something wrong with me?* Those words didn't come out at all.

He snorted and pulled her down to kiss her. A sweet, comforting kiss she sure hadn't expected from the stern cahir. "Little cat, we didn't even discuss sharing you. You're too new to mating. Two males at once can be frightening—and would certainly be more cocks than you were ready for at once. One was enough, I think?"

"Oh." At the teasing quirk of his eyebrow, her tension relaxed. "Yes. It was." She blushed, remembering how Gawain had pressed inside her, hurting her, and filling her, and it had been wonderful.

The memory sparked an internal glow, one she was beginning to recognize. Her need was rising again, even more demanding this time.

She wiggled and realized her stomach rested on a very long, very erect cock. "Speaking of sharing…" She rubbed her pelvis against him, feeling his shaft jerk against her stomach. "It's selfish to keep certain things to yourself."

"Is it now?"

Oh, she loved when she could make him laugh.

"Then take what you need." He ran his hard hands up and down her arms. "I'm all yours."

Her mouth opened as delight surged over her. He was so very…dominant. "Really? I can…do what I want?"

"Aye." He opened his hands, letting her know she was free.

Pushing away the growing urgency, she leaned forward and initiated her first kiss. His lips were firm, and he kissed her back, letting her tongue fence with his...and she found his limits when she started to squirm on him.

Suddenly his hand was wrapped in her hair, holding her while his tongue invaded and plundered without mercy.

He released her eventually...when her head was filled with a hum of desire, and her breasts throbbed for his touch.

"Sorry." His lips twitched. "I can only stay on the receiving end for so long before instincts take over."

That was a good warning, she decided. Rather than answering, she kissed his chin, nipped his jaw, and felt his hands crush her arms before he remembered and released her.

She moved down to lick along his collarbone, tease out the flat nipples...and see if she could make them peak the way hers did.

They peaked, but were still tiny.

His stomach had ridges of muscle, like an old-fashioned washer-board. Farther down, his cock jutted upward from a dark tangle of hair. After giving him a second to object, she wrapped her hands around his shaft.

Oooh wow. Long, ever so long. Satin skin over a granite core, his erection radiated heat. Thick veins twined from the base to the mushroom head, and his woodsy scent was dark and strong here, enticing her to taste.

She licked over him and heard him inhale through his nose.

Her pussy swelled, demanding she straddle him and put him inside.

Not yet.

Instead, she licked around the head and closed her lips around the shaft, feeling him pulse with his own hunger. He needed her, too. Satisfaction seeped into her.

The taste of the salty drop from the tip of his cock made her center clench. She took him deeper in her mouth, sliding him up and down. The vision of how his shaft would feel inside her sent more wetness between her legs.

Sent more urgency through her.

She couldn't wait. "Um."

"Yes, kitten?" His face was strained as he quite obviously kept himself from taking what he wanted.

"Do people do matings this way? Can I?"

Her query was awfully inarticulate, but he understood. His grin flashed. "Aye, tinker. You can...for a while. Then I will take over...and take you."

That warning again.

She better not wait. Straddling him, she tried to figure out how to get the two parts to go together, and he obligingly reached down and held his cock up.

Perfect.

She was wet and slick, and the head slid right in, although the burn of her tender tissues made her suck in air. But need drove her on, and she took more of him, easing down gently as he moved his hand away.

Her center stretched around him—and oh, he felt so good. She rose up, slid down, and...realized he wasn't all in. Leaning forward, she braced her hands on his shoulders. "It doesn't fit."

His chuckle was reassuring. "It will, just take it slow."

He cupped her dangling breasts and ran his thumbs over her nipples.

The added sensation, heat and abrasion, made her wiggle, and she slid back down more.

His purr of approval made his chest vibrate.

Up and down. Oh, she could feel the stretch deep within. Each time she went a bit lower until finally, breathless at the sensation, she felt his groin against her buttocks. "In."

"Aye." His eyes were half-closed with pleasure, his lips

curved, and he looked so different that she leaned forward, lifting up so she could kiss him.

But she went too far and his shaft almost came out.

Laughing, he closed his big hands on her hips, seating her firmly back on his cock...much faster than she'd done it. She gasped at the feeling of the sudden fullness.

Before she could move, he lifted her up and yanked her down again, taking control.

A thrill ran across her nerves. Under her knees, the ground seemed to soften as she gave over to him and let go. Deep in her core, the coil of pleasure began to contract.

He was moving slowly, being careful not to hurt her, she realized, but... "More. I want more."

An eyebrow went up, and his eyes lit. "More you will get." He tried to move his hand down between them, but she was leaning too far forward and his hand was too big.

His eyes narrowed, and then he smiled, a wicked light in his eyes. "No, I think you will take me another way, little cat—one that puts your ass in the air for me."

Before she could understand what he meant, he lifted her off entirely, pulling his cock out and setting her in the grass. She started to roll over to her back, when he grasped her around the waist and turned her, positioning her on her arms and knees.

"What are you doing?" Belatedly, she realized he'd knelt behind her, and her ass was...right there.

He ran his hands over her bottom, massaging her. "Fuck, I adore your ass."

"Uh, thanks?"

Laughing, he flattened his hand under her pelvis, holding her hips up. Then she felt him press his shaft against her pussy.

She frowned. The other males hadn't done it this way. "This isn't—"

"You're going to take me—and you're going to come this

way." He relentlessly pressed in, past the tiny burn of abused flesh at the entrance, and filled her.

Oh Gods.

He purred as he started sliding in and out, going deeper each time, filling her so full she had trouble finding her breath. The way he felt was…amazing. Her core compressed with excitement, with need, and she leaned forward and back, trying to make him move faster.

He laughed. "Push little cat." Gripping her hips, he forced her to the speed he wanted. Controlling her. "I'll speed up soon enough. First, let's get you ready."

As he pressed back in, he leaned forward. The angle changed and he went even deeper, making her gasp.

Bracing himself on one arm, he slid his other hand down her pelvis and over her clit.

The intense burst of pleasure was shocking, and she clenched around his cock, making him groan. His fingers never stopped, circling her clit, teasing over it, even as he continued the slow in-and-out. The pressure within wound tighter and tighter. Her body drew to a razor's edge, and she hung there, quivering.

Then he gripped her hips with both hands and his thrusts grew deeper as he took her, hard and fast. Within seconds, the rhythm took her over, pushing her ever higher, and then…then everything inside her convulsed, shattering her with overwhelming pleasure as she spasmed around his cock.

OWEN WATCHED THE little cat's back bow with her release—so fucking beautiful—and he kept thrusting, keeping her going until the clenching around his cock began to slow.

Then he let his body take over, and he hammered into her with short fast strokes as the pressure built at the base of his spine, until his balls were drawn up so painfully taut that he wanted to bellow out his need. With the last thrust, he pressed deep, deeper, and released. The heat streamed out his balls, through his cock, filling the little cat with his seed.

For the first time, he hoped his seed would find a home. He wanted to see her belly swelling with his cub. Wanted to—By the God, what was he thinking?

He shook the wayward thoughts out of his head and leaned down to kiss her hair.

She was trembling, panting, and her heart was pounding so vigorously he could almost hear it. The new shifter'd had two days of running as a cat, then an entire night of mating. Talk about being exhausted.

"Poor kitten," he murmured, straightening and running his hands over her back. The feeling of the scars from where she'd been whipped flattened his mouth. By the God, he'd see that never happened again.

He frowned as he eased himself out of her. When she started to fall forward, he gently rolled her onto her side. She was half-asleep, and he should get her back to the fire. The moon had set. She could rest now.

But… He'd heard some females, after mating, some wanted to be held. He'd never… And yet…

He lay down behind her and pulled her back against his chest, curling around her to keep her warm, to protect her…to show her that she wasn't alone.

When she sighed and wrapped her hands around his forearms, keeping him close, a tiny sprig of contentment uncurled inside his chest.

Chapter Seventeen

I N THE BACKSEAT of Gawain's car, Darcy sat with her knees against her chest, staring out the window, and trying to understand her life.

Earlier, she'd walked out with the males to where they'd hidden their clothing. Gawain had dashed ahead and fetched spare clothing from his car for her to wear.

Donal and Tynan had left.

Dressed in Gawain's clothes, she was riding back to Cold Creek with him and Owen. Although Owen had offered her the front seat, Darcy had climbed into the back, because she wasn't supposed to be in a car or really, in human form outside of Cold Creek. Was this how a criminal would feel?

She sighed. Life was sure strange. And uncomfortable.

Every time she looked toward the front, Gawain's eyes in the rearview mirror caught hers. Even in a mirror, his intense gaze was piercing, and she remembered the way his hands had felt on her body, the thickness of his shaft, how the muskiness of his scent had increased with his lust.

Her face turned hot with her flush, and she turned her head to stare out the side window again.

Four males. She'd mated with *four* males last night.

Donal had been gentle and kind, Tynan more…bossy. She

was fond of them both, but if there hadn't been a full moon drowning her in overwhelming need, she wouldn't have mated with them.

Gawain, though. Oh, she cared for him too much, under the full moon or not. When he talked with her, looked at her, touched her—it was the same as being plugged into an electrical socket, full of sizzle and heat.

He was fun. Caring. Gentle, yet he had an unsettling core of strength. He matched his cahir blades—beautiful, smooth, balanced perfectly—and deadly sharp. She loved how he'd laughed, eyes dancing with enjoyment of life, even as he mated her so very...thoroughly.

In the passenger seat, Owen turned to look at her, and his dark green gaze ran over her like a firm caress.

He was vastly different from his brother.

Had she ever met anyone so difficult to understand? Still, he'd been open with her. Honest and blunt and...kind.

He was also extremely dominant. If he were a wolf, he'd be the pack alpha. Last night, he'd told her what would happen, what he'd do...what she'd do. And he'd followed through. He hadn't been cruel—on the contrary—but firm with an edgy roughness, and very demanding.

Why did she have to like him so much?

Be honest, timid tinker. She more than liked him and Gawain, even though they were nothing resembling the males she'd daydreamed about as a child. Her fantasy lifemates had been sweet, gentle, funny. Tall and slender. Not huge and muscular.

Certainly not blunt or deadly or...she smiled slightly...*grumpy.*

As a cub, she sure hadn't thought about the fact lifemates would...mate. Let alone might make love to their female at the same time.

At the thought of Owen's rough hands and Gawain's slow,

very thorough touch, warmth rolled up into her cheeks and pooled in her body. Oh *no*, what was she thinking? She could smell how her own body was reacting, which meant the males could scent her arousal as well. She closed her eyes in humiliation.

Owen already thought females were manipulative, greedy creatures, and he'd been kind to her—last night anyway. They both had. But it had also been obvious a full moon mating didn't mean anything more...serious. After all, she'd been with Donal and Tynan, too.

As her spirits sank, the heat zinging through her veins cooled. Gawain liked her well enough, and Owen had said he liked her, but that didn't mean either one would want more than friendship from her. They'd performed their...service...to her last night. Now, they'd return to being her mentors, nothing more. Lusting after them would be inappropriate, possibly even offensive.

She cared for them...too much...and she mustn't. Besides, she'd be leaving town the minute she could. Her mere presence endangered the Daonain.

Looking out the window, she was relieved to see Cold Creek's outskirts, then the small downtown. Gawain slowed and parked in front of Angie's Diner.

"Did we need to pick something up here?" she asked.

"A text came through," Owen said. "Calum said he'd be at the diner now."

"I'd hate to interrupt his breakfast."

Gawain snorted. "Nice excuse, but it won't work. We are summoned, sweetling."

Oh my Gods. She'd washed as best she could in the cold creek water, but it sure hadn't erased the fragrance of sex. Sex with four males. Humans would call her a slut.

She wasn't, was she? *No.* Having sex with multiple males

was a Daonain tradition—and it shouldn't matter if all the males knew she'd been a virgin.

So why did the whole thing feel purely embarrassing?

And now, meeting the Cosantir after everything that'd happened last night? It was too much. Just too much.

Owen opened the rear door and held his hand out for her to take, as if she were a granny incapable of standing on her own. Or a criminal he had to secure to ensure her compliance. *Honestly.*

She scowled. "I won't run."

A smile tipped the corners of his mouth. "I doubt you'd run from anything…except maybe being embarrassed." Even as she stared at him, he hauled her out of the vehicle and headed for the diner. With an iron-hard arm around her waist.

Gawain walked on her other side.

Uh-huh. Criminal. Even if she wanted to run, she'd undoubtedly trip over the rolled-up legs of Gawain's jeans. He'd had to string a rope around the waist to hold them up.

With a sigh, she straightened her shoulders and marched inside.

Sparsely filled, the diner had a wooden floor, blue-checked vinyl tablecloths, and a long glass-fronted counter filled with goodies.

In a back corner, Calum sat with his mate, Vicki. When he saw Darcy, his expression went cold.

He was angry. At her. Her stomach felt as if she'd eaten a mass of wriggling grubs. "Oh, he's going to kill me," she said under her breath.

With his arm still around her, Owen looked down. "You weren't seen by any human, so probably not."

Oh, Goddess. Calum's killing her was a possibility? Her feet stopped dead in the center of the diner. Someone had said Cosantirs had the right of high, middle, and low justice, so

Calum *could* execute shifters.

But, but, but…

Beside Calum, Vicki gave her a tiny smile and made a slight motion with her fingers. *Come.*

Darcy pulled in a breath and tried to locate her spine. If he killed her, at least he'd do it quickly and neatly—not torture her as the Scythe would. As often as she'd thought she'd be dead, shouldn't she be getting used to it by now? Jaded?

Why did she have such a cold feeling in her belly?

Owen dropped his arm from around her waist, maybe so she could walk to her death without looking as if she was being coerced. "Come, little cat. Time to fess up."

Gawain squeezed her shoulder with his big blacksmith's hand. "We won't leave you."

We? Both him *and* Owen?

Owen nodded agreement.

Wow, it was almost like having protective brothers only…not. Because…

Gawain's gaze softened as he touched her cheek with his fingers. As if he, too, remembered all the incredibly intimate things he'd done to her last night.

She flushed and forced her feet forward to the table.

Calum rose politely. "Cahir. Mage." A muscle flexed in his jaw. "Darcy." A quiet gesture was an order for them to take seats.

She took the chair Gawain held out, relieved when he sat beside her.

Owen pulled a chair from another table, so he could sit on her other side.

"Good morning, Cosantir. Vicki," Gawain said blandly, as if Darcy wasn't about to be executed for defying a Cosantir's orders.

Owen nodded to Vicki. He leaned back in his chair, stretching out his legs. "Calum, you look like someone stole your breakfast bunny."

The Cosantir straightened. "Quite observant of you, cahir."

Darcy elbowed the stupid cahir in the ribs and whispered, "*Stop* it. You're going to get me *killed*." Belatedly, she remembered everyone at the table was a shifter with very good hearing.

Owen shook his head. "Nah. As an honorable adult, Calum wouldn't cut down a tree to move a branch out of his path."

The Cosantir's eyes narrowed. "Owen, you're—"

"Do you remember how Breanne ran off to Seattle to rescue her human neighbors?" Owen took a coffee cup from the stack on the table and poured himself a cup. "At least Darcy was trying to save other Daonain."

Vicki's hand was over her mouth, and her eyes were laughing.

The Cosantir wasn't amused. When his...black...gaze focused on her, the bottom of her stomach dropped out. "How badly were the Daonain exposed?" Calum's quiet voice reminded her of how soft a cougar's paws could be...until the claws appeared.

"I was careful and stayed in cat form the entire time. I avoided humans, roads, and camping areas. No one saw me."

"Cosantir." Owen's voice was rough. "She's scraped, bruised, starving, and footsore from staying shifted. It's not her fault she didn't learn the Law or about possible problems. That's on me for not teaching her better."

"I do realize that," Calum said. "However—"

"There should be consequences, aye." Gawain ran his hand down her arm in a comforting move. "However, I might note she's already suffered for her less-than-wise choice. Her first Gathering...as a virgin...was not in a comfortable, warm room with soft cushions and a fireplace, but isolated on a freezing mountain with four males she barely knows."

Virgin. Oh, he just had to put that in, didn't he? Darcy glared at him.

"Jesus fucking Christ," Vicki muttered. "And I thought *I* had problems on my first." She turned to her mate. "I know this isn't a democracy, oh guardian of the territory, but I'm all for mercy in this case."

Calum's lips twitched, and the darkness in his gaze lightened. "You would be."

When his attention returned to Darcy, she fought not to shrink down in the chair. In the *priosan*, Director had ruled with promises of pain. Calum needed no words, no actions. The power was simply his.

"Do you realize how lucky you are in your advocates?" he asked. "It appears you've made friends here—even with the cahir who avoids females. You're finding your place within the Daonain, Darcy, and I'm pleased to see it."

Darcy blinked. Friends? "I…" She had friends?

Yes. Yes, she did.

She looked up at Gawain who smiled, at Owen who didn't, and Vicki who gave her a laughing look. "Thank you all."

"Do you realize the dangers of leaving Cold Creek?" Calum asked. "And will you stay until your control is adequate?"

"Yes, sir." The answer was automatic.

Vicki grinned. "Give me a few months, and I could make a Marine out of her."

The sound Calum made was exasperated, but his arm went around his mate, pulling her closer. "Thank you, no. One of you in this territory is enough for the Gods to handle."

Gawain chuckled, and then his smile fell away. "Darcy found a trace of a scent on a trail near the Twin Sisters, so we'll concentrate around there. Has there been any news of the Scythe?"

"Tynan said someone requisitioned the traffic cameras records from around Seward Park. It's good you two were careful when you entered the park." Calum shook his head. "With no luck in Seattle, they are searching farther afield. They're working their way through the forest towns."

"I'll die first." Darcy heard the quiver in her voice. "I'll make them kill me before I let them take me back."

Owen closed his hand over hers. "They'd have to go through me first." His voice was steady, calm.

"And me." With an arm over her shoulders, Gawain leaned her against his muscular frame. "Relax, catling. You're safe here."

"This isn't a tiny village like Dogwood. Our town has some serious resources," Vicki said. "Speaking of which, my old boss is in Alec's office," Vicki said. "The minute we told Wells about the Scythe, he went into investigation mode. He wants to talk if you're up to it."

"Of course." Wells was the big shot human spy. That was fighting fire with fire. "I'll tell him everything I know."

"Very good." Calum tapped his fingers on his coffee mug. "While the search continues for your Dogwood people, please continue to work with your mentors. Learn to survive in animal form and how to live as a Daonain. As soon as we find out anything about the Scythe or your villagers, I'll let you know."

It wasn't enough—and yet it had to be.

Darcy sighed. If it hadn't been for the need to find her brothers and save her friends, this would have been the most wonderful time of her life. She glanced up at Gawain and met his concerned gaze.

Owen's expression was worried, along with a stubborn expression she was beginning to know. He'd make sure she obeyed the Cosantir. His hand was still over hers—as if he had the right to touch her. Because last night, he had. He'd…*known*…her. Been inside her, bit her, tasted her.

Her shoulders straightened, and she pulled her hand away, moved away from Gawain. She mustn't let herself fall for these males. If the Scythe came for her, they'd be killed—because they'd try to protect her.

She sighed, knowing there was no choice but to let others search for the *prìosan* and shifter-soldier camp. Experienced shifters could look for the Dogwood captives far more unobtrusively than she could.

After the locations were found, then... A chill crept through her. Then it got scary.

Although Calum had been wonderful about letting his people search, she doubted he'd be willing to lose his people while rescuing shifters who weren't his own. The Dogwood males would have to do the rescue of the females, and they needed to know that the females were dying. The risks had changed.

Somehow, she'd have to convince the Cosantir to let her be the one to sneak in and make contact with the shifter-soldiers. She rather doubted the males would believe a stranger.

But, even beyond that, sneaking into the forest camp would be...dangerous. Too dangerous to risk anyone but her. If the Scythe caught a Cold Creek shifter, they'd have a new hostage and—far worse—would know there were more shifters in the area.

However, if she made the contact and the Scythe caught *her*, they wouldn't realize she'd had help.

If they caught her... Wrapping her arms around herself, she tried not to shiver. She'd not let them catch her alive.

To keep Cold Creek and the Daonain safe, this task was hers and hers alone.

GAWAIN SCOWLED AS he watched Darcy follow Calum out the

diner's back door. Since the Cosantir was returning to the tavern, he'd drop her and Vicki at the sheriff's office to meet with Wells.

Gawain and Owen needed to go to the hardware store to order plumbing supplies for the master baths, but still…

"We could have driven Darcy to the lodge," Owen growled, opening the diner's front door.

"My thoughts exactly." Gawain followed onto Main Street. "She's pulling away from us."

"Aye."

Gawain fell into step as they strolled down the street. "Can't blame her. She's new to everything. And last night…" The intensity had left him stunned. Her sweetness and honesty had taken him by storm. It had felt as if everything they were had touched: body-to-body, mind-to-mind.

"Last night was"—Owen cleared his throat and studied the street as if it held the answers he needed—"different."

"Brawd, I've never felt this way before. I know you avoid females, but she's special. She's…she's got a grip on my soul."

To his surprise, Owen nodded. "Mine, too. And…I don't…mind."

That was an admission Gawain had never expected. "What are you saying?"

Owen rubbed his neck in the self-grooming a cat did when uneasy. "Not sure, mage. I want her, aye, and I'd prefer to say the attraction is merely physical, but it isn't. I enjoy being with her. Want to share her with you—for mating and for…more."

As a cub, Gawain had learned to stay silent as a rock if he wanted Owen to talk.

"Females annoy…used to annoy me, but I'm learning they're not all the same. I like some of them. She's one. No, she's more than that." Owen scowled. "Pisses me off some."

Aaand, there was his grouchy littermate. Gawain stifled a grin. "Time to go on the hunt, then. She doesn't get to pull away—unless she really doesn't want us." They'd know from her scent if nothing else. "We'll run the trail and see where it leads."

"Yeah." Owen shook his head. "Probably straight into an abyss."

"There's that optimistic spirit we all know and love."

"Clay-brained cougar." Owen shoved him off the sidewalk.

Stumbling, Gawain caught himself on a parked vehicle. "You puny, pox-ridden, pumpkin-headed panther." As he shoved upright, he froze. Dark van. Tinted windows. Empty. It fit the description of the Scythe vehicles Owen had mentioned. Slowly, he backed away from the SUV.

Had Owen noticed?

No, Owen was already heading into the hardware store. An elderly woman stopped him in the doorway.

After brushing off his shirt, Gawain joined the two.

"Sounds good. I'll bring it over," Owen said to the woman. As she walked away, he grinned at Gawain. "She bought the carving of the stag."

"Great."

Owen's eyes narrowed. "What's wrong?"

"Turn casually and check out the van behind you."

Owen held open the hardware store door for Gawain and used the movement to glance at the van. "Good eye, brawd. Spitting image of the Scythe vans in Seattle. Got that same remote button on the visor."

"I figured." Gawain walked in. The store was empty except for young Warren behind the counter.

Already on his cell phone, Owen said, "Alec, we got a black van by the hardware store. No one's in it, but I'd guess our tinker's *friends* are visiting."

After a murmur from the phone, Owen nodded. "Will do." Pocketing his phone, he told Gawain, "Alec'll warn Calum. We're to visit BOOKS, give Joe Thorson an ears-up, and he'll inform the rest of downtown.''

"Sounds good." Thorson. Right. He'd been the tough old shifter who had helped fight the hellhound two weeks ago.

Lifting a hand to Warren, Owen headed out the door.

Across the street at the small bookstore, the bell over the door tinkled as they entered.

Owen walked to the counter. "Thorson."

The owner looked up from his paperwork. "Aye?" The old shifter had a myriad of thin claw scars on his face, hands and arms—evidence of a lifetime of fighting.

As Owen leaned over the counter to talk quietly, Gawain glanced around the store…and spotted a coffee machine. Just what he needed after the long night. He nodded toward the machine, caught Owen's unspoken request for his own cup, and moved away.

As he walked between bookshelves toward the rear, the scent of a human reached him…along with the stink of gun oil. Was one of the Scythe weasels in the store?

Gawain rolled his shoulders, stopped to peruse a shelf of mysteries, and pulled one out. He raised his voice. "Hey, bro, would you believe I found the mystery you wanted?"

He could hear the stunned silence before Owen called back. "Is the sequel there, too?"

Gawain could only scent one male and see only one shadow at the end of the shelving, unmoving. Undoubtedly, Thorson would confirm. "Nope. Want this one?"

"Nah, I hate cliffhangers. I'll wait for the next and buy them both."

What was the all-purpose word the humans used? "*Whatever.*" After replacing the book, Gawain continued toward the coffee. If he needed to fight, he wanted caffeine first. Then again, having an enemy so close had certainly accelerated his heart—because the human was after Darcy. *My* Darcy.

At the coffee machine, he glanced back. Owen still stood at the counter, and the fury in his gaze was more than a cahir's protective anger.

The catling was rapidly becoming *our* Darcy.

As Gawain set a cup under the spout, the human approached. About five-eleven and bulky with muscle. His brown hair was cut short. His posture was that of an aggressive young wolf, eagerness to fight in every movement. His smile didn't reach his cold brown eyes. "How's the coffee?"

Gawain tasted the dark roast. He'd seen a coffee advertisement last week. What was the name? *Star Stags? No.* "It's not Starbucks, but it's good."

"Great." The human picked up a cup. "I'm lookin' for work. You know anyone hiring around here?"

Clever, wasn't he? Job-hunting would permit him to ask plenty of questions. "Bad timing, I'm afraid. Tourist season is winding down, and most positions here are seasonal."

"Huh. I hadn't thought about winter coming." The man picked up his drink and eyed Gawain. "You don't look like a shopkeeper. You a logger or something?"

Gawain smiled easily. "Blacksmith, actually. I sell ironworks to the tourist shops."

"Wouldn't you sell more if you were closer to Seattle?"

"Some stores there carry my work, but"—how nice he had a logical reason—"there are fewer regulations way out here and less expensive licensing fees for running a forge."

The man's interest in him visibly died. "Yeah, no one wants to pay for licenses."

As Gawain returned to the front, he noted Thorson had disappeared and Owen stood behind the counter. Why the switch? Gawain raised his eyebrows.

Silently, Owen turned his hands over, showing the almost unscarred backs.

Of course. The owner had distinctive werecat scarring. He'd probably grown up somewhere with no healer. The Scythe might have noted similar scars on their captives.

Owen raised his voice slightly. "The old fool's feeling sick and asked me to watch the counter."

"Fool?" Gawain picked up the obvious hint.

"The idiot had supper at Angie's Diner last night. I've warned him before about eating there."

Gawain choked. "If she hears you say that, she'll be pissed." Yeah, she'd rip out Owen's throat out with her bare teeth.

His brother's eyes lit. Damn cahir was addicted to risk, wasn't he?

"Now what?" Gawain asked under his breath. Keep the weasel here? Let him leave? Kill him? Gawain had never killed a *human*, but he was open to new and intriguing experiences.

"Patience, brawd." Owen pretended to fiddle with papers on the counter.

Patience it was. Leaning on the counter, Gawain rambled about the weather, the football season, the increase in gas taxes. When painting the walls last week, he'd protected the floors with newspapers—and read the headlines.

After a few minutes, the weasel approached the counter with a book in his hand. "I'll take this one." He handed Owen a twenty.

Owen took the money and scowled, obviously realizing he had to get change from a cash register.

Technology and Owen…not a good combination. Gawain ducked under the counter, opened the old-fashioned register, and smirked at his littermate. "You should have taken a part-time job when you were younger like I did."

Owen sneered. "Thank you, no."

"You must be brothers. Which of you is older?" the human asked.

Gawain stiffened. Saying they were the same age would be a clue they were Daonain, wouldn't it?

"I am," Owen said easily. "By a couple of years."

The bell rang as the bookstore door opened. Vicki strolled in, one hand on her bulging middle in the protective way pregnant women had. She had a shopping bag in her other hand. "Hey, guys."

Truly, Calum and his littermate had hit gold with their mate—her smile brightened the room almost as well as Darcy's did. She turned that lethal weapon on the weasel, and Gawain almost laughed when the human smiled back.

"Hi there," Vicki said. "I haven't seen you before. Are you touristing or a new resident?"

"Ah, neither, exactly." The weasel shifted his weight under the burden of her sweet regard. "I might move here though. I'm job-hunting."

"Ugh, I don't think anyone enjoys looking for work. What's your occupation? No, wait, let me guess." She tilted her head. "Hmm. Maybe a teacher?"

Terrifying thought.

"Ah, no. I'm—"

"Phooey. Let me see your hands." Laughing merrily, she took one hand and looked at the back, then turned it over to study the palm. "My sister and I pretended to read fortunes at Halloween. Let's see… Your Mount of Venus is on the flatter side, so you're less influenced by emotions.

The human grinned. "Probably right."

"So, maybe business?" Vicki frowned. "Or, no—the Mounts of Mars, inner and outer, show you're brave and into adventurous stuff. Maybe a ski instructor? White-water rafting? Or there are soldiers who have strong Mounts of Mars."

The twitch of his lower lip was like a shout, before the human grinned. "Sorry, ma'am. Nothing so interesting. I'm just a minimum-wage guy. I can run a cash register, stock shelves, do bartending, and wait tables. Basic shit." All places where people congregated.

"Speaking of cash registers"—the weasel turned to Owen— "any chance the old guy here is hiring?"

"Sorry, it's a one man operation." Owen shook his head. "I don't know anyone who's looking for workers right now."

Vicki tapped a finger on her lips. "Let me think. Maybe over at the B&B? No, I think they're good. Or the grocery. No, he prefers to hire high school kids. The tavern only has barmaids, which does seem rather sexist, don't you think?"

Gawain stared. Had she just accused the Cosantir of being sexist?

"I'm not gonna point any fingers," Owen said with a grin. "I think the tavern owner keeps a shotgun behind the bar."

Vicki's eyes widened. "Oh, I'm sure that's just a rumor."

Gawain watched in awe. When Vicki'd mentioned her past as a spy, he hadn't taken her seriously. He should have.

As she babbled away, acting as if she had fewer brains than a tree sprite, the Scythe agent relaxed and leaned against the counter, obviously hoping for tidbits.

"The gas station...well, they use their own kids...and, although teens always insist they're overworked, I don't think some practical experience hurts a child. Have you noticed how whiny the next generation is about doing a bit of work?"

"No shit." The human nodded, totally pulled into the conversation.

"My kid isn't going to be lazy," Vicki said with a decided pat on her big belly.

"Good to hear." The weasel smiled. "Are you going to have a boy or a girl?"

"Oh, my husband doesn't want to know. He wants to be surprised." Vicki pouted. "I think he's awfully unfair. How am I supposed to know whether to decorate the nursery in blue or pink? Or what color of baby clothes to get?" The color of the baby's room was obviously the most important concern in her life.

"Maybe you should go for green or beige," Gawain suggested.

She gave him a shocked stare. "What's the fun in that?"

"Wait till you get married, bro. You'll learn how important women consider these things," Owen told him knowledgeably— as if he'd ever spoken to a female outside of a Gathering.

Gawain managed not to laugh.

"Well, I'm blathering on. I just popped in to grab some decaf coffee, although I have to say, if there's no caffeine in the coffee, it's not nearly as satisfying. But my doctor is all full of telling me how caffeine is bad for the baby and how a sip of wine will make her—or him—be born with no brains or something."

No, she wasn't merely good; she was brilliant.

As the human edged away from her, she leaned forward and patted his arm. "I'm afraid I can't think of anyone looking to hire. But best of luck in finding a job."

Having somehow acquired a disarming waddle, she walked toward the rear of the store.

The Scythe agent picked up his book. "Doesn't look like I'm going to find a job here. I guess I'll try the next town down the road."

"Those are the breaks," Gawain said. "Good jobs are tough to come by."

Owen merely nodded.

As the door closed behind the human, Vicki wandered back with a cup in hand and nary a waddle. Sneaky female.

"Nice act," Owen said.

Gawain watched the human cross the street, climb into his

van, and drive away. "That's it? We're just going to let him go?"

"Actually, no," Vicki said. "My job was to stall him long enough for Wells to place a tracker under his bumper. He'll have people monitoring where the bastard goes."

"Perfect." Owen gave her an approving nod.

The bell rang as Thorson shoved the door open. The old werecat stopped and sniffed. "Damned stinking human. I'll be smelling him all day."

"Poor Joe." Vicki patted his arm. "Wells is in town and said he'll be by later. He wanted to be sure you still had his favorite French roast."

"Another damn human? I'll have to fumigate the place."

"You're just stewing that the spymaster beat your furry ass at chess last month." Owen grinned at Gawain. "The two play every time Wells is in town."

"At least he can play. You cubs lack the patience for a decent game," Thorson said.

Chess? Mother and Hunter, but it'd been a while. Gawain smiled. "I have an adequate amount of patience."

Thorson gave him a skeptical stare. "You any good?"

Gawain ignored Owen's snort and said mildly, "Fair."

The old werecat grunted. "You're on. Anytime during store hours." Thorson rested his scarred-up hand on Vicki's shoulder. "You planning to ever have those cubs?"

"Cub, Thorson. I'm shooting for one. Just one. A single baby. Fuck this *litter* bullshit."

Gawain smothered a smile. The Daonain didn't often have singletons.

Thorson gave her a cynical half-smile.

"Don't even say it." She rolled her eyes. "And, for your question, according to Donal, babies come when the Mother decides and not before."

"Ah, well." Thorson snorted. "Difficult to argue with that

kind of a statement."

"Yeah, the healer's fucking sneaky that way."

Gawain grinned. Calum's mate had the vocabulary of a drunken dwarf.

"C'mon, you two." She motioned toward the door. "Calum and Wells will want a report."

As Gawain turned to follow her and his brother, Thorson cleared his throat. "Come by for a game tomorrow, mage. We'll see if you have more brains than a pixie."

"You're on."

THE STREET FELT cleaner without the Scythe van on it, Owen thought, as they crossed the street toward the sheriff's office. He walked on Vicki's left, pleased Gawain automatically took her right. The van might have left, but neither of them was about to be careless with her safety.

"Joe's delighted to find a new chess player." Vicki raised her eyebrows at Owen. "Is your brother going to get slaughtered?"

With a straight face, Owen said lightly, "Who knows?" Owen had lost a game or two to the old werecat…barely. With Gawain, Thorson would be slaughtered. As cubs, no one gave Gawain enough of a challenge, and he'd taken to playing chess online with other fanatics. "How long since you had a game, brawd?"

"A few months. I've missed it." At a patch of cracked concrete, Gawain put his hand under Vicki's arm to help her.

She scowled. "I'm pregnant, not fucking incapacitated."

Owen grinned.

Her spine was straight, head was up, and she walked a step in front of them as if determined not to slow them down. Yeah, he liked the feisty little female. Honest, blunt, brave. Her mates—and Calum's teenaged daughter—adored her because, despite trying to hide it, she had a tender heart.

He didn't. So why did he wonder how many good people he'd ignored because they were female. He growled under his breath. Fucking self-evaluation was a pain in the tail.

Vicki led the way into the police station, past the reception desk, and motioned to a door on the right. "Alec's out on Main Street, but Wells is in there with Darcy."

Owen stepped into the conference room.

Wells was seated at a long rectangular table across from Darcy. From her pale color, Owen figured the spymaster had quizzed her about the Scythe's *prìosan.*

Calum was pacing up and down the room. When Vicki came in, he growled and pulled her into his arms...very gently. "You…"

"Relax, boss cat." She kissed his chin. "Stalling a dimwitted foot-soldier for a few minutes is hardly dangerous."

Belatedly, Owen realized why the Cosantir was so furious. "You didn't ask her to come to the bookstore?"

"I did not."

Vicki turned to look at Owen. "Wells and I were in here when you called, so we made a plan while Alec notified Calum."

"Ah, right." Owen retreated a step from Calum.

After detouring around the seething Cosantir, Gawain sat beside Darcy...and quietly appropriated her hand.

Good job, brawd. Owen positioned himself behind her and Gawain. Felt right, guarding these two that he… Guarding these two.

When Darcy turned to look at him, he tugged a lock of her black hair and stepped back. Folding his arms over his chest, he nodded at Wells. "Go ahead."

Wells looked from him to Darcy, obviously caught the warning, and his head tilted an infinitesimal degree. The lean spymaster had icy blue eyes, gray hair the color of his tailored suit, and was the most calculating person Owen had ever met. A notepad sat in front of him. "Miss MacCormac was telling me about the Scythe plans." He pointed his pen at Darcy, his eyes narrowed. "Why would competent operatives discuss secrets where you could hear?"

"They didn't. I mean they didn't know I was there."

Owen moved to the side a step so he could see her face. Her color had returned to normal and she'd relaxed...maybe because she trusted him and Gawain to care for her. It was a satisfying thought.

"Explain," Wells snapped.

When she flinched, Owen growled—as did Gawain.

The spymaster sat back carefully. "Forgive my impatience, Miss MacCormac. Discovering a covert organization is manipulating US politics, well, I fear it eroded my manners."

"I understand," Darcy said softly. "To answer your question, the *priosan* staff didn't converse in front of the hostages. However, whenever an outside visitor spent the night, I'd listen outside the window of the guest suite. Director enjoyed having drinks with them in the evenings, and it wasn't long before they were boasting about what they'd done."

"No patrols?"

"Yes, guards walk the grounds. But the floodlights only reach to the top of the first floor. The rooms for the staff and Scythe visitors are on the second floor." She smiled slightly. "Ivy-covered brick walls aren't difficult to climb."

"I see. Nicely done." Wells gave her a respectful nod.

Owen couldn't help but visualize how fucking easy it would have been for the little cat to have been spotlighted like a fly on the wall—and filled with bullets. His jaw clamped down so violently his teeth might start cracking.

"Armed guards, a stone wall around the property, an automated steel gate with a guardhouse, concealed machine gun nests, floodlights." Wells tapped his pen on the notepad.

Vicki scowled "Very third world, isn't it?"

"Once the place is located, managing a rescue without casualties will be tricky." Wells glanced at Calum. "I understand your concerns are only for the captive shifters. My job will include freeing the human hostages."

Calum nodded. "I assumed you would feel that way. But first we have to find them."

Chapter Eighteen

D ARCY WALKED DOWN the stairs from her bedroom in the lodge. What should she do today?

Not shopping, obviously. After the Scythe showed up in Cold Creek last week, the Cosantir had ordered her to stay away from downtown.

Bree and her mates now locked the lodge's front door—in case some Scythe operative showed up—which meant giving keys to their lodgers.

By the Mother, Darcy had caused everyone so much trouble.

Rather than a valuable addition to the town, she was a perilous guest. The knot in her stomach grew. What if the Scythe realized this was a shifter town? What if someone got hurt?

She'd leave, dammit, but she was stuck, caged by Daonain Law and by the need to know when the Cold Creek searchers located her villagers.

Maybe she'd spend the day in the forest. Owen and Gawain had given her permission, as long as she stayed away from the town. She wrinkled her nose. Running the trails alone wasn't nearly as much fun, but her mentors were working on their house, hunting for the villagers, and running their smithing and carving businesses.

Just as well. She wanted to decrease the time she spent with them. Although it hurt to see less of them. Actually hurt as if she'd stubbed her heart on an unseen stone or something.

Stay strong, tinker.

She lifted her chin. Maybe she could talk Bree into going for a run.

As she crossed the main room, a high-pitched shriek came from outside in the back.

Heart hammering, Darcy ran out the back doors. The patio was empty.

At the sound of chittering, she checked the sprite in the spruce tree. The pixie was watching the creek below her.

Darcy followed its gaze and grinned.

Where the patio ended, a long expanse of tended grass rolled downhill. Five cublings around four or five years old were making stick castles beside the burbling creek. *Just look at them.* All fat legs and round stomachs.

Under the water, the silvery undines swirled with delight, brushing up against any fingers that ventured in their stream—and reducing the cubs to infectious giggles. One water elemental sent a thin stream of cold water toward a cubling.

The boy let out a scream and fell backward, laughing so hard he couldn't sit up.

Well, there was the source of the shriek.

Bonnie, Emma, and a younger female lounged nearby.

"Darcy, perfect." Bree walked out of the kitchen, carrying a tray filled with sandwiches and cookies. "I was about to call you downstairs and see if you wanted to join us. Emma and her cub just arrived."

"Is this a special occasion?"

Bree handed her the tray and disappeared back in the kitchen. Her voice drifted out. "We're just taking advantage of such a warm, sunny day. Bonnie, Emma and their cubs adore Zeb's little playground and the creek. You met them already, right?"

"At the Wild Hunt, yes." Curvy, tall, golden Emma was the bard; shorter, brown-haired Bonnie was Owen and Gawain's littermate.

"There are also a couple of wolf pack cubs with today's caregiver. I try to keep an eye on the pack cubs when I can." She reappeared with another tray of milk, iced tea, and glasses. "It's kind of part of the alpha female duties."

Right, Bree was a wolf. But alpha female? "If you're alpha female, does that mean Shay or Zeb is the alpha male?"

"Yes, Shay is alpha, Zeb beta." Bree led the way onto the grass and set the food on a flattened, polished log that had obviously been created to serve as a knee-high serving table. "The pack had a rough time before Shay arrived, but he's got it functioning fairly well now."

"I bet he does." Shay was not only a natural leader, but also the kind of person who took care of everyone around them. Setting her tray down, Darcy looked around.

The three other females sat on blankets strategically positioned out of splashing range. Emma wore her golden hair in a long braid. In jeans and a tank top, a slender redhead in her early twenties was talking to her. Bonnie apparently had monitor duty—her gaze stayed on the children.

"Look, it's Darcy!" Smiling, Emma pushed to her feet and tossed her braid over her shoulder.

Bonnie looked up and waved.

At the table, Emma pulled Darcy into a big hug. Yes, the female was totally a bear. "I hoped you'd come."

The sincerity in her voice made Darcy blink quickly.

"Hey, Bree!" A cub with wavy golden-brown hair, dashed up from the bank. "Bree!"

After some happy hugs, Bree said, "Darcy, this is Minette who belongs to Emma, Ben, and Ryder."

The cubling had beautiful hazel eyes, fair skin, round cheeks.

"Hi, Minette. It's nice to meet you." Darcy glanced at Emma. "I don't think I know Ben or Ryder."

As Emma poured iced tea for the females and handed the glasses out, she said, "I don't think you were introduced, but Ben said he met you here one day. On the patio."

"He's a cahir—a grizzly—and simply huge," Bree added.

On the patio, huge cahir. Darcy gave an embarrassed huff. "I remember. He was there when I got in trouble for being in cougar form too close to the lodge."

Emma gave her a sympathetic smile. "I've been on the receiving end of a cahir scolding; I know the pain. But Ben feels awful that he upset you."

Darcy snorted. "I upset myself. I hate doing stupid things."

Coming up to accept a glass, the redheaded female laughed. "Oh, I know!" She took a cookie from Bree and continued, "I'm Nia. Bonnie and I are the wolf cub-watchers today."

"They look like they'll keep you busy."

Nia rolled her eyes. "I'm rethinking ever having cubs."

"You'll change your mind when you find the right mates," Bree told her.

"The right mates? Not happening." Nia dropped down onto the blanket. "Bonnie, it's my turn to watch. Get yourself a cookie."

Once on her feet, Bonnie called, "Luke, Tyler, come and meet Darcy.

Two young boys about four ran over.

Bonnie beamed and turned to Darcy. "These are my two cubs, Tyler and Luke."

Aww. All bright eyes and bounce. "They're adorable."

"I think so." Grinning, Bonnie put an arm around each tiny body. "Cubs, this is Darcy who fixed your computer, so say thank you."

"T'ank you!" said one. The other gave her a hug.

So, so cute. She crouched down to their size and whispered, "Did you see what's watching you from the big tree?"

They turned and after a second, spotted the pixie swinging on the end of a branch, as if she was trying to get closer to the fun.

Their open delight in seeing her made the pixie do a fancy swing—and another when they cheered in glee.

"Sprites and cubs—they enjoy the same things, have you noticed?" Emma said, grinning.

"Everything is more fun with pixies and cublings," Darcy agreed. "I miss the tiny ones." The littlest in the *priosan* were now teenagers.

"Oh, girl, you're welcome to come and cub-watch anytime your heart desires," Bonnie said. She shook her head as one of her cubs jumped up onto a boulder—an amazing leap for someone so tiny—and pounced on his brother.

Bonnie grinned at Bree. "Shay taught him that leap."

"Shay loves to teach," Bree said. "And it's nice that they're learning some of those skills early."

Darcy scowled at the ground, remembering how she was still messing up her own jumps. She had to do better. When the shifter-soldier forest camp was located, she'd have to sneak past the guards to contact the males. And, if she had to take to the trees, she'd probably fall off a branch and get caught.

Or if the shifter-soldiers caught her scent, who knew how they'd react? She'd need to disguise her presence until she was close enough to speak with them.

Picking up a twig, she twirled it between her fingers. When the time came, she had to be ready to act—skillfully. It was time to work her tail off and master the skills she needed.

She looked up to see Nia nibbling on a cookie and studying her. The redhead said, "You must not be a wolf or you'd have joined us on the last pack run. So are you a bear? Or a mountain lion or panther or whatever term you felines are using these days?"

Emma laughed. "It's not fair, is it? A wolf is a wolf is a wolf, whereas cats are mountain lions or panthers or cougars or puma or…really, you guys have a dozen different names that all mean panther."

"Exactly!" Huffing, Nia pointed her finger at Emma and scowled. "I was *trying* to say that I don't *want* to know all those names. Bards, sheesh." She looked at Darcy. "So, what name of cat do you prefer?"

Such an indignant expression.

Darcy grinned. "I love how *mountain lion* sounds. Only when I'm in a hurry, two words are one too many, so I use cougar mostly, only the humans use that now to mean an older woman hooking up with a younger man, so I use panther now, too."

Nia's vexed look deepened. "Oh my Gods, you're as bad as the bard."

When the laughter broke out, all the cubs turned to see what was going on—making everyone laugh harder.

As the females settled onto the blankets, Bree said to Darcy, "I saw your mentors head off together toward town. Did you escape a lesson today?"

"Gawain has a blade to forge, and Owen's doing something for the Cosantir. No lesson today." Darcy took a bite of cookie. Sugar and chocolate chips and walnuts. *Mmmm.*

"I bet it's a relief to escape," Nia muttered, gaze on the cublings.

Darcy blinked, caught Bree's slight shake of the head, and moved on. "I was going to go explore a new set of trails, but, this is so much nicer."

"Are Owen and Gawain teaching you anything besides hunting?" Bonnie asked before grinning at Bree. "I remember how ignorant our Bree was when first arrived. She didn't know anything about the Daonain or wolf packs. Or anything about Gatherings."

Darcy rolled her eyes. "I'm in the same sad shape."

"I can't even imagine how scary that must be. I'm new, but if you need someone to hang with at a Gathering, just yell." Nia frowned. "Did you attend the last Gathering in Cold Creek? I didn't see you."

Darcy felt her cheeks heat. "I wasn't there. I'd gone to the Twin Sisters to search for my people."

"On a Gathering night?" Nia's tone was scandalized.

"No one had told me about full moons or Gatherings. I guess I was lucky. My mentors as well as Donal and Tynan caught up to me before the moon rose." Remembering how gently the males had treated her...and how intimate it had gotten, her insides melted. Gawain and his laughing eyes and powerful body. Owen, such a mixture of rough and gentle.

Being with them, mating with them, had changed her.

Some forest pinecones wouldn't sprout until burned by fire. She'd been burned—and now love was sprouting in her heart. *Oh no. Don't be a turkey-brained tinker.* She mustn't—couldn't—be in love with them.

She was.

Oh my Gods.

She cleared her throat. "The males were all very kind to me, especially for my first full moon heat."

"Right. I'm glad for you. But, don't expect... Um." Nia's smile was bittersweet. "I found out the nasty way that what a male does under the full moon means nothing once the moon sets."

"What do you mean?" Darcy asked.

"Well, see, I mated Owen, and it was amazing. He was really nice." She shook her head. "Only, I thought he liked me, but when I saw him the next day, he said he didn't like me—or any female—and he hates that he has to fuck us once a month."

"He was awfully rude," Darcy's voice came out hesitant. Would even grumpy Owen have said something so mean?

Nia glanced at Bree. "You heard him."

Bree nodded with a sad look at Darcy.

"He did apologize, though." Nia wrinkled her nose. "Probably the Cosantir told him to."

Bonnie was frowning. "I'm sorry, Nia. Owen is…"

"Oh, it's all right. He was nasty, but I was silly to see more in a mating than was really there." Nia shrugged. "It was a lesson I needed to learn."

But such a harsh one.

Apparently, Darcy had needed the lesson, as well.

She knew he avoided females, although he did like her. He'd said so. However, like wasn't the same as love, now was it?

Nia wasn't the only foolish one. Akin to the cublings, Darcy had been building castles out of mud and had somehow forgotten that matings under a full moon weren't a prelude to a relationship.

Had Gawain or Owen said they loved her? No, they hadn't. The two were wonderful and protective…and her mentors. Nothing more. *Control your emotions, tinker.*

This really was for the best, anyway, since she'd be leaving Cold Creek. Love wasn't in her destiny.

Chapter Nineteen

G AWAIN HAD SPENT the day forging new blades for the cahirs' incoming students, but halted early to clean up at the lodge. Breanne was hosting a dinner party for the cahirs and their families to give Darcy a chance to meet everyone. Apparently, a couple of days ago at a creekside picnic, Darcy had mentioned she didn't know Ben and Ryder.

Gawain pulled on clean clothes, a better shirt than his usual white smithing ones and jeans.

No clothes on the floor meant Owen hadn't yet returned from dragging Darcy out for a quick hunt. Undoubtedly, they'd be back soon.

As Gawain headed down the stairs, amazing aromas were coming from the kitchen. His stomach rumbled.

In the kitchen, Bree was pouring a liquid over a huge roast in the oven.

Hoping to score some food, Gawain asked, "Can I help with anything?"

She closed the oven door and smiled at him. "Not in here. I have everything timed and choreographed. But…"

"What?"

"Well, with the danger from the Scythe, Zeb ordered me to keep the door locked all the time. But I need to be in here.

Could you possibly be the doorman?"

"Sure. Not a problem. I'm an excellent butler."

Obviously knowing males, she handed him a handful of tiny muffins that smelled of sausage and cheese.

"You're a fine female, Breanne." He popped one muffin in his mouth and heard himself start to purr. Two more disappeared. Then all.

"Here. Go play butler." Grinning, she handed him a beer and waved him out of her domain.

Sipping his drink, Gawain settled into a chair near the front door. As he thought of his day and the evening to come with Owen, Darcy, and new friends, contentment was a warm glow in his belly. Cold Creek was a fine town, much more to his taste than Pine Knoll.

Maybe because the ratio of shifters to humans was nicely balanced. The humans kept the shifters aware…at least somewhat…of the outside, modern world. In turn, the Daonain reminded humans there was more to life than money and power.

In another few days, he and Owen would move into their house. Gawain stroked his beard and smiled. Being around his littermate had brought him more satisfaction and…rightness…than he'd felt since they'd parted so long ago. Although the breaking of the bond when Edwyn died had hurt, Owen's departure had been far more painful. Thank the Gods, they were together again.

Then there was Darcy. Gawain wrinkled his brow. The little minx had been avoiding them. At a guess, she was worried about her villagers. She might feel her life was too unsettled to start a new relationship.

Of course, being as she was female and he was male, his guesses as to her reasoning could be completely off the path. The catling needed to share her worries rather than him and Owen trying to guess.

But…she concealed her fears from them. Maybe because the Scythe had isolated the captives, and she'd never learned to share? Or because she was an independent little tinker and a strong female?

Owen wasn't any better about sharing. Gawain grinned. People teased the cahir about being quiet, grumpy if annoyed, and blunt as any dwarf—yet he had a lot of good friends. As he should. He was strong, brave, honest, and—even if he tried to hide it—incredibly kind.

Darcy had seen through all of Owen's bluster to the good male beneath. She liked Gawain, too. Gawain nodded. Truly, she cared for them both.

They needed to discuss those worries of hers. It was time to take the next step to starting a relationship, because, once the villagers were rescued, she was liable to up and leave. He was damned if he'd let that happen. She needed to see they wanted her. He'd have to make sure Owen was ready to run that trail at a fast pace.

The three notes of the doorbell interrupted his planning. Time to be the lodge butler.

Gawain crossed the reception area and opened the door.

An older female stood there. She had the palest of blonde hair and brown eyes.

Gawain's gut muscles flinched as if he'd been stabbed. "Mother."

"I *found* you." Shoving the door farther open, she stalked past him, every inch the annoyed cat. "Why are you here in this scatty town?"

Automatically, Gawain checked the room for breakables that he might need to protect; the lodge was well cubling-proofed— or in this case, *angry-Mother-proofed*. He could tell from the shrill edge in her voice, she was gearing up for an ugly fight.

The bottom of his stomach slid greasily downward. "I live

here," he said shortly.

"No, you don't. You live in Pine Knoll."

"Not any longer. I moved here."

"But…" Her pale white hands clasped together over her heavy breasts. Over the last decade or so, she'd begun to visibly age. Harsh lines of discontent were graven beside her mouth and eyes. Although she'd once been an attractive female, a mean spirit would eventually blight even the most beautiful surface.

She took a step toward him. "But, Gawain, you're my cub. I need you. I need your help."

"No, you don't. You're a healthy adult. Other adult shifters live on their own." Only…she was getting older. He hesitated.

She could spot her prey's weaknesses faster than a pack of wolves, and she never hesitated to take advantage. "Oh, Gawain, I'm out of money, and I don't know what to do." Tears brimmed in her brown eyes. "Edwyn would have looked after me, but he's gone. You're all I have left."

Out of four cubs? Not hardly.

But he certainly wouldn't mention Bonnie, not after the eternity he'd spent in Pine Knoll to ensure his sister was free.

And Mother still hated Owen.

What would she do without Gawain at her beck and call? Whenever she was without one of the numerous males she picked up and discarded, she'd use him for chores, repairs, money, and even emotional support. And if he tried to set boundaries on her use of his time, she'd descend into hysterics in the most public places possible.

The twenty-five years of being her "cub" had taken their toll. Now Bonnie was safe, and he needed to escape before his spirit turned bitter and sour. He probably should have traveled to the far end of the continent to get out of her reach, but the lure of his littermates had caught him.

And now she'd found him.

As she started sobbing louder, Gawain looked at her and felt...nothing. Not hatred, not warmth. Not even a sense of duty remained.

Instead, his first thought was for his littermate. He needed to get her out of here before she saw Owen. *Don't return to the lodge yet, Owen. Stay away.*

Unfortunately, if she didn't get what she wanted, she'd refuse to leave. She'd persist—clinging and crying, talking and talking. Her infantile behavior would escalate until she'd start throwing whatever she could get her hands on.

He sighed. "How much money do you need?"

WITH DARCY BESIDE him, Owen finished dressing in the side room and headed down the hall.

Still in an exhilarant mood, Darcy was dancing, although on feet now rather than paws.

Smiling slightly, he slung an arm over her shoulders and pulled her close. "You did good, little cat."

Her snort held both delight at his compliment—and exasperation. Her pointy elbow jabbed into his ribs. "Don't call me little."

"Ah, right. I forgot." He grinned down into her dark eyes. Fuck, she was beautiful. Her cheeks had rounded out, and her skin glowed with health. Her lips were full, the lower one tempting a male to nibble on the plumpness.

Undoubtedly catching his interested scent, she stumbled slightly, and to his delight, he caught a whiff of her own interest. To see what she'd do, he lifted her arm and blatantly sniffed her wrist. *Oh, yeah.* The scent there not only roused him, but the knowledge that she wanted him made his own feet want to dance.

He cleared his throat. *Not the time, Treharn.* "If you don't like the word little, I could call you tiny. Tiny tinker?"

Her dainty hiss reminded him of Mrs. Henderson's Persian. Yep, *little cat* was the right term for her.

He tugged a lock of her wavy hair in reprimand. "Did you just hiss at your mentor?" He'd never teased a female before this one. Odd how much fun it was.

"Oh, no." She widened eyes as filled with mischief as a passel of pixies. "I would never. Truly. I know better than to disrespect someone of your venerable age."

His jaw dropped. The kitten had just called him old? *Old?* "You are in so much—"

Giggling, she darted down the hallway, around the back of the stairs, and into the main room of the lodge.

At a more leisurely pace, he followed. If Zeb was around, he'd hand her back. Shay or Gawain would enjoy teasing her— or him—but eventually, Owen would have his hands on her again. What could he do to make her eat that insult?

As he rounded the corner, a scent froze his feet to the ground. Loathing filled him.

His mother stood in front of Gawain, accepting a fistful of bills.

Laughter gone, Darcy was within a few feet of them and backing toward the stairs.

Owen couldn't move. He hadn't seen Mother since the day in the Pine Knoll restaurant when she'd been loudly sobbing about her cub being dead. An exasperated customer reminded her she had three remaining cubs—and unfortunately, pointed at Owen who'd just entered the restaurant. By the God, he'd never seen such hysterics in his life.

For twenty-five years, he'd not thought of her. And he'd believed Gawain loved her. His littermate had stayed in Pine Knoll, after all.

Owen might have been wrong.

His littermate's emotions were as easy to read as a fresh-cut trail. Gawain was angry. Frustrated. And almost despairing. Despite his need to protect Gawain, Owen knew any intervention would only lead to a foulmouthed scene, punctuated by screams and wails. Ear-splitting hysterics were Mother's specialty.

He and Gawain were guests in this lodge; fouling the wolves' den with their mother's howling would be wrong.

Owen started to retreat the way he'd come.

The movement caught Gawain's attention.

Mother noted his gaze, spotted Owen, and hatred filled her face. "*You*. You're still alive." She pointed at Owen as if she'd gladly stab him through the heart with her finger. "You're the reason my baby, my Edwyn, is dead. You're more evil than any hellhound."

He was an adult now, full-grown, and still…something in him wanted to curl into a miserable ball like a cubling. Even knowing she wouldn't listen, he still protested. "I had nothing to do with Edwyn's death. I didn't see him that night."

"You lie! I know you yelled at him. Called him names. You're why Phoebe rejected him. Why he drove his new car too fast and crashed it." Her voice shook. "You killed him as surely as if you'd bit his throat out."

No reasoning with her. Owen shook his head, barely managing to mutter the words. "I don't lie. Wasn't there."

"You *were*. Murderer." She launched herself across the room, striking Owen with fists and slaps.

He turned his head and backed away, and she followed…as she always had. He'd never hit her back—she was female.

"This is bullshit. Stop right *now*." Darcy grabbed his mother's arm—and hair—and slung her into a chair.

"You dare! You—"

With a wolverine's ferocity, Darcy hissed and raised her fist. "Owen might not hit a female, but I certainly will." Darcy's voice was a low growl. The little female was under complete control, despite her anger.

His mother burst into pitiful weeping. "You don't understand. He killed my son."

"I very much doubt it. Owen doesn't lie." The certainty in Darcy's voice was a balm over burning welts.

Still—he needed to leave, or Mother would continue ratcheting up the hysterics. He glanced at Gawain.

Snowfall pale, his littermate hadn't moved.

Owen took a step forward. "Brawd?"

Gawain's haunted eyes met his. "She blames you. I didn't know she still did. Owen, I swear, I would have dealt with it."

What the fuck? He shrugged. "She's always blamed me for everything. No matter."

"It does matter." Gawain straightened his shoulders. "Mother, listen to me."

Their mother continued to sob, but…the volume decreased. She was listening.

Gawain took a step toward her. "That night, Edwyn had boasted to Phoebe about stealing. I was the one who called Edwyn names, not Owen. I was the one who yelled at him, knocked him down, and took his stolen goods away. He busted out bawling. Phoebe was disgusted with him and walked away."

Owen stared. He'd always thought—blamed—the female for the fight and goading Edwyn into recklessness. Gawain had fought with him and blamed himself for Edwyn's death?

"No. You're wrong." Mother shook her head. "My Edwyn would never steal. He was perfect."

Owen barely managed to prevent a snort.

"Your Edwyn went into a dwarf's cave and stole his hoard."

"He what?" Owen stared.

"Yeah. I was so pissed-off, I lost my temper." Looking ill, Gawain rubbed the back of his neck. "I took the bag away from him and left it at the dwarf's door. But, considering Edwyn had a brand-new fancy Jeep, he'd already spent a good chunk of the gold, so I had to make it up out of my own savings."

Edwyn stole from a dwarf. Owen shook his head. Nothing was more important to a dwarf than his hoard; females chose their mates depending on the amount of gold. "Edwyn could have started a…a fucking war."

"My Edwyn wouldn't steal. It was you; I know it. You're nothing—just demon-spawn." Mother pushed herself up, spittle flying from her mouth. "You should have been the one who died. I—"

"Oh, honestly." Darcy shoved her back in the chair.

Gawain's face turned implacable. "I'm done. Done being a dutiful son, done giving you money. We are finished. Don't ever come near me again."

Darcy turned and put her arm around Gawain's waist, and comfort flowed almost visibly from her.

"You don't mean it." Their mother stood. "*He's* turned you against me."

Footsteps came from the rear, and then Zeb and Shay moved to either side of Owen. Panting, Breanne leaned on a wall. She must have heard the yelling and run to fetch her mates.

Shay set a hand on Owen's shoulder. "What's going on here, cahir?"

"My mother is leaving," Owen said.

She didn't move, but stared at the cahirs on either side of him. After a second, her gaze focused on the blue scar on Owen's cheek, and her mouth dropped open. "You're a cahir? God-called? *You?*"

"Darcy, if you don't hit her, I will." Vicki stood in the front doorway, one hand on her belly, the other in a fist. "Get her the fuck out of here."

Alec and Calum stood behind her—and Alec chuckled.

His mother gave Vicki a frozen stare. "My cub…cubs…are here, and they owe me. You can't talk to me that way."

"I do believe she just did." Calum moved Vicki back and behind him. Expression deadly, he examined Owen's mother as if he'd found a gnome in the butter. He glanced at Alec. "Is the human influence destroying our race's maternal instincts? No animal would behave so cruelly to a cub."

"You disgusting piece of…" Mother's voice faded at the increased shimmer of power around Calum. Belatedly, she realized she'd spoken to the Cosantir of the territory.

"You have no cubs here. Leave my territory and do not return." His gaze darkened…and he snapped his fingers.

Owen felt a pinging ripping sensation deep within his ribcage. The tattered bond between dam and cub had been severed.

With a shocked inhalation, Gawain put a hand to his chest and stared at Calum.

Gasping, their mother staggered backward a step, two, then fled out of the room…not dropping any of the money. The door of the lodge slammed shut.

For a moment, silence reigned, and then Darcy hugged Owen. "I'm sorry, sweetie, but that woman is a disgusting butthole."

The open sympathy, the anger on his behalf, and having the little female in his arms, not for mating, but purely to give comfort, filled the empty hole in his heart to overflowing.

And she'd called him sweetie.

When Gawain put his arms around both of them, Owen's knotted muscles relaxed.

Gawain chuckled. "Ah…butthole?"

Alec laughed. "Ever noticed how some human-raised females possess rather…earthy…vocabularies?"

"No, but I'm looking forward to learning more." Owen kissed the top of Darcy's head. When he met Gawain's gaze, he saw the same sentiment.

This was a female to cherish.

GAWAIN AND OWEN were hugging her. Darcy wasn't sure how it had happened, but she let herself sink into the pleasure. She rubbed her cheek against Gawain's chest, breathed in his summer meadow scent, and turned to press her forehead against Owen's shoulder. Dark and woodsy. The masculine fragrances mingled together and she snuggled closer, feeling like a kitten in fresh grass.

Can't stand here and hug the males all night. Reluctantly, Darcy looked up at Owen. His gaze was on the door.

What a ghastly, manipulative, foul-mouthed evil excuse for a mother. And Owen had lived with her until his teen years?

No wonder you hate females. Someone should have slapped her spitless years ago.

When the room went completely silent, Darcy realized she'd spoken out loud. She clapped her hands over her mouth—way, way, way too late—and stared up at Owen.

His eyes narrowed…and then his lips twitched.

Gawain burst out laughing, followed by everyone else.

Owen actually grinned. "You've got a cat's own temper, don't you?" He gave her hair a tug. "Thanks for the defense, tiny tinker."

"I like our tinker." Alec gave Calum a friendly punch on the arm. "Brawd, you're getting faster at bond-snapping."

Looking exhausted, Calum gave his littermate a cold look—and Alec only laughed.

"Bonnie," Owen whispered.

Gawain froze, his expression dismayed.

Calum nodded. "Indeed. She will have felt the bond break." He turned to Alec. "Brawd, can you check in with her and ensure she's all right?"

"Aye." Alec squeezed the Cosantir's shoulder. "I'll explain.

From what little she's said about her mother, she'll be more than relieved to be free of her."

Owen's shoulders slumped. "Thank you, Cosantir. Alec."

"What is bond-snapping?" Darcy whispered to Gawain.

"I don't know what the Cosantir has done in the past, but"—he splayed his fingers over his chest—"the bond between me and our mother is cut." His expression seemed torn between sorrow and relief.

Darcy reached up and kissed his cheek before checking Owen. How odd—and sad. His face showed the same two emotions. In spite of the way the horrible woman had treated him, he'd still viewed her as his mother.

She hugged him again. Then frowned. "Calum did this before?"

"Yeah, with Minette's mother, Genevieve," Owen answered. Darcy frowned. "No, Minette is *Emma's* cub."

Owen clarified, "Genevieve and Ryder had Minette, but the cub now belongs to Ryder, Emma, and Ben."

Oh. And the Cosantir had broken Minette's mother-cub bond? "I guess her mother was…"

"Abusive as hell." Owen glanced at Calum. "Calum, about—"

"I'm sorry." The Cosantir's face tightened. "Severing of the bond wasn't my decision."

Not his decision? After a second, Darcy understood. Herne worked through his Cosantirs, apparently sometimes without permission, leaving them with the guilt. Being God-chosen sure wasn't for the weak, was it?

Owen pulled in a slow breath and then shook his head. "Cosantir…Calum…losing the bond was a shock, but also a relief. You have my"—he glanced at Gawain and got a nod—"*our* thanks."

Calum's expression eased.

Owen's lips curved slightly. "Actually, what I was asking is what happened to Minette's blood mother? What if Genevieve has more cubs to mistreat?"

"Word has been passed out to the other Cosantirs. Most females only bear one litter, but if for some reason she is gifted another, she won't be permitted to keep them."

"Good to know. Thank you." Owen glanced at Gawain. "A shame someone didn't remove us when we were cublings, too."

Gawain inclined his head in agreement before a frown appeared on his face. "Maybe. Our lives would have been easier, but...would we be the same people? Lacking a mother's love changed me, made me more open to the blessings of the Mother of All. And you—I saw how your desire to guard the weak grew stronger as you got older. Strong enough for the God to call you."

Owen's face went blank.

Darcy nodded. She'd seen the compulsion in the big cahir, his need to protect everyone in his path. Her gaze met Calum's and she saw the Cosantir had heard Gawain. His nod confirmed what the mage had said.

The pain of their childhoods had forged the two brothers into strong tools that could be wielded by the Gods.

She pulled in a breath, hoping the last ghastly decade had shaped her into someone strong and worthy of the pain.

"All right, people," Bree announced in a loud voice. "Dinner will be delayed for an hour. Everyone—the chef included—needs a strong drink. Let's gather around the fire pit and enjoy the quiet evening."

Shay's laugh boomed out. "Aye, and you have the right of it, *a leannán*. Brawd, if you light us a fire out there, I'll break out the alcohol."

As drinks were being poured, Darcy retrieved her coat and slipped outside. In the fire pit, a newly lit fire crackled in the dry wood. As she dropped into one of wooden chairs across from the stone bench, a swirl of sparks announced a salamander's arrival. The fire elementals adored dancing outside.

Twinkling in the firelight, a few snowflakes drifted down from the black sky. There would be more snow before morning. Darcy pulled in a deep breath, pleased that the icy air off the mountains held no stench of rancor. The last few minutes had been, as the human captives would say, *intense*. Poor Owen and Gawain.

"I hear we missed some drama." Emma walked across the patio and settled onto the curving built-in stone bench across from Darcy. Ben, the huge cahir, sat at his mate's left and gave Darcy a smile. A strange male sat down on the bard's right.

"Did Minette come?" Darcy asked hopefully. The tiny girl was cuter than any pixie and adorably smart.

"No, we dropped her off to have a sleepover with Angie's grandcubs." Emma smiled and patted the stranger's arm. "Darcy, this is Ryder, my lifemate. He works with Ben in the construction business."

Ryder had skin darker than Darcy's, black hair to just below his shoulders, and dark brown eyes. Although tall, he was leanly muscular instead of having the massiveness of his grizzly littermate. He gave her a reserved look. "Good to meet you."

"And you." Darcy smiled. "You have a wonderful cub."

The way his eyes lit with pleased pride changed him from a darkly dangerous male to a proud sire—and she could see why Emma had fallen for him.

"There she is." Owen sat down beside Darcy.

Gawain took a chair on the other side and handed her a mug. "Vicki said you were sampling various drinks. Have some hot chocolate and Bailey's Irish Cream."

"Oh, fun." She took a sip and smiled. The alcohol tasted like ice cream. "This is wonderful. Thank you."

Owen gave her a stern look. "Just remember it'll impair your judgment. No driving cars—or running around in shifter form."

"Yes, daddy."

Gawain let out a hearty laugh, but Owen growled under his breath, curved his hand around her neck in a ruthless grip, and pulled her closer to him.

Uh-oh. She gazed up into aggravated green eyes. "Um…"

He rubbed his lips over hers gently and said softly, "You have a mouth on you, little cat. Good thing it's so kissable."

"What?" Her eyes narrowed.

Walking past, Vicki stopped in her tracks. "Now there's a man who needs his clock cleaned. Need help, Darcy?"

"Tempting, but I think I'll just set his washing machine to flood his house…and all that new flooring."

As Vicki grinned, Gawain sputtered. "Now wait, tinker. I'll be living there, too."

Despite the stern set of Owen's jaw, laughter danced in his eyes. "I'll have to watch my words." When he picked up her hand and kissed her fingertips, her mouth dropped open. Owen was never affectionate. "Are you going to forgive me?" he asked.

"Well, of—" She stopped and frowned. "Maybe when I get an actual apology."

"Fuck, you're smart." His rough chuckle stroked over her almost like the caress of his callused hands. "I look forward to watching you and Gawain play chess."

"What? I haven't played chess since I was twelve." Her lips curved. "Although I did usually win."

Gawain looked at her with keen interest. "Challenge accepted," he said promptly.

"I didn't…" She glared. "The two of you are scary when you team up."

The exchange of satisfied glances between them was…delightful, actually. Since she'd met them, their relationship had changed, evened out, until they now moved together better than a well-tuned engine.

Although it might be better if they didn't collaborate to pick on her. She'd have to check out their new home and see what appliances could be sabotaged.

More voices added to the conversational hum. Alec, Shay, and Bree settled down on the stone bench near Vicki, leaving a space for Calum.

"Bonnie?" Owen asked Alec. "Is she all right?"

"My dispatcher is a tough female." Alec smiled slowly. "She was shaken, but after I told her what happened tonight—and let her know you two were all right—she decided she was more pleased than not."

Owen and Gawain let out relieved breaths.

Wakened by the noise, the resident pixie chirred in annoyance from the tall spruce. A couple of twigs were tossed out.

Shay chuckled. "Now you know why we put the fire pit on this side of the patio."

The pixie clicked her fingernails at him rudely before disappearing into her hole.

The door from the dining area opened, and Calum and Zeb walked out. As Calum took a seat beside Vicki, Zeb leaned a hip on the stone wall beside Breanne. The frown on the Cosantir's face made Darcy sit up straighter.

Alec studied his littermate. "Problems, brawd?"

"Tynan called. He's narrowing down the possible locations of the Seattle prison."

Darcy caught her breath.

Calum regarded her. "When we find the captives, we'll act, Darcy. The cahirs—all of them—have requested they be permitted to rescue the females. Other males here also asked."

Alec snorted. "Thorson demanded, actually."

"We'll get your villagers free," Calum said gently.

Her hand closed around Gawain's. Help. The Cosantir was offering help. She swallowed. "I'll probably have to be the one to contact the shifter-soldiers, or they won't believe you. I can do that."

"Perhaps. We'll make plans when we know what we're up against." His gaze met hers and the depth of understanding there made her eyes burn. "Whatever happens, you won't have to return to the prison, Darcy."

How had he known her deepest fear? How had he *known*? She pulled in a shuddering breath. In so many of her nightmares, she was back there. Helpless. Her voice came out a whisper. "Thank you." Owen stroked her shoulders, and she could sense his courage pouring into her. "It's all felt so…hopeless, sometimes."

"Not hopeless." Vicki shook her head. "Wells stuck a tracker on the Scythe van that came to Cold Creek. Their operatives killed the device within a day, but it gave Wells a start. He's been working his way up the ladder, uncovering people, funding, and locations. There's no one better at digging out information."

"Mmmhmm. I'm sure he's looking hard for traitors to the United States." Maybe not so much for the kidnappers of the Daonain. Darcy couldn't keep the flatness from her tone. The spymaster had his priorities—and they wouldn't include Daonain hostages and soldiers.

"Well, fuck, you're almost as cynical as I am." Vicki grinned. "Wells knows the dangers of having the Daonain exposed to humans—if nothing else, it'd be really difficult to be a godfather to a baby in a science lab, right?" She patted her stomach. "He's in Seattle right now, concentrating on locating your villagers."

"Really?" Darcy swallowed. "Th-thank you. I've been so frustrated with not being able to help."

Owen and Gawain exchanged glances.

"With your permission, Cosantir," Owen said. "Gawain and

I will take Darcy with us when we go scouting tomorrow. And we'll stay out there until we locate that damn camp."

The Cosantir steepled his fingers, considered, and nodded. "Aye, cahir. Go find the camp."

Chapter Twenty

THE MID-NOVEMBER AFTERNOON was cool, but dry...just the way Owen enjoyed. He swiveled his ears toward Gawain and Darcy who trotted behind him. When traveling a distance in a group, panthers tended to space themselves a good distance apart, unlike idiot wolves who would run nose to tail. He couldn't see the other two, but he kept track of their quiet sounds of passage.

They'd had a late start yesterday, because a male had shown up looking for the blademage. He'd traveled from the other side of the territory, and they delayed so Gawain could make him lifemating bracelets.

Since Darcy didn't yet have perfect control, they'd driven partway to the Twin Sister range and parked Gawain's car on a deserted logging road rather than a human parking lot. They'd spent the rest of the day as cougars, traveling fast. Last night, Darcy'd been so exhausted, she'd fallen asleep halfway through eating the rabbit Gawain had caught.

Owen lifted his muzzle to sniff the air. He wanted to find the well-hidden mountain meadow that Tynan and Donal had used as a base when they'd scouted the southeast quadrant.

Catching an acrid urine stench, Owen veered toward it. In wolf fashion, Tynan had marked the tree next to where an almost invisible deer trail began. Without slowing, Owen continued down the trail.

As dusk approached, the air was cooling, and they should get set up. They'd been animal long enough—and he missed talking with the other two.

Stepping out into a grassy meadow, he shifted.

Darcy padded up behind him.

Gawain followed and trawsfurred to human. "Nice place to camp."

"Can you catch Tynan's scent?" Owen asked. His brother's sense of smell was more akin to a big-nosed bear than a cougar, which Owen had made sure to tease him about when they were cubs.

"Let's see." Gawain walked around, casting for the scent. He stopped at a tree at the south end and pointed up. "There, brawd."

Owen climbed the tree, found a dark green, waterproof bag, and lowered it to Gawain.

"How did you know that was there?" Darcy asked.

"Owen called Tynan after Breanne's dinner party, and the cop suggested we use this spot as a base," Gawain said. "Tynan already had a cache here, but since yesterday was his day off, he dropped off extra camping gear and clothing so we won't freeze if we're in human form. In the evenings, it's nice to be able to talk, but this high up, we'd freeze without clothes."

"Oh. Awesome." Her smile could entice the sun to shine on a rainy day. "I missed chatting with you two last night."

Owen snorted. "Little cat, you fell asleep last night in mid-bite."

She laughed, not insulted in the least.

Yeah, he'd grown fond of talking to her, too. "Tonight, we'll discuss what you want to practice while we search for the shifter-soldiers." Owen glanced at Gawain. They'd already come up with a few ideas, in fact.

"Okay." She knelt and started pulling things out of the duffel bag. Sleeping bags—the kind that zipped together into one bed. Clothes for them all.

Gawain divided them into the proper sizes. The longer jeans for Owen. Over-sized shirts and jacket for the blacksmith. Smaller everything for Darcy.

"No boots?" Darcy held up the moccasins and thick socks.

"We'll search in animal form. Clothes are only for our comfort at night."

She eyed the heavy duffel. "It was nice of Tynan to haul it up here."

"Aye, although some of it was already here." Owen pulled on jeans, thermal shirt, flannel shirt, and a down vest. "He keeps some caches in the forests around Seattle for when Donal can join him."

"How long has he been a cop?" Darcy's jeans were snug enough that she had to wiggle her curvy ass to get them up.

That ass. Owen remembered all too well how perfectly her hips could be gripped, how... With a grunt, he looked away and tried to recall her question. *Bad cahir.*

All too observant, Gawain grinned and prompted, "How long?"

Tynan. They were talking about Tynan. "I think he's been in Seattle ten to fifteen years. It must be agony for a wolf to be without a pack."

Her dark eyes held sympathy.

"Poor bastard," Gawain muttered. "Why in the God's forest is he there?"

"Donal told me the God sent his brother there, and he'd know when he could leave."

Gawain dumped the firewood he'd collected near a circle of boulders that would serve as a heat reflector. The high canopy of leaves would disperse the smoke. "He's got more guts than I do."

"Or he's crazier than a ram in breeding season." Owen shook his head. "He can't stay much longer. He told Donal he's not aging as fast as the other officers who are supposedly his age, and it's beginning to be noticeable."

"Oh. I bet." Darcy frowned. "Isn't that a problem in shifter-human towns, too?"

"I'm not sure why, exactly, but in a territory, the humans don't seem to notice the fifty or so years difference in our lifespans. The Mother and Hunter might exert a blurring influence or something."

An hour later, they settled in front of the blazing fire. Tynan, may the Mother bless his name, had included a skin of scotch.

As they passed the skin between them, Darcy drank, although she wrinkled her nose with each sip. Fuck, she was cute. Even better, her defenses were down, which was what he'd been waiting for.

When he nodded at Gawain, his brother drew her into a discussion about good colors for a living room.

Silently, Owen slipped into the forest, stripped, and shifted. *You're not a nice cat, Treharn.* But this was part of being a shifter—and what with being hunted, she didn't have a year to master control.

Gawain noticed the second he sneaked out of the tree line. In a most painful fashion, their mentor had taught them what happened to unobservant shifters. Despite the years, they'd never lost the edgy awareness.

Darcy was as heedless of danger as a sprite focused on a new flower. Tonight, she'd learn attentiveness as well as control.

Owen vibrated his throat in a low growl. Panthers couldn't roar, but this had the same effect.

Her muscles tensed even before her mind comprehended

the danger behind her.

When she turned, he charged with a piercing hiss-spit.

She screamed, the scotch went flying, and suddenly they had a panicking panther encumbered by jeans, shirts, and vest.

Being swift of hand, Gawain had caught the skin of scotch in midair.

Owen chuffed a laugh and lay down in the grass.

He had to give Darcy credit; she stopped panicking faster than any youngster. After only a minute, she realized he wasn't moving. She looked at Gawain who was drinking more scotch, and she gave her own growl.

A second later, she was human again, trying to set her clothes straight. And scowling. "You scared me on purpose."

"Aye," Gawain said. "So, pretty panther, did you trawsfur because that was the wisest choice?"

She sank down on the log. "No," she said slowly. "I didn't even think. I was scared and shifted."

Lesson learned. Owen nodded at her and returned to the woods.

Before her clothes were even put to rights, he did it again.

And again.

When she finally stayed human despite his charging her, he gave her a break.

When Owen, back in human form, approached the fire, Gawain winked at him. In another hour, it would be his turn.

Shivering, Owen took a seat on the log beside Darcy and held his hands out to the flames.

Frowning, she turned. "You look almost frozen."

"Yeah, my clothes were fucking cold when I put them on." The temperature away from the fire was freezing.

Without a thought, she put her arms around him, generously sharing her body's warmth...even though he'd done his best to scare her to death.

He kissed the top of her head, soaking up the feeling of being held as much as the warmth. "I thought you'd hate me by now."

"The thought occurred." She rubbed her hands up and down his back, chasing the chill away. "But after the first times, I realized you weren't doing it for fun." Her lips curved. "Although, I did see Gawain laugh at me a time or two."

"At least that," Gawain said agreeably. He leaned forward and handed Owen the scotch.

Owen took a sip. The liquid slid down his throat and spread warmth into his belly.

Scotch, a fire, and a clear night sky. An evening with his littermate. Darcy snuggling with him. As contentment seeped into him, he pulled her onto his lap.

When she tried to pull away, he kept an arm around her and lifted her chin. "Is that habit or do you really want to move away?"

Actually, she rarely jumped when they unexpectedly touched her now. The trust in that pleased him immensely.

Frowning at him, she opened her mouth. "I…" Then she buried her face against his shoulder. "I don't think you're so cold you need me on your lap."

"Nope. I just want you here." Sounded reasonable to him. Her ass was a soft weight on his thighs, her breasts pressed against his chest, and every breath was filled with her feminine fragrance. Want was a poor word for what he needed from her, but it would do.

When she finally looked up, he smiled at her…and took her lips. There was no full moon heat driving them tonight, and yet, when her lips yielded under his, when she softened and opened to his tongue, the flames were hot enough to sear.

Maybe he couldn't say the words, but as he held her and kissed her, he tried to let his actions convey what he felt. That this was where she belonged. That he cared.

When he finally lifted his head, she was clinging to him.

"So, brawd." Gawain stretched his legs out, amusement and approval in his gaze. "While we search, are we working on anything with Darcy tomorrow?"

Before Owen could answer, Darcy sat up straighter. "I need to learn how to work around the wind." She patted Owen's arm. "The same way you did with those humans in Seward Park. You hid your scent until the time you wanted the dogs to notice you."

Interesting. Most new shifters wanted to practice running down prey. But working the wind was a valuable skill—and necessary for hunting, as well. "All right. Anything else?"

"Everything else?" Her smile disappeared. "Mostly, I want to be able to get up into trees and be able to leap from rock to rock without messing up. And I can't. Cats are supposed to be all graceful, but I swear, I have four left paws."

"Four...what?"

"Human saying, brawd." Gawain handed him the skin of scotch. "Having two left feet is a way to say someone is clumsy."

Owen eyed his moccasin-clad feet, trying to envision having two left ones. "Humans are weird sometimes."

"WHATCHA WORKING ON, O'Connolly?" The question came from an aging detective in the Seattle police station. "It's quitting time, you know."

Tynan looked up from the computer on his desk. "I know. Remember that woman's body they pulled out of the Sound at Lincoln Park? I'm wondering if anything similar happened in the past few years in West Seattle."

"Like murders and shit?" The pot-bellied human was getting close to retirement—and his indifferent expression said his mind was already there.

"Just curious."

"Good luck with that."

The bullpen was never silent, but at least, the nosy detective was gone. Tynan frowned at the map on the computer monitor. Darcy had identified the body pulled from the Sound as one of her fellow captives. Poor lass. She'd not only suffered years of captivity, but also the loss of friends. It was a wonder she was sane.

But she was a strong female.

Now, it was up to him to find her villagers.

When Darcy escaped, she'd run wildly, darting various directions, even doubling back a time or two. She hadn't any notion of the distance she'd covered. However, she'd given him a few tidbits. Sometime during her escape, she crossed over a big river first and then a multilane freeway, which had to be I-5. Also, she knew her general direction had been east, and she'd ended up in Seward Park. West of Seward Park, the river had to be the Duwamish Waterway, which meant that bloody wall-enclosed prison had to be somewhere in West Seattle.

Now, if he were an asshole with a dead body to dump in the Sound, he'd pick a nearby location—a familiar area. Since the dead body had washed up around Lincoln Park, he'd search in the surrounding Gatewood and Delridge neighborhoods first.

He pushed away from his desk and grabbed his jacket.

By the God, he'd find that fecking Scythe prison and get the people—*his* people—out.

Chapter Twenty-One

AS GAWAIN WALKED down the conifer-shaded forest trail, he sniffed. The damp, cool air helped to preserve odors, but he caught no scent of other shifters. There was also no hint of Darcy—which meant she was doing quite well.

Earlier, he'd taught her how to prevent the wind from revealing her presence. Her assignment this afternoon was to circle him as if he were a deer—and not spook her prey.

She'd done better than he'd anticipated.

Back near the rise, he'd caught her scent. He'd have to warn her about unexpected updrafts in the mountains. He'd also spotted a flash of her dark fur twice. Really, she'd improved immensely and was more prudent than others he'd trained. Smarter, too.

Fun, generous, and sweet. She had a beautiful spirit, one that resonated with his.

Now, he wanted more… He'd been patient, waiting for her to work past her fears. Waiting for Owen to see past his prejudices.

The last two nights, they'd all slept together in a panther pile. Tonight, he'd see if Darcy wanted to spend the night in human form. With him.

Owen could join them—or not. Gawain sighed. He really

hoped his brother would. Sharing a female was one of the most rewarding, wonderful joys of being littermates.

But tonight was hours away. To keep Darcy on her paws, he audibly sniffed—and caught the wild scent of a different shifter.

Stopping, he cast about for the source, wishing he could shift to panther form where his senses would be more acute. The breeze brought him news of several deer in the distance. A badger had a hole just off the trail. No sounds of anyone or anything else. He said quietly, "Come in."

Slinking slow, Darcy slid out from the underbrush. Such a small panther. Her fur was several shades darker than his, and she could fade nicely into the shadows.

He indicated the pine in front of him. "A werebear marked this tree. Do you recognize the scent?"

Ears up in excitement, she trotted over to the tree. After a sniff, she shifted. "*Yes.* I didn't know him well, but he's three or four years younger than me and my brothers." She bounced once. "Oh my Gods, they're here. Somewhere close."

Gawain eyed the claw marks. The young male was nowhere as tall as Ben. Probably a black bear. "Tell me how old the scent is."

"I don't have time for lessons. We found them. Let's—"

"How old?"

Her brows pulled together, but she obediently sniffed, backed up, and sniffed again. "I…I'm not sure. The weather is chilly, so the scent would linger for maybe a couple of weeks?"

"Aye." He ran his hand down her arm. "I'd guess over a week, and the smell of his passage is gone. You're not going to track them by scent now."

"Oh." Her shoulders slumped.

Unable to help himself, he slung his arm over her bare shoulders and drew her close. When she sighed and cuddled against him, his heart leaped with pleasure.

"I want to find them so bad."

"I know, *cariad*." He pulled her closer, trying not to notice how very good she felt against him. If she needed comfort, that's what he'd give her, no matter what his body wanted.

After a minute, she tensed, as if recalling her state of undress. Yet, rather than stepping back, she softened against him.

He caught the scent of interested female. *Mmm*.

"Darcy." Her head lifted, her dark eyes met his, and he lowered his head slowly, giving her time to retreat.

She met his lips with hers.

By the God, she tasted like the tart huckleberries from the undergrowth, and he took the kiss deeper, exploring, and letting her explore in return. He filled his hands with her softly curved ass and pulled her up, rubbing his erection against her, smelling her arousal.

Unfortunately, this wasn't the place to take matters further. He pressed light kisses over her cheek and jaw before releasing her. His cock was so hard his jeans felt as if they'd shrunk at least two sizes. "Let's go fetch Owen."

Her eyes were dazed. "Owen?"

Yeah, his mind jumped all over the image of sharing her with his brother. *Stay focused, mage*. "We'll get my littermate, take animal form, and check this path the rest of the way."

"Oh. Of course." She huffed a laugh. "I can't believe the way you make my head go mindless." Forehead against his chest, she nodded. "Let's go get Owen."

She stepped away, prepared to shift back to cougar.

"Want to walk with me on the trail?" he asked.

"Yes, please."

He'd come prepared. Pulling off the daypack, he took out her clothes.

"You are so smart." She took the bundle and…still modest, turned away to change.

The thin sunlight coming through the canopy bathed her shoulders…and highlighted the thin shiny white scars on her back.

Anger surged. Someday, he'd meet the Scythe who'd hurt her…and they would die.

After she dressed, they retraced their steps, moving at a good pace. As they neared the camp, she kept giving him small glances.

His lips twitched. "Ask, Darcy. I won't claw your ears off."

Her lovely eyes were uncommonly serious. "About your mother. She…I know she's your mother, but she was awful. Why did you stay in her town so long? Why didn't you come to Cold Creek sooner and be with Owen and Bonnie?"

He halted as her unanticipated questions hit him like an attacking eagle's talons. He could almost feel his spine snap.

Her gaze fell. "I'm sorry. It's not any of my business."

But if he wanted more from her than a single night, his past *would* be her business. He'd built this trap of ugly memories; it was time to chew himself free. "I didn't stay in Pine Knoll because I wanted to be around her. My mother isn't a likable woman; in fact, if there were shifter vultures, she'd be one. She expects everything to be handed to her, doesn't want to work, and will manipulate, whine, cry, yell, and blackmail to get what she thinks she deserves. Edwyn had the same attitude." Gawain heard a branch snap nearby and started to turn.

"Were you living with her?"

"No, Owen and I moved out at fifteen. He apprenticed to a carver, me to a smith, and Bonnie was safely away in Cold Creek. Edwyn didn't want to learn a trade and so he stayed with Mother and provided the fawning attention she required. He didn't do anything else, so when she was between males, she'd call me and demand money or help with stuff at home. I protested, but"— he hated admitting this—"I always caved in."

"At fifteen." Darcy's expression was thoughtful. "You were way too young to stand up to her."

"Maybe. Owen did all his life, though."

"I get the impression he didn't have much choice."

Gawain shook his head. "I wanted to love her—but I hated her. And I still feel guilty for hating a female."

"You're such a Daonain." Darcy snorted. "I hate to disillusion you, but females don't belong on pedestals. If we behave like assholes, we should be treated like assholes." Her voice was matter-of-fact as she took his hand, lacing their fingers together. "Why didn't you leave when you finished your apprenticeship?"

"If Edwyn had stayed alive, I'd have fled town with Owen the minute our apprenticeships were done. But Edwyn died, and when Bonnie returned for the funeral, our mother preyed on her. Bonnie's a sweetheart without a mean bone in her body, and Mother would have sucked her dry."

Dawning understanding lit Darcy's face. "You were afraid she'd follow Bonnie back to Cold Creek?"

"Aye." Gawain shrugged. "Since it was my fault Edwyn died, I made a deal with Mother that as long as I stayed in Pine Knoll, she'd leave my sister alone—and not hit Owen up for money. As long as Mother had someone to…cater…to her, she wouldn't bestir herself to search for them."

With a harsh rustle of leaves, a mountain lion dropped onto the trail right in front of them. Ears back, fangs exposed, it hissed furiously. Owen wasn't teaching lessons this time. The cahir was furious.

Gawain felt Darcy's magic as she fought the instinct to trawsfur. "Brawd, you're scaring her. Stop it."

The cougar trawsfurred, and Owen stood before them, still spitting mad. "How in Herne's fucking forest can you figure you're responsible for Edwyn's death?"

"When I humiliated him in front of Phoebe, she showed

him her claws and dumped him. That was why he drove off."

"But that—"

"You did right, Gawain," Darcy interrupted Owen. "That poor girl might have ended up with the asshole otherwise. Didn't she deserve to hear the truth before getting manipulated into a relationship with such a loser?"

Gawain scowled. That loser was his brother. And…she was right. Edwyn would have abused Phoebe.

"You stayed…for me and Bonnie." Owen looked like he'd been kicked in the gut. "After I got Bonnie to Cold Creek, I went back to Pine Knoll for you. I thought maybe you'd want to join me—only you were at Mother's house, hauling in her groceries. I thought…"

"Thought I wanted to take Edwyn's place in her affections? Don't make me puke." Anger flickered and died under a surge of love. His brother had come back for him.

Owen scrubbed the scruff on his jaw with his palms. "You gnome-brained *idiot*." His voice rose to a shout. "You put up with her for well over two fucking decades."

"Aye." The words clogged in Gawain's throat. "I'd do it again to keep her out of your lives. At fifteen, Bonnie was too young. Too sweet. You were…" The humans would call it "abused." Gawain swallowed, remembering how there were always bruises on his littermate's body. How Owen's shoulders would hunch against the names she'd called him. How his eyes had grown more and more haunted.

Those green eyes were clear now. Pissed off, but clear.

"You needed a chance to heal, brawd." Gawain wanted to reach out, to touch him—and knew better. All he could do was offer the insight he'd gained. "Every time I helped the master blademage make a lifemating bracelet, I would be bathed in the Mother's love. Feeling real love—not the twisted mess our mother offered—made a difference, gave me balance, but you didn't have that gift. You needed time, brawd. Time away from her."

Gawain didn't know what else to say. He could see the pain and guilt in Owen's face. The protective cahir would see leaving his brother behind as cowardice. The male with such an ugly past wouldn't know how to deal with someone trying to save him pain.

Owen took a step back as if to run, to nurse his wounds in private.

"No, you don't." Darcy grabbed Owen's hand and yanked Gawain forward. "*My* mother taught us that after the yelling, you hug each other. Do it—or I'll hurt you both."

Shocked, Owen stared at her, then his lips twitched.

Gawain almost laughed. The female had bigger balls than an alpha wolf—and she was right. He pulled Owen into a hug.

Twenty-five years. Owen was the taller one now, and all muscle, yet still felt like Gawain's littermate. Despite the years and anger, as Owen's arms tightened and their scents mingled, the scars and damage to their brother bond faded. The energy pouring between them increased to a thick glow.

It felt good. Felt right.

When Gawain took a breath and looked up, he saw Darcy had disappeared, leaving them alone. He gazed after her. Not releasing his brother, he said, "I don't regret staying in Pine Knoll. But gotta say, I missed you. Missed sharing my life with you."

"Aye, me too." Owen's lips curved as he followed Gawain's gaze. "Seems like we might consider sharing a mouthy, bossy, little cat, as well. I'm getting rather fond of her."

Gawain laughed. He was well on the way to being more than fond, but there was time for his brother…and their female…to catch up.

LATER, AS DARKNESS fell, Darcy loped after Owen, followed by Gawain.

Owen always led them on the trails, and he usually took charge, she'd noticed. She'd bet it'd been his and Gawain's dynamic as cublings, even if Owen had been the abused one. Gawain would put his paw down if he disagreed with something, but that didn't happen often. Actually, she understood how Gawain felt. Owen was a good leader, his decisions well thought out. She trusted him—and it was so, so nice not to be the one making all the decisions.

As for running the trails, she preferred being in the middle.

Recently, she'd realized Owen monitored the sounds around him. Whenever she fell behind, he'd slow without even looking around. Behind her, Gawain kept a comfortable distance, not close enough to crowd her, but near enough he could help if she got into trouble. The day she'd miscalculated a leap and slipped off a boulder, he'd been beside her in an instant.

Today… There was no way she could convey how grateful she was for their overprotective presence.

With every mile, her anticipation and anxiety rose. Once, Owen had to take them off the trail to avoid a couple of backpackers. Gawain and Owen had perched in trees. She'd hid in the underbrush and had to endure Owen's disapproving stare. He felt cats belonged in the trees.

Unlike her, most cats didn't fall out of trees.

At the top of a rise, Owen came to a stop.

When Darcy joined him, he glanced at her and lifted his nose. She sniffed. Humans. Food and sweat and garbage. Metallic scents. Gasoline. Gun oil. And under the stench drifted the elusively wild fragrance of shifters.

She took a step forward—and Owen blocked her path, ears

back.

Gawain's heavy paw came down on her neck. *Don't move.*

But, but, but… Her villagers, her *brothers* were there. Reason trickled slowly into her brain—if her brothers were there, so were the Scythe.

Watching her carefully, Owen motioned with his head toward the trail's edge. His glance at Gawain was easy to read. They were to stay here and wait.

No, she needed to go with him and…and she'd probably get him killed. Her heart sank. Owen was called "Ghost Cat" because he could move through the forest without a sound.

She sure couldn't. With a low whine, she nodded.

Gawain chirruped softly and led her off the path. He stopped at a bare patch in the thick underbrush where they could watch the trail.

When they were settled, Owen flicked his ears at them, then sprang into a tree with a power and grace that dried her mouth. A second later, he disappeared.

Waiting was painful.

She tried to lie quietly, but the tip of her tail wouldn't stay still.

Lying next to her in the tall, pink-stemmed salal, Gawain purred softly, put his big paw on her neck again, and started to clean her fur.

She wanted to scold him, to tell him to stop, that she was too upset. Yet the sound of his deep purr, the feel of being pinned down, and the slow lap of his rough tongue filled the tiny space with a serene peace.

THE MOON HADN'T risen yet, and the path Owen followed was dark. His paws made no sound in the thick duff.

The trail ended at an eight-foot wall of side-by-side, vertical logs with the ends sharpened to points. His history books called it a stockade.

The scents were stale. No sounds of occupation came from within. The shifter-soldiers must be out training or on a mission.

Fuck, the thought of disappointing Darcy was a splinter in his heart.

He studied the property with narrowed eyes. Tiny glints of light told him the closest houses were several forested acres away. Aside from the untouched rear, the forest was cleared well away from the outer stockade, and floodlights studded the walls. Anyone approaching would be lit up like a comet in a black sky.

Staying at the forest's edge, he circled to check out the front. A rough dirt road fronted the property, and entry was by way of a long driveway through the stockade gate. Owen would guess that an attack through the front would be lethal.

Growling under his breath, he returned to the rear where the forest grew right up to the stockade. He'd bet the Scythe and shifter-soldiers used the door in the log wall to enter the forest.

He veered away from the floodlights that were pointed toward the trees and dropped down on the trail again. Very well traveled, wasn't it? The idiots were using the same path each time they came and went from the forest. Not a mistake any of Calum's shifters would make. But the Scythe wouldn't notice, and of course, these Daonain had been captured as children.

Quietly, he climbed a tree, going high enough to view the inside of the stockade. Bare earth surrounded two houses. On the right, the building had bare windows with iron bars. A small interior light illuminated barracks-style beds and tables. Clothing was strewn here and there. A few books lay around.

On the left, the house had a very sturdy door, a garage, and a satellite dish. Shutters covered the windows. At a guess, the staff lived there where they had privacy—and could defend themselves against the big nasty shifters.

As he'd suspected, no one was home. This would be a good time to check out the interior.

He moved down to a thicker branch and sprang to the top of the stockade fence, aiming for a flat-topped 6x6 post. He landed, dug his claws into the wood to secure his balance, and jumped down behind the barracks.

An earsplitting alarm went off. *Wah-wah-wah-wah*. A floodlight spotlighted him.

AS A DISTANT alarm went off, Darcy sprang to her feet, ears flat to her head. The sound was one she knew all too well—something had set off a Scythe security alarm.

Owen. They'd caught him.

She'd barely moved before Gawain blocked her. When she tried to shoulder past him, his hiss of discouragement stopped her.

A growl got her nowhere—and if she tried to run, he'd flatten her.

After checking to ensure they were concealed, she shifted to human. "That's a security alarm. Owen's been caught." A tearing sensation ripped through her chest at the thought of him being hurt. Of lethal, sarcastic, gentle, grumpy Owen being shot.

Tears filled her eyes. "What if they killed him? Took him prisoner?" She grabbed the ruff on Gawain's neck and shook the loose skin. "He needs us."

A world without Owen. No, never. Her knees buckled, and she dropped. "Please, Gawain."

Gawain didn't leap forward to save his brother. Instead, his ears pricked up to listen and then he shifted. "Owen was detected, aye. I don't hear anything else—not shouting, not weapons firing." He paused and prompted gently, "Do you?"

He wanted her to sit here when Owen was in trouble? The

cahir could be lying on the ground, shot, bleeding to death.

But…Gawain was right. Firearms would make noise, wouldn't they? Turning her head, she listened.

The blatting noise had gone silent. There was no shouting or shooting. No one screaming. No vehicles. The forest was silent—even the normal noise of the wildlife had stilled as the animals hunkered down in place.

"We'll wait, sweetling." Gawain pulled her close, and she laid her head on his chest, listening to the faster beat of his heart. He was worried, too. She rubbed her cheek against his bare skin, wanting to tell him how much it meant to her to be held.

How much *he* meant to her.

A few minutes later, Owen loped down the trail…and her heart swelled as if unable to contain all she felt. By all the Gods, she was in trouble, so much trouble. The words that must not be said fought to escape. *I love you.*

No, this would never work. Not ever.

THREE HOURS LATER, cup in hand, Gawain sat beside the fire, watching a salamander flirting with the campfire flames.

Last night, they'd zipped all the sleeping bags together to make one large bed and slept on top of it in animal form. Tonight, after they'd discussed Owen's findings, Darcy had been mostly silent, but the strained look on her face showed her emotions had been clawed to shreds. She'd crawled inside the sleeping bag bed and eventually fell asleep.

His heart ached at the pain she'd suffered.

Owen laid another log on the fire and glanced at Darcy. "I expected her to cry when she found out the camp is empty."

"She doesn't give in to how she feels." Gawain shook his head. "Not unless she's protecting someone as she was with us last night. Even then, she's—"

"Controlled," Owen said. "She was furious at Mother, but her voice was clear and low. She didn't hit or throw anything."

Gawain drank some of the hot chocolate they'd made from Tynan's provisions. "She's had a miserable month. Escaping from those bastards, having her first shift, being dumped in a new culture."

"First Gathering. Being hunted. Feeling guilty because she's free and her family isn't." Owen turned to look at Gawain, and his jaw clenched. "Like how I was free when you were trapped with our mother in Pine Knoll."

Yep, Gawain knew his littermate would feel the guilt. "It wasn't all bad. I didn't live with her, and there were long quiet periods when she had a male. And I got to work with the finest master blacksmith west of the Rockies, whereas you had to find yourself a new master carver to finish *your* apprenticeship. Lose the guilt, brawd."

"Yeah, well, it'll take some time." Owen took the hot chocolate from Gawain and sipped. "Did you leave a female back there?"

"No one serious. I had my share of lovers, but"—Gawain gave him a level look—"I always figured we'd share a mate."

Owen froze.

"Assuming you ever get over your unreasoning dislike of females."

"Don't hold your breath." His brother's retort lacked the force of conviction. Owen was changing—as did everyone who lived—and Darcy had a great deal to do with those changes.

No matter what Owen said, Gawain held a great deal of hope for the future. He tipped his head back. The waning moon wouldn't rise until later, and the stars hung low in the coal-black bowl of sky. "What's the plan for tomorrow?"

Owen poked at the fire, sending up sparks, and the salamander gave a pleased twirl. "Back to Cold Creek to report on the camp. I saw personal belongings in the dormitory. They'll be returning."

Then we'll have them. "Any lessons for Darcy tomorrow?"

"Yeah, but I'm not sure how to go about it. You know, cubs take only a couple of days to get used to four legs. So why is she still so clumsy?" Owen glanced over at her, frowned, and rose.

Gawain turned and jumped to his feet.

Asleep, she was thrashing in the sleeping bag. As growing horror filled her face, her hands and feet trembled like a wolf pup dreaming of being chased by a grizzly. "No. No, don't." Her voice was a whisper. Tears leaked from under her closed lids. "I'm sorry. Please, no."

Owen started to reach out and stopped. "Should—"

"Yeah, brawd. We wake her." Gawain went down on one knee and closed his hand over her delicate shoulder. He kept his voice low and calming. "Darcy. You're having a nightmare. Wake up, sweetling."

"No. Please. Don't hurt her any more. It was my—"

The panic in her voice made his anger rise. Gawain shook her gently.

Owen took her hands. His rough voice held a dominance that had never faltered despite their mother's abuse. "Darcy. Wake *up*. Now."

Her lids rose, and her eyes held blind panic. Fighting their hands and the sleeping bag, she struggled to sit up.

"Easy, easy." Gawain sat down and pulled her, sleeping bag and all, into his lap. When Owen started to rise, Gawain growled at him, "Stay here, brawd."

Owen sank down. "I don't know what to do when…"

Tenderhearted cahir. "She's scared, brawd. Sit beside me and let her feel guarded by the males she knows best."

That was all it took. Owen edged closer and stroked her

back. "We're here, Darcy. No one can hurt you now."

Gawain could feel the moment she truly woke. She pulled in a shuddering breath, and with a moan, sagged against him. Shivers wracked her still-too-thin body. "I-I'm sorry. Did I wake you two up?"

"We weren't asleep." Owen tucked her hair back from her tear-damp face. "Tell us…" He paused and rephrased. "Can you tell us what had you so frightened?"

She shook her head.

Owen growled slightly under his breath, and Gawain almost laughed. The cahir did far better with killing than comforting.

He'd learn.

Gawain folded her closer and kissed the top of her head. It pleased him when she pressed closer, letting him give her some of his strength. Was this what the Gods felt when they gifted their chosen? "Catling, sharing a nightmare will remove the claws embedded in your soul."

Her head lifted. Her haunted dark eyes narrowed as she caught the bitter knowledge in his words. "You've had nightmares?"

"Aye. More than a few." Edwyn's car wreck. A feral he'd been forced to kill before the male could slaughter two young wolves. A Gathering fight where two males had torn each other apart over a female.

One of his lovers had been a healer. She'd coaxed him to tell her, and with the talking, the nightmares had eased. "Sharing helps, Darcy."

SHARING? NO. DARCY couldn't talk about the blood, the screams, the guilt. She shook her head. "I c-can't."

Surprising her, Owen kissed her palm, and the scratchiness of his stubbled chin drew her back further into reality. "The night is not the time. You'll tell us tomorrow."

Bossy cat. Why did his order and his light kiss make her want to cry? "I will if... Would you just hold me for a while?"

Owen rose, and oh, the rejection hurt. She pulled in a shuddering breath and—he picked her up. "Strip down, brawd." He nodded at the sleeping bags.

After Gawain shed his clothes and climbed into the bag, Owen set her next to him.

"Closer, catling." Lying on his back, Gawain drew her against his side. He gave off heat like a bonfire and smelled of mountain meadows and sunshine.

She rubbed her cheek against his shoulder before lifting her head to look for Owen.

Gawain chuckled. "He'll douse the fire and join us."

With a sigh of relief, she snuggled closer with her front against his side. She put a leg over the top of his hard thighs, and somehow, it didn't even matter that they were both naked.

A minute later, also naked, Owen slid into the bag on her other side, spooning her with his chest against her back, and his legs behind hers.

Despite the frigid night air, warmth surrounded her. Gawain's heart beat slowly beneath her cheek.

Against her back, Owen's chest moved in and out with his even breathing, and his heavy arm lay over her and Gawain, securing them all together. His voice was deep. "You're safe, Darcy. Go back to sleep now."

"Bossy cat," she muttered...and fell asleep to the sound of their laughter.

Chapter Twenty-Two

THE NEXT DAY, on the way to the car, Owen had told the little cat to find him. If he watched closely, maybe he could figure out why she was such an inept feline.

Lying on a comfortable branch, Owen licked a wayward patch of fur on his foreleg. Having the pretty panther searching for him gave him an odd sense of satisfaction.

There she was.

He had to suppress his purr. Although she was still tiny—not much bigger than a teenaged shifter—the time in Cold Creek had been good for her. Her fur had a sheen, and her flanks were no longer hollowed. Smooth padding covered her ribs, although she had a few more pounds to go. In all reality, she was far more than the "pretty panther" Gawain called her—she was beautiful.

She went past the place where he'd left the trail, halted, and retraced her steps. Finding his trail, she headed into the underbrush. Her paw almost landed on a shrew. Its angry squeak and skittering retreat made her freeze, consternation in every line of her body.

Owen had to smother his huff of amusement.

But—good girl—she hadn't jumped a couple of feet into the air as she had the first few times. Instead, she sniffed and relaxed.

She continued on. Slowly. Really, far too slowly. When he and Gawain had played these games as cublings, they'd loped along, sniffing the air, ears swiveled to catch any sound. They hadn't gone into stalk mode unless they found an active scent.

At this rate, she'd be searching for him for hours.

His tail impatiently flicked up and down as he realized her every step was planned out, as was each pause to sniff.

Planned? For fuck's sake, she was in animal form. Animals didn't plan. Admittedly, a shifter needed some control. The human side never disappeared—unless feral. Part of being an animal was letting instincts rule, allowing the magic to have its sway, and taking joy in the sheer physical nature of a beast.

Darcy, however, was all human and merely clothed in the body of a panther.

He saw the moment she caught his scent and again overruled her instincts. She didn't crouch. She used her eyes instead of her other senses. Following his scent, she should have launched herself into the tree and jumped him. Or chased after him if he'd leaped away first.

But no, she pushed away those urges because she wanted to use her eyes. To *see* him before acting.

With an annoyed hiss, he sprang. In two bounds, he hit her and wrapped his forelegs around her shoulders so he could bite her ear in a reprimand. Then and only then, he trawsfurred.

After a moment, she did the same. As she lay, flattened by his weight, she glared at him.

She pleased his eyes.

Her hair was the blackest of blacks and made a lush waterfall over her high, pert breasts. Muscles flowed in her shoulders and arms. Whatever she'd done in that prison, it hadn't been sitting around on her ass.

Grumbling under her breath, she squirmed out from under him, which he enjoyed more than he should have. Herne's hooves, this wasn't the time to give in to his attraction. It sure wasn't appropriate to remember the last Gathering—taking her, mating with her, how she'd felt around him.

How she cried out as she gave in to her passion.

That thought reminded him of why he was angry. He rose to his feet, folded his arms over his chest, and scowled at her. "I've seen better hunting from thirteen-year-olds with only a day of being a shifter. You caught my scent. Why didn't you attack?"

She jumped to her feet and scowled back "I had to find you first."

"No. Your nose told you where I was, and your body wanted to spring. I saw your muscles tense. But you didn't."

"I… I wanted to see you. To make sure." She looked confused. Adorably confused.

He sighed and motioned her toward a log. "By Herne's holy antlers, Gawain should explain this. I'm not used to having to…"

"Talk rather than kill?" Anger gone, she grinned at him.

"Impertinent cub."

"I'm no cub."

His hand reached out of its own accord, and he traced his fingertips over her shoulder, heading toward the valley between her breasts. Her skin was warm and soft with a mesmerizing silkiness. Her scent was a light musk, holding a whiff of pine from the trees.

As he breathed in, he caught the first hint of her arousal. She enjoyed his hand on her.

"No, he said huskily, "you're no cub." With an effort, he took a step back and dropped his arm.

Lesson. This was a lesson. *Think, Treharn.* Having lived with intellect-driven humans, she wouldn't easily relax into being an animal. Daonain cubs grew up around shifters—Darcy hadn't. "You need to let your animal instincts handle your body."

"But, I thought… Don't you kill Daonain who go feral and let the animal control them?"

He heard Gawain cross the meadow, but kept his eyes on Darcy. "With ferals, the human half is gone and only rage remains."

When she paled, he knew she'd seen a feral in her past. "In animal form, if really needed, the human side can take charge. It's…" He scowled, searching for an example. "When I learned to drive, an instructor sat beside me. I steered—did the driving—but if I screwed up, he could tell me to pull over, and he'd drive."

"Oh." Her brows puckered. "You're saying I should let the animal drive and keep veto power."

"Exactly." Gawain sat down beside her. "You need to sink into the wildness and trust it. This is part of who you are now."

She bit her lip. "I…don't want to let go. I need to be in control."

Owen snorted. "Sounds like our mother." He regretted the words even before she glared at him.

"I am not your mother. I'm *me*, not any other female—any more than you are Gawain. I can tell each male is unique. Why can't you see that females aren't identical?"

He blinked. By the God, she'd delivered a verbal disembowelment—which was exactly what he'd asked her to do if he made an idiot of himself. "You're right; thank you for reminding me."

He couldn't keep from smiling. "You're definitely not like anyone I've met before."

Her glare faded. "I didn't mean to snap at you."

"*I* enjoyed it," Gawain said. "But, sweetling, can you tell us why you won't let go?"

Her color grayed, and fear scented the air. "No."

Owen frowned. The same scent of fear had clung to her last night after the nightmare. She didn't frighten easily, this little female. Had something happened in the past when she lost control? Something that, even now, gave her nightmares? How could he help if he didn't know what was wrong?

By the God, he couldn't stand it when she was frightened. Needing to protect her—even from her own past—he moved closer and put an arm around her.

She gave him a surprised look, then leaned against him and put her head on his chest. Letting him give her comfort. Finest feeling in the world.

As her muscles relaxed, he nuzzled the top of her head and figured some kisses would put her right. He hadn't had a kiss for hours, after all. Tangling his fingers in her hair, he pulled her head back and kissed her, teasing her lips open, then delving deep.

She tensed for all of a moment before melting against him. When he tipped her back into the soft grass and flattened her with his weight, she made no protest. Her arms came around him.

At least she had no trouble losing control when mating. Perhaps because she had no bad memories to overcome.

Owen lifted his head to glance at his brother.

Despite the slight worried crinkle of his eyes, Gawain gave him an amused look. "My turn."

Obligingly, Owen rolled to Darcy's right and propped his head up on his hand.

On her left, Gawain stretched out and, before she could sit up, rolled on top of her. "Kiss me, sweetling," he murmured.

She frowned and looked at Owen.

Ah. She'd been in human hands for too long. "Kiss him, Darcy. We both like your kisses."

Her look of delight was endearing. And then ever so sweetly, she wiggled her right arm under Owen to stroke his back and keep them connected.

Curling her other arm around Gawain's back, she gave him her lips.

Owen smiled. So sweet.

As Gawain kept her occupied, Owen deliberated. Acknowledging she had to give the animal control wouldn't work if her past blocked her. She needed to face her fears to move past them.

Talking was the first step. After all, they were her mentors, the ones she trusted, but apparently, not enough.

Mating could break down barriers and increase trust.

Then mating it would be.

The detour for her lesson had brought them up a steep climb no human hikers could manage. This meadow was private. The grass was soft. The sun was high and warm against bare skin—and there were no shadows to frighten a little female.

Aye, this was the time to deal with nightmares. Lying on his side, he caught his brother's attention with the subliminal hum that meant *I have an idea.*

Gawain lifted his head and waited for Owen to indicate what the plan was.

Darcy was on her back. Owen slid closer until he pressed against Darcy from the side. A glance ensured that Gawain would do the same. Owen set his free hand on her breast, cupping it, kneading it, enjoying the softness that fit in his palm so nicely. It made an excellent way to keep her in place.

Gawain's eyebrows rose, then he simply followed suit.

WHAT WERE THEY doing? Flat on her back, Darcy looked up at the two males who were studying her carefully. Their warm, hard bodies pushed against her. Owen had a hand on her breast, holding her firmly, and obviously enjoying himself.

Gawain's hand was broader. As his callused thumb rubbed over her nipple, her whole body tensed. Anticipation simmered deep in her core.

Two males. She could smell their interest, could feel their erect cocks pressing against her hips. But why were they watching her like that? "No more kisses?"

"Aye. In a bit." Owen's voice was deeper than normal. Huskier. His gaze never left hers as he stroked her breast until her toes curled. "It's daytime, kitten. Warm and quiet and far from anything frightening."

"Ah." Gawain's expression changed to one of comprehension. He leaned down to kiss her forehead. When she looked at him, his gaze was both stern and sympathetic. "Owen's right. It's time to tell us about your nightmare. What haunts your trail, sweetling?"

"No." Instinctively, she tried to sit up, but...the hands holding her breasts simply pressed down. She'd put her arms around them earlier, and now her elbows were pinned under their bodies.

Owen had the nerve to caress her again. "We'll continue kissing after we talk."

She glared. "I'm not in the mood, not anymore, and I'm not going to talk with you. Let me up."

"Sweetling," Gawain said softly. His eyes were the same clear blue as the vast sky behind him. "Didn't you agree to tell us about your nightmare today?"

She *had* agreed. Her voice came out almost a whimper. "I don't want to."

Gawain nodded. "I know. But fears are best faced in the light of day—and with someone beside you."

She had *two* concerned someones. The ice of fear was in her veins, but the sun was hot on her skin, and the males were unmoving guardians on each side. *Talk, Darcy.*

She wet her lips. "My nightmares are memories. Mainly one." She stuck there.

"When did it happen?" Gawain asked. "In the last year?"

The question helped. "Way back. The adults had all died, and they brought us up out of the basement and cages. They were afraid they'd lose us all."

The deadly growl from Owen shook her bones…and was the most heartening thing she'd ever heard.

"We did the yard work, cleaning, gardening, but weren't allowed to talk to each other—to anyone, really—and couldn't touch or be together." *Do the work. Be silent.*

"By the God." Owen looked at Gawain. "Can you imagine what that kind of isolation would do to wolves?"

Gawain's jaw clenched. "Did you talk?"

"Not me… Margery did. She was whispering to Barbara and got caught. The guard—they all carry canes—he started hitting her."

The whacking sound against flesh, Margery's cry of pain. Her begging. I'm sorry. Dropping to her knees.

As Darcy went silent, sliding down into the nightmare, Owen cupped her cheek and turned her head. His eyes were a stern, compelling green.

"Talk to us," Owen said. "Get it out, little cat."

She pulled herself back to reality. "Another guard came and joined him. Having fun, hitting her over and over. She was sobbing, curled up in a ball, and they wouldn't stop." Darcy spoke around the knot in her throat, blinking her burning eyes. "I…I couldn't take it. I knew better, and I still tried to get them to stop."

"Stop it, just stop!" Knocking one guard away. Standing between them and Margery. So angry. Hardly feeling the blows of the canes. "Leave her alone!"

"Of course, you tried to stop them." Gawain wiped tears from her cheeks. "What did they do?"

Sickness curled in her belly, and she shook her head.

When she didn't continue, Gawain's voice held as much steely determination as Owen's. "Give us the rest, Darcy."

Her voice came out a whisper. "They beat me. Broke my arm. My ribs." *A crack. Horrendous pain. Blow after blow.* "Then they kicked me to the ground and went back to Margery. With their fists. Their boots. One held my head up, made me watch. Said she was paying for my interference."

"By the God," Owen muttered.

Darcy swallowed. "They beat her until…until her arms and legs were broken, her ribs, her face. She stopped screaming, and they kept hitting her. I was begging and crying and…"

Snarling, Owen yanked her into his arms, and behind her, Gawain pressed closer, growling low and deep.

The sound of his anger shattered her barricades, and she started to cry. The ugly sobs surged from her depths, spilling out in painful sounds.

Eventually, she realized Owen's embrace was crushing her ribs—and was the most wonderful feeling in the world. Gawain was stroking her hair in long slow strokes.

With a shuddering sigh, she laid her cheek on Owen's wet chest. "I didn't mean to…weep all over you."

"Sounds like you had some stored up," Gawain said. "Anything else in there?"

She pulled in a breath. "A couple of times after that, I acted before thinking, but at least I was the only one to get hurt. Eventually, I learned to restrain my reactions."

"Control. I get it." Owen kissed the top of her head. "Holding back won't serve you well as a shifter. You'll have to find a balance, *cariad.*"

Cariad. Gawain had called her that. And it was what Calum called Vicki. What did it mean?

"Time to wash your face and get a drink." Gawain rose and pulled her to her feet. "I hear a stream over there."

Wiping her face, she took a step. Her legs shook. All of her shook.

"Come." Owen put an arm around her waist and held her steady as they followed Gawain to the trickling creek. The water was crystal clear with a bottom of rounded river stones.

Gawain stepped in and splashed his face and chest.

Holding onto Owen's arm, Darcy put a toe in. The icy water bit her skin, and she yanked her foot back. "Are you crazy? It's freezing."

"Glacier water." Owen grinned. "Go on. Be a brave kitten."

She stiffened. "I'm not brave."

"Yes, you are." He studied her. "I've seen you fight"

The hellhound. "That was different."

Gawain turned. "Different how?"

"There was only one of him and in Cold Creek. The Scythe...they terrify me." She looked down, regretting her honesty, yet they needed to know how much of a coward she was. "When the Cosantir said the cahirs would rescue the females in Seattle—and that I didn't have to go back—I...I almost cried with relief."

Return to the *prìosan*. Just the thought formed a knot of fear in her chest.

"Easy, sweetling," Gawain murmured.

"Being afraid doesn't mean you're not brave." To her surprise, Owen leaned down and kissed her cheek. "Being brave means doing what you have to do in spite of the fear."

She looked at him in surprise. The cahir didn't despise her?

Jumping into the freezing stream, he melodramatically peered all around. "I don't see any Scythe in here. Get in, tiny tinker."

"You... You are so..." She glared at him, unable to believe he'd tease her about her fears. Yet the knot in her chest loosened.

"I am." He grinned. "Get in."

"Not in this lifetime. I'll hold out for a hot shower when we get to the lodge." Males really were insane, weren't they?

Owen glanced at his brother. "Who could resist?"

She frowned. "Resist what?"

The two males bent down with cupped hands—and a wave of icy water drenched her. She shrieked. "You dumbasses. You stupid…" She couldn't find words nasty enough.

"Excellent scream." Gawain was grinning.

"Like a hawk. Very nice." Owen eyed her as if he planned to yank her in.

She hastily backed up.

The male didn't laugh often, but when he did, her heart actually danced. "We won't splash you again. Promise."

Gawain grinned and held out his cupped hands. "You need to drink, Darcy."

They'd never lied to her…and she *had* screeched loud enough to wake the gnomes in the city. She advanced and sucked the water from Gawain's hands. It was cold enough to make her teeth hurt.

The sun was already drying the water from her skin.

Jumping up onto the bank, Owen used his wet hands to stroke the last of the tears from her face. "There. All better."

"Thanks."

A grin warned her a second before he put an arm behind her back, lifted his other hand, and circled her nipple with a freezing cold finger.

The nub puckered into an aching peak. She tried to jerk away, and his arm curbed her.

"Look how it jumps to attention," he told Gawain. He teased the nipple to a long peak.

"You're impossible." She glared up at him.

Bending, Owen took her mouth, pulling her against his

rock-solid body.

Her insides went into a meltdown.

He lifted his head an inch and whispered against her lips, "Now we can go back to kissing." Slowly, holding her gaze with his green eyes, he lifted her wrist to his face, inhaled…and smiled.

There was no denying the scent of her arousal. Against her pelvis, his cock was thickening, lengthening. And oh, she remembered how he felt. Her core dampened, preparing for his entry.

He turned her, and Gawain took her into his embrace. He lifted her chin and smiled into her eyes, watching her carefully as he lowered his head.

Her mouth opened to him, and she wrapped her arms around his neck. He followed Owen's lead, sniffing her wrist, and satisfying himself she wanted them both.

"You could just ask," she whispered.

He nuzzled her temple and whispered back, "Words can be misleading. Scents don't lie."

Moving in behind her, Owen sandwiched her between the males. As Gawain kissed her, she felt Owen playing with her breasts, teasing them, rolling the nipples.

Heat sprang to life within her. Between her legs, she was tingling, swelling, needing. She wiggled against the rigid cock in back, and made a sound. An urgent sound.

"Oh, not yet, little cat," Owen murmured, kissing the curve between her shoulder and neck. His teeth nipped, and his lips soothed the tiny sting.

Gawain framed her face with his hands as he teased her lips and fenced with her tongue. Against her soft belly, his erection was hard and thick, a promise of more.

Both of them would take her.

Her hands closed on Gawain's forearms. "I'm…I don't

know how to do this. I don't want to disappoint you."

"*Cariad*, don't you know we're worrying about the same thing?" He traced a line from her crinkled brow down her nose to tap her lips. "But there is no right or wrong here. We're going to go slow…and simply enjoy what happens. Aye?"

A sigh escaped her. She could do that. "Aye."

Before she could move, Owen scooped her up, holding her cradled against him like a cubling. She grabbed him around the neck and growled.

His grin flashed. "Choose a place, brawd?"

"Over to the left. It's flat with good grass."

"Perfect." Effortlessly, Owen carried her there and laid her down on the lush, cool creekside grass. He knelt beside her on her left. Smiling into her eyes, he laced his fingers with hers, raised her arms, and pinned them over her head. "Here you go, brawd. Enjoy your treats."

"What do—" Before she could finish her question, Owen took her mouth, his tongue plunging deep. He didn't release her hands.

A second later, Gawain caressed her breasts. "These really are a treat." He closed his mouth on her right nipple. His mouth was hot and wet, and he sucked lightly while fondling her other breast. When he rubbed his beard on the underside, the light scratching curled her toes.

Urgency wakened inside her, and the feelings were strange and almost overpowering. She tried to move, but Owen had her hands trapped.

He made a reprimanding grumbling sound and simply kept kissing her.

Gawain switched to her left breast, teasing the nipple with his tongue. He stroked down her waist, over a hip, between her legs.

Her center throbbed in response.

His finger slid between her folds, and she could feel how slick she was.

When her hips lifted and her legs opened to make room for his large hand, Gawain made an approving sound. He kissed her breasts and sat back. "You know, I've missed your taste."

What?

Slowly, he kissed his way down the same path his hands had taken. Her stomach muscles quivered under his soft lips and teasing nibbles.

Owen pulled her arms down and set her hands on his shoulders. "Keep your hands here, kitten. I want to feel your claws."

She stroked over his contoured iron-hard muscles with her fingertips. Why would he talk about claws? She'd never scratch him.

"Nice. Feels good." He licked over her lips.

As he kissed her jaw, his beard scruff scraped her skin, rousing more sensations.

Ignoring his order about keeping her hands on his shoulders, she tangled her fingers in his long thick hair. "Are you—"

Gawain took her clit in his mouth, and the excruciating pleasure consumed her.

"Ooooooh." Her back arched, and her hand fisted in Owen's hair.

Laughing, Gawain licked over her folds. "That was even better than the scream."

"Aye." Chuckling, Owen pushed her breasts together and sucked one nipple, then the other. "Do some more."

"Oh, I intend to." Gawain bent his head, tracing his tongue in circles around her clit. When he stopped to flick right on top of her clit, she started melting into the ground beneath her.

He circled her entrance and then pushed a thick finger inside, stretching her, reminding her of that night when she'd been taken so many times.

Owen closed his lips around her nipple and sucked forcefully on the peak.

An electrifying sensation surged outward.

Before she recovered, Gawain began to suck in light pulls on her clit, and her entire core tightened with need. With urgency.

"Breathe, *cariad*," Owen murmured.

Opening her eyes, she saw he'd lifted his head and was watching her. His hand on her breast sent small zings of pleasure through her with each caress.

She drew in air and lost it again when Gawain licked and flicked his tongue right on top of her clit. Her eyes closed as all of her muscles tensed. Her fingernails dug into Owen's shoulders, and he laughed.

As the pressure in her core increased, every cell in her body quivered, waiting for more.

Gawain didn't stop. His tongue circled her clit slowly, danced over the swollen top, circled, flicked.

A quaking started in her center.

"Now, brawd," Owen murmured. She felt his fingers on her nipples, pulling and rolling them, and the sensation zinged downward, even as Gawain set his tongue over her clit and rubbed mercilessly.

Everything…everything within contracted into a ball, exploding outward in massive waves of pleasure. She felt Gawain's hands on her hips as his tongue teased out more spasms of pleasure until even her fingers tingled with sensation.

"Oh my Gods," she whispered.

She felt Owen's hand against her cheek as he kissed her lightly and gave her a hug. Gawain lay down on the other side, and she loved the feeling of being between them, bathed in protection and…and affection.

They cared about her. She really was certain of that.

She turned to her right, lifting a shaking arm so she could stroke Gawain's face. Touch his tan cheek, run her fingers through the soft short beard framing his strong jawline. "Thank you."

He smiled at her and kissed her fingertips. "You are very welcome, sweetling. It was my pleasure." She could hear his sincerity—he'd enjoyed himself.

She bit her lip. During the full moon, taking Owen in her mouth had been amazing, and he'd seemed to enjoy it. Would Gawain? "Can I do…? To you?" What was it called?

"Use your mouth on me?" Gawain's smile grew. "Oh, aye, you certainly can. It's one of the ways two males can share a female at the same time."

Her eyes widened. *Oh…my.* At the Gathering, Owen had mentioned males shared in various ways, and she'd tried to imagine exactly how it all worked. "How, um, where does everything go and who does what and…?"

Owen laid his callused hand on her cheek and turned her to face him. A slight smile softened his hard face as he ran his thumb over her lips. "Darcy, do you trust me?"

"Yes."

His green eyes lightened, and his voice was gruff. "Thank you. Then, let me arrange everything—and we'll all be happy, aye?"

He'd be in control, not her. She wouldn't like letting him take over…would she? The memory of the full moon night made her rethink. When she'd mated Owen, there had been no question as to who was in charge. Did she want that again?

Oh, yes. As she met his steady, confident eyes, any thought of refusing melted right out of her. "Yes."

He smiled slowly and met her lips with his. His scent filled her with each breath, and he purred as he nibbled on her lips.

When Gawain started playing with her breasts, she felt as if her body was slowly sinking into the grass.

GAWAIN TEASED HIS tongue around Darcy's velvety nipple, enjoying the sound of his littermate's purring. Finally, finally, they'd get to share Darcy—he couldn't think of anywhere else he'd rather be right now.

With a sigh, Owen lifted his head and sat up. "On your back, brawd. This little cat has work to do."

Gawain glanced at him and caught on. "Work is good for a soul." He lay back in the grass, put an arm behind his head, and smiled at the perplexed look on Darcy's face.

"Kneel between his legs, *cariad*." Owen positioned her.

To Gawain's delight, she was completely acquiescing to his littermate's directions. Yes, she was perfect for them.

Owen took her hand and wrapped it around Gawain's cock.

As her flush deepened, her fingers curled in a snug grip.

Gawain inhaled sharply. His cock leaped at the heat of her palm, at the feeling of her small fingers around him.

"There's a good female. You did a bit of this at the Gathering, remember? Now, you can lick and suck, but no biting or teeth," Owen told her. "The more you can take into your mouth and throat, the happier he'll be, but don't go farther than you're comfortable with."

"But, how exactly do I…?" Her worry was obvious. She was so sweet—a female who wanted to do everything perfectly when making someone else happy.

As deep into her need as she'd been for her first Gathering, he doubted if she remembered much of what she'd done.

Gawain reached down and covered her fingers on his cock. He moved her hand up and down, and rumbled in pleasure. "This is the movement, whether you're using your hand, your tongue, or your lips. If I'm purring, I'm enjoying it."

Relief filled her eyes, before she bit her lip. "But what if you're not enjoying it? Or I hurt you? Or…"

Such a worrier. Gawain hesitated, unsure how to reassure her.

With an evil grin, Owen handed a handful of her hair to Gawain. "There. He has a leash to tug if he needs your attention."

The concept would have annoyed some females. Darcy's lips curved in a pleased smile. "Perfect. I can do this." As she regarded him, heat kindled in her eyes.

Elation hummed in his veins at the knowledge that the sight of his body pleased her. To see her arousal as she looked at him was one of the finest compliments he'd ever received.

She stroked his cock, very tentatively. When he didn't scream in agony, her grip firmed, and she pumped slightly more vigorously.

Simply having her hands—Darcy's hands—on him at all thrilled him to the depths, but he managed to hold himself to a light purr.

She bounced in excitement, bent, and licked up his dick. "Mmm." As her small hands played with the fuzz between his legs and around his balls, she inhaled and took him deeper. Her tongue teased his shaft as she clamped her lips around him.

He might combust from sheer overload.

Why didn't she move?

Laughter in his voice, Owen reminded her, "Up and down."

She grunted an acknowledgement and began to move, thank the Mother, and the feeling was…sublime. Without even thinking, he purred louder—and was startled to hear a light purr from her in return.

"Someone likes this…even without the full moon heat," Owen said softly.

Thank fuck.

WHY WAS THIS so…exhilarating? Darcy took more of Gawain's cock in her mouth. Each breath brought her his masculine, musky scent, so much stronger around his groin. She stopped to nuzzle the soft hair between his hip and thigh. With gentle fingers, she caressed his testicles. They were round and hot and heavy.

His purring never slackened.

She ran her tongue up his cock, teased out the fat, winding veins, and licked away the drop of moisture at the top. The taste, like the deep forest at night, made her insides clench.

All right, enough playing. Gripping the base, she tried bobbing up and down. Licking. Sucking.

Gawain's purring grew more intense.

And for some reason, heat engulfed her. Her pussy felt drenched, and her breasts throbbed.

"Don't stop," Owen said, even as he moved her right hand to the ground beside Gawain's hip. The pat on her fingers let her know she should keep her hand there.

Don't stop. She sucked lightly on the head of Gawain's cock, and his breathing hitched. *Oh, nice.* Trying to add variation, she took his shaft almost all the way in her mouth, compressed her lips, and bobbed up, faster than before.

Hard hands lifted her hips up, forcing her to balance on her knees and one hand. When Owen's fingers ran between her folds and over her tingling clit, she gasped.

She lifted her head and looked back. "What are you *doing*?"

"Seems I've heard that question before." Kneeling behind her, he grinned. "This time, I'm playing with a little female's body while she plays with my brother's body."

Securing his grip on her hip, he teased around her clit so knowledgeably that a seething tension began to build low in her pelvis. His eyes darkened, his gaze holding her. "And I'm going to take you. You'll have both our cocks in you, so be prepared."

Her breathing faltered to a halt. Take her…while her mouth was around Gawain's cock. Desire built to a steady pulse between her legs.

She looked at Gawain.

He smiled at her, eyes half-lidded, and with a tug on her hair, directed her to resume. "No biting. But you can lift your head up if you need to scream."

To scream. A shiver seized her. Setting thinking aside, she tried to concentrate on sucking and licking—even as Owen pressed a finger inside before running the slick finger around her clit again.

Hunger churned as the sensitive nub swelled. Her legs started to tremble.

Gawain tangled his fingers in her hair, pulling her head down on his erection.

Even as more heat washed through her, she sucked on the thick shaft. Licked. Sucked. Lifted her head and slid him partway out.

Behind her, Owen moved closer. His cock pressed against her entrance, and even as she took Gawain's shaft deeper, Owen pressed inside.

Oh my Gods. She thought she'd remembered what he felt like, but she hadn't. She was slick with need, and there was no pain, just overwhelming pleasure as he breached her entrance.

As the head of his cock pressed in farther, and her swollen tissues were forced to stretch around him, she felt helpless in his grasp.

Lifting her head, she gasped for air.

He paused for a moment, another, then inexorably continued to advance until he filled her completely. When he stopped, his long shaft was planted deep within her.

As her core throbbed around him, she needed…needed more. She wiggled, gasping as his cock moved.

Laughing, Owen pushed her head down, reminding her of the erection resting against her cheek.

With a giggle, she turned her head and took Gawain's shaft back in her mouth. Sucking lightly, she tongued him, loving the velvety texture.

Owen started to move, in and out, slowly, letting her adjust.

And the feeling...oh, the feeling. Forget adjusting. She rocked back onto him hard and swayed forward to swallow Gawain's cock.

Both males were purring.

So was she.

Fingers curved unyieldingly around her hips, Owen penetrated her, withdrew, and continued, slowly, relentlessly increasing the speed.

Stone by stone, her need built to a mountain in her body.

Then Gawain made a low sound and twisted her hair around his hand to hold her still. "Give us a second, brawd." His voice was hoarse.

Owen paused.

"Sweetling, if you continue, I'll fill your mouth with my seed." Gawain's heated gaze met hers, giving her time to object.

Oh *yes*. She wiggled her delight and nodded.

Gawain's eyes lit, and as he tugged her head down, he pumped in and out of her mouth in short fast strokes. As Owen held her hips still, Gawain's cock hardened, thickened. She heard a rumbling groan of pleasure, and then his shaft was jerking in her mouth. The taste was intense, salty and musky, and she swallowed it down.

The grip on her hair loosened, and he stroked her head gently.

Lifting her head, she used her tongue to capture the last drops and lick him clean. "Mmm."

His eyes were half-lidded and satisfied. "Thank you, pretty

panther." He guided her head down so she could rest her cheek on his flat belly. Closing his hands on her shoulders, he said, "Go, brawd."

Owen chuckled and lifted her hips higher for still greater penetration. He pulled out, sank in, and slowly, steadily increased the pace.

As the driving rhythm set up a merciless throbbing, she clenched around him. She wanted more. Wanted to rock back and forth, but he gripped her hips, and Gawain held her shoulders. As the exquisite torment grew, she could do nothing but moan.

Leaning forward, Owen bit the nape of her neck, holding her lightly with his teeth. His hand reached between them down to her clit. His finger slid roughly over the sensitive nub with each plunge of his cock.

Everything faded except his thrusts and his finger on her clit. Every stroke and thrust increased the pleasure until she hovered at the heights of the most devastating sensation she'd ever known.

Then, he somehow rotated his hips, and his shaft struck a new place inside her. His ruthless finger pressed on her clit.

Everything within her stopped—even the planet came to a halt, then her world erupted into great, glorious spasms of pleasure, exploding outward until the very sky seemed filled with stars and the earth itself disappeared from under her.

As her core spasmed around the hard shaft, Owen pressed deep, deeper, and she could feel him inside her, filling her with his seed.

IN THE HIGH mountain valley, the air was chill, yet the sun beat warmly against Owen's skin. Sound asleep, Darcy lay with her head on his brother's shoulder, pressed against his side, her breathing deep and slow. Cupping Darcy's soft breast in one hand, Owen was curled behind her. He propped his head up on his free hand and drank in the moment. Each breath brought him the fragrance of sex, of this little female, of his littermate, mingling in a way that sent an ache through him. This was why a male lived. Why he fought. To win a female's love and keep her safe.

For this female—for Darcy—he would willingly fight the entire world.

As he looked at Gawain, his contentment deepened. An arm behind his head, his littermate was watching Darcy, satisfaction almost humming from him.

They'd not only shared a female for the first time in decades, but that female was Darcy. She'd liked being with them both. Had cried out her pleasure. And snuggled between them with as much trust as an unweaned kitten.

Had any female ever trusted him so deeply? Had he ever wanted one to?

But Darcy…she was special. So amazing. He loved her ability to laugh, even at herself. Her courage to stand up to him when he was wrong. Her honesty. Her intelligence. Her loyalty to the people she'd left behind. She would show that same loyalty to her cubs. What a fearsome, amazing mother she would be.

What a mate.

But…would she want him? For more than just being God-chosen? Owen wasn't charming. Wasn't particularly good-looking, especially with all the scars he'd accrued over the years.

Then again, Darcy knew him better than any female ever had. She'd seen past the cahir legend to the grumpy, blunt male beneath, and she'd still mated with him when the moon wasn't full.

Did she realize he'd give her the same loyalty he wanted from her?

"I want to keep her," Owen said, his voice barely audible even to shifter ears. "Make her ours."

"Yeah," Gawain whispered. "We should keep her. She needs us."

"Do you think she'd want to…? Does she…? How do we make her want to stay?"

Gawain's lips tipped up. "The question she'll ask, brawd, is if you love her."

DARCY WAS HAVING a happy dream, playing near a lake with two big males. The three of them were chasing each other's tails, batting at ears with soft paws. Hiding in the grass and playing pounce.

A hand jostled her. "Darcy."

One male caught her between his huge paws and the other leaped over her. So fun. Her heart swelled because these were her lifemates, the ones she'd dreamed of forever.

Only…they weren't. These panthers weren't average-sized and sleek. They were huge.

She frowned as her shoulder was shook again.

"Wake up, kitten."

There was such a lovely scent around her. Musky male scents were blended with the fragrance of mating. Mating? Her eyes popped open.

She was lying in the grass on her back. Owen lay beside her.

On her other side, Gawain had his hand on her shoulder.

"Ah." She felt her cheeks heat as her body reported in with the sensitive tingling in her nipples and how swollen her breasts were. There was an aching burn between her legs…and her jaw muscles felt tired. Her gaze dropped to where Gawain's shaft lay quiet. It was still big, actually.

Her lips curved. Mating was amazing. Her whole body felt limp and thoroughly satisfied.

"Darcy."

She jerked her gaze up. "Um, yes?"

Gawain's cheek creased with his smile. "Time to go. The Cosantir needs to set things into motion, now we know where the shifter-soldiers live."

"I'm sorry." She sat up. What was she thinking to have fallen asleep? "We shouldn't have—"

"It was time for a break." Owen rolled up onto a knee and tucked her hair behind her ear. The tender look in his eyes made her breath catch. "We'll eat on the run and make this a long day. You're in better shape, so we should reach the car tomorrow morning."

Gawain rose, pulled her easily to her feet, and did the same for his brother. "Grab a drink, rinse off, and we'll be on our way."

Beside her in the cold water, the males washed themselves off. She managed to stifle her squeaks at the icy water as she cleaned up, moved upstream, and drank her fill.

On the bank, Owen stopped beside her, his expression serious. "While we're running in animal form, I want you to sink deep into the wild."

Let go of control. Apprehension constricted her lungs.

"We're your mentors. We won't let you get so far you can't return." Gawain stood beside his brother.

She shoved the fear down. They were right. Fighting against her animal instincts made her clumsy. She refused to go through life falling off of branches. "I'll try."

"Good." Owen squeezed her shoulder in approval.

"We'll play a game." Gawain grinned. "Follow-the-alpha. You simply do whatever Owen does."

Owen's smile was almost a smirk. "I'll be jumping into trees, off boulders, over logs."

Oh, goody, her favorite things. *Not.* "And you'll be doing all this leaping and jumping, too?" She gave Gawain a skeptical look.

He only laughed. "Not a chance."

Owen turned and jogged toward the forest, shifting into cougar without missing a step.

Wow. She tried the moving-trawsfur—at a fast walk—and her four feet almost tangled into a knot.

"Sink into the wild, catling. Let go." Gawain shifted and ran easily beside her.

At an easy lope, Owen sprang up and into a tree, leaped off the lowest branch, and was back on the trail.

By the Mother, I can't do that.

Yes. She could. She would.

Darcy shut her mind down and let the cat take over…all the way. She looked at the tree. The branch. Her body tensed, sprang, clawed up and onto the branch, then she was down and running the trail.

Taking a moment for a happy spin, she flirted with her tail and heard the low chuff of Gawain's laughter.

Happily, she darted after Owen.

Chapter Twenty-Three

THE NEXT MORNING, as the rising sun shone down on the logging road, Gawain rolled up the sleeves of his flannel shirt, then yawned. They were almost at his car.

Ahead of him, Owen and Darcy were discussing how she could have caught her breakfast quicker. Instincts were good, but knowledge and practice were also needed, which was why cubs got hunting lessons.

As teens, he and Owen had often been assigned to instruct the newly shifted. Even when young, his littermate had been a fine teacher, although cranky if he thought a youngster wasn't trying.

Darcy, though, poured her heart into trying…no matter what she was doing.

Like last night…

At dark, despite the chill air, they'd shifted to human long enough to enjoy a hot, fast mating. Gawain smiled slightly, rubbing the scratch marks on his chest. After a day as a panther, Darcy's instincts had been more animal than human, and she'd clawed him when she peaked. Owen had bite marks on his shoulder.

Seeing her work afterward, she'd turned a brilliant red.

Gawain grinned at the memory. By the Mother, he loved

her.

He and Owen had talked over their hopes after she'd fallen asleep. And they'd tried to make plans.

Gawain shook his head. For decades, he'd made lifemating bracelets for shifters. Shouldn't he have learned the steps of the relationship dance? Then again, most shifters didn't choose a female who was ignorant of mating, let alone lifemating.

"Gawain." Owen looked back over his shoulder. "Let's detour long enough to swing by that camp from the highway. We can get the street address for Tynan and Wells."

"Aye."

An hour later, Gawain could scent the tension in the car as he left Highway 20 and drove down a gravel road. Not much here. A few small farms. A couple of fancier vacation homes.

"We're getting close," Owen said from the back seat. "Darcy, drop to the floor."

"What?"

"They might recognize you."

"Oh, right." She undid her seatbelt and slid down to the floorboard, turning to lay her head on the seat. She'd be invisible to anyone outside.

A wooden stockade type fence loomed farther down the road.

"That's it," Owen murmured.

Not slowing the car, Gawain surveyed the property as well as the surroundings. To his surprise, the gate—also wooden planks—stood open. At the front of one of the houses, males were unloading a van. Excitement surged through him.

"The soldiers are back," Owen told Darcy.

"Really? Oh my Gods." She started to sit up, caught herself, and stayed flat. Her fingers closed in a fist.

Poor catling. To be so close and not be able to act. Gawain patted her shoulder.

Owen met Gawain's gaze in the rearview mirror. "Get us out of here."

"Aye." Gawain took the next corner and the next, returning to Highway 20. His jaw clenched as he thought of the flood-lights, the high log walls. "Breaking them out of there won't be easy."

"We'll manage," Owen said.

Visibly shaking, Darcy crawled back up to the seat.

With a sigh, Gawain reached over and captured her hand, intertwining his fingers with hers. "Breathe, sweetling."

Her attempted smile almost broke his heart.

The drive home was mostly silent.

As they neared Cold Creek, Gawain wasn't able to take the silence any longer. He squeezed Darcy's shoulder. "Are you all right?"

She shook her head. "I hate this. Shifters will have to risk their lives to get the villagers free. But if they do, the Scythe will know there are more shifters. They'll hunt down anyone who helps—and everyone who gets free."

"Let them look." The snarl from the backseat said Owen looked forward to meeting the Scythe.

Darcy was still looking out the side window. "My brothers probably know places to hide. We can go—"

"You're not going anywhere," Owen snapped.

"What?" Darcy turned to stare at him.

Gawain shot his gnome-brained littermate a frown, then recaptured Darcy's hand. "He means we want you to stay with *us*. Live with us."

Be our lifemate. But it was too soon to say that. Even the love words dancing on his tongue would be premature.

Her mouth dropped open, and her gaze was…shocked. Fearful. "Stay in Cold Creek? With you?"

"Aye." Owen leaned forward and gripped her shoulder.

"With us. We want you to stay with us."

"No. I can't." She shook her head hard. "I'd put you in danger."

Gawain winced, not needing to see Owen's reaction. Talk about insulting a cahir.

"We can handle danger," Owen growled.

"Why can't you understand? Once my brothers are free, I have to leave. The Scythe will search for all the shifters who escape, and they'll start with these forests."

Owen's growl deepened. "They won't find you."

"They will."

The way Darcy shrank into the seat like a terrified cubling made Gawain want to shred something. Someone. "Darcy…"

"You don't know the Scythe," she whispered. "They're politicians. Heads of giant companies. Even if we weren't shifters, they wouldn't let us be free, not with what we know. They'll burn the forests to ensure we never talk about them."

The certainty in her voice sent a chill through Gawain.

Like a panicking deer herd, she only saw flight as the answer.

She was wrong. Descended from the Fae wild hunt shifters, the Daonain had never been prey animals—they were predators.

Searching for a reasoned answer, Gawain turned onto the road to the lodge. "Your warning means all the Cosantirs will be prepared. We'll manage whatever comes, Darcy. But we'll manage better with you beside us."

She was shaking her head as he stopped the car in front of the building.

"I can't stay. It wouldn't work." She jumped out of the car and turned.

"Darcy," Owen's rough voice was gentler than Gawain had ever heard. "Don't you know how we feel about you?"

"Don't." Her big dark eyes filled with tears. "I have to leave and keep you safe. We can't… There can't be more."

Pain ripped through Gawain as his hopes began to disintegrate. He held out his hand, willing her to stay. "Catling, we lo—"

"No." Her tears spilled over, and she pressed her hand to her mouth. "You mustn't. Please. There can be nothing between us. *Nothing.*"

She slammed the door shut and ran into the lodge as if all the wolves in the forest were snapping at her heels.

"That…did not go well." Gawain turned toward his brother and saw his misery. Pity slid into his heart, joining his own pain.

His littermate had avoided emotional entanglements all of his life. Now, for Darcy, he'd ventured out of his cave, left himself vulnerable—and gotten clawed.

Life wasn't fair sometimes.

"She's scared, brawd," Gawain said softly. "For us. For Cold Creek." To give her space and time, he turned the car around and headed toward their house. "Females aren't reasonable if afraid someone will get hurt, and she loves us." He could feel it from her, like the warmth of the sun.

At the silence, he checked the rearview mirror.

Owen stared out the side window, face unreadable.

Gawain's chest constricted. His littermate was so fucking unfamiliar with love.

"I know," Owen said, finally. "I know she cares about people. About us. It is one of the things I lo…"—he cleared his throat and said even more firmly—"love about her. She has reasons to be afraid."

"Aye." They needed to discuss what to do. But between Gawain's business and Owen being cahir, they'd never be left undisturbed. "Let's go up to the lake and think this out. Figure out how to reassure her that everyone will be safe."

There was silence from the back.

Gawain parked and got out.

Joining him, Owen gripped his arm and pulled him to a

stop. "Brawd, if we cannot find a path to safety, if she would feel more secure elsewhere, then…we'll go too. Our place is with her."

Love swelled as Gawain stared at the determination in Owen's face. "Aye. This is the trail we're on. We'll run it together. All of us."

WHEN DARCY SLIPPED into the lodge, tears were streaming down her face. At the sound of low voices, she froze and realized the dining area was filled with males, including the Cosantir. They'd see her if she went up the stairs.

Shay or Zeb would follow her to see what was wrong.

Hands over her mouth to keep from sobbing aloud, she veered into the library room to the right. There, she curled into a chair and let the tears fall.

Gawain and Owen wanted her—to stay, to live with them. Oh, if she only could. Love for them pounded through her with each beat of her heart.

She wrapped her arms around herself, wishing she were hugging them close, as she had last night when she'd finally gotten to snuggle, kiss, and touch to her heart's content. Licking and tasting. Feeling the implacable hands guiding her to please them. Being teased and driven out of her mind until pleasure seared away everything. Being held between their solid male bodies. Hearing Owen's rough laugh and Gawain's smooth chuckle.

She loved them—her Owen, so tall and deadly, and her Gawain as muscular as the biggest mountain lion.

To live with them? That would be a dream come true.

And then a nightmare if the Scythe found her hiding in Cold Creek. Horrifying images shattered her. The cahirs would be the first to fall—*her* cahir. Gawain would charge into battle, too. Her friends, the townspeople, everyone would die—or worse. The Scythe would capture some. Put them in cages. Nightmarish memories and fears blurred together until she felt screams building up in her head.

No, no, no. The minute the villagers were free, she *had* to leave with them. She and her villagers would hide…somewhere…and this town would be safe.

She'd have to stay away from Owen and Gawain until then, or her resolve wouldn't hold. Because there was nothing she wanted more than to be with them. Forever.

With a determined breath, she wiped her eyes. *Be strong.* It was her job to ensure that her males—and yes, all of Cold Creek—were safe. "Take care of them for me, Mother of All."

Chin up, she walked out of the library and across the lodge. She didn't know where Owen and Gawain had gone, but since neither male had carried a phone on their trip, the Cosantir didn't yet know they'd located the shifter-soldier camp.

In the dining room, the cahirs were gathered around a table. Like a caged animal, the Cosantir paced back and forth beside the windows. Everyone looked up as she entered.

"Darcy." Alec's expression was grim. "Where is Owen?"

The room stank of fear and anger. "What's happened?"

Alec made an impatient noise.

"Owen and Gawain dropped me off and left. Maybe they went to their house?"

Calum paused in his pacing, glanced at the big grizzly cahir, and tilted his head toward the door. Ben hurried past her, pausing long enough to pat her shoulder gently.

"What's happened?" Darcy repeated.

Calum looked at her, rage streaming from him. "The Scythe took Victoria."

The words took a second to penetrate, then stabbed deep.

No. Oh, no, no, no. Not Vicki. Dear Mother of All, she was pregnant.

The front door of the lodge opened, and someone strode quickly across to the dining room.

The scent of human reached Darcy, and she growled before recognizing Vicki's former boss, Wells.

The spymaster stepped past her and spoke to Shay. "The sergeant is missing?"

"Aye." Shay turned to the Cosantir "Wells is in one of our cabins here—for the cubs' birth, and I asked him to join us now. We could use his help."

Visibly struggling for control, Calum was staring at a wall map of Seattle. Without turning, he merely nodded.

Darcy's hands clenched into fists, hating the Scythe with every drop of her blood.

Joining his brother, Alec leaned against him, silently sharing fears, strength, and support. After a minute, he cleared his throat. "Brawd, can you tell Wells about the note?"

Calum took an audible breath. When he turned, his lean face was icy cold. "A typed note addressed to me was found on the counter in Angie's Diner. It says they have Victoria, and if I don't turn myself over to them, they'll kill her and the baby. A van is waiting for me on Main Street."

Alec's low growl was echoed by the cahirs.

"Are you positive she's been kidnapped?" Wells's face showed no expression, but his icy blue eyes held murder.

"Yes. They took her, stole her from our town. From *us*." Alec's voice rose, and he slammed his fist down on a table. With a loud crack, the wood split down the middle.

Shay gripped his shoulder. "Easy, *a brathair-faoirm.*"

Like a furious cat, Alec strode across the room and back…and then said in a controlled voice, "She'd gone to visit Evangeline, an elderly human living on the outskirts. Three male humans captured Vicki there and knocked Evangeline out. She called the minute she woke. I tracked the scents to a car."

Oh Vicki. Guilt made the whole room darken. *I brought this down on them.* Was Vicki all right? Pregnant or not, she wouldn't have surrendered; she'd have fought.

Wells echoed her thought. "I'm surprised the humans survived."

Alec's smile was vicious. "From the amount of blood— human blood—on the floor, one didn't."

"That's good to hear. Now…from what Darcy has said about her previous captors, the Scythe don't bluff. They will kill the sergeant if they don't get Calum." Wells leaned forward and flattened his hands on the table. "I'm not Daonain, but it seems unwise to let these power-hungry bastards have a Cosantir."

As the cahirs nodded, Darcy felt cold sliding into her belly and recognized it as fear.

"It would, indeed, be unwise." Calum's gaze was cold. Stark. "However, the God should have enough power, even in a city, to kill me as soon as she is released. They will get nothing—"

"By the *God,*" Shay shouted. "Don't even talk like that."

Zeb growled, low and dark. "Have some faith in your cahirs, Cosantir."

Reaching out, Alec shook Calum. "Think, brawd."

The Cosantir hissed at him, then bowed his head and pulled in a breath, visibly trying to overcome the fear for his mate.

Darcy bit her lip. The Scythe knew the value of hostages, especially with the Daonain. A beloved female in danger would drive the calmest shifter to become an unthinking animal.

"Forgive me, cahirs." Calum's voice was rough.

Every one of his warriors bowed a head.

Including Zeb who held a phone. "Tynan, we need a location for the female villagers' prison, right the fuck now."

The room went silent as the Seattle cop's voice came

through the speakerphone. "You're in luck. I correlated my info with the Scythe van's tracker log that Wells sent me. I'm pretty sure I found the property."

Darcy clasped her hands together, hope rising.

"Odds are they'd take Vicki to that prison." Alec scowled. "But if we free her and the other captives there, the Scythe will cut their losses and kill the shifter-soldiers. Their location isn't—"

"We found the forest camp," Darcy interrupted. "And the males are there. We saw them this morning."

"It appears we have ourselves a hunt." Shay ripped the map of the Twin Sisters area off the wall and laid it on a table.

"Two hunts." Zeb joined him at the table. "We need to attack each place at the same time."

"Aye." Calum tapped his fingers on the map. "But how do we get into the Seattle prison and kill the guards before they turn on their hostages."

Wells spoke up. "I'm not fond of open frontal assaults, especially against anything with concealed machine gun embrasures."

"Trouble is, getting anyone in from the rear is...difficult." Alec shook his head. "That blackberry thicket perimeter is damn clever. Only a cat shifter could use the trees to get over it. But fruit tree limbs and two hundred pound cats are a bad combination."

"By the time we get organized and drive there, it'll be nearly dark." Zeb scowled. "If the grounds are floodlighted, even feline eyes can't compensate enough to see through tree shadows. You won't be able to see well enough to assess the branches."

Alec's shoulder slumped. "Wait until tomorrow? That won't..."

As the cahirs talked, fear skittered across Darcy's nerves. They mustn't postpone an attack. The Scythe wouldn't permit a delay—they'd push Calum by hurting Vicki and her unborn cubs. But even if Calum turned himself over, they'd never let Vicki go.

Yet Alec was right. Most of the fruit tree branches were too small to support a full-grown male shifter. An experienced shifter might have been able to follow her scent through the trees—but too much time had passed.

A shifter could use her scent to get through the trees now...if she went back in.

Terror wrapped fingers around her body, squeezing the air from her lungs. She *couldn't* go back. No.

But Vicki...Vicki was her friend. Had stood up for her against her mate. *"I know this isn't a democracy, oh guardian of the territory, but I'm all for mercy in this case."*

"I need to show you." Her voice was not even a whisper.

The cahirs had shifter hearing. And they all turned toward her.

Wells frowned. "Did you say something?"

She wrapped her arms around her waist. "I can get back in the same way I got out. And the cat shifters can see well enough—and smell well enough—to follow me in the dark."

Zeb growled. "No, little female. You're not going back there."

Oh, she wanted to agree so, so badly. Tears filled her eyes. "We can't let them kill Vicki or her babies. And you need me to get in." She pulled in a shuddering breath.

Zeb studied her with black eyes and then glanced at Alec. "To risk a female is...wrong. But we need her."

"By the God." Staring at her, Alec gripped the table. "I don't want..."

"You must," she whispered. "For Vicki."

After a long moment, he nodded. "Aye. We need you."

There was no sense of victory, not with the paralyzing fear lodged in her bones. *Don't think about returning. Not now.* "But what about the shifter-soldiers?" *My brothers.* "Can we get them out and remove their trackers? The camp has a stockade fence and floodlights. Owen set off an alarm and—"

"Wait." Alec paced away from them, stared out the window for a moment, and rubbed his hands roughly over his face. When he turned, his expression held only a cold resolve. He walked back and picked up Zeb's phone. "Tynan, you know about human security systems. Take charge of breaking the shifter-soldiers out. Tonight. Collect what you need, get moving that direction, and we'll send you help."

"My brothers and their friends won't believe anything you say," Darcy said toward the phone. "They'll think it's a Scythe trick. A test."

"Those Scythe feckers could well make a male suspicious." Tynan was silent for a second. "Right then. Darcy, did ye wear those clothes I left you and did you re-hang the bag?"

"Yes. And yes."

"Then I can convince your lads." He paused. "Alec, were you saying the poor shifters will have to carve the GPS devices from their bodies?"

"Aye. Then and there," Alec said.

"Right. Consider it done."

Wells cleared his throat. "How many of the shifters from here will assist in the two attacks?"

Shay answered, "Should be quite a—"

"Not as many as you think," Calum said.

The cahirs looked at him in surprise.

"Somehow the Scythe learned about me and Victoria. Do they also know Cold Creek has other shifters? We must get the elderly, females, and cubs to safety."

Tensing, Zeb and Shay turned toward the kitchen and the sounds of Bree cooking. They wouldn't leave their mate to be taken.

"In that case," Alec said, "how about those trained shifter-soldiers that Tynan is going after? They could be useful at the Seattle prison."

"Too far to get them there in time to help," Zeb said.

Wells frowned. "Not if I can arrange a helicopter."

Calum nodded. "Do it. The males would want to be part of getting their sisters free."

"They would," Tynan said over the phone. "But can they? Cutting out the trackers will leave them bleeding and limping."

"Send Donal," Calum told Alec. "He can heal them enough that they can fight."

Tynan grunted. "You explain it to him, then. My littermate hates patch jobs."

Alec pulled out his own phone and swiped a number. "Donal, we need you. Meet us at the lodge—and come prepared for a battle out of the territory. You'll be doing quick and dirty repairs."

"Out of the territory?" Donal's sonorous voice came from the speakerphone. "By Herne's holy prick, where am I to get the energy to heal? Do I look like a Gods-benighted battery? And you want me to—"

When Alec thumbed the speaker off, the cursing faded to an indistinct rumble.

The cahirs...except for Alec...were grinning, and even Darcy felt her lips curving up.

"That's my tactful brother." Tynan chuckled. "What's the location of the forest camp?"

"It's off Highway 20." Darcy explained how to get to the stockade from both the road and the mountain meadow.

"Got it. Alec, the females' prison camp is in the Gatewood area of West Seattle." Tynan rattled off the address.

Shay bent over the map and circled the spot with a pencil. "If the cats follow Darcy in, they can deal with the machine guns."

Follow Darcy in. Her stomach was one frozen knot.

"Attack after dark," Zeb said.

Shay nodded. "If we can kill the floodlights, we'll have an advantage."

"Kill the power to the neighborhood," Wells suggested.

The cahirs nodded agreement.

"How do you want to time the attacks? One first or…" Tynan asked.

"Simultaneous," Zeb said. "Keep them too busy to think—or harm anyone."

"Shortly after dark is probably the longest I can stall them." Calum looked at his cahirs. "I will arrange to surrender myself just before the attack, so they will believe everything is going their way."

"Why would they wait for you?" Wells asked. "I wouldn't."

"They can't calculate when their note will reach me…which is why we could have this meeting. In a minute, I'll take my phone into the mountains and call them from there. Once I call, they'll understand it will take me a while to return to Cold Creek."

Wells gave a nod of approval. "Nice. They'll track your phone's GPS and confirm your location. They won't do anything to the sergeant until they know you won't show up. It'll give us time to—"

"I will show up."

Zeb growled. "Cosantir, no need to risk yourself. They will be armed and—"

"When I enter the Scythe car in Cold Creek, I will be in the heart of my territory."

Darcy's mouth went dry as she saw the power flickering around the Cosantir. And the fury banked in his black, black eyes.

She wouldn't want to be the Scythe soldiers trapped in a vehicle with the chosen of the God.

"Brawd…" Fear showed in Alec's green eyes before he sucked in a breath and turned to Darcy. "Darcy, we'll stop by our place. Vicki's black sweats will work well for sneaking around—and shifting unexpectedly. You'll ride with me."

She rubbed her damp palms on her jeans. "Okay."

Alec shot Wells a look. "If you ride with me, we can finish planning on the way."

Wells tilted his head. "Of course. Let me get supplies from my van."

As Darcy moved toward the door, she saw Alec put a hand on his littermate's shoulder, and her heart broke for them.

I'll get her back for you. I will. She blinked hard and walked out onto the porch.

Thank the Gods that Owen and Gawain weren't here. They wouldn't be in danger.

And yet, everything inside her wished they would be with her.

AS OWEN AND his brother loped back down the mountain trail, he was satisfied with their planning on how to reason with Darcy. The mountain lake had been peaceful, easing his emotions, and letting him think clearly.

Gawain had pointed out that Darcy hadn't rejected them. She was simply terrified that the Scythe would hurt the people she loved—including him and Gawain.

The thought, true or not, that she loved him was enough to make his heart stutter.

They'd figured out some ways to ease her worries. If all else failed, they'd leave with her, maybe take her into Canada. Zeb,

Shay, and Ryder had traveled extensively before settling in Cold Creek, and they'd know safe places. Most territories would be delighted to welcome a blademage, a tinker, and a cahir.

Regret nagged at him as he ran. He loved the Cascades. Loved this territory. Loved Cold Creek. Few Cosantirs were as evenhanded—or as powerful—as Calum.

Fucking Scythe. By the God, he really wanted to shred the weasels into bloody tatters of skin and flesh. Growling, he leaped a log and increased his speed.

With an annoyed chuff, Gawain kept up.

They wouldn't get to see Bonnie's cublings grow up. That hurt. Well, maybe someday he and his tiny family could return and…Owen almost stumbled. Maybe they'd be bringing back cubs of their own.

Behind him, Gawain hissed. He'd scented something or someone.

Owen slowed and smelled a bear even as he spotted it. Coming fast. Huge. A grizzly.

Ben.

Gawain moved forward to trot beside Owen as they met the cahir.

Ben trawsfurred without coming to a complete halt. "Need you now, cahir, at the lodge." His Texas accent was thick in the gasped words. "The Scythe has Vicki. They want to trade her for the Cosantir."

Vicki. The unborn cubs. The Cosantir. Fury blasted through Owen, and he snarled, his paw lifting, claws out.

Ben jerked his head. "Go."

Owen took off, running down the trail, Gawain right behind him.

If your officer's dead and the sergeants look white,

Remember it's ruin to run from a fight;

So take open order, lie down and sit tight,

And wait for supports like a soldier.

Wait, wait, wait like a soldier…

This was proving to be a thoroughly fucked-up day—and reciting Kipling wasn't helping. Vic snorted. *Wait for supports?* She despised waiting for backup and always had.

Sitting on the floor behind a bolted-down metal bed, Vicki scowled at her cell. For fuck's sake, she was tired of being dumped in windowless basements. A recessed space held a tankless toilet. There was no other furniture. The bed's blanket and sheet were now on the floor with her.

She leaned her forehead on the mattress. God, but she hurt like hell.

When they'd arrived at Darcy's prison, the asshole beside her in the backseat had jumped out to talk to the gatehouse guard. Vic'd slid out and dashed for the gate. As her pursuers caught up, she'd deliberately fallen, and due to her *I'm-a-bowling-ball* shape, she'd landed hard and collected some ugly scrapes. Being backhanded by the pissed-off guard hurt worse.

None of the damage was important. She'd left her scent and her blood near the gate, and she counted the action a success.

The fight when she was kidnapped sure hadn't been. God, she hoped Evangeline was all right. Vic shook her head. That sweet old woman had walloped one of the assholes with a table lamp. She hadn't hit him hard enough though.

Vic had done better. She'd grabbed a table knife and rammed it into the biggest bastard's heart. Unfortunately, the third attacker had knocked her off her feet.

She lifted her arm and grimaced. The shoulder joint still worked…barely. If she hadn't had to guard her belly, she might have dealt with all three. "Dammit, kid, you sure screwed up my skills," she whispered and rubbed her stomach.

He, she, or they had screwed up her escape, too. Big-time.

With a sigh, she looked down at the soaking-wet jeans she'd removed.

Her water had broken…because she was in labor. *Congratulations, Sergeant, it's official. You're royally fucked.*

Good thing she'd assisted in a couple of births when undercover in third world villages. At least she knew the basics—starting with a person didn't deliver babies when wearing jeans.

She'd be giving birth in a basement. As a captive. She rolled her eyes. Over the past months, when she'd whined, Alec would laugh and say mothers loved to tell their cubs all the trouble they'd caused when in the womb. Apparently, Alec and Calum's mother had busted an ankle, and she'd never let them forget.

Well, you little terror…or terrors…you're going to get an earful from me.

Another labor pain caught her. *Oh, fucking god, it hurts.* As her stomach turned to concrete under her hand, she heard footsteps in the hallway. *Can't scream, can't scream.* She gritted her teeth.

The door opened. One of the bastards who'd escorted her to the basement stood in the doorway. This one had tried to cop a feel, and she'd planted a fist in his gut. He'd stayed out of reach since.

If you come in, I'll kill you. She'd try her damndest, at any rate. She let her gaze convey that.

He sneered. "You think hiding behind the bed will keep you safe?"

Speaking would mean unlocking her jaw. And screaming. Sweat broke out on her forehead as the contraction lasted and lasted.

"It won't, bitch." His coarse laugh held ugly anticipation. "The Director will be down after he finishes his supper. He says you'll give him good information, or we'll rip that freak out of your belly and cut its fingers off in front of you."

You can try, asshole.

With everything except her shoulders and head concealed by the bed, she fingered the knife in her ankle sheath. When they came for her, she'd do what she had to do. For as long as she lived.

"Filthy beast." Annoyed by her lack of reaction, he left, slamming the door behind him.

Calum, Alec, hurry. Please, please, please hurry. I'll wait as long as I can.

But they didn't even know where this place was.

As fear flooded her system, she curled on the floor and let the pain take her.

Chapter Twenty-Four

THE NIGHT WAS moonless, thankfully, which meant Ryder couldn't see Darcy trembling like a leaf.

Tynan's address had been the right one. This was the stone *prìosan* that had held her captive for over ten years. She stood outside the stone wall on the west beside Ben's littermate, waiting for Alec.

When they'd arrived, Alec had wanted to get an idea of what they were facing. To look through the huge wrought-iron gates. So, after dropping him off a block away, she and Ryder had driven around the corner, parked up the hill from the property, and found themselves a dark shadow in which to wait.

"There he is." Ryder's voice was a whisper in the light breeze.

Earlier, as she and Wells were climbing into Alec's car, Ryder had slid into the back seat and said simply, "My bro, Ben, said you needed another cat."

Another person to help. She'd wanted to hug him so hard.

Looking as if he didn't have a care in the world, Alec sauntered around the corner and up the hill. He eased into the gloom of the overhanging tree. "I caught Vicki's scent." His quiet voice couldn't conceal his anger. "Close to the front. She must have made a run for the gate, fell deliberately, and left her scent behind.

Darcy shook her head. Vicki had probably panicked and… No, Vicki was a Marine. A spy. There was no panic in that female. "She's probably planning her escape even now."

"Let's save her the trouble," Ryder murmured.

Darcy pulled in a breath. Vicki wasn't the one who was panicking, Darcy was. Her heart was hammering violently enough to hurt, and even her bones were shaking.

She swallowed past the constriction in her throat and whispered, "See the walnut?" She pointed to the tall tree on the other side of the wall.

The males nodded.

"That's the tree closest to the wall. I'll wait for you in the branches." If she made it.

As if he could hear her doubts, Alec squeezed her shoulder. "You'll do fine, sweetheart." Pulling out his cell phone, he sent a text to Wells and Tynan. *Going in now.*

Darcy stripped and stuffed her black tank top and sweatpants into a tiny bag.

The males disposed of their clothes in a black garbage bag and left it under the tree. Tynan said it would look as if the garbage collector had missed a bag.

"Ready?" Ryder stood beside her. His skin was dark enough to blend in with the shadows, and he'd tied his shoulder-length black hair back. "I'll be right behind you."

The knowledge helped, even as she wished it were Owen and Gawain with her. But no. *Stay away, my males. Be safe.* She thought of them being hurt, being shot, falling. *Dying.* A shudder ran through her.

No, don't think about dying. She forced her lips into a smile that probably looked more like a grimace. "Try to keep up, cat."

"The Mother be with you," Ryder whispered.

"The Hunter guide your paws," came from Alec.

She trawsfurred...and hesitated. What if she missed the top? Overshot and fell to the ground?

Then her memory gave her Gawain's calm voice. *"Sink into the wild, catling. Let go."* Just pick a target, and let her animal get her there. *I can do this.*

With the bag of clothes in her mouth, she sprang into a full-out run. At top speed, she leaped to the top of the wall and into the walnut.

A second later, Ryder landed on an adjacent branch. His jaws were clamped around a cotton bag.

As she shifted to human, Alec came over the wall and settled onto another branch.

Instead of birds, the walnut was overflowing with cougars. She suppressed her laughter—because it would turn to hysterics—and looked around.

The interior compound hadn't changed at all, had it? The front lawn was flooded with light as were the sidewalks in back. The wide tangle of blackberries around the inner perimeter lay in darkness...because no one could walk through the head-high thorny mass.

Touching Alec's furry neck, she motioned toward the grounds and the closest three-story manor house. "That one has the human hostages." The lighted windows of the second manor house—Zoo Hall—seemed a long way away. She pointed to it. "I forgot to tell you, the stairwell on the far end probably has less traffic. The west side stairs are what the staff uses."

Alec nodded. He already knew which hall was which, since they'd planned everything with Wells on the drive to Seattle. After she'd drawn maps of the grounds, Ryder had used his phone to snap pictures and send copies to the others, including Tynan. Everyone had memorized the plan.

So why was she still sitting here, clinging to a branch, like...like a cub too terrified to move?

Alec rubbed his muzzle against her and purred. Comfortingly. She knew he was half-crazy with worry for Vicki—but he'd still spotted Darcy's fears and tried to help.

His courage bolstered hers. "Thanks," she whispered and shifted to cat.

Here goes. Carefully, she leaped to the next branch, taking the same path she'd used for her escape. Her claws closed on the bark, and the tree shook. She froze. *No. Stop thinking and worrying. Stay in the wild.* She whipped her tail back and forth, rode the slight sway of the branch, and leaped again.

Over the sea of blackberries, she jumped from tree to tree. Followed by the males, she worked her way around the corner and beside the back wall. There—that was the tree that had grown up near the inside edge of the brambles, almost reaching the lawn. She jumped to it and sprang off the branch, over the thorn tangle, and landed on the grass.

One soft thump sounded. Another. The two cougars were beside her.

Alec butted his furry head against her shoulder as if in thanks, then loped beside the thicket toward the far end of the property.

Ryder nodded his head at her and trotted toward the three underground machine gun nests in the front lawn. Wells had given him grenades to toss into each gun barrel slit, because there was no other access to a concrete box. When entering, each set of two guards would deadbolt the rear door behind themselves.

Her chest squeezed with fear for the brave shifter…because it was a *horrible* plan. After the first explosion, the rest of the guards would know what had happened. They'd know his targets and would shoot him before he could sabotage the next pillbox.

But she couldn't help. She had her own task.

She trotted toward the east, moving silently in the lush grass.

Halfway down the back wall, she reached the toolshed—and the industrial generator on a concrete pad next to it. When the power went out, the generator would kick on and restore power—as well as the floodlights.

After shifting to human, she dressed, then slipped her hand into her pocket and pulled out Gawain's gift—the multi-tool. It sat in her palm, familiar and heart-warming, and she used it to jimmy open the generator's circuit box.

Like that fancy spy, James Bond, in one of Gawain's movie choices, she had a special device from Wells. Smiling evilly, she set the spymaster's box inside.

And pressed the button.

THE MAGIC GIFTED by the Mother tingled in Gawain's veins—and not in a pleasant way. Rubbing his arms, he walked beside Owen outside the Scythe's stone wall. Every few feet, he bent and sniffed. The scent from panther paws—Darcy, Alec, and Ryder—was very fresh. They couldn't be more than a few minutes ahead.

Darcy had volunteered to return to the prison that terrified her...no, Shay said she'd *insisted*. "By the God and Goddess, she's got courage," Gawain whispered.

"Aye," Owen muttered.

Damn the evil humans that had started this. His anger was a low roar, hotter than the flames in his forge. They'd get her out—get them all out.

Darcy's scent trail ended.

"Here." He looked up. On the other side of the wall, a tree rose high into the night sky. "That has to be the walnut tree."

After leaving their clothing in the black garbage bag with Alec and Ryder's, they jumped the wall and landed in the walnut.

Pleased the fruit trees grew close together, Gawain checked the scents. The three cougars' trail through the long orchard was clear. With Owen following, he leaped to the next tree. And the next. Around the corner. Along the back.

Midway, he stopped, confused for a second at the abrupt change in direction. Ah, a tree had been planted close to the lawn—and was obviously the exit to the bramble patch. He jumped to it and down onto the grass.

When his brother thumped onto the lawn, Gawain turned, and they exchanged head rubs.

Be safe, brawd.

Staying in the shadows, Owen loped toward the far manor house. His job was to help Alec get Vicki out and then assist Darcy with the villagers. Gawain saw Owen pause at a small building near the back wall. Was that the generator?

Gawain took a step in that direction, wanting to find their mate.

But Owen picked up speed and disappeared into the night. Darcy must have already moved on.

With a huff, Gawain crept toward the front, skirting the floodlit sidewalks, and freezing whenever a guard appeared. He needed to find Ryder before the cat pitched a grenade in a machine gun pillbox and set all hell loose.

There was a better way, if it worked. If he was in time. His muscles were tense, expecting the first explosion.

Then he saw a cougar, belly to the ground, creeping beside a hillock. Thank the Goddess, Gawain had made it in time—assuming the male would stop.

Gawain gave a slight hiss, hoping it would be enough. It took a second hiss, but the cougar froze and turned its head.

Gawain moved enough Ryder could make out his shape.

The male turned and retraced his steps.

Gawain motioned for him to follow and led the way to the

dark recessed stairwell at the back of the embrasure. At the bottom of the stairs, he shifted and whispered, "When I yank the door open, you eliminate whoever is inside. Quietly."

No noise. No warning. Much better plan.

The cougar stared at Gawain's empty hands, and if a cat could look skeptical, this was one.

Ah, well. The magic Gawain had requested of the Mother still burned in his veins. If he was lucky, there would be enough for all three sites. Setting his palm against the cold metal plate, he reached out to the deadbolt and sang the song of steel.

Obedient to his will, the metal slowly softened into jelly.

At his feet, the cougar waited, tail twitching with doubt and impatience.

With a grim smile, Gawain yanked the door open.

HER FIRST TASK completed, Darcy had stayed in human form and sneaked across the grounds to Z Hall, evading the patrols. Her fear increased with every step she took toward the source of her nightmares—Z Hall. Now, crouched behind the waist-high privet hedge, she'd frozen completely. *I can't do this.*

Alec had gone after Vicki. Darcy's job was to get her female villagers down to the back door.

She forced herself to look up at the tangle of ivy covering the wall. Little Alice was up there. And Margery. This was their chance. She couldn't leave them.

Pulling in a breath, Darcy set her jaw. On the third floor, every window was locked shut to ensure no hostage would jump to her death. On the second floor, some of the staff's windows were cracked open to let in fresh air.

Darcy wiped her clammy palms on her thighs, picked the nearest window, and started climbing the vines.

Reaching the second floor, she slid through the window, walked across the dark room, and jerked back. *Oh Goddess.*

In a pool of blood, a human lay staring up in death. His throat had been ripped out.

Swallowing down nausea, Darcy took a step forward and stopped. Over the stench of blood, she could smell a shifter. Not Alec. That was Owen's scent.

Her heart did a fast flip of joy before fear enveloped her. Owen. *Here.* Where Owen went, Gawain would go. *No. Please no.* The Scythe would shoot them, lock them up, kill them. Her Gawain and Owen would *die.*

Her body shook as terror consumed her—memories of slaughtered bodies, staring eyes, the stench of death, screaming and moans and…far worse…silence.

She fought for control. *Stop.* A shudder ran through her. If Gawain and Owen were here, they had their tasks.

So did she, something no one else could do. Her villagers needed her—she was the only one they'd trust. The only one they'd follow without panicking. *Must go.*

Wiping sweat from her face, she edged around the body, through the door, and hurried down the hallway.

Opening the door to the stairs, she came face-to-face with a guard.

For years, she'd watched the weapons practice in the yard. Had tried to duplicate their moves. Now her body responded instinctively. Strike to the throat, silencing him. Kick to the balls to bend him over. Hammer-fists on the back of the neck.

At the crunch of bone, she gasped. She'd hit too hard. Wells had said, *kill anyone you see*, but she'd never, never planned to.

He lay on the floor. Heart slamming into her ribcage, she stared at him, bitterness and sorrow filling her.

Keep going, tinker. You have work to do.

As she dragged the human into the janitor's supply room,

her mouth was so dry she gagged when she tried to swallow. She'd had no choice. He'd have yelled for help. The village females would be killed. But...this wasn't her. She fixed things; she didn't break them—didn't break people. She swallowed again.

No time to stop. Her people needed her. Beside the body was a mop in a bucket. Grabbing it, she stomped on the handle and broke it in half. There, she had a weapon.

Running now, she fled to the stairs and upward. On the third floor, she eased open the door.

Feet up on the desk, a guard watched a movie on his tablet.

She sprang across the five-foot gap, swung the mop handle, and cracked him right across the head. The chair tipped backward, spilling him out.

Don't look. Don't think about the feeling of something breaking or the sound. Trembling, she snatched the keys from the desk and pushed the green button to open the door to the hostage hallway. Trotting through, she unlocked the first door and whispered urgently, "Into the hall. We're getting out of here."

Trained all too well to stay silent, the village females, from fourteen to twenty-four years old, peeked into the hall, saw her, and suddenly she was surrounded.

"Thought you were dead."

"They said they caught you."

"Said you screamed."

"You died."

Hugs and whispers and more hugs and tears.

Keeping her voice low, she said, "I escaped and found other shifters. We're breaking you and our brothers out at the same time. You need to do what I say. Is everyone here?"

"There's a new female in the basement," someone said.

"No, two females," a tiny female corrected. "An older one

and the pregnant one."

In the basement. They meant Vicki and someone else. Alec planned to check all the cells down there. "A friend is freeing everyone down there."

She looked at the group surrounding her. "Listen. We'll go to the ground floor, out the back door, and hide behind the building." It would be better if she could take them through the trees and off the grounds, but they were weak with captivity and lack of food. Despite her practice climbing ivy and doing exercises, she'd almost fallen that day she'd escaped.

Alice tugged on her arm and whispered, "What about the alarms? The floodlights? The guards? We'll—"

"The lights will be gone, trust me. I'll handle the guards." *I hope*. She firmed her grip on the mop handle, carefully ignoring the dark stain on one end.

Spotting Margery, she said, "Can you bring up the rear and make sure everyone stays together?"

Margery's face still carried scars from the beating she'd gotten because of Darcy's mistake. She still limped. But her answer was calm and sure. "I can."

Idelle, also older than Darcy, stepped out. "Can I help?"

Oh, she did adore these females. "Stay in front with me. If we run into a guard, I'll attack. You get everyone out."

Lips pressed together with determination, Idelle nodded. "I will."

Darcy led them down the stairs.

NOT BOTHERING TO shift to human, Owen padded down the stairs in the *zoo*. The air drifting from the third floor held the fear-filled scents of females, and the concrete beneath his paws carried the stench of pain. With every inhalation, more rage filled his heart.

He didn't smell Alec, though. Had the cahir taken the stairs at the other end of the building?

The first-floor door handle rattled.

Above on the steps, Owen went immobile, only the tip of his tail lashing.

Two guards entered the stairwell, chatting about the capture of a freak who had cried, screamed, and babbled information. They laughed.

Were they talking about the Cosantir's mate? About Vicki?

With a snarl, Owen sprang. A slash through one's trachea silenced him, so Owen could bite through the other's spine. Turning back, he finished the first.

As he looked at the mess, his ears flattened against his skull. Not good. The next human on the stairs would run into the gore and dead bodies. The lights better go out soon.

He turned and trotted down the stairs.

The basement had a guard station, but the guards obviously didn't expect trouble. He killed them both.

After shifting to human, he grabbed a key ring and tried to open the metal door behind the desk. There was no keyhole. What the fuck was the key ring for, then?

Wait. Before dropping him and Gawain off, Shay had run through the information Darcy'd provided about the compound. He'd mentioned a button on the desk.

There was a green button beside the monitors. He punched it, and the door lock snicked. When he pushed the door open, he flinched at the stink of loosened bowels and terror and blood.

The basement was where the Scythe did their *experiments*, Darcy had said.

A snarl lifted his upper lip.

He took a step and scowled at the door. The lock. What happened when the power went out—or if someone entered?

He tossed a body into the doorway to hold the door open and then punched the red desk button. When the door lock extended out, Owen slammed a metal chair down on the deadbolt. Metal rang on metal—far too loudly—but the newly bent deadbolt would never fit into the strike plate box again.

No one was going to lock him in this fucking place.

A sniff of the corridor air told him that Vicki was nearby. He stiffened when he caught another familiar scent—one that belonged to someone who couldn't possibly be here.

Stretching before him, the long corridor was studded with doorways and intersecting halls. The first door stood open. Empty. The next three were the same.

Finding a closed door, he unlocked it and stepped inside. No guard. No Vicki. Only an aging blonde female lying on a blood-soaked bed that was bolted to the floor.

Burn marks, fingernails gone, blood—everywhere. If not for the scent, he wasn't sure he'd have known her. Her hands held her stomach, holding in her intestines. She'd been cut open—and the smell of death was in the room.

Her blackened eyes were swollen to mere slits, and she looked at him without recognition. "Don' hurt meeee."

As he crossed the room, pity swamped his lingering bitterness. He went down on a knee beside the bed. "Mother."

"O-Owen?" Her pale skin took on a blue cast as her spirit prepared to return to the Goddess. "They hur' me." She tried to focus. "I tol' them…"

"Told them what?" But he knew. "About Calum and his mate?"

Her infinitesimal nod held agreement. And guilt. "Shouldn't have…"

They'd tortured her for the information. "I think the Mother will find forgiveness for you." Odd how he could now find his own forgiveness.

She reached out blindly, and he took her hand. "Didn' tell them."

"Tell them what?"

"About my cubs. 'Bout you or Gaw—" Her breath wafted out, and her spirit went with it.

For a long, long moment, he couldn't move. *Mother.* His mother.

"Peace to you on your journey back to the Mother," he whispered finally. As he rose, sorrow was a heavy stone in his chest. In her final moments, she'd stood strong for her children.

The thought of leaving her body in this foul hole frayed his control.

He had to. He let anger bury the grief and turned toward the door. The Cosantir had entrusted him with this hunt—he would not fail.

Where was Vicki?

He tracked her scent to the far end of the hallway. Another locked cell. When he opened the door, he saw a bed lacking sheet or blanket. The room was empty except for the overwhelming stench of fresh blood.

No. By the God, he *couldn't* have come too late. Despair ripped at him, and he groaned.

Dark hair hanging over her face, someone sat up from behind the bed. "Get lost, asshole. If you come near me, I'll rip out your eyes and stuff them up your nose." Her voice was tight.

Vicki. Pride in his Cosantir's mate choked him until his voice came out hoarse. "Bloodthirsty female, I think I'm feeling sorry for Calum."

She pushed the hair out of her face, and her eyes widened. A bruise darkened one swollen cheek, and blood had dribbled down her chin from a split lip—but her smile was beautiful. "Damn, it's good to see you."

"Right back at you." He stalked over to help her up and

froze at the sight of blood smearing the floor. Beside her, blood and tissue soaked a ripped-up sheet. She wore only a white button-up shirt. Also bloodstained. "How badly are you hurt?"

Her laugh held no humor. "I'm fine. This shit is supposed to be normal, although I think whoever said that was a sick fuck." Rather than giving him her hand, she slid a blanket out from under the bed and handed him…a baby.

"Hunter's hairy balls." He froze, holding the tiny mite, wrinkled and red and covered in white stuff. "You gave b-birth?"

"Dude, I hate to tell you, but the storks don't really deliver babies."

"Storks?" What did birds have to do with birthing? Was she hallucinating? He frowned at her in concern.

"Give me your hand. I need help to stand up."

Without thinking, he did as she said—and realized she had another baby tucked into a sling made from the rest of the sheet. A third was cradled in her free arm.

"Three?"

"A litter." She actually growled at him. "My men actually gave me a litter. Multiple babies. Jesus, I didn't think the labor bullshit would ever stop."

When she released his hand, she stood for all of a second before her legs gave out. He grabbed her and held her up with an arm around her waist.

She snarled. "Yeah, I'm going to kill Alec. And Calum. More than once."

Who knew that a person could find a smile in such a Gods-benighted hell? Owen grinned.

Resettling the cubs, she looked down at them. "You timed it well. I just managed to feed them all—talk about a clusterfuck. I thought they were supposed to just latch on, you know? But they might sleep for a while. Maybe." Her expression turned grim. "Have you got a plan to get out of here?"

"Aye. Darcy led shifters in to handle the machine guns. When your spymaster shuts down the power to the neighborhood, more shifters will attack."

"Places like this have generators."

"Darcy will kill it."

Her expression filled with concern. "Owen, she was a captive here. Coming back might be more than she can take."

He smiled at the certainty filling him. "That little female will get the job done or die trying."

"I guess you would know." A smiled tilted a corner of her mouth. "You've changed, cahir."

Ignoring her comment, he frowned. "We've got to get you to the rear of the building and then to the garage." Only how? Her legs wouldn't hold her. He couldn't carry the female *and* the cubs. "If you shift, you'll have four legs—and animal strength."

That left the cubs. "Maybe we can rig up a harness for you to—"

"You carry my babies. I'll fight in animal form."

He started to shake his head.

"I can." Her expression turned deadly. "Nothing and no one will hurt my babies. Cahir, you get them out, no matter what happens to me."

Owen stared at her, and his eyes stung. This was the mother love of which bards would sing. "All right."

THE METAL MELTED, and Gawain pulled open the door to the third and last machine gun enclosure.

Still in panther form, Ryder streaked past him into the room. A scream was cut off abruptly.

The scent of death wafted out.

Wearily, Gawain leaned against the concrete wall in the dark stairwell as the remnants of the used-up magic stuttered through his body. Using his powers here, far from forests and the Mother, was like pushing water upstream.

"You okay?" Ryder had shifted to human and stood in the doorway.

"Tired." Gawain motioned to the room. "Did you disable all the guns? We don't want—"

"It's done, my friend." A white flash was Ryder's smile. "That spymaster guy told me what to do."

"Good enough." Despite his exhaustion, Gawain felt impatience flooding through him. His job was complete. Now he needed to find his brother and Darcy. Find them and guard them, the two people he loved most in the world.

He started up the stairs.

Ryder's hand clamped on his shoulder. "Gawain, I know what you're feeling. Nonetheless, we wait for Ben's signal."

Ryder and his brother ran a building company, Gawain knew. With Wells' help, the big grizzly cahir and his shifter crew were stealing heavy equipment from a nearby construction site to dozer down the nearest utility poles. If successful, the same dozer would bash through the front gate, providing a way in for Shay and the other volunteers.

Another minute ticked by.

Boom!

The sound was somewhere between a gunshot and an explosion. The floodlights flickered. Off. On. Off. Darkness filled the area.

"By the God, that was a transformer blowing. They *did* it." Ryder slapped his arm. "Let's go, mage."

Gawain trawsfurred and leaped out of the stairwell. Almost to new moon, the skies were dark. Although the humans would be blind, the ambient light from the surrounding city gave ample light to a shifter.

Hunting time.

OUTSIDE THE SHIFTER-SOLDIERS' forest camp, Tynan had spent a fair amount of time up in a tree.

Thanks to Owen's warning, he'd studied the motion detectors that monitored a ten-foot area inside the fence wall, calculated the probable blind spots, then cautiously slow-motioned his way in. Pissed him off, too. Maybe werecats enjoyed creeping an inch at a time, but he was a fecking wolf.

Once past the motion detectors, he ghosted to the barracks building, killed off a poor excuse for a guard, and stepped up to the door. The interior was dark; evidently, shifters had a lights-out time.

The door was locked. Wasn't it nice he'd learned to pick locks in his early days as a cop?

A minute later, he slid into the room.

The sound of the door—and his scent—alerted the males inside. Thuds sounded as they jumped from their bunks in the dark.

"Dogwood villagers," Tynan said in a voice only another shifter would hear. "Darcy sent me to get you out. We're freeing your females in Seattle—right now. We need your help to finish at the prison."

"Darcy is out?" One male moved forward.

The next voice was harsh. "Bullshit. It's a trap, Patrin."

"We can't—" A third voice held frustration and anguish. "They'll kill our females if we escape. How can we trust what you're saying?"

Aye and Darcy'd figured they'd have this reaction. "Now that Darcy is out of the city and off the pills, she's the shifter she was meant to be." He pulled a shirt from the tiny pack he'd carried around his neck. "Smell."

The one named Patrin snatched it. Inhaled. "By Herne, she's shifted. She's a cat, Fell."

In the shadows, a male joined Patrin and sniffed the shirt. "Darcy. She's healthy. *Healthy*." The male choked on the last word.

Another asked, "The females are being rescued?"

"The Seattle attack has been launched. We need you to destroy this camp—and then we go to help free the females."

Patrin said quietly, "You don't get it, wolf. We all have trackers in our arms. They'll know if anyone leaves this area."

"I do get it. And by the way, you each have two trackers, not one."

The male's curse was low and foul.

Tynan continued, "Once the guards are down, we'll cut the trackers out and leave them in this building to keep the Scythe content. You'll get patched up on the way."

In the dim light, Patrin held up his hand, stopping the others. "The staff holes up in their own house. Locked and bolted. You have a plan?"

"I've got more shifters to create a diversion at the north edge." Tynan smiled slightly. "Darcy assured us that if we got the guards to open their doors, you'd deal with them."

Fell's laugh was low and deadly. "Our sister is correct."

As Owen carried his armload of tiny cubs out of the cell, the power went out—and the corridor turned pitch black. Well, *fuck*. Even a feline couldn't see where there was no light at all.

Vicki didn't slow, just kept going, following the scent trail Owen had left on the way in. Owen followed her.

Lights appeared at the end of the corridor as several humans with flashlights dashed into the guard station. The lights paused at the desk area. "Jesus Christ, the bastards got Jones and Morris."

"The door's o-open." That human sounded ready to flee.

"Yeah, and if they're still in there, I'm gonna fill them with lead." A pistol trigger clicked.

The lights moved toward the corridor.

Vicki broke into a run toward them.

She couldn't take them on alone. He'd have to leave the cubs in a room. Owen shoved open a door—and a huge tawny shape shot past him.

Alec had arrived.

As Vicki reached the men, a man yelled in pain. A flashlight danced wildly before falling.

Cubs in his arms, Owen hastily stepped into a side cell as gunfire and shouting filled the air.

The cub in his right arm squirmed, not liking the noise. "I don't like the noise either, youngling," Owen murmured. By the God, he wanted to fight, not stand here, helpless.

A feline *mrow* reverberated down the corridor. *All clear.*

Owen jogged toward the sound. At the guard station, the floor under his bare feet was wet and slick. Ignoring it, he ran up the stairs, following the scent of Alec and Vicki.

IN THE BACK of Z Hall, Darcy had gotten the females hidden behind the privet bushes before the lights went out. Once everyone was safe, she'd stripped and returned to cat form—hearing the gasps, then delighted murmurs of the females.

The grounds were dark, and angry shouts came from the front. "Someone fucked with the machine guns, killed the guards."

"Get those lights on!"

With heavy footsteps, two guards pounded between the two manor houses toward the generator. *Thank you, Wells.* The spymaster's "gift" was designed to fry every circuit in the board.

Tonight...darkness would reign.

Crouching low, Darcy crept out of the bushes far enough to monitor all approaches. Her tail twitched nervously as she scented the cool night air.

From the front came the sound of a roaring vehicle, then a horrendous crash. Metal whined and clanked. The engine stopped abruptly.

As planned, Ben and his construction crew had rammed the front gates with a bulldozer.

Shots rang out. Individual shots—not the rat-tat-tat of machine guns. But still...bullets. *Oh, Mother of All, keep our shifters safe.*

The back door of Z Hall opened.

Darcy dug her claws into the earth, bracing to spring.

A cougar female ran out the door. *Vicki?* Alec, also a cougar, was right behind her. Both were drenched in blood. Ignoring her mate, Vicki looked right and left. On guard.

Alec shifted to human and bent to stroke his mate, rubbing his face against hers. "By the God, are you all right?" he whispered.

Her purr was a soft sound under the yelling and shooting coming from in front.

In human form, Owen appeared in the door, moving funny, as if walking on eggshells. His arms were filled with...*babies.*

Darcy stared.

All his attention on his mate, Alec frowned. "You're...thin, *cariad.* What—"

"Hey, Alec. I think these cubs belong to you." Spotting the females in the bushes, Owen motioned them over and handed off the cubs to Margery and Idelle.

Staring, Alec straightened. "Mother's blessing, Vixen. We have cubs?"

The wonder in his choked voice sent a surging joy through Darcy.

When Alec moved toward the steps, Owen blocked him. "Cubs come later, cahir. We need to get everybody to the garage." After using the Scythe's vans to transport the hostages, they'd abandon the vehicles somewhere in the city.

Alec sucked in a pained breath. "Aye, let's get them out of here. I'll take the lead. Vixen, stay by the cubs. Owen, left flank. Darcy, you bring up the rear. Let's go."

As Alec started away from the manor, the female villagers remained crouching under the hedge. Darcy understood all too well. Gunfire, guards everywhere. They'd been prisoners too long—and wouldn't follow a strange male.

Darcy shifted to human. "Come on. It's time to move to somewhere safe." She waved for the females to come out of the bushes. "Hurry."

Step by step, Margery ventured out, and Darcy felt her heart swell with pride. No one on the planet was as brave as Margery. She was followed by Idelle, then the rest.

Darcy turned. "Alec, I'd better lead."

"Aye. I'll take rearguard."

Staying human so the females wouldn't panic, Darcy led them along the back wall of the manor, scouting for danger. Soon they'd have to cross a long wide patch of lawn to get to the garage in the back east corner. Between intervals of gunfire, shouting, and screams from the front lawn, she could hear the soft footsteps of her villagers behind her.

As she moved out and away from the far side of the manor, one of the babies started to cry, a thin, high wailing. Someone shushed it.

"What the fuck!" a man shouted. "What was that?"

The sound came from her left. Heart pounding wildly, Darcy cringed as several guards appeared along the manor's east wall.

A flashlight caught her full in its beam. "That's the one that escaped!" It was Huber—the guard who'd raped Fenella.

Hatred flamed in her heart—and was swamped by fear. If the guards reached the back of the manor, they'd see the line of females behind her.

She saw the dark glint of pistols. They'd kill her friends.

Never.

Darcy sprang forward and sprinted directly away from the villagers. *Come on, chase me.*

Like a poorly led wolf pack, the guards mindlessly tore after her, their flashlights flickering on her and past her. Pistols barked, their shots going wild.

It was her nightmare in the park again. A tinny taste filled her mouth. Her bare skin was too visible. *Hide, must hide.* The need to trawsfur into a dark panther and disappear into the shadows wracked her.

Visible was the point. *Run, tinker. Lead the guards away from the children and babies.* Her muscles flinched with each gunshot blast.

Not far ahead of her, two more guards appeared. "Get her!" Muzzle blasts sparked in the darkness as they shot at her.

She felt a tugging on her arm. A bullet slammed into her thigh, and her leg buckled. She went down, rolling over and over.

Terror filled her. *Not again.* She tried to push to her feet.

A man landed on her, flattening her to the ground. His stench increased her fear. Huber. He ground her face in the dirt.

"You fucking abortion." His breath was foul, his weight horrible. As she struggled frantically, he ran his hand over her bare shoulder and made her shudder with revulsion. "You brought them freaks here."

A flashlight beam danced over Huber and her. "You got her. Good—" The human's high shriek ended abruptly.

A startled, choking grunt came from someone else. Heels thumped on the ground convulsively.

Another guard skidded to a stop. "One of 'em got Conklin." He turned in a circle. "Jones? Parker? Huber, the fucking beasts are all around us!"

"Christ Jesus." Huber's breath panted on her cheek. Gripping her hair, he yanked her head up in the air and pressed his knife to her throat.

Terror engulfed her. There—the door to the wild, to the trawsfur. With all her control, she fought the change. If Huber realized she was shifting, he'd cut her throat immediately.

In the shadows to her right, tawny fur flickered past.

From the front, another cougar bounded directly toward them. *Gawain*. Snarling madly. All his attention was on Huber.

The guard beside Huber whimpered in terror, raised his pistol. Aimed.

"No!" Darcy struggled. The knife cut deeper into her neck.

The redhead hesitated, looking at her.

"Shoot!" Huber yelled.

From the right, a cougar leaped over Huber and landed on the other guard. The pistol blasted—and then Owen bit out the guard's throat.

"Jesus!" Huber screamed. "You freaks, get back or she's dead! I'll—" His knife pressed viciously against her throat. Burning pain seared her skin.

Still a cougar, Owen let out a chilling scream-snarl.

And Darcy saw Gawain shift to human, pull his sheathed blade—and throw.

Huber shrieked and dropped his knife. Releasing her hair, he yanked Gawain's blade from his forearm.

Free. Desperately, she shoved up and scrambled out from under him.

As she tried—managed—to stand, Huber disappeared beneath two enraged male cougars. His scream was cut off.

Dead. Darcy swallowed. He was dead…and he'd never rape or hurt another female again.

Shaking, nauseated, hurting, she took a step toward Gawain and Owen. In the middle of her worst nightmare, they had come for her. *Saved* her.

As her strength failed and she collapsed, she heard the whap-whap-whap of a helicopter making a landing.

NAKED IN HUMAN form, Tynan loosely tied the bag with his clothing around his neck. The helicopter touched down, and he jumped out, ducking his head against the wind from the blades. The grounds within the stone walls were dark. The little female had done her job. Tynan's gut sucked in at the ugly noise of battle. Gunshots and yelling, screams of pain, shouted orders…but there was no rat-tat-tat of automatic weapons.

In wolf form, Fell and Patrin leaped to the ground, and then the rest stormed out and onto the grounds. As they spread out, littermates ran together, targeting the sounds of gunfire and the flashlights. The healing time had been too short, and some limped as they ran. A few remained in human form and carried cans of gasoline since Calum had ordered them to burn the manor where the Daonain had been held. Wells had requested the other building burn as well.

Tynan checked the helicopter. The last male out was his littermate, the damn fool. Healers were too valuable to risk in a war zone, but Donal had the stubbornness of a donkey. He insisted a battle was exactly where a healer was needed.

Tynan scowled at him. "We'll head for the garage where the hostages and wounded will be. Follow me—and remember to duck."

His damn littermate simply chuckled. Carrying a backpack of medical supplies, he joined Tynan.

Needing the greater mobility, Tynan shifted to wolf and trotted across the wide lawn, cursing the lack of fecking cover. Bodies scattered the lawn, and the stench of bowels and blood hung thick in the air.

A massive grizzly swatted a guard, flinging him into a building.

Two wolves in a well-coordinated attack took down another guard.

A lean old panther chased after another guard. Was that the old werecat who owned BOOKS?

A shot rang out from the vine-covered building—and the panther snarled. His forelimb darkened with blood.

Tynan turned.

Rifle barrel resting on the sill, a sniper knelt in a first floor window. Growling, Tynan leaped through, hit the guard's shoulders, and knocked him onto his back.

Then the cop part of Tynan watched as his wolf instincts took over and tore the human to pieces. As the guard under his paws died, Tynan thought of the others who would also die today—without recourse to any laws. He found no pity or remorse in his heart.

It appeared his time as a law enforcement officer was at an end.

THE LITTLE CAT had gone down. Fear was a cold ball in Owen's gut. As Gawain prowled in a circle around them, Owen shifted and dropped to his knees beside Darcy. A hand on her ribs let him know she still breathed. "She's alive," he whispered, knowing Gawain would hear. *Alive, alive, alive.*

In cougar form, Alec loped over.

Having seen him and Vicki wipe out two guards coming from the rear, Owen gave him a grateful nod.

Alec looked at Darcy, and his ears tipped forward in a query.

"She'll be all right." She *had* to be. Owen pointed in the direction of the garage. "Get the group moving. We'll catch up."

The cougar nodded and gathered his charges. Now out in the open with nowhere to hide, the females seemed willing to follow with the cougars.

Owen turned his attention back to Darcy. Where was she hurt? In the dark night and against her olive skin, blood seemed to be smeared everywhere. He made a sound of frustration…and her eyes opened.

Thank the Mother. His heart had almost failed when he saw her struck by bullets, saw her go down.

"Owen," she whispered.

He couldn't keep from snatching her into his arms and breathing in her *morning-after-a-rain-shower* fragrance. "I thought you were dead." His arms tightened until she squeaked.

A second later, Gawain trawsfurred and wrapped his arms around both of them. "By the Hunter and the Mother, you two almost gave me heart failure. Don't do that again."

The tiny chuckle from the half-smothered female was the sweetest sound in the universe. "Nice knife-work, blademage," she whispered.

Damned if it hadn't been. Owen smacked his brother on the arm. "Damn right."

"I'm going to have nightmares about missing that throw for months," Gawain muttered.

Owen pulled in a breath. Fuck, what was he doing, letting

down his guard? "Gawain, tend her wounds while I keep watch."

"On it," Gawain said in a rough voice. "Where are you hurt, catling? Darcy?" After a second, he said, "She's out cold."

Owen's gut clenched. He forced himself to stay on guard in human form in case he needed to speak.

"Three wounds. Neck's just a thin slice. Thigh and arm. Nothing life-threatening, brawd," Gawain whispered.

Owen closed his eyes for a second…and kept circling.

He recognized Zeb and Shay's scents a second before the two wolves trotted by. They paused, ears up.

"We're good. Keep going," Owen said softly.

As they disappeared, Owen spotted the first flames shooting up in the house where the shifters had been captive. Wells should be moving the human hostages out of the other house. Very soon, the grounds would hold only burning buildings and the dead.

At a hint of a sound, he spun.

A wolf stalking the shadows was about to jump Gawain.

Snarling, Owen sprang first, shifted to cougar midair, and landed in front of the damn dog.

The wolf froze.

Trawsfurring back, Owen planted his feet, badger-furious. "For fuck's sake, you sprite-brained fool, we've got shifters in human form. Sniff before you leap." Had battle fever taken the idiot?

He spotted another wolf, deeper in the shadows.

Owen scowled at that one and folded his arms over his chest.

The first wolf shifted and walked forward cautiously. Sniffed. And relaxed. "Sorry, you were downwind."

Not in a mood to be forgiving, Owen glared. "That is my littermate you were about to attack."

"Ah." The male moved to one side to be able to watch Darcy and Gawain. "Apologies. But that's my sister." His sentence ended in a growl.

Owen blinked. *Well.* He kept his voice low. "Are you Patrin or Fell?"

"Fell. You know Darcy?"

Not the time, not the place. "Talk, later, wolf. She's hurt, unconscious, and I need to get her to the transport before cleanup starts."

The male's face turned dangerous. "We'll take her. She's—"

A voice came from the shadows, probably Patrin's. "That scar on his face means you're a cahir, right?"

Owen nodded.

Fell took a step back. "Guard her well, then, cahir."

The other male's voice was low. "We'll be nearby, clearing your trail."

As the two shifted and darted away, Owen frowned. They'd been adolescent shifters indoctrinated into senseless human savagery. Would they be able to adjust to Daonain ways?

A small groan sounded, high and sweet, and Owen turned.

Darcy's eyelids fluttered, and she looked around. *Yes.*

Unable to keep from smiling, Owen asked, "Gawain, if you're done, can you carry her?"

"I can think of nothing I'd like more."

The tiny snort of laughter was Darcy's.

By the God, he loved her.

Chapter Twenty-Five

S OMEONE'S VOICE HAD wakened her. Darcy blinked, trying to remember where she was and why she was wrapped in a blanket and lying on the floor. Other females were sitting or lying nearby. Her villagers.

The room held brown and green upholstered couch and armchairs, long drapes, and a television. This was what Wells called a "safe house".

Now, she remembered. Owen and Gawain had tucked her into a black van packed with hostages. All the vans, loaded with females and the wounded, had driven to the front gate. Far down the street on both sides, emergency vehicles were flashing lights. The downed utility poles and power lines had blocked traffic.

One female asked, "Then how will we get out?"

"Watch." Grinning, Shay'd stomped on the gas, driven straight across the street, over the curb, across a front lawn, scraped between two houses and into a backyard. The van convoy had torn through residential properties, flattening fences and landscaping, to finally emerge onto a quiet street blocks away.

Such a getaway.

"There she is." Owen's voice.

Relief poured through her, and she struggled to sit up.

"Lie still, catling." With his littermate beside him, Gawain knelt and pressed her back onto the blanket.

She breathed in their scents, feeling the hard knot in her belly unwind. "Are you all right?" Darcy touched the blood-drenched rag around Gawain's arm.

"Nothing serious." Gawain checked the rough bandage he'd put around her leg.

Owen tilted her chin up to look at the one on her neck. He scowled. "You got the worst of it." The snarls beneath his words showed how he felt about her getting hurt.

She tapped his nose as she would a puppy. "I'll be fine."

"Donal was supposed to heal everything." Owen glared around as if he'd drag the healer over himself.

"He was—"

"He's tapped out." Tynan walked over, set down a box, and crouched beside her. "In a city, this far from the Mother, he's weak. He knew he would be, but insisted on coming anyway. Even exhausted, he was able to locate and remove the females' trackers."

Gawain grunted. "I'd forgotten the hostages here had trackers. I'm glad someone remembered."

"He couldn't heal the females—and that pissed him off. I sent him back to Cold Creek with the worst of the injured. Once he recovers some energy, he'll be able to heal them—at least enough to keep them alive."

Darcy shook her head. "Poor Donal. I bet he hated not being able to fix everyone."

"The idiot ran himself so dry he passed out," Tynan said.

"Fuck." Owen blinked. "Healers have died doing that."

"Aye." Scowling, Tynan pushed the box toward Gawain. "He left us the supplies he brought. Clean your group's wounds, wrap them up, and hand off the bag to the next person."

"What's the plan for the Dogwood villagers?" Gawain opened the box.

"After the shifter-soldiers arrive and get a bit of time with sisters, the females will go to Rainier Territory for a couple of weeks. The Cosantirs in Washington and Oregon are working out who goes where. Some of the people have family elsewhere, some don't; some will have preferences." After smiling at Darcy, Tynan headed into the crowd.

"If the soldiers are here, have you seen my broth—" Burning pain jolted her, and she hissed at Gawain who'd pulled the gauze off her arm. "*Ouch*. Donal was nicer."

His lips twitched. "No, he wasn't. He dug a bullet out of you, remember?"

Well, okay, but still…

Gawain kissed her lightly. "I am sorry I hurt you." His blue eyes showed his worry.

Guilt washed through her. "I shouldn't have snapped at you."

Owen snorted. "I kind of enjoy seeing you in a temper…but I can gag her if you prefer, brawd."

"*What?*" She glared…and then she saw the strain in the cahir's face.

Seeing her in pain was upsetting him. Jaw locked, he moved his grip from her hand to her forearm, keeping her arm immobile.

"You're such a mean cahir," she said to try get a smile.

It didn't work, but he rubbed his knuckles lightly over her cheek.

Trying not to show how much Gawain's efforts hurt, she gritted her teeth and suffered. As her newly dressed arm throbbed and burned, she wanted to whimper when he started on her thigh. She gave him a beseeching look. "We could just skip my leg."

Owen was the one to kiss her this time. "Puppy-dog eyes. Very nice. Nevertheless, we're still going to clean it up."

He waited a second—and kissed the pout off her lips as well.

If she'd had the heart, she'd have smacked him on the nose. Yet the merciless jerk hugged her when—as she'd thought—the dressing really, really did hurt.

As Gawain finished the wrapping job, Owen pulled her against him and said in a rough voice, "It didn't look too bad."

She rubbed her cheek on his shoulder. "Honestly, I think it hurt you worse than it did me." And now that her eyes weren't blinded by tears, she noticed Gawain's face was just as grim.

"You shouldn't have been there," Gawain said. "We know how you felt about that place, and you went in without us."

"Then you got hurt with me right there." Owen's voice was like a badly tuned motor—rough and ragged. "Should have been me."

Such guilt. Her heart warmed with love. After stroking Owen's cheek, she pulled Gawain down for another kiss. "If you hadn't been there, I'd be dead. Instead, we're all alive. I'm happy."

Some of the bitterness in Owen's eyes lightened.

"Rescue of both the forest camp and the females accomplished. Guards dead, houses burned. Got a lot of wounded, but no one died. I'd call it a success." Gawain ran his finger down her cheek and smiled.

As Gawain passed the first aid box to the females nearby, the front door opened. Males in black vests and cargo pants, carrying firearms entered.

The soldiers looked around expectantly, and happy shouts echoed through the room as they spotted their sisters.

"Darcy!" Two males—her *littermates*—charged across the room. As Owen and Gawain moved out of the way, her brothers dropped to their knees beside her.

Patrin with his olive skin and long black hair. Fell with his blue eyes and short sandy hair.

"Oh, Mother of All, you're here. You're free and alive." Joy welled up in her so strong she was drowning in it.

"You're safe," Patrin whispered, as if to reassure himself. His smile didn't show in his eyes—and hadn't for the last five years. Ever so gently, he pulled her into his arms.

When he released her, Fell was there. A burbling brook frozen into silence, her brother rarely spoke. He studied the dressings on her arm and leg, nodded approval, and leaned forward to kiss her cheek. Then he frowned at her. "You didn't belong there."

"What?"

"In danger."

Seriously? They were actually together again, finally—and he was using some of his hoarded words to criticize her? The urge to cry warred with the urge to smack him.

She settled on the second option and smacked the side of his head.

Not even a flinch. He growled. At one time, he'd have yelped and laughed.

Breathing past the ache in her heart, she growled back. "I *did* belong there."

"She's the one who discovered the captives had two trackers." Gawain's tone was very even.

Owen's tone wasn't polite at all. "She escaped, helped us find your prisons, and saved every benighted one of you. Show some fucking *gratitude*." The pride in his voice made her eyes sting.

Both of her brothers scowled, shook the insult off, and she got two more hugs.

"Thanks, *chwaer*," Patrin murmured.

Fell simply gave her a squeeze…and she mourned for his lost words.

"Cahir, mage, a moment," Alec called from the center of the room.

As Owen and Gawain joined him, Patrin's eyes narrowed. "I saw the cahir. What's a mage?"

"A blademage." Darcy looked after him and didn't…quite…sigh. Gawain had earned all those muscles the hard way.

As if he felt her gaze, he met her eyes and winked.

The flush of heat ran from her head to her toes. After a second, she turned to Patrin. "He's a metalsmith with extra magic so he can make cahir blades and sheaths and the lifemating bracelets."

When Alec said something, both Gawain and Owen glanced at her, turned back to Alec with scowls, and whatever he'd suggested was turned down cold.

The sheriff laughed, agreed, and wrote something on his clipboard.

Owen gave him a narrow-eyed look, one that promised retribution, and stalked back to Darcy.

Such a cat. Deadly and snarly and ever so softhearted. She almost sighed again.

He stood over her, his arms crossed over his chest. "We're heading for Cold Creek. With you."

"Good." She frowned. "What about Patrin and Fell?"

Gawain glanced at her brothers. "It seems the spymaster has asked the Dogwood males to help him with a project for a while."

Patrin nodded. "We agreed."

"When done," Gawain said, "your brothers will be assigned to Cold Creek."

"Assigned?" Patrin asked slowly.

"For safety and to help you all reintegrate with Daonain life, the Dogwood villagers are being scattered throughout the towns in Oregon and Washington," Gawain said. "Once things quiet down, you can move where you want."

Her brothers exchanged glances. "Makes sense," Patrin said. "We'll be with Darcy, though?"

"Aye." Owen's tone was inflexible. "She lives in Cold Creek."

Grumpy cat. But she loved what he'd said. "*She lives in Cold Creek.*" Not "assigned", but she *belonged* there.

NURSING BABY TOREN, Vic burrowed deeper into the blankets on the couch. *Thank you, Zeb.* He'd carried her in from the van, set her on the couch, and told her to stay where he put her. Two-thirds of Cold Creek were terrified of the deadly cahir—never realizing he had a soft side. The wonder in his face when he'd seen the babies had almost reduced her to tears. He'd scrounged up tiny boxes for baby beds, ripped up a blanket for bedding, and lined the beds up on the coffee table. After moving the table right next to the couch, he'd sent someone off for diapers.

She'd wondered for—oh, all of a moment—why he and Shay hadn't stayed behind to fight. But, of course, they'd been ordered to get the captives out. Any Cosantir—and any Daonain male—would put the females' safety first.

Calum. Worry hummed inside her like a swarm of bees. Zeb had said Calum had planned to hand himself over to the Scythe. No wonder they'd left her alone. The so-called Director had wanted to ensure he'd nabbed Calum before damaging her.

"Please be safe, you stubborn cat," she whispered, aching to be with him. The overprotective cat must have been going crazy, not being able to come after her. How he must be resenting the duties of the God—even as he fulfilled them. Her lips curved. She wouldn't have loved him so much if he didn't have that bone-deep sense of responsibility.

The sucking at her breast stopped, and she looked down. Toren had a tiny fuzz of dark hair covering his head and blue-gray eyes. Donal had warned her that babies' eyes often darkened, but oh, this boy totally had Calum's genes. "Look who I'm bringing you, Calum."

Much more smoothly than with the first fumbling efforts, Vic eased her nipple from the baby's mouth and checked the other two. She still wasn't sure if she was horrified or proud. *Three fucking babies.*

Good thing she, Alec, and Calum had chosen a couple of extra names—just in case. For two, they'd used the Daonain tradition of honoring an older friend by selecting a name that was similar, yet unique.

During the long hours in the concrete cell, it had been a comfort to be able to call her babies by name.

Reaching over to the coffee table, Vic touched Sorcha's tiny hand and ruffled the fluff of golden hair on her head. The baby's eyes opened—blue eyes that already held a hint of green. "Yes, Alec had a hand in making you, didn't he?"

Smacking her lips, the girl fell back asleep.

Next to her in his box-bed, Artair kicked his tiny feet. His face wrinkled in frustration. Brown hair. Eyes already brown. He not only looked like her, but also demanded prompt action when he raised his voice.

Smiling, she scooped him up.

At the door, another set of soldiers came in, followed by Wells—and damned if Joe Thorson wasn't beside him.

Joe had a bloody bandage on his forearm, but the old cat looked fine and fierce. Both of them looked around and—when they spotted her, the relief in their eyes almost made her start crying.

Again. Fucking hormones.

They made a beeline for her, and then Wells was close enough to see over the back of the couch. He stopped dead, eyes on the bundle in her arms.

Thorson bumped into him. "Stupid human. Can't you even walk without—" His gaze followed Wells's.

"Sergeant," Wells said. "You had the baby?"

Blinking back more tears, Vic laughed. "Babies, sir. Plural." She reached out to pat Sorcha and Toren.

Just like Zeb, the two merciless killers turned all gooey. Boy, if she could synthesize the baby-effect, she could end every war on the planet.

"You have babies." Wells touched his finger to Artair's tiny hand.

There would never be a better time.

"Arthur Wells," she said in a formal voice—a command voice—and held up the baby. "Here is your namesake, Artair. Will you serve as his *caomhnor?*"

Damned if she'd ever seen Wells at a loss. After a second, he took the baby as competently as he did everything else. When he held tiny Artair against his chest, she lost the battle with tears.

"What's a *kuheev-rore,*" he asked in a gruff voice.

Thorson had crossed his arms on his chest. Buddies with Wells or not, the werecat took infinite pleasure in taunting the human spymaster. He smirked. "It's a—"

"Joe," Vic said softly and picked up the black-haired baby. "Joe Thorson, here is your namesake, Toren. Will you serve as his *caomhnor?*"

As Joe tucked the baby into the crook of his arm, he stared at her—and she knew why. She was giving him family. More bonds to tie him to the earth. More people to love. He swallowed, and his voice came out as rough as she'd ever heard it. "Aye. I will serve as his guardian-protector, teaching him and loving him for as long as my heart beats and the blood flows in my veins."

She felt the first tear spill down her cheek.

"Yes…" Wells cleared his throat, and his words came out clear and strong. "I will serve as Artair's guardian-protector, teaching him and loving him for as long as my heart beats and the blood flows in my veins."

IN ALEC'S CAR, Owen rode shotgun. Behind him were Darcy, Vicki and her cubs, and Gawain. Owen was amused to see how good his littermate was with the tiny cubs.

It was good to be headed home to Cold Creek—and sooner than he'd thought.

Alec hadn't planned to leave until all the hostages and soldiers were gone.

Owen had watched the cahir call Calum to report in…and seen his growing concern as he spoke with the Cosantir. After ending the call, Alec had turned over everything to Shay, Zeb, and Ben.

He'd said Vicki and the babies needed to get back to Cold Creek. When Shay told him to take extra protection, Owen had volunteered, which meant Gawain and Darcy had come.

When Vicki had protested the need to hurry, Alec looked grim, saying Calum needed to see she was all right.

The thought of a Cosantir losing control was…not good. And by the God, Owen understood how frantic Calum must feel. When Darcy had been hit by bullets and gone down… He'd come very close to going on a killing rampage. He'd never felt such fear. Such rage.

Knowing a mate was safe wasn't the same as feeling her, seeing her, hearing her, breathing her in.

Even now, Owen couldn't stop checking on Darcy. For the hundredth time, he looked over his shoulder. She was snuggled to Gawain's side, holding a baby on her lap, half-asleep. Just watching her breathe was more comforting than he would have ever imagined.

As the car approached Cold Creek, Owen spotted a vehicle parked on the shoulder, barely off the road, in fact. The van was black with darkly tinted windows. "Alec, that's a Scythe vehicle."

Alec braked.

"Looks empty." Alec scowled. "I can't stop, not with…" He glanced at the passengers in the back. The babies and females. Putting them in danger wasn't acceptable.

"Drive past and let me out. I'll run back and see what's up." If the Scythe were off in the woods, he'd wave Alec away and do some hunting.

Owen approached the vehicle from the rear, since the car was pointed toward Seattle. Moving up, he glanced in the back. Empty.

Looking in the driver's side, he realized the car had occupants, after all. When he opened the front door, the escaping scent was so filled with fear that he jerked back a step.

But the two dead humans posed no threat. The driver and passenger were slumped over each other, with no signs of injury. No blood. Just stark terror in their faces.

After a second, Owen slammed the door shut…because the scent lingering in the back was that of a very angry Cosantir.

The Cosantir had turned himself over to the Scythe. Had probably been bound and shoved into the back seat. By these two humans.

"You poor bastards," Owen muttered, remembering the look on Calum's face when he'd said, *"I will be in the heart of my territory."*

FINALLY HOME. VIC realized Alec had parked the car in front of the side gate. Oh, hell, it was a long walk around the side and up the stairs to their second-floor rooms. And she was so…fucking…exhausted. It was taking all her strength to sit upright.

Gawain jumped out and helped Darcy out.

Vic swung her legs around and found her way blocked.

"Soldier or not, you're all in." Darcy turned to Alec. "You carry her. The guys and I will bring in the babies."

Alec raised his eyebrows and grinned at Owen. "You're going to have your hands full with this one." A minute later, Alec took Sorcha from Vic, handed the baby to Owen, and scooped up Vic.

She rested her head against his shoulder and sighed. "Normally, I'd belt you one for carrying me around."

He rested his cheek against her head for a second. "Not today?"

"Not today. Thank you."

"Vixen, you have no idea how much I need to hold you…for a long, long time. It'll be a while before I can shed my fear, and Calum is even worse. He already—he didn't sound good when I spoke to him."

Oh, fuck. Calum's first mate had been slaughtered by a human. Vic kidnapped by humans…no, he wouldn't be a happy camper. "Let's get in there."

"Aye." Alec led the others around the side of the house and up the stairs. The door was ajar, and he pushed it open and walked into the living room. The room was dark and silent.

Calum was on the couch, head in his hands, and power was

so thick around him she could almost hear it rumble.

"Brawd." Still holding her, Alec went down on one knee beside the couch.

Calum looked up, and his eyes were black and unseeing. "Did you lie? Is she—"

"Oh, Calum." Vic reached out. When she put her hands on each side of his face, he gripped her wrists in an unbreakable hold.

"Victoria."

"Here, brawd. Hang onto her for a bit." Alec set her on Calum's lap.

"You're here. Alive." The arms that came around her felt like finely forged steel as he wrapped her in his strength and power. When he bowed his head and rested his cheek on the top of her head, she felt the tremor go through him.

And the shimmering heat of the God slowly diminished.

After a minute, when he let her take a breath, she asked, "Have you been sitting here all this time?"

"Aye." He lifted his head and slid over so Alec could join them on the couch. "After I…disposed…of the Scythe agents, I had nothing I could do—and too much anger to be trusted around anyone. I could only"—his words descended to a low deadly growl—"wait."

She rubbed her cheek on his shoulder. "Yeah. Waiting is the worst. I'd rather be shot at any day."

Alec snorted. "It really bothers me that I know you mean that."

"Are you unhurt?" Calum asked, finally releasing her enough to look at her. His eyes were returning to the silvery-gray she loved.

"Just tired. Um…" She glanced at Alec, and he nodded. "How about a nice surprise for a change?"

Calum's lips curved. "About the captives?"

Damn, he *was* off his game. His powers of observation rivaled Wells's, and he hadn't even noticed she was a hell of a lot lighter.

"Huh, I guess you could call them the most recent of the captives." She looked over his shoulder and motioned to the three standing as far away as they could get without falling down the stairs.

Owen—brave cahir—came first and went down on one knee in front of Calum. "Congratulations, Cosantir," he said gently. "The clan increases." He held Sorcha in the curve of his arm.

Calum went deadly still. "You—"

Gawain went down on one knee next to Owen. "Congratulations, Cosantir. The clan increases." Toren kicked his pint-sized feet and made a burbling sound.

Darcy joined the brothers. Her smile was brilliant as she turned Artair so he could look up at his sire. "Hey, Cosantir. You did good."

Vic snickered. Yeah, she really did like this woman.

A second later, there were pounding footsteps on the stairs.

Jamie burst into the room. "You're back! MomVee, are you okay?" The girl skidded to a stop beside Darcy, and her eyes widened.

"Fucking-A, Daddy, we've got a whole litter!"

The knot in Vic's stomach unwound as Calum's dark beautiful laugh rang out. "We do indeed, kitten." He planted a hard kiss on Vic's lips and whispered in her ear, "Thank you, *cariad*, for keeping yourself and our cubs safe."

Chapter Twenty-Six

JUST OVER A week after the rescue, Darcy was curled up in front of the fire, watching two salamanders dance in the flames. She'd been in the game room earlier, enjoying a talk with a couple of the Dogwood females whose brothers had been badly wounded.

The front door opened, and Darcy looked up to see two annoyed males stalk in the front door. They spotted her immediately.

Run!

Heavy footsteps thudded behind her as she fled across the room and up the stairs—giggling uncontrollably. She darted down the hallway, into her room, and spun to shut the door.

Too slow.

An angry cougar shifter picked her off the floor and tossed her onto the bed. A knee beside her hip, he came down on her, squishing the air from her lungs with his heavy body. Gripping her wrists, Owen slowly stretched her arms over her head, immobilizing her.

She couldn't stop grinning. From the way they'd entered the lodge, she knew the prank had worked.

Gawain closed the door behind him and shook his head. "For someone with such an innocent face, you have an evil streak, my pretty panther. Calum was appalled to have his meeting broken up by wayward *farts*. What did you do to our phones?"

"You're going to pay, little cat." Owen's deadly growl reverberated in her ear.

She burst into another giggling fit and felt his lips curve against her cheek. It hadn't been easy to set up the farting app to start making bowel noises on both phones at the same time, but…hey, she was a sneaky cat, and Ryder had been delighted to help.

Gawain gave her a regretful look. "She's out of control, brawd. We can't allow our student to treat her aging mentors with such disrespect." He lit a candle on the dresser.

Aging mentors? Seriously? She almost strangled on a laugh. "Oh, sorry. How could I forget about your advanced years?"

Gawain's eyes narrowed at her syrupy sweet tone.

"But, let me assure you, you two cats have still got it…even if you don't remember what *it* is." Ignoring the choked noise Owen made, she assumed a sad expression. "Then again, these days, maybe the only thing turning hard on you is your arteries?"

"That does it." Gawain ripped his shirt over his head, and oh, talk about powerful muscles.

Her mouth went dry at the voracious desire in his eyes.

"She is very disrespectful, aye." Owen ran a finger down her cheek. "She should be naked before I beat on her."

"Beat on me? I don't—"

"Let me help with that." Finished stripping, Gawain gripped the hem of her jeans as Owen undid her jeans button.

"Hey!" Excitement rising, she pushed at Owen. "Two against one isn't fair. Besides, I was hurt. Shot—remember?"

Owen laughed. "Donal healed you, remember?"

She scowled.

Ignoring her struggling, he unzipped her jeans. "Now,

brawd."

Gawain gave a yank, and her jeans came right off. Dammit.

With ruthless hands, Owen rolled her far enough to grab the back of her T-shirt and pulled it over her head. He grinned at Gawain. "Why don't you pin her down while I get ready?"

"My pleasure." Stark naked, Gawain came down on her, hands gentle, but he didn't need to fight—his sheer weight pinned her to the bed. And as she squirmed, she felt his erection lengthen against her bare belly. He rumbled a laugh. "Fuck, you feel good."

"So do you. Always," she whispered. "Does this…need…ever go away?"

The sun lines at the corners of his eyes deepened. "Lust alone will fade. Lust when mixed with love? Never."

Oh, she was in trouble, because she was so filled with love for them it was difficult to breathe.

He tilted his head in query.

Instead of talking, she wound her arms around his neck and pulled him down for a kiss. He teased her lips with his tongue, his teeth, then dove deep inside, possessing her with an intensity that sent her mindless.

"I call dibs on these, brawd," he said, moving down to kiss her breasts until she was arching up for more. "I can think of several ways to punish our female."

Now naked, Owen pushed her knees apart to make room for himself. He settled between her legs and licked over her pussy, looked up…and smiled.

And she knew then, that her need for Owen and Gawain would never disappear.

Chapter Twenty-Seven

S MILING, GAWAIN BREATHED in the sweet scent of female. The sun was streaming in the window, but the catling was still sound asleep. They'd worn her out last night. May the Mother save him, but Darcy was amazing. Beautiful. Generous. Sweet. *Ours*.

He hated to leave her, even for a few hours. After kissing her rosy lips so lightly she didn't rouse, he rose and reluctantly pulled on his clothes.

Grumbling under his breath, Owen eyed him, then rolled off the bed and dressed. "No more early morning deliveries," he muttered to Gawain.

"Agreed." But Ryder was ready to bring over the furniture he'd built for the female bedroom. Over at Ben and Ryder's, Owen had been working on the headboard every moment he could spare. It was time.

Darcy's room—Darcy's *bed* was finished.

Gawain tucked the covers around her. She liked sleeping with them; she'd said so.

The rest of the house was clean, furnished enough to live in, floors gleaming, walls ready to paint or wallpaper—ready for her. He glanced around the room, noting the vase displaying bright yellow and orange leafed branches, the myriad of candles, a bowl filled with pinecones. He wanted her living in *their* house, doing her nest making, adding the warmth of her touch.

When she joined them, their house would have a heart.

It was time to move out of the Wildwood Lodge. The cabins and interior rooms were filled with villagers who were assigned to Cold Creek as well as the injured shifters who needed Donal's care.

He grinned at Owen who was pulling on his soft, high leather boots. "Let's go get our cat her bed."

Owen's green eyes lit. "Aye."

LATER THAT DAY, Owen walked into the Wild Hunt with his brother. Behind them came Tynan and Donal. The tavern was more crowded than normal, considering it was only four in the afternoon. The Daonain were still discussing the past events and making plans for the future.

"Now there's a lovely sight—one I haven't seen since I left Ireland." Tynan nodded to the left.

Owen followed his gaze.

Near the fireplace, Calum's daughter Jamie held brown-haired Artair. Vicki sat beside her, feet up on the short game table.

Her face soft with delight, Darcy cuddled another cub with a golden fuzz of hair. Even though he'd seen the little tinker only a few hours before, his heart still lifted.

"Darcy's here," Gawain murmured in pleasure.

Owen moved closer, rubbing his shoulder against his littermate's. *Ours.* Would she accept them? His hopes had risen. She'd been in their bed every night since the rescue.

"Joe's going to have those cubs reading before they learn to talk." Smiling, Donal pointed toward the window where the bookstore owner, Thorson, held Toren in his uninjured arm. As the grizzled old cat talked, the cub's eyes were fixed on his face as if taking in every word.

"Aye, he will." Chuckling, Owen glanced around.

Calum was behind the bar, his faint smile apparent as some shifter told a story, hands waving in the air. Having the Cosantir in his usual place was oddly heartening, indicating all was right with the world.

"Beer?" Donal asked Owen.

"In a bit. We have a female to harass first."

Donal laughed and headed toward the bar with Tynan.

Owen followed Gawain toward Darcy.

When she saw them, the way she brightened sent his heart to bouncing like a mountain goat within his chest. Her loose black hair shimmered in the light from the window, and when he bent to kiss her, he couldn't help running his fingers through the soft waves. She smelled of a light clean shampoo and her own feminine fragrance, and he nuzzled the curve between her shoulder and neck to savor the scent.

After collecting his own kiss, Gawain went down on his haunches beside the infant in her lap. With an expression of wonder, he carefully touched the infant's round cheek. "She's so tiny," he murmured.

Seated next to Darcy on the couch, Owen stroked a finger over the cub's hand—and was startled when the tiny fingers closed around his. "She's got a grip on her." He grinned at Vicki. "Takes after her mother, doesn't she?"

Mother. The word no longer tasted like cinders in his mouth. Only a lingering sorrow remained.

"Sorcha is going to kick butt and take names." Vicki bumped shoulders with Jamie. "She takes after her big sister."

Jamie grinned. "Damn straight."

Gawain glanced over at Vicki. "Do we know anything about

what happened with the Scythe prison in Seattle?"

"Yep. Wells called with a report." She smirked. "The manor where I was held was gutted by the fire. Nothing was recovered. The other manor isn't in much better shape"

Owen grinned. He'd never seen anything burn as fast as those two houses. "Good to hear. What else?"

She continued, "The human hostages were quietly returned to their families, and the FBI is openly investigating. They think a hostage's family must have hired a mercenary group."

"That's not far from the truth," Gawain noted.

Vicki scowled. "Unfortunately, the person called Director wasn't on the property at the time. He's in the wind."

When Darcy shivered, Owen put his arm around her. She'd tried to hide how much the fighting and death in Seattle had unsettled her. She was getting better and, by the God, it made him feel good when she'd said sleeping between him and Gawain drove away her nightmares.

"Any idea what will happen next with the Scythe?" Gawain asked Vicki.

"Wells will track the rest down, and I think he's planning something with the Dogwood males." She frowned. "He's not exactly sharing though."

Silently appearing, Calum plucked the mite from Jamie's lap, cuddling the tiny male cub against his shoulder.

"MomVee," Jamie whined. "He stole my baby."

"*Our* cub," Calum murmured and kissed the top of Jamie's head. "As are you, kitten." With a smile, Calum rubbed his cheek against the baby's and leaned on the armrest next to Vicki and said to the group, "Donal reports the wounded are ready to travel. I've made arrangements with the other territories to house everyone, including the females, currently in Rainier Territory."

He looked at Gawain. "Owen says you enjoy driving. If you are amenable, I'd like to you to transport the Dogwood females to their new homes. Owen will accompany you to ensure their safety."

After a startled second, Gawain bowed his head and gave the formal answer. "Your will, Cosantir. When do we start?"

"I believe Bree would gut me if I sent you away before her Thanksgiving dinner tomorrow. Will Friday suit?"

Gawain glanced at Owen for his nod and answered. "We'll be ready."

"I'm glad." Darcy's lips curved, and she rubbed her shoulder against Owen's. "The females will finally be able to start their lives. And they'll get to meet Daonain guys. They're in for such a lovely surprise."

A lovely surprise. Pleased, Owen squeezed her.

"Speaking of meeting guys, full moon is coming." Vicki frowned up at her mate. "My darling Cosantir, although I love you, if you even think of mating, I'll hurt you."

Calum burst out laughing. "Indeed. No worries, *cariad.* There will be no heat for you for a couple of months, at least. Remember, if you're not interested, neither are we."

Her eyes narrowed. "What if other females are interested in you? Two months is a long time."

"Time is irrelevant when you're lifemated. The only female Alec and I want to mate with is you."

"Huh. Sometimes this Daonain stuff isn't all that bad." With a soft smile, Vicki leaned against her mate.

Turning toward Owen, Darcy bit her lip. "I've never been to a big Gathering. It was scary enough with only four of you. And I don't really want..."

Owen drew her more snugly against him.

Kneeling beside her, Gawain set a hand on her knee, brow drawn with worry. "Darcy."

Calum's expression turned gentle. "I will be there, Darcy, and will keep an eye on you."

Although her worried look didn't ease, she smiled back. "Thank you."

Uneasiness trailed cold fingers across Owen's nape. A Gathering? How the fuck could he stomach seeing Darcy—*his* Darcy—get escorted to the mating rooms by other males? Just the thought sent possessive rage streaming through his veins.

The muscles in Gawain's cheek had gone taut.

They were fucked.

Chapter Twenty-Eight

DARCY SAT IN Angie's Diner, drinking coffee and tearing a donut to shreds. Rain ran in clear rivulets down the glass windows. The diner was almost empty. Apparently, the noisy storm had discouraged people from venturing outside.

After a swallow of coffee, she resumed tracing her finger through the brown liquid she'd spilled on the table. She wasn't really hungry. Bree had made huge omelets for breakfast. Of course, that had been hours ago.

Face it, her appetite had fled because the full moon was tomorrow. As Vicki would say…*god fucking dammit all to hell*.

Gawain and Owen weren't back.

Honestly, they'd been gone…forever…delivering the Dogwood females to the various territories. Okay, four days. She'd heard from them only once—using Shay's phone—but like Tynan, they were being exceedingly cautious about being traced. She agreed. Once the Scythe rebounded from losing the *prìosan* and forest compound, they'd start a hunt for their lost shifters.

Ice filled her belly at the thought. She still wondered if she should have disappeared into Canada as she'd planned. At the time, she'd expected the villagers would all hide together. Scattering made more sense. Probably.

She sighed. The days were long and dull without her guys.

How long could she last without hearing Gawain's big laugh or being wrapped in the muscular blademage's arms. She missed Owen's low growl and how the ever-so-deadly cahir would nuzzle her cheek. And, oh, she missed mating with the both of them.

Hunger slid into her bloodstream as she remembered the ways they'd made love—sheer carnal sex, loving sex, slow sensuous sex, fast, pounding sex, and every other variation they could think of. Sex in bed, on the floor, in mountain meadows, in the shower…although—she grinned—the lodge shower had been a bit small for the three of them.

Being with them and loving them fulfilled something in her.

She shook her head and took a sip of coffee.

As she set the cup down, she smiled at the cell phone sitting on the table. It was a present from Vicki. One evening when the females had gathered at the tavern, Vicki'd tried to thank her for going into the *prìosan* to get her out. In return, Darcy'd tried to thank her for the clothing, the friendship, for standing up for her, for…

They'd decided friends didn't keep score.

This morning, Vicki'd handed over the phone with a smirk and reminded Darcy they weren't keeping a tally. The Cosantir's mate had a seriously devious nature.

Leaning back, Darcy finished off her coffee. The rain still fell outside…and her walk back to the lodge would be dismal. Maybe she'd run across the street to BOOKS. She was getting more repair jobs and could afford to indulge in a new book. Really, she'd probably be able to make a good living here in Cold Creek.

Her phone rang, shrill in the silent diner, and she spilled her coffee.

She picked up the cell and swiped the ANSWER. "Hello?" Must be Vicki since no one had her number.

"Darcy?" The voice was familiar—and unexpected.

"Patrin." She frowned. "How did you get my number?"

"The Cosantir's mate gave it to Wells so we could call you."

Vicki, you're an amazing friend. "Good for her. How are you guys?"

"We're good." After a moment of silence, Patrin said, "You're on speaker, so…on the rare occasion Fell might speak, you can hear."

Over the phone came a *smack* and a yelp. Darcy grinned. Fell had obviously walloped Patrin.

"When are you two going to be done with whatever you're doing?" she asked.

"Not sure," Patrin said. "Wells said something about a mandatory night off, but didn't explain what or when. Soon, I think."

"Good. Since Owen and Gawain have moved out of the lodge, Bree's holding their room for you two."

"Those the two males who were with you at the safe house?" Patrin asked.

"Mmm-hmm." Her lips curved. *Mine.*

"They seemed concerned about you. Awfully fucking concerned." Patrin's voice held a growl.

"Well, we're…" Mating more often than rabbits? Sleeping together? "Um, they're my mentors in learning how to be Daonain again."

"Oh…good. Very good. I'd thought—"

"And I care about them," Darcy added. "A lot."

"A lot?" Fell's dark voice came over the phone.

"Yes. I do."

"*Chwaer*…" Their word for her—sister—made her smile, despite Patrin's disapproving tone. Oh, she had missed them.

"Darcy, being stuck in prison, you never learned about guys. How they think…" Patrin was obviously trying to keep his voice even. "And you're all by yourself in Cold Creek with no one to protect you from assholes who will take advantage."

She rolled her eyes. "I'm fine in this town, thank you. And Gawain and Owen aren't assholes. If you call them names, I'll be seriously pissed off at you."

The silence sounded…bad. As if her defense of her males had backfired.

"Darcy, we'll return soon," Patrin said finally, "and have time to spend with you. We can catch up on everything from the past."

"Sounds wonderful. I've always wondered about your missions." Although from eavesdropping on the Scythe leaders, she knew far more than her brothers realized. The shifter-soldiers had specialized in stealing, in destruction, and in assassinations. "Um, guys. You haven't exactly been around females either, have you? Should I be giving you the same lecture?"

"Well…" Patrin cleared his throat.

"Oh my Gods, you have?" She straightened. "When? After you were released or before?"

"Before." Patrin was getting as close-mouthed as Fell.

But hadn't they'd been stuck in their compound? She frowned. "How did you manage to meet women?"

"When the Scythe human soldiers trained us overseas, they were careless. In the evenings, they'd pay women to join them, not knowing how well we hear, how much we can see in the dark. When we were finally sent out on our own, we…did the same now and then."

Gawain said Daonain females never wanted humans, but that young testosterone-laden males who were unsuccessful at full moons would sometimes mate with human females. Her brothers had never been around Daonain females; they probably still didn't know the difference. "I see."

"So, yeah, we know how males think about females. And you need…" Patrin pulled in an audible breath. "We love you, *chwaer*. You're a beautiful woman."

"And too fucking sweet," Fell growled.

Patrin said, "We just want you to be happy."

"And safe." Fell again.

Her eyes filled with tears. Patrin and Fell had changed so much. She'd seen them with the other shifter-soldiers. Their "men." Her brothers were the alphas in charge of the deadly group. Even Wells treated them with respect.

"I am happy," she said. Although she'd be a lot happier if Gawain and Owen would get their tails back to Cold Creek. "And I'm very safe. You two just finish up your job and get back here so you can start your lives, too."

"Yes. We'll see you soon, *chwaer*," Patrin said gently.

Chapter Twenty-Nine

THE DAMN SOFTWARE convention had lasted way too long, and Heather Sutharlan was tired. Being surrounded by humans for days would stress anyone, even a sociable wolf like her. It was good to be back in the Gods' territory, even if this wasn't her own Rainier Territory.

Behind the Wild Hunt Tavern, she loped up the outside steps to the second floor where Vicki lived with her mates.

Alec let her in. "Hey, Heather. They're in Vicki's room doing those exotic things you females like to do during your Gathering pregame."

"You are so full of it." With long familiarity, she punched his arm. Back when they were cubs, Alec and Calum had run with Heather's littermates…with Heather trying to keep up. She'd never succeeded, and not because she was female, but because Alec and Calum were tricksy cougars and her brothers were bears.

A single wolf rarely won if going one-on-one against bigger, stronger felines and bears. Seemed like she still owed Alec and Calum a few sneaky pranks as payback.

Giving her an easy grin, Alec handed her a beer and waved her toward Vicki's bedroom. "Got a new female in there for you to take in hand."

"So I hear. Darcy, right?"

And why would that question make the big cahir laugh?

Heather tapped on the door and heard Vicki call, "Come."

Tears prickled Heather's eyes with her relief. Her friend's voice was still strong and unchanged. She'd survived a violent kidnapping and kept right on going.

That's one tough kitty. Heather'd liked the younger female the moment they'd met. Vicki might be a cat, but her style was as blunt and straightforward as Heather's.

Entering, she gave a quick glance around the room. Bree and Emma were on the bed, Angie in the armchair, and a black-haired female by the dressing table. Vicki sat in a new rocking chair with…with…

"A *cub*?" Heather rubbed her face, afraid her eyeballs were protruding from her skull. "You had…"

Vicki wore an evil feline smirk. "Three babies, no less." She nodded at the bed. "That's Toren."

The blanket in Bree's lap held a baby. A tiny, tiny baby. Even as Heather's fingers twitched, desperate to hold the cubling, her belly felt empty. Barren. Although her moon-courses were still steady, so many, many years had passed without life kindling within her that she'd given up hope.

Her expectation of finding lifemates had also died.

And those weak, useless emotions had no place in this room. It was time to rejoice with her friend. "Three cubs? Truly the clan increases."

Vicki's gaze was gentle. The observant cat had undoubtedly noted Heather's momentary despair. During several Wild Hunt evenings, they'd indulged in tongue-loosening brews, and Heather had perhaps shared more than was wise.

Because Vicki was the sister of her heart if not blood.

Beside Bree, Heather leaned down to touch the cub's tiny hand. "Toren, may the Lord and the Lady bless you with courage and a life filled with love," she said softly.

In the armchair, Angie cleared her throat. "Heather, this is Artair." She drew back the blanket to reveal a beautiful cubling with brown eyes.

Heather brushed her fingertips over his soft round cheek. "Artair, may the Lord and the Lady bless you with strength and a joyful heart."

She turned to Vicki. "And who do you have?"

Her friend's lips curved. "You ran with Alec and Calum as a child. You were one of my first friends here, taking the time to explain all these fucking Daonain traditions and helping keep me sane."

Inexplicably, Heather found her throat was tightening.

"So, speaking of traditions, Calum and Alec say the custom is to do this with the first meeting."

"Do what?" Heather frowned. Maybe Vicki had spoken too soon about being sane.

"Heather," Vicki rose and handed Heather the golden-haired infant she held. "Heather Sutharlan, this is Sorcha whose name means *radiant*. Here is a cub for your arms and your heart to hold. Will you serve as her *caomhnor?*"

"Oh." *Oh my Goddess.* Heather's escaping breath carried joy. Sang of her acceptance. And as she gathered Sorcha closer into her arms, she felt a sweet aching tug deep within her chest as the new bond of love settled in place.

As the ancient words came to her, her voice was thick and full of tears. "Aye. I will serve as her guardian-protector, teaching her and loving her for as long as my heart beats and the blood flows in my veins."

DARCY FELT TEARS spilling down her cheeks at the joy in Heather's face. At the peace in Vicki's expression as she patted Heather's arm and resumed her seat.

Bree and Emma were sniffling.

Angie's eyes were damp, but she lifted her glass of wine. "To cublings. The clan increases."

Everyone lifted their glasses. "The clan increases."

Wakened by the noise, Toren kicked up a fuss about wet diapers, and by the time he was changed, everyone was settled again. Emma made the rounds with more wine.

As Darcy sipped hers, she gave a happy sigh. Celebrations and family and babies.

And wasn't it simply amazing to be *free* and able to drink wine, dress up, and gossip? Like a normal female.

She smiled at Heather who was still snuggling Sorcha. The female from Rainier Territory was around five-eight and slender with a thick mass of red-brown hair held back in a braid. She wore nice jeans, a snug golden top, and expensive cowboy boots.

Seeing Darcy, she smiled, open and comfortable. "You must be Darcy. Welcome to the Territories."

"Thank you. It's nice to be here."

"So, Heather." Bree waved a hand at Darcy. "Since she was a captive, she doesn't know makeup, and we told her about your mad skills. Can you help get her ready?"

Heather grinned. "Absolutely. Makes me feel like an artist." She handed Sorcha back to Vicki, grabbed her bag, and pulled a chair over to join Darcy at the dressing table.

Darcy glanced around, rather surprised that a bedroom was big enough to fit them all comfortably. Darcy looked around. "This is a great room, Vicki."

A painting of the forested mountains around Cold Creek set a peaceful tone. An old-fashioned quilt of blues and greens was echoed by a green handmade rug on the hardwood floor. The well-filled bookcase occupied one wall, a dark wood dressing table with a beautifully carved mirror another. "But I didn't realize a female would have her own bedroom and each male would have a separate, complete apartment."

Vicki rocked gently as she nursed Sorcha. "Most littermates share a house, and each person has their own bedroom. This room was originally designed for the female, and as with most shifter houses, the male bedrooms had surrounded it. But since Calum and Alec didn't share Calum's first mate, they remodeled the floor into two separate apartments. Now I'm here, and they're sharing everything again. Alec doesn't use his apartment much."

Heather stroked a dark brown shadow on Darcy's eyelids. "Every mate-set chooses how they arrange the bedrooms. Some female bedrooms are huge, and the males join her there. That's assuming they share in bed, since some shifters prefer one-on-ones."

Breanne studied Vicki's queen-sized bed. "I don't think you, Alec, and Calum would all fit on there."

"We don't. The guys have huge beds, and we usually all sleep together in a pile. They decided this room is mine alone." Vicki's lips tilted. "They know I sometimes need space—and wanted me to know if I came here to sleep, they'd honor my wishes."

"Your mates are so nice. But"—Darcy frowned—"if you join them in their rooms, when do *they* get to be alone?"

Heather started applying mascara. "I like your Darcy, Vic. She reminds me of Emma—always wanting to know why."

Emma grinned at Darcy. "Well, I need to know *why*. You want to know *how* everything works—and how to fix it. Together we could rule the world."

Darcy smiled back. Oh, she did love these females.

Vicki burped Sorcha, handed her to Angie, and took Artair. "Your turn, munchkin." She looked over. "Alec never wants time alone. The guy's totally gregarious. When Calum needs solitude, he heads into the mountains. He has some places in the forest he visits and just…sits. I asked him once, you know, as a joke, if the Gods visit him there, and he said, 'Not always.'"

Bree stared. "Whoa, that's a little scary."

Darcy stared. "Uh-huh." Then again, how *did* the Gods communicate? Was it in thoughts or images or…

"Here, your makeup is done." Heather spun her around. "What do you think?"

"You're an *artist*." Darcy stared at herself. "My eyes look huge."

"Mmmhmm. You have gorgeous eyes; they deserved to be played up." Heather tucked her kit away.

Sipping her wine, Angie scrutinized Darcy. "Very sexy. We did well."

The women had decided Darcy's jeans and shoes would do, but she'd ended up in an emerald green tank top of Heather's. The shirt was thin and not too low-cut, but somehow—when worn without a bra—appallingly revealing.

Vicki pursed her lips. "I better warn Alec there will be males fighting over her."

"Very funny." Darcy reached for her glass and realized no one was laughing. "You're making a joke, right?"

"New and gorgeous female. Still wide-eyed. Yes, the males will work to get your attention any way they can." Emma gave her a serious look. "You need to remember, Darcy, everything is up to you. If the gnome-brains want to fight, and you're not into battles, walk away and find a male more to your liking."

There were only two males to her liking. But she'd gone by their house earlier, and everything was dark. Why, why, why hadn't they returned?

"Hell, we need to get moving." Vicki rose. "If we're late for the Daonain meeting, Calum will be displeased."

"Meeting?" Darcy asked.

"Meeting first, then Gathering."

Gathering. Please, Gawain and Owen, get back. Please.

IN THE BACK of the pool table alcove, Owen sat on a bench against the wall. The fucking tavern was packed, cheek to jowl, with shifters. He'd hoped Darcy would be here but so far he hadn't gotten a glimpse or sniff of her in this crowd.

There would be time when all the non-single Daonain cleared out.

He wanted to hold her, to talk with her, to hear her laugh. And, although the full moon wasn't even up yet, he wanted to be inside her. To sandwich her between him and Gawain and take her, over and over.

But tonight was the Gathering. He and Gawain would have to see her go off with other males. Touch other males. Mate with other males. And he wasn't sure he could. All his instincts called for him to claim her and fight anyone who thought to touch her. A low growl escaped him.

Beside him on the bench, Gawain glanced over. Obviously understanding Owen's thoughts, he gave a low snarl of agreement.

They were so fucked.

Out of sight near the bar, Calum reported the happenings of the past month, made introductions, and all that. *Blah, blah, blah.* Owen ignored him as he would a scolding blue jay.

Would Darcy be happy to see them?

A hand clamped onto his shoulder, and he realized Gawain had stood up.

"What?" Owen growled. *I'm thinking here.*

"Calum welcomed Darcy to the clan—and the meeting's over." Gawain yanked Owen to his feet. "Let's go find our female."

THE DAONAIN MEETING had ended, and most of the mated shifters departed. Vicki, Bree, and Angie—and the babies—were still over at the fireplace sitting area. Emma had jumped up on top of the bar so she could strum her guitar and flirt with her lifemates, Ben and Ryder.

With Heather, Darcy'd stayed near the door. Feeling the full moon humming in her blood, she knew the Gathering would start shortly. Hoping against hope, she'd looked around during the meeting and hadn't seen Gawain or Owen.

She was stuck at a Gathering without them. Would be mating...without them. Her stomach churned queasily.

Someone came in the door, and she held her breath.

Not Gawain and Owen—Patrin and Fell had entered.

"Hey, guys!" She gave Fell a big hug—and got the same back. "I'm glad you're back. Are you two all right?"

Patrin pulled her into his arms for his own hug, then held her out at arm's length. "What the fuck are you doing in this place?"

"I'm attending the Gathering, of course. It's the law, remember?"

"What law?" Disapproval darkened his face. "Do you realize what happens here? *Chwaer*, it's not a good place for a little female."

Her lips curved. He was cute, all brotherly concern and acting as if she'd barely been weaned. Actually, she understood since sometimes she forgot he and Fell were adults and not twelve. "I don't think—"

"How about we take you back to the lodge?" Patrin's question was more of a demand.

"Yeah. We can talk." Fell took her arm.

Fell *talk*? That'd be the day. That he'd even offered showed his worry. Still, she couldn't leave. She knew the law, even if they didn't yet. As she shook her head, she spotted two males making their way through the room, overtopping the mostly male population. Her heart did a slow somersault in her chest. *Owen and Gawain?*

When she started toward them, Fell's grip tightened.

Patrin stepped in front of her, making himself a barrier. Back to her, he glared at Owen. "She's leaving. Use someone else to get your rocks off."

Darcy thumped his shoulder. "What did you just say?"

Patrin glanced back. "We heard a bit about this full moon shit. It's an orgy, *chwaer.*"

"What's an orgy?" Owen stepped closer, forcing Patrin to look at him.

And Gawain quietly circled to approach her from the side. "Darcy." He held his hands out. His blue eyes were warm, and the sun lines beside his eyes crinkled with his smile.

"Oh, I am *so* glad to see you." When she tried to go to him, Fell didn't let her go.

Her hand fisted. *No, don't hurt him, tinker.* After all, her brothers had always been over-protective. As Gawain's eyes narrowed ominously, she told him, "Hold on."

She turned and stared up at Fell. "Let. Go."

His hand fell, but his expression turned grim. "*Chwaer,* no." He touched her hair. "No orgy for you."

"Darcy, you don't know these guys. They want only one thing from you." Patrin backed up to take her other side. "We love you. Let us—"

"Guys, I have to stay here tonight."

"What's going on?" Holding Artair, Vicki approached, her gaze assessing. Jamie was beside her.

Ignoring Vicki, Fell scowled at Darcy. "*Chwaer,* you're leaving."

Beside Vicki, Jamie put her hands on her hips, confronting Patrin and Fell. "Leave her alone. She's not in your fucking army, so you can't tell her shit."

"Oh, fuck, Jamie, your language," Vicki muttered. "Calum's going to kill me."

"He is considering that possibility," came the soft deep voice as the Cosantir strolled up.

Oh, Mother of All, why was there nowhere to hide? Darcy almost cringed. If prison had taught her anything, it was to avoid attracting attention from the person in charge.

Calum frowned at his daughter. "We'll discuss appropriate language later. What is the problem here?"

Jamie pointed at Patrin and Fell and said indignantly, "They said our Darcy has to leave right now."

"Did they indeed." As the Cosantir regarded Darcy's brothers, the power of the God shimmered around him. "The moon is rising. Were you planning to break the Law?"

Patrin frowned. "We're not breaking any law. We simply came to get our sister."

Darcy saw Calum's eyes darken.

Oh, no. "Cosantir, please." Darcy jumped between Calum and her brothers.

His dark, dark gaze fell on her. "Aye?"

"Patrin and Fell spent a decade with humans, learning to kill and nothing else. And…as I told you, my brothers and I never knew anything about the Daonain even before we were captured."

Fell flinched.

"They don't know what a Gathering is. They think it's an orgy. Please, my brothers need instruction rather than…" She bit her lip, unable to continue. *Don't kill them, please, Cosantir.*

Before Calum could speak, Alec's infectious laugh sounded. The sheriff clapped a hand on Calum's shoulder. "Don't kill her littermates, brawd. It's a pain in the tail at a Gathering to have to clean up your mess."

Calum shot his brother an unreadable look, then his lips twitched and his eyes lightened to gray. "An orgy? Instruction is needed, indeed. Alec, please assign mentors to our new Daonain."

Patrin's eyes narrowed. "We already know how to shift."

Alec gave him an easy grin. "That's just the beginning. You need to learn to live within the Daonain traditions and Laws. How a female chooses a male, how you know if she's interested, what the next step is."

Her brothers looked blank, and Darcy remembered how Owen had lifted her wrist, how his first inhalation had given him the scent of her interest.

"With help, you two might not step on your own tails tonight." Alec looked around. "Joe. Can you take them on? Give them the Laws of Gathering—as well as etiquette for male/female interactions. I doubt they'll ignore you."

Joe Thorson, the grizzled owner of the bookstore, stalked out of the crowd. The old, lean cougar was scarred from the tips of his fingers to his face, and Darcy knew no one interested in survival would ignore him.

Eyes narrowed, he scrutinized Fell and Patrin before he turned. "Do you wish me to take on this task, Cosantir?"

Calum inclined his head.

Thorson bowed slightly. "Your will, Cosantir."

And Darcy knew Thorson had delivered his first lesson—how a shifter should deal with the God-chosen guardian of a territory.

From Fell's intent expression, he was absorbing the lesson as quickly as he did everything else. Her brothers were brilliant...when they weren't being over-protective idiots.

Owen and Gawain moved forward.

Fell blocked their way.

Oh, honestly.

Even as Darcy kicked her brother hard enough to make him grunt, Thorson's hand fell on his shoulder. The old werecat growled, "A female chooses who she wants, cub."

Darcy realized the Cosantir was still watching.

Patrin cleared his throat. "Sir. We heard how she talks about these two. They saved her life and she's obviously... Well, she hardly knows them. She's so young and—"

"Oh, honestly, you dumbasses," Darcy snapped. "I'm the same age you are, and I do know what I'm doing."

Fell's brows drew together. "Don't want you to get hurt, *chwaer.*"

"Sweetie, you're not experienced, and it's easy to get confused about sex," Patrin said, shooting a glare at Owen.

She snorted. "Guys, I escaped the prison well over two months ago. I've already experienced a full moon Gathering."

Patrin's mouth dropped. "You...what?"

"Did I mate with more males than Gawain and Owen?" she asked lightly. "Yes."

"And it was an honor to be with you on that, your first Gathering Night." Donal stood nearby and gave her a slight bow.

"It was." Tynan smiled at her.

She grinned at the two.

"Just so you know, female, there are others who'd be delighted to be with you tonight," a burly shifter said, stepping forward.

"I, too, would be pleased to fight for your favor." A bear-sized shifter presented himself. "You have other choices, you know."

Choices. The masculine scents and sounds from the gathering males swirled around her. As she breathed in, she remembered her first Gathering. All the males had smelled unique and tantalizing, like a banquet of wonder, and she only had to choose which to sample first.

No one smelled interesting tonight.

She shook her head and sniffed again. Even Tynan and Donal weren't a temptation. Her feet moved her back a pace.

Calum studied her. "Is there a problem, Darcy?"

"I'm just…" She shrugged. "Not really interested in anyone tonight. Can I have some wine instead?" She could buy Owen and Gawain a drink. She frowned and realized Owen no longer stood in front of Patrin. Where did they—

"There is always wine." A corner of Calum's mouth lifted, and he glanced behind her. "However, might you find an interest in those two?"

She turned and Gawain and Owen stood behind her. Their scents washed over her…and suddenly she was drowning in need. Her blood scalded her veins, fogged her mind, and her words came without thinking. "I always want them. Every minute of every day. Especially now."

She flung herself into their arms. "I *missed* you."

Side-by-side, they caught her, and she was lifted off her feet and hugged forcefully enough her ribs creaked. Her arms wound around two necks, fiercely gripping their hair.

And she kissed them. *Owen, Gawain, Owen, Gawain.*

When they let her down, she took Gawain's face between her hands and pulled him down so she could look in his deep blue eyes. Would he—did he still…?

Her brothers were wrong, and she was right. Her instincts—human and cat—said *leap.*

"I love you," she said firmly and kissed him again.

Turning, she reached up to Owen, and he was already bending to her. Hands on his clean-shaven jaw, she looked into his forest-green eyes and saw her answer already there. "I love you,

Owen."

As cheers resounded through the room, they squished her again—and she heard them. Gawain's smooth voice, "I love you, sweetling. Love you so much."

And, to her astonishment, Owen's gravel voice was right there, too. "I love you, Darcy."

When they finally let her go, she saw that Fell and Patrin were staring.

"Now, brawd, we do it now," Owen growled.

But he didn't grab her. She blinked—and looked down to see her two males kneel in front of her.

Owen took her hand. "We love you, Darcy. More than anyone like me could ever say. But I'll try to tell you how much I love you—through this life, and in all our lives to come."

Oh, she knew how incoherent he felt, because when she tried to answer, the words stuck in her throat.

Gawain's clear blue eyes were deeper, wider than the entire sky, filling her universe. "We love you, Darcy. Our lives aren't complete without you with us. Be our lifemate and share our love and lives from this day on."

Their voices blurred together, dancing back and forth in a rumbly, growly chorus of wonderment.

"You can fix anything that is broken, including our hearts."

"We'll help you leap any obstacle in your path.

"We'll never boss you around. Much."

"No nightmare will find you when we're with you."

"We'll love you until the last star falls from the sky."

"Yes," she whispered. "Oh, yes."

As they rose, they gathered her in, claiming her with lips and arms for all the world to see.

"Let's go home." Owen took her left hand, Gawain her right.

To one side, Vicki was smiling beside a grinning Jamie.

Bonnie had her hands over her huge grin, her eyes filled with happy tears.

Darcy barely had a chance to smile at them before her mates led her out of the building to the sound of such cheering it was surprising the building still stood.

IN THE LIGHT of the rising moon, they'd walked down the hill from the tavern and into their gravel drive. With his arm around Darcy and his heart light enough to slip out of his chest, Gawain turned toward the barn instead of the house.

"Brawd?" Owen frowned.

"We have lifemating bracelets to make. Let's do it now."

Owen studied him and grinned. "Aye. I can think of nothing better."

Their little catling's eyes lit, and she nodded.

After picking up bracelets from the barn, Gawain led them outside to his ritual area. In the dark night, he could hear the splashing of the stream within the circle of river stones. The moon was full, and the area was awash with power.

Needing to feel her again, Gawain hugged Darcy to him. "I've missed you."

"Me, too." Like a cat, she rubbed her cheek against his chest, leaving her fragrance behind, marking him with her scent. He breathed her in and handed her to Owen to hold.

Without any hesitation, his brother wrapped his arms around her, pulling her close, and laying his cheek on the top of her head. The bond was there, oh yes, it was.

This was a good lifemating.

Just by being in their lives, she'd changed them for the better, opened them, healed them. And they'd been good for her as well.

He couldn't help but smile, just looking at her. Her dark eyes were wide, her lips curved. Happiness radiated from her.

Gawain lit the brazier, added incense, and felt the elements merging—earth and water, fire and air. Holding the bands over the spiraling smoke, he added the fifth—spirit—and opened to the Mother.

This time...

By the Mother's grace, this time when She touched him in inquiry, the names and images of the potential lifemates included *himself*. His own elation danced through his heart and to her.

To his surprise, he felt his brother move forward to join him, and instinctively, they pulled Darcy between them so they stood connected, shoulder to shoulder to shoulder. Owen and Darcy's joy mingled with his own, flowing to the Mother.

He could feel Her delight. And then Her power flowed through him, magicking the lifemating bands, and filling him and his lifemates with her love.

Darcy leaned into him.

Tears were in Owen's eyes.

Gawain squeezed his brother's shoulder. "That's a Mother's love—and our cubs will have that from their mother." He handed Owen a lifemating band and watched wonder fill his brother's eyes for the band still resonated with the Goddess's gift.

Slowly, Owen's smile appeared. "Darcy." His voice was rough. Husky. He took her hand and slid the bracelet onto her left wrist before kissing her. "By the God, I love you so fucking much."

She was blinking back tears now.

Gawain bent and kissed her and added his bracelet next to his brother's. "I love you, Darcy."

After a minute of looking at the bracelets on her pretty wrist, she took the heftier male bands. One went on Owen's left wrist with a kiss and the second on Gawain's with another kiss. "I love you two, enough for this lifetime and many, many more."

As the full moon's power started to make itself felt, the scents of arousal filled the air.

SHE WAS WITH her males. Lifemated. Together. Finally. Darcy couldn't stop smiling. Her feet seemed to be inches above the ground as Gawain and Owen led her into their house, up the stairs, and down a hallway.

Owen's arm was behind her back.

Gawain was holding her hand, pulling her forward. "Darcy." He sounded...worried. "Owen has the left room, I have the right one, and if you like it...want it...this is your room."

She almost laughed. "If you're here, that's all I need."

Owen squeezed her waist. "We left it mostly unfurnished so you could decide how you want it to look."

The room was even bigger than Vicki's. Carvings of flowering vines circled the doors and windows. The balcony faced the east, and the first glow of the Mother's moonrise lit the glass door.

The only furniture was a bed standing between two windows.

She touched Owen's beautiful carvings on the headboard in wonder. Three cougars snoozed on a rock under a crescent moon.

The footboard showed a female cougar leaping into a tree with her mates watching. She could almost see the laughter on Owen's whiskered face and the approval on Gawain's.

Her eyes widened at the size of the bed.

Looking at it, she understood her males' hopes and dreams. They hadn't given her a small bed to sleep in alone, but a giant one big enough for a towering cahir, a huge blademage, and one small mate.

They knew her so well. Given her choice, she'd never sleep alone again.

She took a breath as urgency filled her blood.

"What? We can change something, anything." Gawain squeezed her shoulders.

A line furrowed Owen's brow. "We'll burn the place down if you want. The only nonnegotiable point is that we stay together."

"Burn it down?" She realized she'd been so lost in her dreaming she'd missed seeing their worry. "I love it," she said firmly. "But…"

Owen growled. "Speak clearly, little female. What's wrong?"

Ah, her grumpy cat had returned.

And the rough, dark sound of his voice made her insides quiver. "I was just thinking we're overdressed—and it's the full moon—and we need to try out that bed."

With a shout of laughter, Gawain leaned forward and whisked her top right off.

Owen had already knelt to strip off her jeans.

A second later, she landed on the bed—bare-ass naked.

As they joined her, she wrapped her arms around them and breathed in their masculine scents. Her happiness filled her heart, the room, the universe. "I love you…my mates."

THEIR FIRST MATING was fast and furious.

The second slower.

Now Owen lifted his head so he could watch the candlelight flicker over Darcy's face, so he could see the way she looked when he ran his tongue over her clit, the way her lips parted as she pulled in a breath. How her back arched up when Gawain sucked on her nipples.

She had the heart-stopping beauty of a crystal-clear snowy morning in the mountains.

"You are so fucking beautiful," he murmured.

She blinked, obviously trying to remember if they'd been

talking. He loved how she gave herself to making love—how she gave of herself, because she trusted them. And loved them.

By the God, she *loved* them. Would he ever stop feeling this sense of elation?

He licked over her again and felt her hips trying to squirm. She was slick and fragrant with her arousal. Using his thumbs to open her more, he flicked his tongue over her clit.

Over the past weeks, he'd learned what she liked. And Darcy, who gave back as generously as she received, had figured out the same about them. Every time was better.

He wanted to take the next step. During their shared showers, he'd worked on stretching her, preparing her to take them both at once. The way her excitement increased with his fingers in her back hole, she'd enjoy a cock even more.

And if she didn't, he wouldn't mind. She was far more important than some variation in the mating act.

He rose up to kiss her before returning to her pussy, scratching her inner thighs with the faint stubble on his chin. He grinned when he saw her toes curl.

As he and Gawain continued, she gave a delightful moan. Under his hands, her hips wiggled. "More, please, Owen, please." She gripped Gawain's long hair, pulling him down to her breasts.

With a rumbling chuckle, Gawain licked one breast, turning his head to check if Owen wanted to order something. He didn't mind taking direction—actually enjoyed it.

Even better, the bossy little cat didn't want to be in control, not when mating.

Owen considered. In their earliest adventures, he and Gawain had worked out a silent routine. Did his littermate remember?

Balanced on an elbow, Owen closed his fingers around his brother's ankle and squeezed once.

Gawain's head came up. He frowned, lowered a hand out of Darcy's field of vision, and held up one finger. He remembered.

Grinning, Owen nodded. Raised fingers or squeezes indicated the method of choice. Taps would coordinate their efforts. One finger, one nudge, or one squeeze meant: *lick until further direction.* He saw Gawain's tongue run in a circle around Darcy's nipple. Owen lowered his head and ran his own circle around a pink clit that was growing more and more swollen.

Darcy's tiny purr stuttered with excitement.

Deciding to move them on, he gave Gawain's ankle two squeezes—for sucking.

As Gawain sucked once on a nipple, Owen sucked on Darcy's clit. Her gasp was most satisfying.

Time to coordinate. *Tap. Tap. Tap. Pause. Suck-suck-suck-pause.* Not being female, he had to wonder what it felt like to have a nipple and clit rhythmically sucked on at the same time.

He squeezed once, and they played with licking for a minute.

Two squeezes. *Tap tap tap, pause. Tap, tap, tap, pause.*

Between his lips, her nerve-ridden nub poked out from under the hood, swollen to hardness. Her hips pressed up for more. Her purr alternated with moans.

Time to end this before she got too frustrated. He squeezed Gawain's ankle three times and caught his littermate's grin. *Bring down the prey with whatever it takes.*

Gawain bent to her breasts, using his hands, his mouth, his tongue—even his teeth.

Her back arched.

Owen bent to his own trail, penetrating her with a finger as he licked a circle around the swollen nub. Thrusting slowly, he savored the satin heat around his fingers. His cock was rock-hard.

He added another finger, pumping faster as he laved and sucked.

Her core tightened around his fingers, and her breathing changed to long pauses between gasps.

Setting his tongue at the top of her clit below the hood, he rubbed…hard.

Her spine arched upward, her thighs closed on his shoulders as if to hold him in place, and he could feel her center contracting in spasms around his fingers. "Ooooooh, oh, oh, oh."

Laughing, he sucked again—and set off her wail again.

This—this made him feel like the luckiest male in the territory.

As her muscles went limp with occasional quivers, he licked his fingers and nodded to Gawain. "Let's try it the way we talked about."

"Aye." Eyes lit with heat, Gawain helped Owen reposition her on her knees and elbows in the center of the bed.

Owen ran his hands over her shoulders and back, enjoying the way her waist widened into a beautifully round ass. Her skin was silky smooth except for the tiny ridges of scars. But the humans who'd hurt her were dead. It was time to celebrate life. He leaned forward and kissed her shoulder.

As he straightened, she grinned over her shoulder at him. "Doggy style? Are kitty shifters allowed to do this?"

"I believe the original term was the *panther pose*," Gawain said in a pompous voice. He handed Owen a condom, glove, and lube packet.

"What's that?" Darcy almost toppled over trying to see.

"Extras. Humans can be canny, at times." After condoming up, Owen squeezed lube on his gloved fingers, spread more on her puckered anus, and slowly inserted one finger.

"OH. OH." THE surprise of his finger pressing through the narrow rim and up inside her anus sent a shudder through her. Her nerves in her pussy and clit were extremely sensitized now, yet he'd bypassed them, going straight for her back hole.

Her nipples puckered into a throbbing ache.

"We've done this in the shower, remember?" Owen's rough voice was amused.

This position was more vulnerable and exposed than she'd realized, and she tried to swivel her butt out of danger.

He held her in place with a firm grip on her hip. His finger slid out and back in, deeper this time.

"Oh Gods." Her skin turned to goosebumps at the strange sensation.

Gawain sat beside her hip, one hand resting on her back. "Breathe, sweetling."

Breathe, how? There was almost no air in the room—and even less when Owen used two fingers. The increased diameter burned slightly, but his slickened fingers slid in and out easily.

Gawain ran a hand down her stomach, and his fingers grazed her swollen clit.

She jumped—and Owen laughed. "She almost squeezed my fingers off. Do it again."

Owen's firm strokes in her ass, Gawain's caressing her clit— at the same time—sent tremors of excitement coursing across her body. Her shivers increased as they held her in place—Owen gripping her hip, Gawain's arm latching around her waist—as they played with her.

"All right, kitten, I'm going to go slow." Owen's fingers slid out.

He was going to…*what*?

Something pressed against her anus—something bigger than his fingers.

Oh Gods, his shaft. Her fingers curled against her palms. She knew they had intended this…eventually. *Now*?

Slowly, he breeched her opening, blazing a trail of fire in her back region. His cockhead stretched her to the point of pain before it was finally in. He stopped. "That's the hardest part, *cariad*. Are you all right?"

Firmness and caring. Orders and concern. What she'd wanted all her life.

"Darcy?" Gawain asked.

She turned her head to look at him. He looked like a god, burning blue eyes, tanned skin, all muscles—and all hers.

His eyes narrowed, and he stroked her hair. "Catling?"

"I'm so fine."

His grin appeared, white within his light brown beard. He glanced at Owen and nodded.

Owen pressed in, slowly penetrating her. His shaft was ever so long...and she giggled.

Both males froze.

"What?" Owen's voice was hoarse. "Have we've driven her crazy?"

"I'm just so glad it's you and not Gawain back there. He's very…"

Gawain gave a shout of laughter...because the girth of his erection *was* impressive. Owen was longer, Gawain thicker.

Even as he laughed, Owen continued to press in, deeper and deeper until his thighs rested against the backs of hers. His groin pressed against her buttocks.

So strange. She gave a wiggle and squeaked as his cock moved inside her. Her whole back area was throbbing around the burning intrusion, yet her clit was tingling, her nipples tightly bunched and aching.

She knew Owen was waiting—and finally, she nodded. "I'm good."

"Thank you, little cat," Owen said, his voice rough. "For your trust." He slid out and in, slowly, adding more lube, wakening new nerves until everything back there seemed alight. "Ready, brawd?"

"Mother of all, yes." Gawain had his hand wrapped around his thick erection. She really loved his cock, and she licked her lips, wanting her mouth there.

"Not this time, pretty panther," he said.

Owen curled over and above her, his chest against her back. Wrapping one arm low on her pelvis, and the other over her breasts, he rolled sideways and over onto his back, landing on a pile of pillows. His shoulders and head were supported by the pillows so he was propped slightly up. His ass was on the bed—and his shaft was still in her back hole.

"What…" Squirming against the feeling of being impaled, she lay on top of him with her back against his chest and her head in the hollow of his shoulder. His long legs hung off the mattress—and his feet undoubtedly touched the floor.

Her feet, of course, were dangling in the air.

She turned her head to glare up at him and saw only the bottom of his jaw. "What are you *doing*?"

Owen chuckled. "I do enjoy each time she asks that question. Want to tell her, brawd?"

Gawain walked to the end of the bed. His lips curved. "He's giving me access, aye?"

Access to… Oh my Gods.

As Gawain stepped between Owen's knees, he put an arm under her left leg, catching her knee in the bend of his elbow. With his other hand, he guided his shaft to her pussy, pressing lightly against her entrance. "Are you ready, Darcy?"

She looked up at him. His trim beard covered a strong jaw. Thick muscles widened his chest and shoulders. His biceps bulged as he held her leg up in the air beside his waist. Had there ever been a more gorgeous male? And his deep blue eyes were full of heat—and love—for her.

She managed a nod. Barely.

Owen fondled her breast with his left hand and the other

cupped her mound. He lifted his head to whisper in her ear, "Breathe, kitten."

Gripping his left forearm to anchor herself, she sucked in a breath.

Gawain pressed in slightly—and her breathing stopped. *Oh Gods.*

He stopped. "Look at me, Darcy. You'll tell me if it hurts."

Staring up into his perceptive eyes, she managed to nod.

"All right." He held her gaze trapped as he relentlessly filled her.

So full. So damn far in.

When he was balls-deep, he stopped and studied her.

Everything inside her was stretched and throbbing. Overwhelmed, she couldn't think, could only cling to Owen's arm as he fondled her breasts. His other hand slid lower to stroke her clit lightly—and at the exquisite sensation, everything tightened.

No, she was already too full. Oh, Gods!

Owen's laugh made his chest shake beneath her—made her jiggle on his cock and gasp at the burning, tingling, amazing feeling. Too many sensations.

Gawain lifted her other leg over his shoulder, leaned forward, and braced his hand on the bed. His erection slid out and back in more forcefully.

She gasped as searing, electrifying pleasure shot through her.

Smiling slightly, he did it again.

Oh Gods, she was so full. Owen didn't move—which was good since she might have had a heart attack. She could barely manage one cock.

Instead, he slid his finger over and around her clit, and heat zipped up her spine. Her clit swelled and throbbed. Her pussy clutched around Gawain even tighter.

"Our catling." Gawain ran his hands over her legs, stroking her. "I love sharing you with my brother. Love giving you my seed." He moved slowly, in and out, simply enjoying her, and grinning every time she wiggled and moaned.

He sped up slightly and every thrust felt so…different with Owen's shaft inside her, too. Her nipples gathered into aching peaks, and Owen laughed and pinched one.

When her lower half contracted, they all groaned.

Gawain started thrusting fast and forcefully. "Join us, brawd. She's ready."

Keeping his hand on her clit, Owen set his other arm around her waist in a hard, unmovable band, and slid partway out of her ass.

She gasped.

Tilting his pelvis, he plunged back in.

Oh, oh, oh. At the ferocious pleasure, everything within contracted around both cocks.

Both males kept moving. Owen slid in, Gawain out. Gawain thrust; Owen withdrew. Their merciless pace increased, and then Owen's fingers rubbed over her clit.

Her core clenched, and excruciating pleasure fireballed inside her, pouring through her, sending her flying. Her whole body shook as she came.

Without a pause, Gawain continued thrusting as Owen pistoned into her from behind—and ceaseless waves of molten pleasure rolled over her, as endless as the tide.

With a low groan, Gawain gripped her harder, and she felt his shaft spasming inside her.

A second later, Owen did the same with a low growl. His arms tightened around her as he kissed the side of her head. "Thank you, my mate."

Still embedded deeply inside her, Gawain leaned forward to kiss her, rubbing his cheek against hers like the cat he was. "Thank you, my mate."

Her arms felt boneless as she put them around his neck and

took herself a proper kiss.

"Stay put for a minute." He withdrew and lifted her up, and she gasped as Owen's softening erection left her ass. Solid and sturdy, Gawain set her on her feet and held her against him.

Owen laughed, patted her butt, and rolled off the bed to go clean up.

Gawain lay back on the bed with her in his arms. "Thank you, Darcy, for letting us share."

She considered teasing them by saying she didn't like it. But…even if her lying abilities worked, they knew better. She'd never come so long and hard before. In fact, it had been amazing to be sandwiched between them, both cocks inside her, feeling…everything. "Thank you for making it lovely."

Owen returned, crawling in to snuggle behind her, warming her with his superheated body.

The bed was the perfect size for all of them.

Exhausted and delighted, she squirmed until Owen moved forward, squishing her against Gawain's side. Pinning her between them.

Purring in pleasure, she settled her head on Gawain's shoulder, feeling Owen rubbing his chin on the top of her head. Gawain's hand rested on her shoulder.

As the last glimmer of the moon disappeared from the window, she gave a happy sigh. This…right here…was where she belonged.

Chapter Thirty

A SUNDAY IN the second week in December was the day of their official house and business warming. As anticipation burbled inside him, Gawain trotted down the stairs and into the living room.

A flash from the huge brick fireplace caught his attention. In the blazing fire, two golden and red salamanders were twining and spiraling in a wave of sparks. "Be welcome to our home," he murmured.

They blinked beady eyes and continued their dance.

Slowly, Gawain turned, reveling in the happiness and contentment that filled the aged house. Earlier, he'd noticed a small nose poking out of a kitchen baseboard hole. Apparently, the OtherFolk had decided their family was stable and happy, and some housekeeping brownies had moved in. He'd have to remember to set out cream and cake for them tonight.

Gawain smiled. He couldn't wait to tell his mates.

From the kitchen came the cheerful sounds of females talking and laughing. A whirr from outside said Owen was sliding open the big barn door. In a few minutes, the house and barn would start to fill with their guests.

Were they ready? He studied the rooms and nodded in satisfaction. Their house had become a home.

Gawain had owned more than enough furniture to fill the rooms and stock the kitchen. But despite the furnishings, the house hadn't been a home...until Darcy moved in. Now, her bright red coat hung in the foyer. She'd bought a large round, hand-crocheted rug from her friend Rebecca, and the dark red and brown colors warmed the living room. A table with a chess set stood in one corner. Books sat on end tables, and a knotted piece of crochet work spilled out of a basket.

She'd taken one of Gawain's early metal artworks and hung it above the fireplace. Beneath it on the mantel were candles and one of Owen's carvings. From Emma's house had come lush foliage plants. He hadn't realized how such small embellishments could change an entire house. Curtains, rugs, pillows, artwork, throws, plants, even bowls of fruit left out so a person could grab something in passing.

He and Owen had stood back and let their mate transform the house into a den that rivaled those created by werebears. All in less than two weeks.

Tilting his head, he smiled, because, in addition to the furniture, each room now held memories. Like Darcy's giggles when she'd discovered he was ticklish. How Owen's eyes lit when he realized they'd saved breakfast for him. Their new ritual of arguing over the dinner menu, then cooking it together. The sound of Owen's laughter when Darcy pounced on him in bed and demanded a morning kiss. The fun they'd had wallpapering the dining room...and Darcy's adorable hisses when they'd tried to get the glue out of her hair in the shower.

How many memories could they create in a lifetime?

Lifting his nose, he sniffed and smiled at the scents from the kitchen. He'd done his part, whipping up the only two appetizers he knew how to make. Owen had added another. The rest they'd hired Bree and Angie to provide. Now, Darcy and her female crew were setting up trays and drinks.

With a cub in a backpack, Vicki walked into the living room and put a platter of mixed hors d'oeuvres on the coffee table. "Hey, Gawain." She grinned. "Holding an open house is a great idea to get your businesses started. I think everyone in town—human and Daonain—plans to come by."

"Good to hear." Gawain appropriated the cub, checking the hair color. Black, so this was Toren. "I'm surprised Thorson let you hold his cubling."

"I made her beg." Joe Thorson stalked into the room. Even as he touched the cub's round cheek, he frowned at Gawain. "I want a rematch."

"How can you be upset about losing one game of chess?" Vicki snorted. "You're always complaining no one can give you a decent game."

Thorson barked a laugh. "You and Calum can. You're just too busy." He nodded toward Gawain. "This one loves the game."

True enough. And Thorson hadn't been easy to beat. Gawain anticipated many quiet, winter evenings with this canny cat. "I do love the game. Rematch tomorrow night? At the tavern?"

Thorson nodded, his lips twitching up in almost a smile.

As Calum came out to join his mate, Gawain seized the moment. "I've wanted to thank you, both of you."

Calum raised an eyebrow.

"Sheltering Darcy, making us both feel welcome in town, offering us this house, rescuing her villagers, helping them find new homes. If there's anything I—"

"No need." Vicki shook her head. "There's no—"

"Aye. A debt is owed," Thorson interrupted. "Cosantirs don't take payment, but for balance, you could make the Cosantir's mate one of your fancy cahir knives. She lost hers in that Scythe demon hole."

Balance—the age-old Daonain Law of Reciprocity. It'd been a while since Gawain had heard it invoked.

Vicki shook her head. "That's not necessary."

Actually, he rather thought it was. And from the way Vicki's eyes had lit, he'd have made her a knife anyway. But it would be good to achieve balance as well. He bowed his head in formal acknowledgement. "The balance is fair. Accepted."

IN THE KITCHEN, Darcy surveyed the wealth of appetizers and felt inadequate. "Gawain made food. So did Owen. I didn't...because I don't know how," she grumbled. "I only remember a few things from when I'd help Mum."

"I know the feeling." Emma patted her shoulder. "But I found it's not difficult to learn to cook the basics and, if you mess up, there's Angie's Diner."

Angie chuckled. "True. But I'd also be happy to teach you. Anytime you're at leisure, drop in. I love having minions to boss around."

Bree popped a tiny quiche in her mouth. "Let Angie instruct you on the real food, and I'll teach you how to make the sweet stuff. I miss having you around the lodge."

Friends. Warmed, Darcy smiled.

Bonnie slid an arm around her and murmured, "I know a lot of Owen's favorites. I'll teach you those."

Unable to resist, Darcy gave her a hug. "You're all on."

OWEN HAD SLID the barn door wide open, and he nodded in satisfaction. The three "shops" were ready for viewing. To the left were Gawain's forges and metalwork—with all magical items tucked away. One of the forges was stoked up enough to warm the barn despite the snow outside. In the back right, Owen's carvings filled the shelves and crowded the floor. Darcy's front corner of the shop showed all the equipment and small appliances she was currently repairing.

"You got this?" he asked, looking at Hector.

"I got it," Hector said confidently. Two days ago, the young shifter had appeared at the barn with Calum's daughter Jamie and had asked Owen for carving lessons. Owen wasn't calling him an apprentice…yet…but the kid had a talent.

And, since the cub was broke, they'd hired him to show off the barn during the open house.

"If Jamie's at the house, I'll send her over with some food and drink," Owen said, getting a wide grin. Ah, young love.

At the house, Owen spotted Gawain in the living room, talking with a group of people. Bree was talking with Vicki, so Calum was probably around somewhere, too.

With a screech high enough to break glass, Tyler charged across the room followed by two more mini-monsters—Luke, and Ben's cubling, Minette. All three were fucking cute.

A second later, they were climbing him like a tree. Smothering his laugh, he looked down at the three. "Who can show me where the Cosantir is?"

They dropped off with small thuds.

"I can." Tiny chest puffed up with importance, Tyler took his hand and dragged him into the dining room.

Calum was there, talking with Wells and Tynan.

"Excellent job, young male." Owen lifted his nephew, tossed him in the air, and got a screech of delight.

After a quick hug, the whirlwind dashed back to his friends. "Unc Wen threw me in the air and catched me!"

Turning, Owen gave a slight bow to the Cosantir and nodded to the other two.

Wells had baby Artair in one arm and was letting the cub suck on his finger. "Treharn."

Owen looked at Calum. "Since we visited my cabin, then got buried in open house details, I haven't heard what's going on with the Scythe. Is Darcy going to be safe, or should we consider moving to Canada?"

Calum glanced at Wells. "I believe this question is yours."

The spymaster looked up from his namesake, and his pale blue eyes turned cold. "Although there are no guarantees in a war like this, Treharn, we plan to locate all the members of the Scythe. And they will be weeded out by the appropriate people." His gaze turned to the front door where Darcy's brothers had just entered.

"I see." The shifter-soldiers would eliminate the humans who had trained them to be killers. There was irony. "In that case, we'll stay put and be cautious."

And help thin that Scythe herd until it reached a stable population of zero.

Owen bowed slightly to the Cosantir and headed off to tell Gawain. He'd best keep an eye on Darcy in case those brothers of hers gave her trouble. Although…she'd done pretty good all by herself.

He smiled. He and Gawain had a fucking amazing mate.

IN A CORNER of the increasingly crowded living room, Darcy set down another platter of food, turned, and bumped into Patrin. Fell stood right behind him.

She stiffened, feeling awkward. By the time she'd looked for them the day after the Gathering, they'd already returned to Rainier Territory. "Uh. Hey."

"Darcy. Listen…we…I…" In frustration, Patrin ran a hand through his hair. "I'm sorry, Darcy. We were out of line."

Fell put his hand on her shoulder. His scarred face held misery. "Sorry, *chwaer.*"

Looking up at him, she wondered if he ever laughed anymore? At one time, he'd had the best laugh.

"After you left that night, we talked and had to admit we

wouldn't like seeing you with any male." Patrin gave her a rueful smile. "The old werecat told us about your guys…uh, your mates…and I guess they're pretty close to being good enough for you. Can you forgive us?"

"Of course." She felt their relief in the strong hugs she received. "So are you here to stay now?"

Fell shook his head.

"We're off again." Patrin's dark eyes turned cold. "When we're done, there won't be any more"—he stopped—"I mean, eventually things will be settled, and we'll have time to get to know each other again."

She studied them. Their eyes were still haunted, but much of the sick despair was gone. "That'll be good. I need you back here so I can start picking out nice females for you."

Fell's black stare made her grin.

"We're so not talking about that." Deliberately looking around, Patrin said, "You have a nice house—and we saw the barn. That was a hell of a nice job of turning it into workspaces."

"Nice sign, too," Fell said.

"Yeah, tinker's a good name for you."

She frowned. "What sign?"

"By the barn," Patrin said.

"There's no sign there."

"Yeah, there is." He opened the front door and pointed across the snowy expanse of yard.

The glossy dark wood sign was chest high, even bigger than the one on the highway. Owen and Gawain's businesses were spelled out in elaborate lettering: *"Carvings by Treharn"* and *"Full Moon Metalwork."*

But this new sign had another name boldly displayed above the other two businesses: *"The Tinker's Repair Shop,"*

The Tinker's Repair Shop. Even before Darcy had moved in, her mates had built her a workbench and shelving in the corner across from Owen's. Added a worktable and chairs. Every day, more tools appeared.

Now she was official and on the sign. Her heart felt as if it was swelling in her chest.

"They didn't tell you? Huh." Patrin started to grin. "I could get to like them."

A corner of Fell's mouth actually tilted up.

"You're both dumbasses." She shoved Fell into Patrin and went to find her lifemates.

Owen and Gawain were standing together in the living room.

Her speed increased.

Seeing her leap, Owen braced. His powerful hands closed around her waist, and she was lifted and spun around. When he stopped and lowered her, she grabbed his shirt and wrapped an arm around Gawain's muscular neck. And she kissed them and kissed them.

"It's been all of fifteen minutes." Gawain was laughing. "Did you miss us that much?"

"Don't care," Owen muttered. He nuzzled her temple. "I'll take it."

As her heart turned into jelly, she ran her hand over his cheek. For all of her days, she would delight in giving him the love he so desired. Then she gave Gawain another kiss and answered his question. "I always miss you, even after a minute. But this was because I just saw the sign. It's beautiful."

"Calum told me he was pleased you'll be here to keep the town running." Gawain tucked a lock of hair behind her ear. "We're so fucking proud of you."

Each beat of her heart reverberated with her happiness.

"So, during the day, we'll work in the barn." Owen gathered her closer. "And when work is done, we'll be together."

Together. Darcy's eyes filled with tears. Her trail had been long and filled with pain and fear and grief, but somehow she'd climbed out of the shadows and into the sun.

Now, in a house filled with friends and family, she stood sandwiched between her two beloved lifemates, breathing in the scents of belonging and love.

Sometimes dreams really did come true.

~ The End ~

Daonain Glossary

The Daonain use a conglomeration of handed-down languages from the British Isles. Some of the older villages still speak the Gaelic (Scots) or Irish Gaelic. Many of the more common (and mangled) shifter terms have descended from Welsh.

Errors and simplification of spelling and pronunciation can be attributed to being passed down through generations…or the author messing up. Below are a few of the more common words and terms used by the shifters.

a bhràthair: brother
A brathair-faoirm: brother in arms
a chuisle mo chridhe: pulse of my heart
a leannán: sweetheart, darling
a mhac: son
brawd: brother
cahir: warrior
caomhnor: protector/guardian of children
cariad: lover, darling, sweetheart
chwaer: sister
cosantir: guardian or protector
dùin do bhuel: shut up
mo bhràthair: my brother
mo charaid: my friend
mo chridhe: my heart
mo leannán: my darling / my lover
prìosan: prison
tha gaol agam ort: I love you
trawsfur: transform or shift

Want to be notified of the next release?

Sent *only* on release day. Sign up at:
www.CheriseSinclair.com/NewsletterForm

Have you tried the
Masters of the Shadowlands series?
Club Shadowlands
Masters of the Shadowlands: 1

Available everywhere
Get Club Shadowlands now!

Her car disabled during a tropical storm, Jessica Randall discovers the isolated house where she's sheltering is a private bondage club. At first shocked, she soon becomes aroused watching the interactions between the Doms and their subs. But she's a professional woman—an accountant—and surely isn't a submissive …is she?

Master Z hasn't been so attracted to a woman in years. But the little sub who has wandered into his club intrigues him. She's intelligent. Reserved. Conservative. After he discovers her interest in BDSM, he can't resist tying her up and unleashing the passion she hides within.

Excerpt from
Club Shadowlands

A N ETERNITY LATER, Jessica spotted a glimmer of light. Relief rushed through her when she reached a driveway studded with hanging lights. Surely whoever lived here would let her wait out the storm. She walked through the ornate iron gates, up the palm-lined drive past landscaped lawns, until finally she reached a three-story stone mansion. Black wrought iron lanterns illumined the entry.

"Nice place," she muttered. And a little intimidating. She glanced down at herself to check the damage. Mud and rain streaked her tailored slacks and white button-down shirt, hardly a suitable image for a conservative accountant. She looked more like something even a cat would refuse to drag in.

Shivering hard, she brushed at the dirt and grimaced as it only streaked worse. She stared up at the huge oak doors guarding the entrance. A small doorbell in the shape of a dragon glowed on the side panel, and she pushed it.

Seconds later, the doors opened. A man, oversized and ugly as a battle-scarred Rottweiler, looked down at her. "I'm sorry, miss, you're too late. The doors are locked."

What the heck did that mean?

"P-please," she said, stuttering with the cold. "My car's in a ditch, and I'm soaked, and I need a place to dry out and call for help." But did she really want to go inside with this scary-looking guy? Then she shivered so hard her teeth clattered together, and her mind was made up. "Can I come in? Please?"

He scowled at her, his big-boned face brutish in the yellow entry light. "I'll have to ask Master Z. Wait here." And the bastard shut the door, leaving her in the cold and dark.

Jessica wrapped her arms around herself, standing miserably, and finally the door opened again. Again the brute. "Okay, come on in."

Relief brought tears to her eyes. "Thank you, oh, thank you." Stepping around him before he could change his mind, she barreled into a small entry room and slammed into a solid body. "Oomph," she huffed.

Firm hands gripped her shoulders. She shook her wet hair out of her eyes and looked up. And up. The guy was big, a good six feet, his shoulders wide enough to block the room beyond.

He chuckled, his hands gentling their grasp on her arms. "She's freezing, Ben. Molly left some clothing in the blue room; send one of the subs."

"Okay, boss." The brute—Ben—disappeared.

"What is your name?" Her new host's voice was deep, dark as the night outside.

"Jessica." She stepped back from his grip to get a better look at her savior. Smooth black hair, silvering at the temples, just touching his collar. Dark gray eyes with laugh lines at the corners. A lean, hard face with the shadow of a beard adding a hint of roughness. He wore tailored black slacks and a black silk shirt that outlined hard muscles underneath. If Ben was a Rottweiler, this guy was a jaguar, sleek and deadly.

"I'm sorry to have bothered—" she started.

Ben reappeared with a handful of golden clothing that he thrust at her. "Here you go."

She took the garments, holding them out to keep from getting the fabric wet. "Thank you."

A faint smile creased the manager's cheek. "Your gratitude is premature, I fear. This is a private club."

"Oh. I'm sorry." Now what was she going to do?

"You have two choices. You may sit out here in the entry-way with Ben until the storm passes. The forecast stated the winds and rain would die down around six or so in the morning, and you won't get a tow truck out on these country roads until then. Or you may sign papers and join the party for the night."

She looked around. The entry was a tiny room with a desk and one chair. Not heated. Ben gave her a dour look.

Sign something? She frowned. Then again, in this lawsuit-happy world, every place made a person sign releases, even to visit a fitness center. So she could sit here all night. Or…be with happy people and be warm. *No-brainer.* "I'd love to join the party."

"So impetuous," the manager murmured. "Ben, give her the paperwork. Once she signs—or not—she may use the dressing room to dry off and change."

"Yes, sir." Ben rummaged in a file box on the desk, pulled out some papers.

The manager tilted his head at Jessica. "I will see you later then."

Ben shoved three pages of papers at her and a pen. "Read the rules. Sign at the bottom." He scowled at her. "I'll get you a towel and clothes."

She started reading. *Rules of the Shadowlands.*

"Shadowlands. That's an unusual na—" she said, looking up. Both men had disappeared. Huh. She returned to reading, trying to focus her eyes. Such tiny print. Still, she never signed anything without reading it.

Doors will open at…

Water pooled around her feet, and her teeth chattered so hard she had to clench her jaw. There was a dress code. Some-thing about cleaning the equipment after use. Halfway down the second page, her eyes blurred. Her brain felt like icy slush. *Too cold—I can't do this.* This was just a club, after all; it wasn't like she was signing mortgage papers.

Turning to the last page, she scrawled her name and wrapped her arms around herself. *Can't get warm.*

Ben returned with some clothing and towels, then showed her into an opulent restroom off the entry. Glass-doored stalls along one side faced a mirrored wall with sinks and counters.

After dropping the borrowed clothing on the marble counter, she kicked her shoes off and tried to unbutton her shirt. Something moved on the wall. Startled, Jessica looked up and saw a short, pudgy woman with straggly blonde hair and a pale complexion blue with cold. After a second, she recognized herself. *Ew.* Surprising they'd even let her in the door.

In a horrible contrast with Jessica's appearance, a tall, slender, absolutely gorgeous woman walked into the restroom and gave her a scowl. "I'm supposed to help you with a shower."

Get naked in front of Miss Perfection? Not going to happen. "Thanks, b-b-b-but I'm all right." She forced the words past her chattering teeth. "I don't need help."

"Well!" With an annoyed huff, the woman left.

I was rude. Shouldn't have been rude. If only her brain would kick back into gear, she'd do better. She'd have to apologize. Later. If she ever got dried off and warm. She needed dry clothes. But, her hands were numb, shaking uncontrollably, and time after time, the buttons slipped from her stiff fingers. She couldn't even get her slacks off, and she was shuddering so hard her bones hurt.

"Dammit," she muttered and tried again.

The door opened. "Jessica, are you all right? Vanessa said—" The manager. "No, you are obviously not all right." He stepped inside, a dark figure wavering in her blurry vision.

"Go away."

"And find you dead on the floor in an hour? I think not."
Without waiting for her answer, he stripped her out of her
clothes as one would a two-year-old, even peeling off her sodden
bra and panties. His hands were hot, almost burning, against her
chilled skin.

She was naked. As the thought percolated through her numb
brain, she jerked away and grabbed at the dry clothing. His hand
intercepted hers.

"No, pet." He plucked something from her hair, opening his
hand to show muddy leaves. "You need to warm up and clean
up. Shower."

He wrapped a hard arm around her waist and moved her
into one of the glass-fronted stalls behind where she'd been
standing. With his free hand, he turned on the water, and
heavenly warm steam billowed up. He adjusted the temperature.

"In you go," he ordered. A hand on her bottom, he nudged
her into the shower.

The water felt scalding hot against her frigid skin, and she
gasped, then shivered, over and over, until her bones hurt.
Finally, the heat began to penetrate, and the relief was so intense,
she almost cried.

Some time after the last shuddering spasm, she realized the
door of the stall was open. Arms crossed, the man leaned against
the door frame, watching her with a slight smile on his lean face.

"I'm fine," she muttered, turning so her back was to him. "I
can manage by myself."

"No, you obviously cannot," he said evenly. "Wash the mud
out of your hair. The left dispenser has shampoo."

Mud in her hair. She'd totally forgotten; maybe she *did* need a
keeper. After using the vanilla-scented shampoo, she let the
water sluice through her hair. Brown water and twigs swirled
down the drain. The water finally ran clear.

"Very good." The water shut off. Blocking the door, he

rolled up his sleeves, displaying corded, muscular arms. She had the unhappy feeling he was going to keep helping her, and any protest would be ignored. He'd taken charge as easily as if she'd been one of the puppies at the shelter where she volunteered.

"Out with you now." When her legs wobbled, he tucked a hand around her upper arm, holding her up with disconcerting ease. The cooler air hit her body, and her shivering started again.

After blotting her hair, he grasped her chin and tipped her face up to the light. She gazed up at his darkly tanned face, trying to summon up enough energy to pull her face away.

"No bruises. I think you were lucky." Taking the towel, he dried off her arms and hands, rubbing briskly until he appeared satisfied with the pink color. Then he did her back and shoulders. When he reached her breasts, she pushed at his hand. "I can do that." She stepped back so quickly that the room spun for a second.

"Jessica, be still." Then he ignored her sputters like she would a buzzing fly, his attentions gentle but thorough, even to lifting each breast and drying underneath.

When he toweled off her butt, she wanted to hide. If there was any part of her that should be covered, it was her hips. Overweight. *Jiggly*. He didn't seem to notice.

Then he knelt and ordered, "Spread your legs."

Get Club Shadowlands now!

Also from Cherise Sinclair

About Cherise Sinclair

Authors often say their characters argue with them. Unfortunately, since Cherise Sinclair's heroes are Doms, she never, ever wins.

A *New York Times* and *USA Today* Bestselling Author, she's renowned for writing heart-wrenching contemporary romances with devastating Dominants, laugh-out-loud dialogue, and absolutely sizzling sex.

Fledglings having flown the nest, Cherise, her beloved husband, an eighty pound lap-puppy, and one fussy feline live in the Pacific Northwest where nothing is cozier than a rainy day spent writing.

Connect with Cherise in the following places:

Website:
CheriseSinclair.com

Facebook:
www.facebook.com/CheriseSinclairAuthor

Facebook Discussion Group:
CheriseSinclair.com/Facebook-Discussion-Group

Printed in Great Britain
by Amazon